I0707594

Small Town Secrets Book II

SHADOWS OF THE PAST

JULIE ANN KEADY

Two Penny Publishing
850 E. Lime Street #266
Tarpon Springs, Florida 34688
TwoPennyPublishing.com
Info@TwoPennyPublishing.com

For permission requests and ordering information, email:
Info@TwoPennyPublishing.com

Paperback: 978-1-950995-97-4
Hardback: 979-8-9901524-7-2
eBook also available

Library of Congress Control Number: 2023912605

FIRST EDITION

For information about this author, to book event appearance, or media interview, please contact the author representative at:
Info@TwoPennyPublishing.com

endorsements for the small town secrets series

"The intricate plotting is great!"

SUSAN in Massachusetts

"I LOVED it!! Well done!! I read it every night before I went to bed and looked forward to reading it each night, a sign of a great book! I cannot wait for the next one."

SANDY in New York

"I really enjoyed it!"

ANNE in Virginia

"I could not put it down!! Can't wait for your next one!"

DOLLY in Florida

For Andrea, Camilla, Alysa, and Cassie:

The "A" sisters never believed this would be finished,
but the "C" sisters always believed. Through it all,
each of you were supportive and helpful.

table of contents

preface

Small Town Secrets is a purely fictional story. The seeds were planted in my overactive imagination while I lived in a small town, considered to be a village. The culture shock of living in a small rural community was a warm welcome after living in more densely populated areas where it could take as long as two hours or thirty minutes to travel the same thirty miles, depending on the day of the week and time of day.

I loved the slower pace with the friendly atmosphere. Many of the homes were built well over a hundred years ago. And on a street close to the heart of the town were a few houses so grand, I often joked about living in the grandest one. I agreed with my friend, I could never afford it. These few houses were so majestic as they appeared to weather many storms over generations. How could anyone ever afford to live in these homes that were once built to hold many generations and servants? Such elaborate houses are no longer made like these.

And as I continued to plan my walks past these homes, I imagined the history of these families and the secrets they held. I wondered if there were secret passageways and if the current home owners were friends, family, or enemies. Were they the founding families of the town? Were the current occupants related to the original owners? Were there skeletons hiding literally or fictionally deep inside that only a few knew of the details?

Many years later, I finally organized my thoughts and the Small Town Secrets Trilogy was created. The name and state is never mentioned because Small Town Secrets could be anywhere in the United States. And like Clara Noelle, I am also hearing impaired and a physical therapist.

But that is where our similarities end and her story (totally fictional) begins.

Here is *Shadows of the Past*, book two of Small Town Secrets Trilogy.

Julie Ann

prologue

35 Years Ago

"*Finally, silence,*" *Evil thought as he stepped away from his wife. He had been annoyed that the whole process took longer than expected. He would never have guessed she would drag it out for as long as she did.*

"I need to calculate the dose better next time," he thought as he hid the vials and syringes.

Pacing the room, he debated what to do next. Should he yell out for the staff or sneak out to let someone else find her?

Which would be better?

As Evil stepped closer to the window, his blue eyes caught sight of movement in the window of the house next door. Paused in his internal debate, he reached for his binoculars, adjusting for the distance before bringing them up.

"Well, well, well. Look who is finally turning into a sexy little lady," he thought as he watched her peel off her clothes.

Standing in her soft pink bra and matching panties, she appeared to study her face in the mirror. When she stepped back, Evil studied her perfect body, so much like a barbie doll. He was pleasantly surprised by his response as she seemed to be dancing to music he couldn't hear.

Reaching down to open his pants, Evil watched with renewed enthusiasm as the young woman reached into the shower to turn on the water. Her sweet ass swung to an unknown beat as she danced around the bathroom. To his utter delight, she unsnapped her bra from her back with the movements of her shoulders, causing her tits to jiggle as her hips swayed. Somehow, the pink panties fell to the ground and he groaned in pleasure as she stepped into the shower.

In his mind, Evil was behind her in the shower. He could feel her wet skin's softness as she rubbed against him. He could hear her groaning as he felt his release.

"Oh, the little barbie doll has undoubtedly grown up," he smiled. "But she isn't just any babydoll. She's my babydoll," Evil sighed with pleasure.

When he opened his eyes, his fantasy vanished, and he was shocked to discover he was back in his room with his wife lying on the bed, her vacant eyes watching. Evil sighed again with irritation. Even dead, she could ruin his pleasure. Evil closed his pants before heading down the old servant staircase.

Decision made. "Let someone else find the damn body," he thought as he faded into the shadows.

A week later, Evil followed his babydoll as she walked beside her unofficial betrothed. He wasn't surprised the young man was leading her into the woods. Any boy his age would. Evil was careful to remain far enough behind not to be seen, but close enough that he wouldn't lose them.

The initial annoyance that they had taken the longer trail faded once he saw the flowered meadow. He understood. The April showers brought the May flowers. Evil watched in amazement as his babydoll's feet stepped on a rug of wildflowers of every color. The musical sound of her laughter encompassed Evil's senses as she twirled around with the sunshine beaming down on her face. Her smile made him smile. He remained in the shadows of the dark woods as the boy sat at the center of the field, leaning back on his elbows, and watched with a stupid grin on his face. Tired of dancing, she dropped down beside him.

Hidden in the shadows, Evil remained mesmerized as the two whispered before the boy leaned down to kiss her. Surprised, his brows furrowed at the sight of his babydoll allowing such a passionate kiss. He shifted his weight to get closer, but a twig snapped beneath his feet. The sound echoed in the silence of the forest. Evil quickly ducked as the boy's head turned in his direction. The boy immediately stood. With his eyes looking towards the treeline, he reached down for her hand to assist her onto her feet before guiding her back down the hill.

Evil muttered a curse at his recklessness, spooking the boy. Both his babydoll and the boy were much more observant throughout the return towards home.

A month later, Evil was once again hiding in the shadows of the garden. Before him, his babydoll sat quietly on the bench reading a book. The garden was the perfect spot. The sunshine highlighted her beauty as she smiled to herself. The rosy aroma surrounded her. She was so beautiful with her long chestnut hair and soft, clear skin, like a babydoll.

"My babydoll," he smiled as he corrected himself.

He reached down to adjust his pants when he heard footsteps behind him. Expecting to see a servant, Evil's eyes grew wide, and he was startled to see the boy of the house.

"Damn it! The kid is too smart for his own good," he thought.

"What the hell are you doing here? This is private property. You don't belong here."

"It may be private, but it's not yours yet," Evil dismissed.

The boy's eyes looked down and then over the man's shoulders, taking in the details of the scene before him and fully understanding the significance.

He lowered his voice but kept his tone harsh. "She's young and spoken for. You have no business with her. Leave now."

Evil stepped back into the shadows without a word, letting the boy believe he had the best of him.

"I'm telling you, Father, it's not normal. He's not normal. He wanders around in the shadows when we hang out, spying on the girls. He's supposed to be an adult but doesn't act like one. He's more immature than his younger cousin. He's a freak and needs to be monitored," the teenage boy reported.

Graham Hawks was a busy man. After spending a long day at the office, he continued with his paperwork on his desk at home. He was reading a memo while he debated his response. The words of his son were heard but not the meaning. When his son's hands slammed onto the desk before him, the words finally broke his concentration.

"He was responding totally inappropriately while he watched Susannah from the shadows. If I didn't stop him, he could have been arrested for indecent exposure to a minor, minimally."

Graham looked up over his glasses from his memo. "What do you mean, exactly?"

"He was watching your daughter while he played with himself. Is that clear enough for you?" Aaron Hawks spat out with frustration.

A week later, Graham's son was dead.

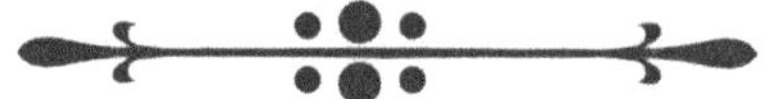

Nine-year-old Clara Noelle Gibson sat at the top of the landing of the grand staircase. Leaning forward with her elbows on her knees and her hands holding her chin, she struggled to eavesdrop on the conversation below.

Being hearing impaired, listening from nearby, let alone from the stairs, was never her strong point. But her friends, Lila, Rachel, and Shannon, had all assured her it was the only way to know what was really going on.

Adults might not outright lie, but they rarely told the whole truth, and there was already proof. Not even four weeks after her mother's disappearance, her father's "lady friend," Felicia Thompson, was already trying to move into the house.

Closing her eyes, Clara struggled to hear the adults below.

"Carl, seriously, you need to face the facts. Susannah emptied her bank accounts and packed her clothes. What more proof do you need? She's not returning home!" Felicia stepped closer to touch his cheek. "It's time we started our lives together out in the open."

"Felicia, I've told you before it's out of my hands," Carl sighed.

He would never admit it aloud, but he was relieved she couldn't officially move in. The lengthy on-off relationship served its purpose when they were married – no expectations or commitments beyond the moment. It was so much easier. Everything changed when his wife suddenly left him just weeks ago. Felicia quickly had the unrealistic assumption of being invited to move into the Hawks House. She left her clueless husband and child without first discussing it with him. Living with Felicia had never been a goal of his.

When Felicia cornered him in high school, her hypnotic blue eyes and enchanting smile always melted him on the spot. And Carl would let her have her way. He never understood how it happened. Eventually, it became apparent she had an ulterior motive. He tried, as the years passed, to break away completely but she always reeled him back in. Carl was suffocating. He wondered how her invisible tendrils hooked into him could be removed, allowing him to finally be free of her unrelenting demands.

Carl remained still, his blue-green eyes alert, waiting, and uncertain of what she would do with his daughter nearby. His adventurous side marveled at her drama, previously entertaining him. Their relationship was like the Argentina tango, each of their steps calculated and fierce with, of course, dramatic flair. He became bored and annoyed with her ridiculous illusions over the years.

He much preferred the waltz with his wife, slow and elegant. Her words never had hidden meaning and she, usually, always followed through. Living with Susannah was never exhausting. It was easy and carefree with hidden unexpected pleasantries. Something Carl had taken for granted until his wife was gone. He missed Susannah.

But back to the issue of the house, her most recent demand. The rules have always been clear and were extensively discussed before his marriage to Susannah—the Hawks House stays in her family. It goes to any of her children but never to him if the marriage were to dissolve. It would remain with Susannah. Always. This told Carl his wife would return to her family home as she always did. And if he were to move out, the marriage would not survive. Remaining in the house gave him a fighting chance to save his marriage.

"Oh, no, it isn't! Lee is your cousin, dammit! He will be on your side and help you fight this! You need to grab this opportunity by the balls! Take control and own up to living here as the master of the Hawks House!" She turned away, gesturing towards the elegant antiques surrounding them. "The trust gives the option of having servants and allows us to redecorate. We should so do it! And the jewelry, where is it? I know Susannah kept the jewels locked away. Did she take them, or are they here? Where is the safe?"

Felicia's eyes roamed the room as if the late Graham Hawks would be stupid and naive enough to store such valuables in the most public spaces of the house. Likely the same thought passed through her mind. Her eyes rose to the ceiling as she tried to recall the various rooms on the second floor from her limited time upstairs.

Carl knew Felicia well enough to expect the comments about redecorating the house and the servants, but the family jewels? Even he knew nothing about the location of the Hawks' jewelry. Of course, he had heard comments as a child in reference to what the Hawks women wore. Even portraits of elaborate, expensive gems on the women were hung throughout the house, but his wife never talked about them. He had no interest in them. Carl realized Felicia had just tipped her hand and he knew exactly what she was after.

"I keep telling you that's not the way the trust works. The house always stays with a descendant of a Hawks. That part is ironclad, with no opportunity for debate. The money and the estate," Carl gestured around at the priceless antiques collected over generations throughout the house, "will never be for me to remove or sell. It all went to Susannah on her thirtieth birthday. That's a separate trust. Every single antique in this house is documented and insured as Susannah's, the rightful owner.

Until her birthday, she couldn't do anything but rearrange it. The jewelry is also insured and locked away in the vault at the bank."

The last part was a lie, maybe. He had no idea where the jewels were hidden. Carl wouldn't put it past Felicia to take a sledgehammer to the walls in search of a hidden safe. He suppressed a smile at the image of her finely manicured hands swinging at the old walls. He could have her arrested in that case. Except he didn't have the desire or energy for that kind of dancing. Way too exhausting.

"If your *lovely* wife," Felicia couldn't withhold the sarcasm, "abandoned you and that brat of yours, it gives you the leverage to fight this in court and divorce her. You can become the rightful owner of the house and the estate."

The startling sound of Carl's laughter echoed in the room, an unexpected reaction to both. Felicia's eyes grew wide in surprise, not the response she was anticipating. And Carl had to sit, amused by her ideas.

"Felicia, after all this time, you really don't know me at all. I would never initiate a battle I have no chance of winning. Why would I? I have this right now! This is my legal address. My legitimate child upstairs is the rightful heir to the estate. I will always have access to this house without initiating a lengthy and costly war. I already have it. I am already here!"

Before Carl could finish, Felicia stormed out of the room. His laughter followed in her wake.

Felicia was headed out the back door towards her car but stopped when Lee, the next-door neighbor, appeared in her path.

"Lee, you need to fix this! I left my husband so I could live here. You promised me years ago I would one day be Lady of the Hawks House!"

At six feet, Lee Howell, the current district attorney, stood a few inches over her five-seven height. With his blonde hair neatly trimmed to the latest fashion and piercing blue eyes looking at her, he was amused by the whining woman before him.

"Felicia, I warned you not to be so brazen. You overplayed your hand way too soon. I don't control the trust. I warned you to be subtle. You know, clever and quiet. Stay a night and casually leave a few things here and there until you are, in every sense, living there. All this, over the course of time, as in a year or more, with you caring for the home and the child. Instead, you publicly leave your husband and try to move directly into the Hawks House? While both you and Carl are still legally married to others? And then you demand servants and the remodeling of the house? You brought unneeded attention to the fact that the current heir is not present to make the decision of keeping Carl's mistress out of the house. The outcome was to be expected. You've been legally instructed to never make this your legal address nor to even stay overnight as long as a minor lives here. How else could this have ended?"

"What was I supposed to do? Stay in the house with constant reminders of the bitch? It was supposed to be *me* living in that house! I was supposed to be the one making all the decisions involved with running the household! It was my right!" Felicia shouted.

"Yeah, well, your right to be the lady ended before it even started years ago when you were stupid enough to get caught with another man. You really expected Aaron Hawks, the heir to the Hawks Estate at the time, to simply look away? It's all a useless argument anyway. Aaron is dead. If Carl is who you want, stay with him." Lee shrugged. "You can't be living here as a legal resident. That ship has officially sailed."

Without listening to any further argument, Lee turned to walk away. His smile grew wider at the sounds of Felicia's demands to help her, always entertained by her perception of his power. How could she honestly believe he had the power to control not only the trust but the running of the Hawks Estate?

Lee heard about the complicated trusts set up by Susannah's father years ago. Most surprisingly, his children would receive their trust at the age of thirty. Such an interesting age, not the usual twenty-one. Lee shook his head as he continued inside to visit with his cousin, Carl.

Cousin was a generous word, Lee thought. Carl's mother dated Lee's Uncle Edwin for years before her death, leaving the young eight-year-old child to be raised by the hard-working man. His uncle always claimed he didn't know Carl's biological father, raising the boy as his own.

Carl wasn't a bad kid. He had the charming charisma and good looks of a movie star, so Lee's been told by many people. He just didn't have the motivation to work it to his advantage. That was where Lee's role came into play. Already married to his second wife, Kathleen, he wasn't available to offer his hand when Susannah came of eligible age for marriage. Instead, he paved the way for his cousin. Obviously, with strings attached. What didn't come with strings in life?

"What are you doing here? I'd think you'd have more exciting things to do tonight." Carl's chipper tone was obvious as he finished cleaning up the kitchen. "I didn't ask her to move in or make demands from the trust. You told me to keep a low profile, and I'd be able to remain living here until Susannah gets her act together and returns home."

"You really think she'll be back?" Lee wondered, reaching for a beer in the refrigerator.

"No reason for her not to. Over the years, even before we were married, Susannah would be gone for weeks at a time. She always comes back," Carl reasoned. With the last dish in the dishwasher, he joined his cousin at the kitchen table. "I want to hire a private investigator, someone to find her."

Lee's eyebrows went up in surprise. "Private investigator? Do you have money for that? It could be a hefty price."

"Money well spent to have Susannah back, don't you think?"

"I can certainly understand why you'd prefer her over Felicia." Lee kept his answer simple while he considered. "Tell you what, how about I pay for the PI? I have connections from my days in the city. Where do you think she'd go?"

Before Carl could answer, the men were interrupted by Clara's voice, yelling from the front of the house, "Dad, Mrs. Foxwood is here!"

Leaving his cousin, Carl went to the foyer to ensure his daughter had everything. "Clara, did you pack your toothbrush? Extra hearing aid batteries?"

Clara was nodding as she ran out onto the porch, her bag strapped over her shoulder.

"Allison, are you sure it's alright to have her stay the weekend?" Carl met Lila and her mother halfway up the path to the house.

"Carl, absolutely," Allison nodded with a smile. Being a slim woman in her mid-thirties, she was the adult version of her daughter, her auburn hair pulled back from her pale freckled face. She turned her blue eyes to wink at Clara. "As long as you don't mind us putting Clara to work. You're alright with her helping in the barn with the horses?"

"That's fine. I'm sure she'll have more fun than hanging out with a sitter here at the house." Carl's hands went on his daughter's shoulders. He waited until she was looking up before he spoke. "You listen to Mrs. Foxwood and behave. Have fun."

"I will, Dad." Clara hugged her father before getting into the minivan behind Lila.

Once Allison slid the door closed, she turned to Carl. "If you have time, come out to the farm. You can check out Clara's progress with riding and go for a ride yourself."

"Naw, it's been too long since I've been on a horse. The last thing I need is to be thrown off and break my leg," Carl dismissed the idea. "Thanks again for everything. I really appreciate it."

"Anytime. Like I said before, anything we can do, just ask." She squeezed his arm before stepping around to the driver's side. "Alright, ladies, we are on our way to get the groceries before heading home."

At the store, Clara walked beside Lila, who was following her mother as they planned the weekend.

"It's too bad Shannon couldn't make it. She went with her mother to the city to visit her grandmother," Allison began. "Lila, why don't you and Clara go get the chocolate, marshmallows, and graham crackers and then meet me up front?"

"Alright," the young girl agreed, grabbing her friend's hand and steering her toward aisle seven.

Clara allowed herself to be pulled in the opposite direction but soon paused, her green eyes finding Zachariah Thompson, Felicia's husband or soon-to-be ex-husband. Clara watched his reaction when he turned to Mrs. Foxwood, calling his name. A smile spread over his face. His eyes looked past her shoulder in Clara's direction. Embarrassed, she quickly turned away. When she turned down the aisle, Clara peeked back toward the adults and bumped into someone.

"Oh gosh! I'm so sorry," Clara turned back, startled to realize she had run into Dallas Thompson, Felicia's son. Apparently, he was here with his dad. "Dallas, I'm sorry. I should have been looking where I was going."

Dallas, two years older than her, had placed a hand on her shoulder to steady her. He smiled. "Clara, I should be apologizing to you. I wasn't looking. How are you doing?"

"What do you mean?" She was quickly defensive, annoyed by everyone thinking of her as the girl whose mother didn't love her enough to stick around. But then she remembered who she was talking to–Felicia's son. The woman was trying to move into her mother's house and take her mother's place. Not once did the woman consider bringing Dallas, her own son.

"I haven't seen you in a while," his voice trailed off. His blue-green eyes were glazed with sadness.

Placing a hand on his arm, she spoke, "No, Dallas, I didn't mean to be rude. I'm just tired of everyone tip-toeing around me. I guess you know what it's like."

"I guess," he allowed a slow shrug. "You probably see my mother more than I do since she's moved into your home. We're almost siblings."

"Like brother and sister?" Clara was momentarily startled by the suggestion. It wasn't a bad one. It could make having Felicia around worth it. Dallas has always been friendly and protective when his cousin Danny was around. "I never even thought of that. Does that mean you'll move in too?"

Dallas' laugh was harsh. "Doubtful. It would be too much for my mother."

"Clara?" Lila called as she came around the corner but stopped when she saw the two talking. "Dallas, hello. How's your summer going?"

Dallas turned to look over and noticed her hands were full. "Hi, Lila, can I help you with all that?"

Before she could answer, he loaded everything into his arms. "Looks like someone's having a bonfire tonight."

"Yes, we are! Clara is staying the whole weekend. We are going to have a bonfire each night. You should join us," Lila invited as the group headed toward the front of the store.

"I don't think your brother would like that," Dallas smiled at the invitation, despite how Lila's brother treated him as if he were a public enemy numero uno. He marveled at how the women in the Foxwood family didn't seem to have any problems with the Thompsons, or at least he and his dad.

His eyes fell onto the mother talking with his father as Lila softened her voice.

"I'm sorry Rob blames you when your only crime is being a Thompson," she whispered. "I don't even know what started it all. Do you?"

"I think the original dispute was over land a while back," he answered truthfully—he had his suspicions on the current dispute. "Everything else was added fuel."

In the parking lot, Dallas sighed when he walked over to his side of the truck. Clara looked so sad. He knew she tried to cover up her pain. He was annoyed all over again at the secrets from the past. Lila Foxwood will only talk to him when her brother's not around. The irony was killing him. No one knew the secret—well, except his biological parents. He wasn't a true Thompson, only in name. His last name should have been Gibson. When his parents broke up and his mother moved out, the house was on Thompson land. *She'd never be able to get her hands on it*, he thought. At least her relationship with Carl Gibson was now out in the open. It would allow Clara and him to finally be friends. They weren't soon-to-be step-siblings. No, Clara's already his younger half-sister.

Stupid small town secrets.

The early morning sun was barely over the mountains when Clara was awakened to the smells of bacon, coffee, and cinnamon. Her eyes were instantly opened. Noting Lila was not in bed beside hers, Clara jumped out and was immediately dressed before grabbing her hearing aids as she followed the breakfast smells to the kitchen. She was at the Foxwood Farms for the weekend, so she wasn't going to waste time in bed or inside, for that matter.

As expected, the Foxwoods had the typical breakfast spread out on the table. This morning, there were towers of pancakes, a platter of scrambled eggs and bacon, and an assortment of muffins to choose from.

"Good morning, Sleepyhead," Rob, Lila's older brother, greeted. Still standing, he pulled out a chair for her to sit. "Just in time for breakfast before we return to the chores."

"Return to the chores? I overslept? Why didn't anyone wake me up?" Clara was horrified at the idea of oversleeping.

"Clara, don't worry, we left chores for you," he assured with a smile once he was seated on her left. He scooped up half the tower of pancakes for himself before handing her the plate.

"Clara, what would you like to drink?" Mrs. Foxwood listed her options and then handed her a glass of juice. "Don't be shy with the food. There's plenty."

"I don't usually have a big breakfast at home," Clara admitted, debating a second pancake before handing the plate to Lila on her right.

She had her eyes on the muffins. Nowhere in this world could better muffins exist! The flavors varied each visit, but today, they made her favorites– cheddar bacon and lemon blueberry! She could smell them the instant she entered the kitchen.

Allison doubted Clara had any home-cooked meals since her mother left, not counting the meals at the farm or Taylor House. No doubt Rachel's mother and grandmother kept the poor girl fed when it wasn't the Foxwoods.

"What are we doing today? Plowing the fields? Picking the vegetables or fruit? Changing the horseshoes?" Clara suggested with the optimism of a child not raised on a farm.

"Shoveling shit out of the stalls," Chase, Lila's cousin, blurted out.

Chase was between Rob and Lila in age but also lived on the farm with his father. Their relationship was closer to siblings than cousins.

When he looked up at his aunt, he paused, caught by her stern glance, and immediately apologized before correcting himself. "Cleaning up horse manure from their stalls."

"Really? I'll help!" Clara was too excited to understand manure. As long as it involved the horses, she was game.

True to her word, Clara had working gloves donned and a pitchfork in her hand an hour later. As instructed, she scooped up everything in the stalls and laid fresh bedding down. Clara put some hay in each stall for the horses to eat when they came back to their stalls. She swept the barn and assisted with the refilling of the water troughs. She loved every minute on the farm.

When the chores were completed to Mr. Foxwood's satisfaction, four of the horses were prepared for riding.

As the horses were led out of the barn, Mr. Foxwood turned his attention to Rob. "No racing the horses today. Clara's skills are still new. That also means *no* jumping. Stay off the more difficult trails."

"Yes, sir," Rob agreed. No one would be thrown from a horse on his watch.

unfair

6 Years Later

"Clara Noelle, what's this I'm hearing? You let Eric fail the chemistry exam?" Her father asked during dinner on a Thursday evening in early October. Between his excessive work hours and Clara's typical high schooler's life, it was the first meal they shared in over a week.

"Dad, I didn't let him fail. He doesn't do his share of the work or the homework. How is it my fault he doesn't know the information for the test?" Clara snapped as she reached for a biscuit. "This stew's delicious. You made this?"

"Clara, we've been over this. He's your lab partner. This was arranged for you to help him pass the class," Carl sighed. After sampling the stew himself, he answered her question, "I wish I made this. No, Felicia brought it over. Since it's pretty good, I doubt she made it."

Clara almost smiled at her father's joke. "Dad, Eric needs to be doing his part! He doesn't participate in the labs nor does his homework. I can't push my paper to the edge of my desk so he can cheat off my test!"

Her father threw his hands up. "Why not?"

"The teacher will know! If she doesn't see it, she'll be suspicious if we miss the same questions."

"Again, so what?"

"Dad, why are you never on my side? If I get caught cheating or helping someone cheat, that could cost me an acceptance to my college of choice. And honestly, Eric's taking the class for the third time. He should be helping me! Not me doing everything for him!"

"Three times?" He paused, his spoon in the air. "Hell, even I passed chemistry the first time. I didn't realize he was so lazy. I thought he was a smart kid."

"Yes, he failed last year and tried again during summer school, but he didn't go to the labs and failed again. I'm learning chemistry for the first time, and I have to work at this. It's not fair to me to have to learn it and feel comfortable teaching someone else. Honestly, if Eric wanted to learn so badly, he should do his homework and pay attention in class. Or his parents should hire a tutor that actually knows the information better than me."

"You better come up with something soon. Eric failed the test and is now benched for this weekend's soccer game," Carl warned with an edge to his voice, and leaned back in his chair with his arms crossed.

"Not like the team will suffer for it," Clara muttered under her breath.

"Clara, I've raised you to be better than that. You are a smart girl and a straight-A student. No reason you can't help someone, especially a close friend. When you see him at school tomorrow, arrange a time that works for you both so he can take the makeup test and be off the bench by next weekend's game."

"He's allowed to take a retest?" she asked, brows raised.

The chemistry teacher made it clear at the beginning of the year that someone had to be sick with a doctor's note or in the hospital to be considered for a retest. Not participating in the lab work would not be a good enough reason.

"Yes, his father talked to the teacher. She's going to allow him to retake the test on Wednesday, so you better get with the program," Carl instructed his daughter.

"I have a cross-country meet on Tuesday after school. Eric better be available over the weekend."

"You may have to miss it to make sure he's prepared for the test," her father warned.

"Dad, it's not fair that he screws up, and I have to suffer and miss out on my life. It's not fair!" Clara, now no longer hungry, stood up from the table with her bowl to rinse at the sink.

"Now's as good a time as any to learn that life isn't fair," he mumbled quietly.

Clara wondered if she really heard the words or imagined them. She turned from the sink to face her father. "Mom would never have made me miss what's important to me for someone who doesn't even attempt to try."

"Clara, we will never know, now will we? Your mother left *us*, not just you. She left both of us. So that puts me in charge, and you will make sure Eric passes all his tests for the remainder of the year. Is that understood?"

Carl left the room, leaving his daughter to clean up the kitchen.

Saturday evening, Clara had just returned from her cross-country meet. She smiled to herself as she packed an overnight bag and a school backpack. The course had been challenging; the 3.2-mile race had its share of steep hills, but she was able to tackle them with confidence and lost her opponent, literally, in the dust. The other girl tried to make it up at the last stretch to the finish line, but Clara was able to hold her own and push through to beat her, shocking no one more than herself by coming in second for her team—she's only a sophomore and the youngest team member! The other girl was a senior, which made the win all the better.

Once her bags were ready, Clara headed down the stairs and out the back door, still wearing her uniform–she was going to shower at Rachel's. Going into the garage for her bike, she wanted to hurry in case her father returned home. As she was walking her bike out of the garage, a car pulled into the neighboring driveway.

"Hi, Clara! Are you off to a race?"

Clara looked up once on the seat of her bike. Heather Emerson had just pulled up and was going to the trunk of her car. Before Clara could answer, Connor came out to assist his mother with the groceries.

"Hi, Clara. Running away from home again?" Connor teased with a grin.

"What?" Clara looked down, seeing her backpack over her shoulders and her overnight bag across her chest. "No, my race was earlier. I'm on my way to Rachel's for the night. I have a study session with Eric if he shows up."

"You and Eric have classes together? I thought he was a year ahead of you," Heather asked as Connor's eyebrows went up in question.

"Just chemistry class," Clara grumbled heavily. "He failed last year and the summer class. Now I have to tutor him."

"Why you?" Connor wondered.

"My dad told me to," Clara sighed in defeat. "He told me it's the good thing to do. So, instead of wasting a Saturday night waiting for him, Eric has to come over to Rachel's when he's ready, and Mrs. Mackenzie can see I really am doing my best with what little I have to work with."

Connor burst out laughing, "He's not a good pupil?"

"Hard to tell. Eric doesn't do any of the lab work, and I'm the one who gets punished when he fails a test and gets benched. But at least I'll be with Rachel for the rest of the night. Mrs. Mackenzie will have my back."

"Didn't the soccer team win? Not like they missed him on the field," Connor jeered.

His mother gave him a look, and he responded with a shrug and a laugh. "Seriously, Mom, they still won by over ten points."

"That's what I told my dad. He wasn't amused," Clara agreed, relieved to have someone else on her side, even if it was only Connor.

Eight years older, he was back and forth often from the city, still training to be what he called 'the best trauma surgeon.'

"I'm sorry it ruined your hot date with the boyfriend," Connor teased.

As intended, the annoyance became obvious. "I don't have a boyfriend!"

"Rob Foxwood isn't your boyfriend? Didn't I see you two together at the pizza parlor last night after the football game? And you were in his truck for a ride home? Well, I hope it was a ride home," he lowered his voice, raising his eyebrows in question.

"He's not my boyfriend," Clara insisted again as she started up on her bike. *He's too busy flirting with everyone else*, she thought to herself.

"Don't worry, one day, he'll be paying attention to you," Connor assured her as if he could read her thoughts.

Not likely, Clara thought as she peddled away to Rachel's, only two houses down. She and Rachel were hoping to ride to Main Street later for ice cream if Eric showed up for the study session. Her father's comment, 'life isn't fair' still irked her. In her heart, she knew her mother would have encouraged her by saying 'help those in need,' the real reason she agreed to help Eric. Heck, the poor kid didn't have any help from his own family. His grandfather lived with them, and he's a pharmacist. Why couldn't he help?

Her mother also used to say, "Sometimes, they may not even know they need it or are wired to not ask for help." Clara always suspected her grandfather was the one her mother was thinking of.

Clara blinked to prevent her eyes from watering. She really missed her mother.

When Clara turned her bike up the Taylor House driveway, she waved to Gigi, Rachel's muted grandmother, sitting on the front porch. Every evening, one could find Gigi sitting out there with a cup of tea, waving at the neighbors. Sometimes, Rachel and her friends would join her. Clara continued to cycle around the house to park her bike next to the back porch.

"Clara! Finally!" Rachel greeted her at the door but paused, surprised to see her friend still in her cross-country uniform. "You haven't even changed yet?"

"Heck no! I just got home. The meet was almost two hours away. I didn't want to chance Eric arriving early while I was still home showering and him telling our dads I didn't show up. Then it would be my fault. Here, you can let me know if he actually arrives and keep him here while I dress."

Rachel nodded her head in agreement as she helped her friend with a bag. Her long blond hair was perfectly pulled back into two french braids, and her beaming smile reached her blue eyes in understanding. Growing up on the other side of the Howell House, Rachel also saw the various sides of Eric's personality. He was an expert at playing to his parent's expectations.

"Clara, how are you?" Rachel's mother, Beth, asked from the sitting room, but then she noticed her uniform. "You just came home from your cross-country meet? How did you do?"

Excited to finally be asked, Clara gave the short version of the race.

Beth smiled. "Congratulations! You beat a senior? That's wonderful! Have you had anything to eat today?"

"Yes, Mrs. Mackenzie. I've been eating all day, including on the bus ride home," Clara answered, following her friend up the backstairs to Rachel's room.

"We are allowed to get ice cream later, right?" Clara tossed her bag onto a chair, quickly getting her things for a shower. Since she was so often at Rachel's, most of her stuff was already here. Rachel nodded as she faced her friend. "Yes, after our study session." She reached for a bathrobe. "Smart idea having the study session here. Then my mother can tell his parents you really are trying to help. Do you think he'll show up on a Saturday evening?"

"We'll find out, won't we? I can't miss Monday's practice or my cross-country meet on Tuesday." As she removed her hearing aids, she continued. "Let me know when he gets here."

Twenty minutes later, to Clara's surprise, Eric knocked politely on the back door, precisely on time, and was escorted by his father, Lee.

"Beth, thank you for hosting the study session. Times have certainly changed since we were in high school. Study sessions on a Saturday evening?" his father asked.

Beth laughed, "I know, that was my first thought, but with the kids' hectic schedules, when else can they meet up together? Each is on a different sports team and is constantly on the go. Can I get you a cup of coffee or tea?"

"No, thank you. Kathleen and I are heading out to a fundraiser this evening." Lee turned towards his son. "Eric, work hard. Clara, thank you. Here's something for your time."

Clara eyed the folded twenty-dollar bill. "Thank you, but I can't accept it."

"Of course, you can. You can treat your friends to ice cream later," Lee suggested with a wink.

Three hours later, Clara and Rachel were riding their bicycles down Main Street to the ice cream parlor. The study session went better than she expected. Clara had instructed Eric to make study notes on index cards. To her surprise, he complied without any of his usual whining. She suspected it was Mrs. Mackenzie's presence that kept him in line. Unfortunately, they had to meet again the following day in the afternoon and Monday night.

Eric had offered to give them a ride to get ice cream, but they declined. Even though the town was small, their bikes were quicker compared to walking. And with Eric, you never know if he's going to abandon you, leaving you to walk home later.

When they arrived at the ice cream parlor, it seemed half of their high school was already hanging out. It took a few minutes in line before they could order.

"Hi, Clara and Rachel. What would you like?" Dallas asked, working the counter.

"Hi, Dallas, we'll each have a medium twist in a cone with rainbow sprinkles," Clara ordered. Rachel was standing beside her but talking to their friends behind them.

Dallas nodded with a smile before turning around to prepare the cones. When he returned, Clara handed over the newly earned twenty-dollar bill. Instead of taking it, he shook his head.

"No worries. It's on me."

"Are you sure?" Clara was surprised by his generosity. She knew he was no longer living with his father. Something happened during the divorce, causing a major rift. Clara didn't know any details, nor did her friends.

"It's barely five dollars," Dallas dismissed. He lowered his voice, knowing Clara would be able to read his lips. "Be careful, Danny's here."

Clara's green eyes widened with surprise as she nodded. The warning was clear. Danny Thompson, Dallas' cousin, was in Clara's grade. And for some reason, he'd taken his easy teasing up a notch from when they played in the sandbox to terrorizing her on the playgrounds. One time, Danny used a slingshot to aim for the front wheel of her bike, causing her to fly over the handlebars. Another time, he swung the merry-go-round so fast before she could hold on, causing her to fall. In middle school, he pushed her into a pool before she had removed her hearing aids. And another, he'd grab her purse from her desk and toss it between friends. She had been so worried he'd open it and see her tampons inside, but Shannon had assured her if he had seen the tampons, Danny would have been more embarrassed. And she was right. He had opened it up to see "what does a girl keep in these things" and promptly turned red, returning her purse without another word.

Often, when they were younger, Dallas would intercept them and redirect his cousin with ease before Clara would start crying or get hurt. The crying always led to more humiliation.

She nodded her head. "Thank you. I appreciate it." She grabbed Rachel's hand to lead her away from the group where Danny was.

However, Eric was already sitting within that group, and true to his nature, he waved to Clara and Rachel, calling out her name.

Danny looked up and smiled at Clara.

Clara was convinced he was thinking of some way to terrorize her tonight. She sighed miserably—maybe not such a great evening out after all. Instead, she had the shock of her life. Danny Thompson did the one thing she never expected. He asked her out. Clara almost died on the spot.

The following day at breakfast, Clara was quiet as she sat with Rachel and her family. She had instructed Rachel to not discuss the Danny situation in front of the adults. So far, Rachel was keeping mum, but the spark in her blue eyes showed how much Rachel wanted to discuss it further than the "I don't want to talk about it" the night before. Once they were finished, she returned to her house to complete her chores and get her laundry done before the next study session with Eric.

Wanting to be done with chores, Clara quickly put all her school clothes on hangers from the dryer before running towards the front of the house, up the front stairs, and to her room to hang them. Later, she stuffed her socks and underwear in the drawers before grabbing her school bag. She headed down the front stairs again before hurrying out the front door and down to Rachel's house.

From the Howell House, Lee watched Clara running past the house with amusement. *She's so like her mother*, he thought, bringing his coffee up for a sip. Once she was out of sight, he turned towards the staircase. Before he could call out his son's name, Eric was already flying down the steps.

"I'm going to be late!" he yelled as he rushed out the door his father had just opened.

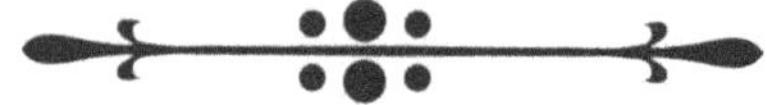

3 girls' day

Later, after the somewhat successful study session, per Rachel's opinion, Clara was reserving judgment until after Eric's retest score was received before she commented. When Shannon arrived, they spent the afternoon reviewing Rachel's wardrobe, debating her outfits for the week. The plan was to head over to Clara's next.

"Don't you have P.E. class on Tuesdays and Thursdays?" Clara asked. "If you wear the skirt, will you pack your sneakers or did you leave them in your locker?"

"Oh, good point! Why didn't I just leave them there last week?" Rachel wondered, replacing the outfit with a different skirt and blouse, then handing them to Shannon before disappearing into her closet for a pair of shoes. "What about this?"

"That would work," Shannon decided. "Are you leaving your legs bare or wearing colored tights?"

The friends continued for another hour before everyone agreed on Rachel's outfits for the week. When they were finished, the friends walked the two houses down to Clara's, laughing as they talked.

Shannon groaned loudly at the sight of Clara's bedroom and closet. "Clara Noelle! What happened here? Nothing is organized! Again! How can you live like this?"

"Easy, I close the door." Clara stepped forward to demonstrate, closing the door with Shannon inside the closet. Rachel laughed. "Now I don't see it."

"Funny." Shannon opened the door before turning around to pull all the clothes out of the closet. She quickly sorted them on the bed. Once finished, she methodically placed everything in 'proper order' with similar garments together, then sorted by color from light to dark.

"Do you do this on purpose?" Rachel whispered.

"Not really," Clara admitted. The two were sprawled out on beanbag chairs, watching Shannon mutter to herself. "She enjoys reorganizing so much. Why should I waste time? What else would we do here?"

Rachel laughed. "I like my stuff organized, but Shannon takes it up a notch."

"Serious OCD!" Clara agreed.

Shannon paused in the doorway with her hands out. "I am standing right here."

"Shan, you're doing great! When you're finished, we can rearrange Clara's room," Rachel suggested.

"Oh, we should!" Shannon almost jumped with excitement. "Rach, find something good for us to listen to while I finish this up. Clara, you need another dresser, something with deep drawers. With more drawer space, you won't have to shove so much into a small space. It'll help keep you organized."

Clara, still sprawled out on the beanbag, looked around the room. "Where would another dresser even fit?"

Shannon paused to look around. "Maybe in the closet? It's a good size, and there's all this wasted space over here."

Once the closet was complete, she started organizing the top drawers. Clara and Rachel roamed the other upstairs rooms looking for another dresser that met Shannon's strict requirements.

After looking in all the rooms, they returned to the second room. Rachel found the perfect tall antique dresser suited for the task. After emptying the drawers onto the shelves in the almost bare closet, they lifted it. The heaviness surprised them.

"I can't get my side up," Clara laughed. "There's nothing to hold onto. I can't believe how heavy this thing is!"

"I know! Should we call the guys over? Maybe Danny Thompson?" Rachel teased.

"Oh, don't ever bring that up." Clara paused to groan as she pulled out the drawers. "I told you last night, never talk of it again!"

"Never talk of what again?" Shannon asked from the doorway.

Rachel laughed again before quickly catching their friend up on the night before.

"Danny Thompson asked you out? What did you say?" Shannon was surprised, not because of all the horrible things he did to her, but because she often hung out with a Foxwood. The Foxwoods never hung out with a Thompson, never!

Clara had the last drawer sitting on the floor before she stood up. Choosing to ignore the subject, she changed it. "Rach, help me. This dresser should be lighter now."

"I'm impressed," Rachel commented when she lifted her side. "Not only is it lighter without the drawers, we now have a place to easily grab onto it. Clar, you take this strong independent woman stuff seriously."

"Rach, you're raised in a three-generation female household. You're the one with the role models," Clara dismissed.

"True that," Shannon agreed, giving instructions as her friends carried the heavy dresser into the hall.

"What are you girls doing?"

"Hi, Mr. Gibson. Clara needs more drawer space so we're moving this dresser over into her room," Shannon explained over her shoulder.

"Need help?" he volunteered.

"No thank you, we have this," Rachel gasped over her shoulder.

Clara, being hearing impaired, didn't even know her father had returned home until she looked up after placing the dresser in the closet. "Oh, hey, Dad! Shannon and Rachel are over."

"I see that. Are you all staying for dinner? Should I order a couple of pizzas?"

Clara looked towards her friends, each giving a subtle nod. "Sure, that'll be great. Can we have the Hawaiian one?"

Her father nodded. "No problem. The money will be on the table by the door. I'll be leaving soon for work. How's the studying going?"

When Clara didn't answer because she didn't hear, Rachel tapped her shoulder and gestured toward her dad when her friend looked up. Carl had to repeat the question. "As good as could be expected. I have my assignments all caught up, and I worked with Eric yesterday and today. We'll meet again before practice tomorrow after school."

"Good. You all have a good night. Don't stay up too late. It's a school night." Carl paused at the doorway to look around the cramped room. "Clara, if you need more space, you could switch rooms. You can even have your own sitting and study rooms. No reason you have to have everything confined to the smallest room in the house."

Shannon's green eyes lit up at the suggestion of moving and reorganizing multiple rooms, but Clara was already shaking her head. "No, it's too late in the evening for something like that. Way too much work."

After he left, her friends challenged her, "Why not switch rooms? There has to be what, five others you can choose from?"

"I could have any room in this house, true, but the other rooms aren't all set up to be bedrooms. I don't want to reorganize and move all the heavy stuff. Everything's ridiculously old and heavy." Clara would not admit, even to her best friends, that she liked being able to look out at Connor's bedroom window. Ever since she was young, looking over to see his light on always gave her comfort, especially after her mother's disappearance. With a quick glance at the clock she announced, "Besides it's almost six, I'm getting hungry."

"I can stay over and work until it's finished," Shannon offered.

"I don't doubt you would. I want to be in bed and asleep by nine," Clara explained. "You are certainly welcome to stay overnight, just no switching the rooms."

An hour later, they were sitting on the floor in Clara's bedroom eating pizza, discussing their thoughts on the newly rearranged room.

"I think this layout gives you the most floor space," Rachel commented. Shannon was nodding in agreement as she continued, "I still can't believe how we always eat up here, in your bedroom! We should at least be eating downstairs."

"Why?" Clara wondered before biting into another piece of pizza.

"The bedroom is for sleeping and relaxing. Downstairs has the rooms meant for eating properly," Rachel patiently explained, not for the first time.

"Rach, when have we ever done anything properly in this house?"

"She's not wrong," Shannon laughed. She marveled at how laid back Clara's father was. He would simply check in with her and then leave her to do her own thing. Rachel had her mother and grandmother constantly hanging around and reminding her of the proper thing. Her own grandmother was always on her about her schoolwork and chores. Lila had it the worst, or the best, depending on who's viewpoint. Lila had both parents, her brother, cousin, and uncle always around with limited privacy.

"Oh, shoot! I need to get home." Rachel was suddenly aware of the time, getting late for a school night.

The friends quickly cleaned up and followed Clara towards the front of the house, down the grand staircase. Clara's friends never asked why she didn't use the back staircase that went directly into the kitchen, it never dawned on them to wonder. They continued out the side door to the trash bin. After the pizza box was tossed, they made their way past the two houses to walk Rachel home.

"I think you should consider switching all the rooms around on the second floor," Rachel suggested. "You could take the larger room two down from yours, it's much bigger. Well, except the closet."

"When would we have the time? Shannon and Lila have soccer, you have cheerleading, and I have cross-country. Our fall seasons are barely over and we all jump into volleyball. I can think of a hundred things more exciting to do than rearranging all the rooms," Clara dismissed.

"Like what?" Shannon challenged as the group walked past the Howell House.

"Good evening, Clara," Lee seemed to appear out of nowhere from his porch. "I wanted to thank you again for giving up so much of your time this weekend to help Eric with his chemistry. Here's your payment for today and the rest of the week."

Clara hesitated to take the envelope but Shannon had no reservations. She reached out to accept it for her friend. "I'll make sure she gets this somewhere safe."

Lee's sparkling blue eyes turned towards the teenage girl he knew the least. His eyes widen slightly at the familiar green eyes. He smiled, "Thank you, encourage her to splurge on something fun. Clara, there will be a big bonus for you *if* Eric gets a minimum of 80 percent on his test Wednesday."

"I'm not making any promises," Clara warned, her voice clearly showing her lack of optimism.

Lee laughed. "I understand. Ladies, have a good night."

The friends were silent as they continued down another house to Rachel's. After ensuring she was safely inside, they continued walking towards Shannon's home that she shared with her grandmother. After she packed a quick overnight bag, they returned to Clara's.

Shannon and Clara sat on the side of the bathtub, both faces covered heavily in a mask, as they discussed the sleeping arrangements. "I'm just telling you, once the lights get turned off, it gets really spooky really fast. You can have any bed you want or sleep in mine with me."

Over the years, Clara and her friends had determined her house to be the creepiest. Lila had suggested it was because the older decor and age of the home gave off the haunted vibe. Rachel and Shannon had quickly agreed. Once everyone was settled, they would usually hear strange noises.

On this night, Shannon had decided she was old enough to brave the night in a room alone. Hell, if Clara could do it almost every night, so could she.

Once they each said good night, Shannon went to the room next to Clara's. She turned off all the lights and crawled into bed.

Shannon wasn't sure how long she had been asleep when she was awakened by the sound of footsteps. At first, she thought it was possibly Clara but then she heard other sounds, like the scraping of wood on wood.

Tossing her covers aside, Shannon slowly tiptoed to the door, quietly opening it to peek out. Not seeing anything in the dim hallway lit by random nightlights, she remained still and listened again. Shannon swore she could hear footsteps coming from the wall. *No, that's not right,* she laughed at herself. All the ghost stories they told each other were getting to her.

Shannon slowly stepped out into the hall, her bare feet were soft on the old wooden boards, but the creaking with each step seemed to echo into the night. She inwardly cringed at the idea of waking everyone up.

Everyone? Shannon thought, Clara would never hear this and no one else was here. Or was someone else here? A sudden chill brought goosebumps to her arms. Where was the draft coming from? She was looking over her shoulder as she continued forward, not seeing anything but dark shadows. Clara was right, this house was creepy as a haunted house on Halloween!

She stopped mid-step at another sound from overhead. Shannon shook her head, Clara would never be upstairs this late in the night alone. Not in this house!

Decision made, Shannon quickly ran into Clara's room. After closing the door, she lifted the covers and crawled in next to her friend.

As her heartbeat slowly returned to normal, Clara whispered, "You lasted longer by yourself this time."

· · · ·

Evil was surprised at the resistance when he tried to open the door. What is going on? He pushed his shoulder into the door to give it a good shove. After a minute, he realized something was blocking the door. What did his Babydoll do? Was she blocking him out on purpose? What about their plan?

He sighed heavily, reminding himself this wasn't the only entrance, just the most convenient. He retraced his steps up to the next floor. Relieved to have access, he quietly made his way toward the back staircase. When he looked down, he paused in surprise, his Susannah was back!

In the shadows below, he could see her walking in a short nightshirt, not her usual style but it was definitely working for her. As he started down towards her, the step under him creaked. "These damn old houses," he thought with annoyance, glancing towards his feet.

But when his blue eyes returned below, he realized, sadly, it wasn't his Susannah. So startled, Evil paused in his steps. Hidden in the shadows, he watched as the young girl built so much like his Susannah, looked over her shoulder before quickly disappearing into the bedroom.

Evil smiled with anticipation, less cautious about the old floorboards as he descended the stairs. When he arrived just outside the bedroom door, he paused to listen. Not hearing anything inside the room, his hand went to the doorknob and he slowly turned.

As he was about to push open the door, he heard the unmistakable sound of Carl's truck pulling into the driveway.

"The bitch said she had plans with the stupid fool after work! Why is he home?"

Evil softly cussed the poor timing and misfortune. He quickly debated waiting until the man was asleep before continuing into the bedroom. Evil watched from the shadows of the back staircase leading down into the kitchen.

Carl had turned on the lights before talking over his shoulder. "Can I get you a beer or a glass of wine?"

A woman at least ten years younger stepped in, her eyes were wide as she walked through the doorway leading to the dining room. "I've never been here before. This place is huge!"

Carl came up to hug her from behind. His lips trailed down her neck before she turned. The two embraced. It was a few minutes before Carl seemed to remember where he was. His eyes glanced up towards the landing of the stairs, so close to his daughter's room. Confident Clara would not hear him, he still preferred a door. He grabbed a bottle of wine already chilling and two glasses before leading the woman towards one of the front rooms—the furthest away from his daughter's bedroom with the most privacy.

Two hours later, Carl was on the floor near the fireplace, covered in only a blanket, watching his lady friend get dressed. He sipped the last of the wine before he spoke. "Are you sure you have to leave now? We have a few hours before the sun comes up."

She turned. "Next time we do this, it should be a non-school night. I'll only have about four hours of sleep as it is."

She squatted down to kiss him. "Thank you for a surprisingly wonderful night! Call me!"

Leaning on his arm, Carl watched as his daughter's chemistry teacher disappeared out the side door.

The next afternoon at lunch, Lila and Rachel listened intensely to Shannon's version of the previous night. "I kid you not! I was so spooked I had to crawl in bed with Clara!"

Lila studied her friends before asking, "Could it have been Clara's father?"

Clara groaned as she admitted, "Of course it was! It's so annoying!"

"He had a woman with him," Shannon whispered; everyone but Clara was leaning forward.

"That's the big news? Carl Gibson had a woman with him?" Lila was disappointed. "He's been seeing Dallas Thompson's mother since, like forever!"

"Yes, he has," Shannon agreed. "Which is why this part is so crazy! It wasn't her. It was Clara's chemistry teacher."

"What?" Rachel was horrified. "Isn't she married? How could her husband not know she wasn't home in bed next to him? Do you think they're having marital problems?"

"It's certainly a given," Shannon answered. Her eyes looked over at Clara. "Clara, it's not embarrassing to know your dad has a sex life."

"It's not so much that he has one," Clara sighed again with annoyance. "It's that he's a homewrecker and we are sitting here *talking* about my father's sex life!"

"Maybe she and her husband have an open marriage," Shannon suggested optimistically. "Your dad may not be a homewrecker."

"You're only suggesting that to make me feel better," she dismissed. Clara leaned forward with fake excitement. "I have an idea, why don't we talk about Lila's parents' sex life?"

Lila blushed at the mere suggestion, but before she could answer, Shannon spoke. "That would be too boring! Her parents are only sleeping with each other and likely in the same position for the last ten years!"

"You both saw her dad actually having sex in the parlor? You know what position?" Rachel was horrified all over again. "Ewww!"

"No, we didn't watch them!" Clara almost shouted with frustration. "We aren't peeping Toms! Can we please get off the subject?"

Lila studied Clara's face and gasped, "Clara, you've seen other women over at the house, haven't you?"

"Who else?" Shannon asked excitedly.

Before Clara could answer, Chase, Lila's cousin, stood at the table.

"Hey, everyone!" Chase greeted as he sat. When no one spoke, he looked around the table; Rachel's face was pink with embarrassment, Lila and Shannon looked amused, and Clara looked seriously annoyed. "What are you all gossiping about now, Clara's father's sex life?"

He knew he had hit it on the nose when Rachel gasped, her face turning even pinker.

"How did you know?" Shannon laughed.

"And tell you my secret? All right," Chase chuckled. "First of all, Rachel always turns that shade of pink when you all are talking about sex. Clara looks embarrassed and annoyed while both you and Lila are amused. What else could it be?"

Chase paused to drink heavily from his milk carton. He looked around the table when he placed it down on the tray. "So, who is it?"

When none of the girls spoke, he looked at Shannon. "Oh, come on, you won't tell me?"

Later in the afternoon, Shannon walked beside Clara toward their last class of the day. Her hand reached over to her friend's arm. "Clara, I'm sorry I embarrassed you at lunch. That wasn't my intention."

"I know it wasn't. It's my fault; I opened the can of worms by venting about my dad's previous visitors. I just can't believe Chase guessed it," Clara admitted. "Don't worry. I'm not upset with you, just my dad. He keeps doing this, and it's freaking annoying!"

Before Shannon could respond, they were distracted by shouting at the end of the hall.

"What's going on?" Clara asked.

As they got closer, Rob Foxwood was shoving Danny Thompson back. "You stay away from her, you hear me? You don't look at her, talk to her, and sure as hell don't even think about her!"

"Or what? I didn't think you two were even an item, especially after who I saw you with the other night!" Danny yelled back.

Before Rob's fisted right hand could swing, Chase bravely stepped in to push his cousin back. "Come on, man; he's not worth it."

Similarly, Dallas was standing in front of Danny. "Walk away, man."

Danny smiled when he saw Clara near Rob. "Clara, baby! Did you tell him about Saturday night? We had a good time, didn't we?"

Rob was about to shake loose from his cousin to throw the well-deserved punch, but Clara was suddenly standing before him.

"What the hell are you doing?" Clara's soft voice stopped Rob's wrestling Chase as his steel blue eyes met her furious green. "You trying to get kicked off the field for the homecoming game? Or expelled from school? Are you really that stupid?"

"Why didn't you tell me he asked you out?" Rob demanded, his voice also lowered.

"Why would I? Who I talk to is none of your business," Clara firmly informed him. "I decide who I talk to, not you. You are my friend, got it? Not even my own father decides who I can and cannot talk to."

Without waiting for a response, Clara dismissed him by walking away, running literally into Eric.

"What's going on? Are you alright?" Eric asked, eyes looking around at the crowd dissipating.

"Fine, why?" Clara's words were clipped.

Eric shrugged. "I don't know. You looked pretty pissed off. Are you ready for chemistry class?"

"No, I'm getting fed up with chemistry," Clara admitted with a shake and a sigh.

Eric laughed as he casually placed his arm around her shoulder. "I hear you."

"What the hell is she doing with Eric Howell?" Rob growled, unable to move his feet toward class.

"Tutoring him in chemistry. They're lab partners," Shannon explained as she redirected him toward his class.

"Why didn't she tell me? Is she tutoring Danny too? Is that why she's hanging out with them?"

"Rob, let it go," Chase suggested. "Clara's right. You aren't her keeper."

"Do you think anyone would notice if he disappeared in the night?" Rob wondered out loud.

"His mother, definitely," Chase offered, relieved the excitement was settling.

Shannon laughed. "What do you have in mind? Need a lookout?"

"Don't encourage him," Chase cautioned. "He likely already has different ideas depending on the day of the week."

4 need help

15 Years Later

Friday Evening Before Labor Day

Shannon Doyle sat in the passenger seat of her car, lost in her thoughts as her friend Clara drove toward home. She could not grasp the facts on the paper in the envelope beside her. She had a biological family. And, most freaky of all, she knew her half-brother and half-sister. How did she not see this before? The evidence was always staring back at her as if she were looking in a mirror. And in retrospect, everything now made sense. All the odd similarities and mannerisms.

The sound of gunshots echoing brought her back to the present as the car suddenly began to rattle. Shannon looked around with confusion. They were twenty minutes from town, and the rough turn was ahead. As she opened her mouth to warn Clara of her fast speed, the driver's window shattered.

Shannon's scream sounded as if it belonged to someone else. Her arms instinctively came up to protect her face from the million tiny pieces of glass blowing into the car. When she felt it was safe to lower her hands, the vehicle slanted downward, missing the turn. Shannon screamed again seconds before their impact into the massive tree as the airbag shot out, pinning her to the seat.

She could only see flashes of green and brown from the trees out her side window as the car bounced back and continued down the slope, rolling repeatedly. When it finally stopped, Shannon was too dazed to realize the car was on its side, Clara's side.

Several minutes passed before Shannon was able to start thinking clearly enough to try to open her door. It wouldn't budge.

"Good God, Clara! That was scary as hell! Thank God for airbags," Shannon stated once she could breathe. "I can't open my door. What about you?"

It was another moment before she realized the only sounds were her voice and wheezing. And the wheezing wasn't her.

"Clara? Clara? Did your hearing aids go flying off your head?" Shannon chuckled at the old joke among the friends.

There was no response.

Panic quickly grew as Shannon fought to push her airbag out of the way. Using her sunglasses to puncture it, she could finally survey the scene.

To her horror, the car was on its side. Clara lay below her, unresponsive in her blood.

Shannon's brain finally processed the gunshots she heard. "Clara?"

After a moment of panicking screams trying to get Clara to answer, Shannon finally remembered to call for help. She struggled to reach her cell in her back pocket.

Devan Mancuso, an undercover agent, was sitting at his cousin's desk with his feet elevated when he glanced at his caller ID. He was tempted to let it go to voicemail but thought that would be too childish.

"Yes, Shannon," he answered with a bored tone.

"Devan, help me! She's been shot! She's been shot, and there's so much blood! She's not answering me. Help me, please!" Shannon's panicked voice cried over his phone.

Devan immediately sat up, hitting the speaker button to alert his cousins, both deputies, while he spoke calmly. "Shan, slow down. Take a deep breath. Breathe. Good, now tell me, where are you?"

After she paused to breathe, Shannon was suddenly more focused. "In my car. Clara was driving. We were heading back from the city going west towards town on route 20."

He looked up at Joe and received a nod, confirming the first responders were notified. Devan found himself saying a prayer, remembering the sharp turn in the road had a history of fatal accidents.

"I heard gunshots, and the tires blew. Clara tried to control the car, but her window shattered. Dev, she's not answering me. I don't know if she's breathing! I need help. I need you to help me, please," Shannon lost all control, consumed by panic.

Devan was already out the door, riding shotgun in his cousin's cruiser. He focused on keeping his ex-girlfriend calm as he silently prayed, his mind wandering with many questions. Starting with who the hell was shooting at them? And why? It was the worst section of the road.

The cousins, Rob and Chase Foxwood were wrapping it up for the day. They owned the construction business renovating Clara O'Reilly's childhood home, the Hawks House. Chase's commute was two houses down, where he arrived at his girlfriend Rachel's home, the Taylor House. The other workers discussed stopping in at Memories for a drink, but Rob decided to return home instead.

The scanner in his truck reported a rolled vehicle close to his family farm. Since Rob was still an active volunteer paramedic, he headed to the crash site. It was a frequent spot for accidents due to people often going too fast to make the sharp curve ahead. The locals knew the hidden dangers, but not the young teens or tourists. Without knowing who the victims were, Rob still said a silent prayer.

Dr. Connor Emerson was more than ready to sign out for the day. It had been a long night with an early call to return to the hospital. He had about an hour before the next surgeon would arrive to relieve him, allowing him to return home at a decent hour. The earlier shenanigans with Tiffany, an ex-girlfriend from last spring, made him realize how lucky he was to have Clara. Connor missed seeing her throughout the day.

Lila Foxwood, an ER nurse and close friend of Clara's, had just informed him two females were involved in a single-vehicle collision on route twenty. The first was already en route. The report was the first patient appeared to have minor injuries and was easier to get out. The second was unconscious and more challenging to extract.

Connor nodded his understanding as he gowned up while heading to the ambulance bay, preparing for the worst but hoping for the best. He prepped his nephew, a first-year resident, Dr. Joshua Emerson, for the chaos about to begin as the first ambulance pulled up.

Connor and Josh were surprised to see Devan open the back doors of the first ambulance. He jumped down to assist Shannon on the stretcher.

"You have to help her, please!" Shannon frantically yelled repeatedly.

Connor rushed ahead to begin his assessment. Her blood pressure was slightly elevated, as was her heart rate, not unusual following a crash. Her pupils were reactive, and no evidence of internal bleeding, but there was deep bruising from the seatbelt and many superficial cuts, likely from shattering glass. He had just enough time to yell out orders to get her to radiology for a CT scan of her head and spine before returning to prep for the second patient.

Devan insisted he remain at Shannon's side, especially when she reported hearing gunshots. His cousin, Joe Mancuso, had stayed behind at the scene, and a recent message confirmed the car had multiple bullet holes.

What the hell, Devan thought as he followed Lila, transporting Shannon down the hall.

Joel Montgomery, a city cop from Shannon's past, was suddenly in front of him, blocking his path. "What the hell were you doing, letting her travel out of town without a proper escort? If anything happens to her, this is on you."

Devan shoved the pointed finger aside. "Why the hell would I think that's my responsibility? To keep Shannon safe? Safe from who? Hmm?"

Devan shoved the detective into the wall as he struggled to contain his temper. His voice was dangerously soft when he continued, "She and I broke up the weekend you two started up again. I have pictures of you two kissing at the motel. If I am going to be responsible for someone's safety, you should at least have the professional common sense to tell me what the hell was going on instead of hooking up in secret. What the hell are you going to tell your boss?"

Joel's face paled. "You broke up? Where the hell has she been staying?"

"No idea; we didn't end it on a happy note," Devan answered as he hurried to catch up with the stretcher.

As Connor changed his gown, he instructed Josh to follow up with Shannon's test results. He recommended, at minimum, overnight observation. He was to be notified if there was anything concerning.

Josh nodded his understanding as both freshly gowned physicians returned to the door in time for the arrival of the second ambulance.

Both were surprised to see Rob Foxwood walking along the stretcher. The female patient was unconscious. In his doctor mode, it took Connor a moment to process that Shannon was the first patient and Rob was escorting the second patient. Lila was working here in the ER and accompanied her friend to radiology…

Rob watched Connor as he approached the stretcher, unaware that it was Clara. She was strapped to a backboard wearing a cervical collar.

Blood covered her face, left shoulder, and chest. The bloody spot on the sheet appeared to be growing. Her face was unrecognizable, but her wild curly hair identified her, despite being matted with blood.

Rob knew the instant Connor realized it was Clara. His face turned pale as he touched her cheek, mumbling softly, "Baby, what the hell happened?"

That was when Josh paused in his steps, suddenly unable to focus as he watched his uncle caress Clara's cheek. To his amazement, Connor quickly shifted back into his doctor mode. Josh followed in his wake.

Connor was at the head of the stretcher. They lifted her onto the ER gurney on his call before he began his assessment. A glance at the monitor already hooked up. Her heart rate was up. Oxygen saturation was dangerously low. Her blood pressure was low. Pupils were active and responding. Connor pulled out his stethoscope to listen to her lungs and realized her left lung was not exchanging air.

One nurse cut off her clothes while another inserted an IV line into her right arm. He noted that the left arm and leg were splints due to suspected fractures. Connor was shouting out orders, preparing to re-inflate her lung. He initially thought maybe a piece of a fractured rib had embedded into her lung, but with the amount of blood on her chest, he shifted his thoughts to a piece of glass. Cleaning the area before sticking the tube in, he realized that glass didn't cause the injury to the lung.

"What the fuck?"

Josh looked up at the unexpected comment. His eyes met Connor's before looking down at the circular wound. *Shit, is that what I think it is?*

Connor shocked everyone present when he stopped the procedure and ordered the portable x-ray. Within minutes, imaging confirmed his fear. He shouted out new orders to call the OR and notify the anesthesiologist. Clara needed to be prepped for emergency surgery to remove a bullet before her lung could be re-inflated. During the elevator ride, he looked closer at the wound on her left arm, also a gunshot wound.

How did a motor vehicle accident suddenly turn into multiple gunshot wounds? Where the hell were Clara and Shannon? Who the hell was shooting at her? Why?

His focus returned as the elevator door opened and everyone prepared for surgery. Connor was scrubbing when he heard overhead, but didn't attempt to process, a code blue called in radiology.

Across town, Rachel MacKenzie was squatting beside the bed, staring at an empty syringe on the floor. She had vaguely noticed Chase returning home and getting into the shower across the hall. Her brain was telling her to call Devan, but she debated as she tried to justify what it could mean.

"Rach?" Chase called from the doorway. His tone had her instantly looking back over her shoulder as she stood up.

The look in his eyes stopped any further comments as he walked closer. Rachel felt a moment of panic as he reached for her hands.

"Chase? What is it?" She stepped back in panic.

"Rob just called. We need to get to the hospital. Clara and Shannon were in an accident," Chase whispered as he reached for her hand, guiding her towards the door.

"Chase, what happened?"

"Clara missed the curve on route 20," he simply answered.

"No! Don't say it!" Rachel almost screamed as she grabbed his arms.

"They are alive and at the hospital. Clara's going into surgery right now," he explained. Chase didn't tell her about Rob's panic as he broke down, giving grueling details of Clara's delayed extraction from the car. Nor the slight panic he observed in Connor's eyes, confirming the seriousness of her injuries.

a long night

It was well into the night when Connor came out of the operating room. With heavy feet, he slowly advanced to the waiting room. Physically and emotionally drained, he hoped to keep himself together long enough to update Clara's friends.

Dallas, Lila, Rob, Chase, and Rachel stood up when he approached. He opened his mouth, but no words came out as his eyes met everyone in the semicircle.

Connor sat on the first chair and pulled his surgical cap from his head. He was leaning forward onto his knees as he stared at it. "She tolerated the surgery."

He heard Rachel gasp in relief as he continued, "We stopped the bleeding, re-inflated her left lung, and removed two bullets. One went into her side, causing a puncture to the lung and internal bleeding. The other was in her left arm, fracturing her humerus. She also has a fractured left clavicle, two left pelvis fractures, and a femur fracture. The orthopedic is consulting now and will likely recommend surgery once she is stable and able to tolerate it. The CT scan of the brain isn't showing any bleeding. She has a concussion. Her spine appears to be clear of injuries."

Pausing to take a deep breath, he dreaded to say the next part out loud. Connor looked at each one, "I need to know who will be her healthcare surrogate, the one that makes any medical decisions until she has recovered enough to wake up and make them herself. We need to have it in her chart."

Connor could not say out loud that she had a rough night ahead, and the possibility of her not being around when the sun rose was genuine. And if she survived the weekend, Clara would still have a long recovery and more surgeries soon.

Rachel and Lila both had tears flowing down their faces as they listened. Everyone was silent, attempting to process the information.

While everyone was quiet, the blanket blocking the reality of the situation fell. Connor started to panic. His eyes were wide as his hand ran through his hair.

"I have no idea where Reese and Hailey are or who is with them, do any of you?"

Lila stepped forward to sit beside him, holding her arm around his shoulders in a partial hug while she explained that the kids were at home with Michelle, the babysitter. She agreed to stay through the night until she and Dallas arrived in the morning. The friends had all talked. Each was more than willing to help take care of the children and do whatever else was needed.

Lila had suggested they wait to see what Connor wanted. "Anthony and Joe Mancuso are camping out in the family room as we speak."

No one talked about why the protection of two deputies was necessary. When Clara's friends heard about the shooting, they were confused. Why would anyone want to shoot Clara? Could it have been a stupid, tragic accident? Someone hunting illegally too close to the road? But Rob was at the scene of the accident. He saw the multiple bullet holes. The car was obviously the target. But the events that followed in the radiology department finally made it clear.

Clara wasn't the target.

Shannon was. The shock was too much to process.

"Connor, when can we see her?" Rachel asked.

"Only two at a time for fifteen minutes. It'll take a while for them to transport Clara to the unit from recovery. The nurses need to remove all the glass from her hair and wash the blood. Once she's settled, you can start sitting with her," Connor answered.

He allowed a hug from Rachel when he stood up before heading towards the ICU. Connor wanted to supervise the transfer to ensure she was comfortable and well cared for. He paused when his brother came up beside him.

Matt Emerson had been sitting with his son, Josh, in a more isolated area. He breathed easier once he heard the initial report. He wondered if anyone had noted the irony of the spot where the accident occurred. Clara's uncle died in an accident on that exact curve of the road over thirty years ago. That accident had taken the lives of three other recent high school graduates. Though, he was not involved in the accident, the catalyst drastically altered his life.

Matt looked at his brother to gauge how he was holding up. Connor looked horrible. "She's going to be alright. You got her over the first hurdle. Getting out of the car alive is half the battle. She's a fighter." He touched his shoulder and squeezed.

Connor looked at him, seeming unable to speak as Matt wondered if similar thoughts had crossed his mind.

"I'm heading home with Josh but will return in the morning. What do you need from your place? Text me the list. And anything else you need, just say it." He waited until his brother nodded before he continued. "Where are the kids?"

"Home, safe with the Mancusos and the babysitter," Connor answered restlessly.

"Alright, head back in there and give her my love," Matt instructed.

Word spread quickly through the small town about the horrible accident. Many people knew Clara as the little girl whose mother ran off when she was a child or the new physical therapist at the nursing home. Shannon was the woman back from the city who worked in the bank.

As the weekend progressed, many townspeople gathered to discuss the accident. Interestingly, no one seemed aware of the gunshots that caused the accident. A turf battle began between the FBI, the local sheriff's department, and the city police.

Connor monitored Clara's vitals at the nurse's station as he worked on her visitation list on the computer. For now, only her five close friends were allowed to see her while she was still asleep. Connor would ask Dallas, Clara's older half-brother, about having their father on the list, but personally, his vote was a no.

The restrictions were placed into the computer just a few minutes before Carl Gibson entered the hospital. Security would not clear his request to see his daughter, nor would they confirm if Clara Gibson was a patient.

"I am her father! I have a right to be here and know how she is doing!" Carl demanded.

"Sorry, sir. My computer does not show any Clara Gibson currently at the hospital," replied Bear Johnson, the nighttime security guard. He was aware of Clara's current status. He was relieved to learn she was out of surgery and in the ICU.

When Bear returned from escorting Mr. Gibson from the lobby, the other guard commented, "Bear, it says right here Clara was admitted. She's now in the ICU. Why didn't you tell her father? He has a right to see her."

"Ryan, what is the policy?" Bear challenged his partner.

"Only those on the list can access information and get a visitor's badge."

"Right, do you see Carl Gibson's name?" Bear asked.

"No, but you and I both know that was Clara's father. Hell, we both went to high school with her," Ryan argued.

"Yes, you are correct. That was Clara's father. I played pool with Clara this summer, she beat me in the double-or-nothing tournament. She's still exactly as we remember her in high school. She's still short, has wild curly hair, and is as sweet as my grandmother's apple pie. All the same except for one thing," he paused to see if his partner would catch it. When he didn't, Bear pointed to the computer screen. "Her current name is Clara O'Reilly. Tell me how a father doesn't know his daughter's last name, and I'll tell you why he's not on the list."

"Shit, you're right," Ryan commented. If Bear had not been at the desk, he would have allowed Mr. Gibson in with a visitor's pass and lost his job.

• • • •

Neither guard saw a man dressed in a housekeeping uniform sneak past during the commotion. Evil came in with an employee badge but never swiped the time clock. He slowly approached the intensive care unit, stopping for a housekeeping cart. Evil understood people were easily persuaded to see what they wanted and would not look further than the housekeeping uniform and supplies.

He remained in the shadows as he watched his babydoll being transported into her room. He was about to follow, but a nurse pulled the curtain around her bed and informed him the room was currently off-limits. To avoid being recognized, Evil continued towards the breakroom to hide. He felt a slight panic as he debated what to do.

Unaware of the actual circumstances of the accident, he felt useless without any action plan. Evil was left to watch the movements of feet below the privacy curtain as the nurses did their jobs. Remaining in the shadows, Evil awaited an opportunity to approach his Babydoll.

He needed to know if he could continue ahead with his plans. The loss of control was keeping him awake. If she dies, so will his dreams! Everything they worked towards will once again be out of his reach. "Oh, Babydoll, you need to fight! We will be together soon."

It was early morning when Lila and Dallas left Clara's side to check in on the children and possibly bring them back to see Connor for a few minutes. It might help him. As they headed into the parking lot, Bear joined them as his shift ended.

"Dallas, Lila, I heard about Clara. How is she doing?"

"Hanging in there," Dallas answered.

"Hey, listen, I don't want to intrude, but I just wanted to pass something on to you. I'm sure there's a reason, and it's just on the off chance it was an oversight," he hesitated uncomfortably.

"Bear, what is it?" Dallas tried hard to keep his irritation down.

"I heard you and Clara have the same father." Seeing Dallas nod, Bear continued. "Well, your dad came in around three this morning and demanded to be allowed in on a visitor's pass, but his name wasn't on the list. I knew, even without asking for ID, who he was. He wasn't pleased to be excluded from the list. I acted dumb and told him there was no Clara Gibson here at the hospital," he shrugged slightly. "I hope I didn't cause any trouble."

"He asked for Clara Gibson, not O'Reilly?" Lila clarified as she exchanged looks with Dallas.

"Alright, thanks for the heads up, Bear. I think you have answered whether he should be on the list or not. For now, he stays off. If anyone else tries to get in who's not on the list, you text me right away," Dallas replied, shaking Bear's hand as he led Lila out to the car.

Rob left late morning, needing to return to the farm to ensure everything was running smoothly. At the first chance, he went to get himself a shot of whiskey to help him forget the sight of Clara trapped in the car, covered in blood. The first few moments were the worst of his life, waiting until the first responders could confirm if it was a rescue or recovery.

The announcement that Clara was still breathing was music to his ears as he slowly sat on the ground, waiting until the firefighters could free her from the car.

Chase had a hard time pulling Rachel from Clara's bedside. He had explained Connor needed to sit beside her for a while.

"Connor?" Rachel softly called as she approached the nurse's station. *He looks horrible*, she thought. "We are going to head out. We'll be back later."

Connor nodded. "I'll call you if there are any changes."

Rachel nodded as she stepped over to hug him.

"Rachel, do you know why they were in the city yesterday?"

"No idea. Michelle said it was last minute on Thursday evening. She figured you knew about it," she responded.

"She probably meant to tell me. I was home late. Clara was already asleep. I was called back to the hospital before dawn. We spent the day playing phone tag," he explained quietly before Rachel and Chase walked away.

Connor had kept his distance at the nurse's station, allowing her friends to take turns sitting beside her. He did go to her bedside every hour to assess her drainage lines and tubes and ensure no signs of internal bleeding. After her friends left, Connor could finally sit alone beside her bed. Exhausted, he leaned forward on his elbows, held her hand, and watched her sleep.

When the fatigue of two sleepless nights won out, Connor lowered his head onto the bed to rest his eyes. He was not aware when Clara first opened her green eyes. She was feeling hazy as she looked around with a slight panic. Her eyes rested on Connor, sleeping beside her in the chair pulled close to the bed. She touched his head and smiled before falling back to sleep.

Josh was sitting at the nurse's station looking over charts when the alarm on the monitor went off. At the realization it was Clara's, he quickly ran. It was signaling her heart rate was dangerously elevated. As he entered the room, Josh saw Clara was awake. He went in to assure her she was alright. But when Clara's eyes found Connor sleeping beside her, she smiled. Reaching with her right hand, she touched his hair before her eyes turned toward him. He thought she saw recognition before she closed her eyes.

In the background, her monitor dimmed as her heart rate returned closer to normal. He remained at the doorway, watching her sleep as her hand fell onto Connor's.

Connor remained by Clara's side into the second night. The only time he left was to visit with Reese and Hailey. Rachel and Chase sat with Clara. While Connor brought the kids into his office to eat lunch together.

Connor explained their mother's injuries and her need to stay in the hospital. He told them he would see them everyday he stayed with Mommy. They were to remain at the farm. Not understanding the reason, they were excited to be able to see the horses each day.

After the children left, Connor resumed his position beside Clara. He held her hand as he reviewed her scans on the tablet. His mind reviewed the orthopedic recommendation to surgically repair her left humerus and femur. It was a discussion he planned to have with Rachel and Lila.

Connor felt everyone's eyes following his every move as he remained close to Clara. He knew most of it was the small town response of those hiding behind the mask of concern. Most were just being nosey. He also expected the medical director to intervene soon. Connor would not be allowed to continue as lead doctor on Clara's case.

Neither Connor or Josh were aware of the housekeeper remaining in the shadows. Both would have recognized him if they had only glanced his way. As it was, little Hailey recognized him when she was leaving the area. She smiled and waved as she walked past.

waking up

It was very early on Labor Day, and the sun was not yet up when Clara opened her eyes again. She looked around at the multiple machines with lines and wondered what had happened. And then her green eyes met Connor's.

"Hey, beautiful!" Clara read his lips as he reached into his chest pocket. Connor pulled out her hearing aids. She attempted to assist, but her left arm was too painful, and the right arm appeared to be anchored with IV lines.

Once she could hear, she noticed the constant beeping of the machines beside her and soft chattering outside her room. While the light was dim, there was a faint glow from the various devices. Her panicked eyes returned to Connor in question.

"Clara, you were in an accident. You're at the hospital, but you are going to be alright. How's your pain?" he asked softly.

Clara attempted to speak, but her voice was hoarse. He reached for a cup beside him and assisted. "Small sips."

"Where are the kids?"

"At the farm with the Foxwoods. Everyone has been taking turns. If you're up to it, Lila will bring them in to see you," Connor answered as he gently stroked her hair.

"I'd like that," she whispered before falling asleep.

• • • •

Evil remained in the shadows, debating how to help his baby doll. He grew tired of waiting for the seat beside her to be vacant. He desperately needed to be close to her and to be reassured she would live at least until December 25th. Everything they've been working towards would soon be rewarded. He didn't think he had the time or patience to start from scratch. Again.

And when he was about to give up, the fool did leave her side. Evil quickly grabbed the wet floor sign and the mop, closing the privacy curtain slightly once he entered her room. He held her hand for a moment as he spoke, "Babydoll, you need to stay strong! Fight! We are in the home stretch now. There are only a few more months before we're together. We'll have it all, just as I've promised."

Evil smiled as a code was called for the room next door, giving him a few more minutes. "What can I do to help you?"

His smile grew when Clara's green eyes opened and met his blue. She opened her mouth in panic when she recognized the fierce blue eyes, but Evil quickly reassured her in his soothing voice. "Hey, Babydoll, you are awake! You gave me such a scare! For a moment, I thought you were gone. I'm so glad you're going to be alright."

He squeezed her hand again, saying, "Tell me what you want, and I will do it! Anything, and it's yours."

Clara's eyes squinted in confusion. "What?"

"Tell me what I can do!" He babbled, not realizing his words were again lost on her deaf ears. She didn't have her hearing aids on. She was trying to read his lips, but the angle was wrong.

"I know! How about I redo your bedroom and bath? I know the perfect person to help! It'll be completed before you return home. I need to leave. Get well soon, Babydoll!" Evil leaned down to kiss her forehead before fading into the shadows.

Clara blinked, and when her eyes were open again, Evil was gone. Was he ever there, or were her childhood nightmares still haunting her? Lifting her head, she searched the dim room. Seeing no one, she relaxed back onto the pillow. Fatigue won out, and she fell into a deep slumber. The incident quickly faded in her drugged haze.

Despite the sudden chaos in the owners' lives, the Foxwood Farms continued to operate as expected with the presence of the O'Reilly children.

Rob, usually up early, stood at the large kitchen window that overlooked the mountains towards the back of the farm. He sighed as he lowered his coffee mug. Typically, the daily event of watching the sunrise centered him. It somehow gave him an optimistic hope for the day and humanity in general, something he had never shared with anyone except Clara back in middle school and Shannon just a few weeks before. To his amazement, neither had laughed at him. Instead, each had remained beside him and agreed. Watching the sunrise was indeed therapeutic.

But not today, he thought as he replayed the last few days in his head. Rob couldn't even sum up his emotions about seeing both of his close friends trapped in the car. To his disappointment, Shannon had immediately allowed the bartender to calm her. After everything she told him about the breakup, Shannon still preferred the other guy. Rob was alright with that as he assisted with freeing Clara, relieved she was still among the living. The panic he contained deep in the pit of his stomach was almost unbearable while they all waited into the dark hours of the night to hear the outcome of the surgery.

Rob's fist clenched as the now familiar SUV pulled around the back of the house. Not even a minute later, his sister was immediately at the driver's door.

How had these two become so attached in such a short time, he wondered for the hundredth time in a few weeks.

Rob had been too immersed in Clara's return last spring. He never really thought about his sister hooking up with the wrong guy. Based on the interaction, he was confident it was longer than the volleyball season.

"Uncle Rob, Uncle Dallas is here!" Reese shouted from behind.

"Yeah, I see that," he answered miserably as the young children joined him to look out the window.

"Can he go riding with us? Can he please, Uncle Rob?" The three-year-old boy asked while his little sister of twenty months stood beside him with a big smile, nodding her head of short curls.

"Maybe he doesn't know how to ride," Rob wondered optimistically as he turned towards the young children. His heart clenched as he looked at the boy with his mother's eyes and the girl, a mini version of her mother, except for the sky-blue eyes and blond hair.

"Oh, but you can teach him! You're the best rider here," Reese declared.

"How would you know?"

"Mommy said so! It must be true. Mommy is always right. Are we going to see Mommy and Connor today?"

"Probably later in the day. Today is Labor Day, so you don't have school today. Are you alright to stay here with me?"

"We want to stay here with you and the horses. We can do school any day," the young boy answered, not understanding the holiday.

Rob agreed; it was daycare. He could always drop them off tomorrow before work or stay home with them. He had not decided yet. Not wanting to be the bad guy, he watched the children practically dancing in place as he sipped from his coffee. "What are you two waiting for? Go ask them already."

He sighed with annoyance as Reese and Hailey ran out ahead of him, cheering excitedly toward the newcomer. Rob simply continued towards the barn to start saddling up the horses.

In the city, Detectives Andy Sanders and Jim Walters were at their desks reviewing what they knew regarding the death of Jason O'Reilly. He went missing last January, but it was May before his remains were discovered. No one reported the man missing because the killer covered his tracks by sending messages to the wife and employer, giving time for the forensics to fade. His body showed evidence of a struggle with defensive injuries. Multiple stab wounds and blunt force trauma suggested a significant amount of rage and a personal connection.

They could not prove the theory of the wife's involvement. There was no proof she had a lover hidden away or even a jealous ex-boyfriend that couldn't let her go. No disgruntled clients that could not account for their whereabouts during the time in question. They could not find anyone in the city that wanted Jason dead.

Andy, the younger detective, was hopeful Jason's cell phone would lead them to the killer. The number was being monitored in case the phone was turned on. The cell towers would be able to triangulate the killers where about.

But his partner was not optimistic. "If the killer is smart, he tossed the phone the moment he learned the body was discovered."

"How's the Jason O'Reilly case working out?" Joel Montgomery was standing in the doorway of their office.

"Hey, Montgomery, heard you had some trouble with your case," Sanders greeted.

"Yeah, I just had my ass chewed. The case literally backfired," Joel answered. His anger was evident. "What's the latest with Jason O'Reilly?"

"You said his name with a bit of familiarity. Did you know the guy?" Walters asked.

"Yeah, I did," he shrugged as he tried to maintain a professional distance. "The girl I was seeing last year is close friends with his wife. We all hung out together."

The homicide detectives looked at each other before the younger one asked, "What is your take on the wife? She's young, beautiful, and smart. Do you think she could have been involved in his death?"

"Hell no! She's as honest as they come. They were tight and totally devoted. My girl introduced them to each other back in college." Joel looked at them both. "You don't have any other leads?"

"We can't find anyone in this city that would have motive to kill him. The wife and kids inherit life insurance," the older man answered. "She would not have had the strength to do it herself, and we can't connect her with any secret lovers. There doesn't seem to be any connections with anyone."

"We're now trying to determine who would want the wife back in her hometown, but we found something off about O'Reilly's own connections to the town. We're about to drive out to talk to her," Sanders reported.

"That's not going to happen anytime soon. Clara was shot while driving on route 20 which caused her car to roll down the ravine. She suffered a couple of gunshot wounds plus the injuries from the accident. She's critical. It's been touch and go. Last I heard, she hadn't woken up yet. My case has now expanded to murder for hire. She had the misfortune of being behind the wheel of my witness's car," he answered sadly.

Joel sighed with annoyance as his emotions threatened to surface. The new developments in his complicated case brought him back to the city. He needed to talk with his boss and coordinate the next step of his investigation.

Last spring, his undercover assignment collapsed when Shannon's employer discovered someone in the company leaked information from the police side. Unfortunately, the mole labeled Shannon as the company snitch. Joel knew for a fact Shannon knew nothing of his investigation, not even his being a cop. They met at a gym over a year ago, after he went undercover at her work. She knew nothing, nor did he use her as a source.

And now, she was suffering the consequences of his mess. He couldn't fight the attraction. Honestly, he didn't even try.

Joel needed to find the mole in the police department.

Shannon was getting restless in isolation, away from her friends. Unable to sleep since the accident Friday night, she paced the small room in her new pajamas. Any other time, Shannon would have laughed at the absurdity of her new wardrobe.

The recent discount store specials purchased on her behalf early Sunday morning were the complete opposite of anything she would have ever bought, let alone worn. But when she verbalized her opinion, Joel made it clear he didn't want to hear about it.

And to add insult to her temperamental state, his actions made her feel guilty about everything going on right now.

It was her fault Clara, one of her best friends, was in the hospital, fighting for her life.

But Clara's not just a friend, she's actually my sister! My maternal half-sister. How did we not see this sooner? We have the same biological mother. Susannah Gibson is my mother. All those years I played over at her house, did she know I was the baby she gave up for adoption at birth? Did she even hold me?

Shannon stopped in front of the mirror to study her face. Her hair was a redder shade of brown, with no curls. Her face was shaped similarly to Clara's, and the green eyes were the same.

But her height, type A personality, intelligence, and love for math and money were similar to Jason's, her paternal half-brother. Shannon thought with a heavy sigh. She never considered that they were such close friends so quickly because they shared DNA.

She thought tangibly that it certainly explained why their relationship never crossed the line. Never dawning on her until now. Shannon never looked at him as anything but a friend. Did he ever wonder why? But they still had differences. He was the quiet, introverted nerd. He always sat in the back of the classroom and watched with those intelligent sky-blue eyes, never raised his hand but always knew the answers when called on.

And the moment he laid those eyes on Clara, he was smitten with her. Shannon smiled at the memory. She was able to read his thoughts. *Was that some kind of sibling connection?* she wondered. Who was their biological father? Did the father have the matching blue eyes Jason shared with his daughter or a different color altogether?

The sounds of a car engine had Shannon pause in her restless pacing.

Joel pulled directly into the attached garage. Once the garage door was closed, he retrieved the groceries before getting his suitcase. He paused before entering the house. He was relieved his boss allowed him to keep the safe house a secret.

The trip into the city was longer than he expected. The paperwork alone was a nightmare. He was surprised his boss agreed and encouraged him to list the information of another safe house. They needed to catch the damn mole in the department. It was ruining an almost two-year undercover assignment. Everything he had on this stupid ass was potentially going down the drain. Except the foolish fuck was stupid enough to get caught following Shannon into the hospital. Big mistake. Not a stretch to prove he was connected to the Boss.

But to prove he was only following orders was more complicated, especially since he was now in the small town morgue. After causing the accident then having the stupidity to follow Shannon into the hospital and attempt to kill her, the enforcer deserved what came to him. Unfortunately, dead men don't talk.

"It's about time. I was starting to get worried," Shannon's voice was soft as she met him in the kitchen.

"Nothing to worry about. I told you I had to go into the city and talk face-to-face with my boss out of the office. He agreed to my plan," Joel explained before he returned to the garage for more groceries.

Shannon's eyes widened at the amount of bags before unpacking them.

"You bought a lot of stuff. How long are we going to be staying here?"

"As long as necessary. Hopefully, the seeds are planted, and we will find the damn mole," Joel answered.

"How long will that be, Joel? I need to get back home! Clara needs me," Shannon's voice betrayed her guilt.

"Shannon, this was not your fault," Joel started, turning away from the groceries, but she quickly cut him off.

"It's my fault, and you know it. I should have listened to you. You've been warning me about the danger since last spring." Her hand ran through her almost shoulder-length hair, longer than he's ever seen it. He liked it long.

"Shit, even Clara cautioned me. And now she's the one fighting for her life!" Her volume increased.

Joel remained quiet, pulling her in close for a hug. There was no point adding to her guilt. She already knew the consequences of her actions. And if he were honest, he was relieved that Shannon was not the one in the hospital fighting for her life, something he would never verbalize.

"How is Clara?" Shannon asked into his chest. "Is she awake? She must hate me!"

"Cautiously stable," he answered. "She was going in for another surgery this morning."

7

first day home

Clara Noelle O'Reilly sat in her wheelchair, looked out the window, and sighed. Her heart was heavy as she pondered the loss in her life. It has been three weeks since the accident. Everything had changed, and yet so much remained the same.

Her body had undergone four surgeries. Clara had forty-eight staples in various places with stitches on her face. She had significant bruising, still a dark purple along most of the left side of her body, while the discoloration on her face was a pale, sickly yellow. Until a week ago, she occasionally found small pieces of glass in her hair, difficult to remove as the small splinters seemed to weave themselves into her curls. Clara had yet to have a proper shower with flowing water from above.

Using her right foot, she reangled her wheelchair to better see her children below, playing outside at the daycare. Clara attempted to shift away from the pain, but any movement caused more pain elsewhere. Her pelvis was fractured in two places, minor injuries that would heal with time. Her left thigh was also broken but surgically repaired. The surgeon assured her she could apply full weight onto her legs, and the pain would gradually fade. Her dominant left arm was broken, as well as her left collarbone. While the final surgery was on her left arm, she was not to bear any weight or move her shoulder at this time. It was to be kept in a sling.

As a physical therapist, she knew these restrictions were temporary, and the pain would gradually fade. But as the patient, Clara was often too overwhelmed by the pain to complete the simplest tasks, like walking and getting out of bed. Forget the more complicated activities such as going to the bathroom or brushing her teeth. Granted, she could easily use her right hand, but her coordination was horrible. For these reasons, it had been suggested she go to her rehab facility to get stronger until she could complete these tasks independently. Clara refused.

Her friends all believed going to the Foxwood Farm would be the best solution. There was plenty of space without the stairs. Everyone could rotate around the clock and assist with the children. Clara refused this option as well.

She wanted to return home to her place. Eat in her kitchen and sleep in her bed. Clara wanted her children to be sleeping down the hall in their beds. Most importantly, she wanted Connor sleeping beside her.

A month ago, she took all these things for granted. Clara didn't think this was too much to ask. But apparently, it would take a miracle. Today, her prayers were answered. She was finally getting discharged home.

Connor agreed she would recover better at home surrounded by her children. He officially moved into her place. Connor was taking the first week off to assist her each day. Afterward, he would bring Reese and Hailey to daycare in the morning. Depending on his schedule, either he or her friends would bring them home.

· · · · ·

Evil glanced at his watch before he quickly got to work. Once the new sheets were on the bed, he arranged the new comforter with the ridiculous extra pillows. While he preferred keeping the bed simple, Tiffany had assured him the extra pillows were necessary.

The thought of the interior decorator brought Evil mixed feelings. She was surprisingly helpful in the redecorating but disappointing in the bedroom. He was surprised her talents were limited. He understood why the foolish doctor had to let her go. And to think Tiffany thought she would be hired to redecorate his house! He would only admit to himself that Evil considered it for a second, only to see his wife's reaction.

The sudden chuckle surprised him as he remembered the last expression on Tiffany's face. It made the whole hassle of taking time out to prepare the room so worth it. He paused long enough to relieve himself before he grabbed the towels.

A quick glance at the clock reminded him of the limited time. He already had the furniture set up, with her clothes properly organized in the closet.

An hour later, Evil slowly walked around the bedroom, pleased with the results. Surprisingly, this part of the plan went smoothly. Everything was ordered and delivered on time. He had the walls freshly painted a similar shade. With the new bedding in place, her bedroom looked perfectly precise. "Babydoll will be pleased," he thought smugly.

As he stepped into the bathroom, he nodded his head with approval. The soft lavender was definitely the right shade to go. Calm and soothing to help his Babydoll heal. He mentally groaned at the memory of all the time spent scrubbing the splattered paint from the tub. It had taken hours! Placing the last towel on the rack, Evil stepped back to admire his work.

He admitted to doubts about the mermaid theme, but it worked! The new painting had all the colors from the lavender walls, the green towels, and the area rugs with the mismatched miscellaneous items on the counter.

Returning to the bedroom, Evil's eyes stopped on the new loveseat. His mind immediately listed several uses as he sighed with anticipation. The mermaid theme did not carry over from the bathroom, but the colors did.

In less than a month, he had accomplished so much! The shower chair was in place and new mats for the floor. The hefty cost of the new items for the bathroom and bedroom would be worth it. Evil would be rewarded for the added luxury before too long. December 25th was getting closer every day. But it was worth it! His Babydoll was coming home!

Evil gathered the packing before vacuuming the rug once more. All he needed was to drop off the new books in the baby's room before he stepped out of the house.

Connor paused at the door, watching Clara. He was still recovering from the image of her all bloody and unrecognizable after her accident. There had been so much blood that he didn't even recognize the woman he had known for nearly three decades and slept beside throughout the summer. The realization of her being in a vehicle that crashed head-on into a tree and rolled down a ravine after being shot twice was very difficult to accept.

Being the trauma surgeon present when she arrived at the emergency, Connor performed the initial surgeries until she stabilized. After the first weekend, he was forced to step down as her doctor. Understandable, all things considered.

Connor had just completed the discharge process. He had her medicine schedule, follow-up appointments, home health therapy schedule, list of restrictions, and recommendations. Clara's bags and flowers were already loaded into his SUV.

"Hey, beautiful, are you ready to go?"

Clara turned in the wheelchair and smiled as she nodded. When the nurse came to transport her down the hall, she wanted to resist, but Connor's expression suggested she simply go with the flow.

Connor's vehicle was already parked outside the lobby. While he opened the passenger door, she locked her brakes and lifted the footplates with her right foot before slowly standing up. She remained still as she allowed the pain in her pelvis to subside before she pivoted on her right foot and slowly reached back to sit. Again, she needed a moment before scooting into the seat.

Connor waited patiently before reaching in to buckle her seatbelt. As he reached across, she touched his cheek. "Thank you."

He kissed her before standing and closing the door. It was all the reassurance he needed. This was the right plan for them.

While driving home, they stopped at the pharmacy before pulling into her driveway. As he walked around the hood, she opened her door and slowly scooted herself to the edge of the seat. Eventually, Clara stood, grabbed her quad cane, and slowly walked to the porch. Without a word, Connor kept his arm around her waist as she slowly negotiated the four steps onto the porch and then a final step into the house. She slowly lowered herself onto the sofa when she entered the family room.

"Clara, do you need anything? I'm going to empty my rig." Connor watched as she slowly scooted back. He noted the wincing and made a mental note to check on her last pain dose. She seemed to be having too much pain. "I'll get you a pain pill when I get back."

"I don't need another pain pill. I'm fine," Clara responded, her eyes still closed as she gingerly shifted her weight.

"Could have fooled me. What is your pain right now?" he challenged.

"Does it really matter?" She sighed when she finally reached a comfortable enough position. Her eyes opened when she continued, "It's any number between one and ten at one place or another on my left side. My body feels like it's been shot, crashed, and rolled, used as a pin cushion and advertisement for a staple gun. No amount of pain meds will resolve all that right now."

Connor remained quiet as Clara, for the first time, vented her frustrations. He squatted down beside her, trying to assess her need for further pain meds. His knuckles gently caressed her cheek as he whispered. "I don't like seeing you in pain."

"Would you rather I be an accident-prone zombie addict?" Clara demanded, looking into his soothing brown eyes. After a moment, she reached for his hand with her right. "Trust me on this. I'm the one with the pain. I should be the one to decide if another pill is needed. I know how it works. Right now, I just need a minute to catch my breath."

Connor nodded his agreement before stepping outside. After a few minutes, he had everything out of his vehicle and was bringing the bags upstairs. He had taken a few minutes to unpack their things. He was officially moving in.

While it wasn't the first time he'd been in her room since the accident, it would be the first time overnight. It had been only the first weekend to grab a few things quickly.

Connor noted with surprise the bathroom was sparkling clean, free of paint stains in the tub. He assumed one of her friends saw the task of redecorating the bathroom, confident they had cleared it with Clara during their visits to the hospital. He had overheard Rachel and Lila discussing ideas. Everyone had been eager to help care for Reese and Hailey, and ease her transition home.

It was certainly an extravagant touch, redoing her bedroom and bath. He chuckled when he opened the closet to hang his clothes quickly. *Someone is a bit OCD*, he thought, looking over the rearranged organization of Clara's clothes. Not only were the similar articles of clothing grouped together, but they were also organized by color and use. Casual flowed to professional to dressy with more formal wear at the end.

He wondered tangibly as he hung his clothes; it must be Rachel. He worked beside Lila. She was organized, but he would never label her as OCD. Next, he went to his few drawers to complete his unpacking. Clara's clothes were placed into the hamper. Unable to resist, Connor pulled open one of Clara's drawers. Smiling again at the order, *I give her a week before this is all messed up*, he chuckled.

When Connor returned downstairs, Clara was still sitting on the sofa with her eyes closed. Assuming she was asleep, he went into the kitchen to get them each a drink.

With her eyes still closed, she was aware of his presence as he sat across the room. "Connor, if I agree to let you carry me upstairs, will you rest with me?"

When he didn't answer right away, she opened her eyes. He slowly stood up. His hand accepted her right hand to assist her with standing before he picked her up.

Once they were upstairs in the hall, her eyes sparkled as she stated, "I may need you to help me change into something more comfortable."

Connor paused in his step as he looked down and grinned. "Beautiful, I told you I'll do anything you need. Just say it."

A couple of hours later, Connor was surprised he'd fallen asleep beside Clara. He reached for his cell, noted a text from his mother, and then read the one from his brother. "Oh, shit!"

"What's wrong?" Clara asked, feeling refreshed after her nap in her own bed. She had meant to ask about the new decor.

"Matt is here," Connor announced, sitting up to pull on his jeans.

"Of course he is. I'm not dressed!" Connor heard Clara say as he left the room. *And her spunk is back,* he thought with a grin.

When he opened the front door, Connor was surprised to see his brother standing on the porch surrounded by grocery bags. "What's all this?"

Matt paused in the process of handing him bags. "What the hell have you been doing?"

"Nothing. Why?" Connor answered, accepting the bags before following his brother into the kitchen.

"You're without a shirt; jeans aren't even closed, no footwear, and your hair's a mess. Were you raised with barbarians? You're lucky I arrived before your mother. She would disapprove of you rolling Clara around in the sack so soon," Matt teased.

"It wasn't like that! We were only resting," Connor answered defensively as he peeked through the bags.

"Uh huh, that's what you're going to go with? Well, how is Clara doing?" He stepped around his brother as he announced, "I'm going to head up and say hello."

"Give me a minute to help her get dressed first," Connor answered without thinking.

Matt laughed. "It wasn't like that? Why doesn't she have any clothes on?"

"She wanted to be comfortable. Clothes aggravate the staples," Connor answered as he chased after his brother.

Within moments, the brothers were wrestling in the hall when the light suddenly flashed on. "Why are you two horsing around?"

They both immediately stood straight up. Clara stood outside her bedroom wearing an old pair of sweatpants and oversized flannel.

"Clara, you are looking better each time I see you," Matt announced as he kissed her forehead.

"Matt, it's very kind of you to lie," she answered, accepting his arm as they strolled together towards the stairs.

"No lies. I'm sorry for the intrusion. Connor's mother insisted on having groceries delivered. She and my dad will be here soon with dinner," he explained.

"Dinner? Did she make it?" Seeing the nod, Clara inquired, "Is Connor's mother a good cook?"

"Not too bad." They stopped at the top of the stairs. Matt watched as she closed her eyes and breathed. "Do you want me to carry you down the steps?"

"No, I need to do it. It just takes me a bit of time," Clara explained as she opened her eyes and smiled softly.

Matt realized she likely didn't want to be watched, so he excused himself and continued down the steps. Connor took his place beside her as she slowly navigated down. Once they were on the first floor, he handed her the quad cane as she continued to the sofa. He was relieved she agreed to a pain pill as his parents arrived.

Clara watched Connor interact with his family, always fascinated, even as a young girl. After his mother instructed the covered pan to be placed into the oven and where to place the flowers and bags, she entered the family room.

"Clara, you must be happy to be home. I hope we aren't intruding. We wanted to stop over and assist you both with getting settled," she explained.

Clara slowly stood up to receive the hug before they walked into the kitchen together. "Mrs. Emerson, you are never an intrusion. I am always happy to see you. I didn't realize you were both in town."

"Clara, please call me Heather. Dan and I wanted to see the children. Matt's boys have been growing up so fast. And I hoped to see yours, but they aren't here?" She did not comment that they had been in town since the weekend of the accident.

"Lila and Dallas will be dropping them off soon," Clara answered when Connor gave her a questioning look. "She called and offered."

"Connor Daniel Emerson, why are you not dressed?" Heather demanded as she finally realized her son was wearing only his jeans. But when she heard her stepson laughing, she continued, "You know what, don't answer that. Get upstairs."

Connor had no choice but to do as instructed. He kissed Clara on the top of her head before heading out, shoving his brother as he passed.

Heather paused momentarily to watch her son interact with the younger girl from next door. When did Connor fall so hard for her? She had not even been aware of his interest in Clara until Matt had explained the details of Eric's arrest last June. She doubted the relationship until she and her husband entered the hospital that first week. Connor was beside himself with worry. She could see his love and devotion as he reluctantly stepped away to greet them at the entrance of the ICU. His clothes were disheveled, his hair messed up, nor had he shaved in a few days. But the look in his eyes said it all. Clara Noelle was the love of his life. She should have known. The two were always close. Connor always knew before she did what was happening in the young girl's life.

"You didn't need to bring over groceries," Clara was saying as she attempted to stand.

Seeing her grimacing in pain, Heather motioned for Clara to remain seated. "Nonsense. Shopping is what I do. And we are all family; we help by doing what we do best. If you need a painter, I would be able to tell you who to call, but shopping, I can always do."

"Thank you, Mrs. Emerson. I do appreciate it. It'll take some of the strain off Connor."

"Clara, please, call me Heather," the older woman repeated, sitting down beside her. "We've known each other all your life. If you need anything, and I mean anything, please don't hesitate to ask. It can be bringing groceries, babysitting, or even knocking sense into Connor if he's difficult."

"If anyone is to be knocking sense into Connor, it should be me," Matt stated as he and his father returned with more bags.

"Matt, please hand me the green bag," Heather instructed as she placed it on the table for Clara to open.

Clara was hesitant at first but smiled softly before peeking inside. She pulled out a soft purple pajama set. They would most likely keep her comfortable and warm without aggravating her incisions.

When Connor returned downstairs, Lila and Dallas had arrived with the children. Reese was so excited to finally be home! He stepped through the front door and yelled, "Connor, I'm home!"

"Hey, Reese, Hailey!" Connor squatted down as the children ran towards him. When he stood up, he was holding the young girl. "I have a big surprise for you. Thanks for picking them up. We really appreciate it."

"Is it a puppy?" Reese wondered.

"No, better," Connor informed the children.

"What's better than a puppy?" the boy asked, following into the kitchen. He suddenly paused when he realized there were strangers in the room.

"Mama!" Hailey squealed as Connor lowered her to the floor. Both children ran to their mother.

"Mommy! You are home! Do you have to go back?" Reese's green eyes were wide with concern.

"No, I'm here to stay, just like you both," Clara answered with a smile as she hugged them each with her right arm.

Seeing Clara wince as the little girl tried to climb into her lap, Connor picked her up to gently place her down.

"Heather, Dan, you know Lila but have you ever met Dallas Thompson?" Clara made the introductions before she further explained. "He is my older half-brother."

Matt was pulling beers out of the fridge when he heard the announcement. His eyebrows shot up in question at his brother. Connor simply shrugged but gestured they'd talk later. Dallas observed the exchange.

Heather initially had concerns about her stepson's reaction. She knew his feelings towards Clara's father very well and worried Matt would take it out on Dallas. Regardless, she invited the couple to stay for dinner. Josh soon joined them when he stopped in to drop off papers for Connor to sign. Heather purposefully invited her grandson to stay, realizing she was overstepping her place, but it guaranteed Matt would behave himself.

As it happened, she worried for nothing. Dallas made a great impression. She knew of him as a child, but Heather never interacted with him until tonight. She and her husband were surprised to learn he served in the army and currently worked as a ranger at the federal park. Who knew a child of Felicia Thompson and Carl Gibson would turn out so well?

After dinner, Lila and Dallas assisted with cleaning up the kitchen while Clara slowly made her way to the family room to be more comfortable. The children and Heather followed as she gave presents and announced the circus would be in town later in the week. They were both excited to go to the circus. Hailey started roaring as she pretended to be a lion.

Clara smiled and relaxed, watching Reese and Hailey sit with Heather as she read them a book. She closed her eyes and fell asleep. The exhaustion of her first day home finally won over.

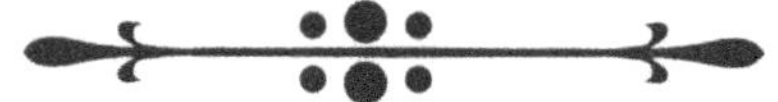

    SHADOWS OF THE PAST

A week later, Connor was returning back to work. He waited patiently at the bottom of the stairs while Clara slowly descended the steps. Both the children were beside him, counting with each step, cheering her on.

"Seventeen steps, Mommy!" Reese announced.

"Go, Mama, go go," Hailey stated as she hugged her right leg.

"Yes, it certainly was. Sometimes it feels like there's more," Clara paused to catch her breath as Connor handed her the quad cane. She slowly walked to her recliner chair, easing herself down before each child kissed her goodbye.

"How could there be more steps?" the boy asked. "We count every day, and it's always seventeen."

The young girl talked with words only her brother seemed to understand.

"No, Hailey. The man can't add steps," he assured his sister. "We would hear him if he did."

"Are you sure you'll be alright?" Connor asked, looking over everything on the table beside her. She had her large water bottle, cell phone, light breakfast, tissues, and hot chocolate.

"Mommy, I can stay here with you," Reese offered as he sadly hugged her.

"Reese, don't you have your field trip to the Foxwood Farms today?"

"Yeah, but I can go anytime. Uncle Rob told me I didn't need to wait for an invitation," he shrugged. He wondered about the man his sister often talked about. No one seemed to know anything about it. Was she making it up, or did he really exist? Maybe he was with the Easter Bunny and Santa Clause. They only came around if everyone was asleep.

Clara watched as Connor mouthed, 'Uncle Rob?' trying not to laugh. "Sweetheart, I think you would be bored staying home with me, but I appreciate the offer. I'll be alright. And when you get home tonight, I want to hear all about your day. You too, Hailey."

Connor leaned down to kiss her forehead. "Text me if you have any problems."

Clara nodded as she slowly scooted back into her seat, watching him and the children leave. Once she was alone, she ate while sipping her hot chocolate. She had scrolled the news feed on her cell. Then she forced herself to complete her exercises. She thought having a home health therapist instruct her on what she already knew to do was stupid. Clara canceled the home health visit.

After the exercises, she slowly walked through the dining room and into the kitchen. She used the bathroom, grabbed a bag as she returned to place the dirty dishes inside, and returned to the kitchen to rinse.

When Clara returned to the family room, her cell chimed a text. It was from Connor, asking if she was alright and needed anything. She assured him she was fine. As she sat, Clara debated sending a text to Matt. Now was a good time to have him stop in since Connor, for some reason, got all weird when his brother was around. After pressing send, she received a response. Matt stated he would stop in around two. Clara thought that was perfect. It gave her plenty of time before everyone returned in the early evening.

Once she was settled back in her recliner, Clara became restless. She didn't want to watch TV. *Maybe if I had something to read*, she pondered. Not interested in the magazines beside her, she thought about her mother's journals upstairs.

Forgetting her cell, Clara slowly made her way up the steps and down the hall to her room. As always, she contained her annoyance at Connor's welcome home gift. He totally rearranged her closet and drawers, repainted the walls, and changed her comforter set. Even the theme was different. While she did like the mermaids and the colors, Clara was surprised Connor had made the changes without consulting her. He didn't even say anything about it. And neither did she. Mostly because she was too exhausted to have what she knew would be a heated discussion. *Don't even get her started on the changes in the bathroom*, Clara thought as she limped to the new loveseat, replacing the chair. She needed to rest for a few minutes. Her eyes looked over the color scheme and the perfectly made bed.

Smiling at the thoughtfulness, Clara was reminded, again, of Connor's A personality. Knowing him all her life, he had always been organized with everything meticulously planned. A wonder, really, that they got along so well. She was the opposite, not a slob, but Clara rarely planned things ahead of time and lived in the moment. Her day wasn't ruined if the bed wasn't made or dishes were in the sink. Chores always got done, eventually.

All was going well until she squatted down toward the box on the floor. She literally saw stars as she had to push into the doorframe to brace herself and slowly slide back up onto her feet. She did not doubt if she allowed herself to sit on the floor, she would never be able to stand up independently. Pausing for a few minutes, leaning into the closet wall, Clara thought it interesting her closet had enough room for an adult to stand. She looked around her room, and her eyes stopped on the bed.

She debated taking a nap. *Better not*, she thought. One of Connor's rules was that she did not attempt the stairs alone. She needed to return downstairs to her recliner. If she slept too long and he found her upstairs, he might not leave her alone again.

Clara slowly pulled from the wall and limped back down the hall. When she was on the tenth step, she was too exhausted to continue further down. Her body didn't have enough rest between the exercises and the stairs. Using her right hand on the rail, she slowly lowered herself down onto the step and rolled onto her right side. *I'll just rest a few minutes*, she thought, closing her eyes.

Two hours away, Shannon was panicking as she looked around the kitchen. What was she thinking? How could she suddenly prepare a five-course meal on her own? The eggplant parmesan was finally in the oven; the apple cobbler was cooling on the counter; the salad, the easiest to assemble, was already in the fridge next to the homemade dressing. The minestrone soup was simmering on the stove. The caprese appetizer was the only thing left.

Noting the time, Shannon quickly sliced the mozzarella and then the tomatoes, debating the arrangement on the plate. Once basil leaves were placed, she wondered if she should pour the balsamic vinegar or wait. *Wait*, she decided. She needed to get the table set.

But when she opened the cabinet to get the plates, she realized she used every dish and pan in the house to make the meal. *Shit, how the hell did Lila and Rachel always make cooking look so easy?* She wanted nothing more than to call one of her friends for advice.

As she began to fill the sink with soap and water, Shannon heard the sounds of the garage door opening. *Shit, he's back! What am I going to do?*

Moments later, Joel entered the kitchen, pausing in surprise at the sight before him. Dirty dishes cluttered the small galley kitchen, with spilled red sauce splattered on the stove and floor. And most interesting,

Shannon stood at the sink with her hair puffed up from the heat, her face flushed, and various stains all over her clothes.

"Honey, I'm home?" he joked as he looked around the kitchen in amusement.

"What? No, it's not like that," Shannon answered with frustration. "Joel, I'm not trying to impress you or even try to get back with you."

Joel's eyebrows went up in question.

"Honestly! I'm bored out of my mind," she dragged the words out as she turned to retrieve the dishes to wash before setting the table.

"I didn't know you could cook," he admitted, lifting the lid on the pot. "Smells good."

"I don't know if I can cook; we haven't tasted anything yet." Shannon was quickly washing the dishes. "I'm not trying to impress you. It's just I'm bored. I figured you'd be hungry when you stopped in. I don't have anyone else to talk with! You won't let me call any of my friends."

"Shan, we've been through this! There's a contract out on you," Joel explained again. His heart ached, as always, when he visited with her. "I can't protect you if one of your friends leads the killer back here."

"How long will this take? Joel, why does my life have to be on hold while everyone else is living their lives?" She all but tossed a pot into the drying rack. "I have no one to talk to, nothing to do but cook and bake for no one but myself and whoever else comes once in a blue moon to visit. It's killing me."

He remained silent, what could he say? They've had this conversation many times before.

"The worst part is, I do not know what he was doing!" Shannon was referring to her previous boss, who was arrested for money laundering and child labor, among other things. She was only one of many accountants working for his company. She had been kept on the legal side of his operation, working with real legitimate clients. "My life is on hold until the bastard's trial? I can't work, go to the store, contact my friends, or even access my own damn accounts!"

The sound of the timer caused her to turn around and stare at the oven before she turned back with a sigh. "Dinner's ready. Give me a few minutes to set the table."

A few minutes later, both were seated at the table with the caprese platter between them and a bowl of minestrone for each. Shannon watched as Joel sampled the soup.

"This is actually pretty good," he announced.

"Really?" Shannon's face lit up in surprise.

"Yeah, it is," Joel assured her as he continued to eat. "Why won't you tell me why you went into the city last month?"

"It's personal," she answered. When she looked up, Shannon was surprised to feel her stomach clench with nervousness. She missed the relationship they shared a year ago. They would each talk about their day over dinner. It seemed like a lifetime ago when he was undercover at her company. Granted, the meal was usually take-out or at a restaurant.

"Shan, you complain about no one to talk with, and I'm sitting right here, enjoying this crazy meal you made. Tell me, why were you and Clara in the city that day?"

"It's a long story."

"We have time." Joel leaned back in his seat.

Her eyes held his while she debated what to share. "Alright, last spring, the week of the arrest, was tough for me. Out of the blue, I was fired and treated like a criminal. Escorted out of the building. The only thing missing was the handcuffs when you all came running in to make the arrests."

"Shan." Joel had already heard this and wasn't in the mood to rehash it again.

"Let me finish. I'm only telling you so you can understand my frame of mind," Shannon quickly cut him off. "That was also the week I started to read my grandmother's journals. I was adopted. All my life, I thought of myself as an only child with two parents that passed young but started parenthood late. After my grandmother was gone, I had no one. Over the summer, I had this crazy idea of having my DNA tested. I was curious to see if I had any biological family.

"The Thursday before the accident, I received my results. I have half-siblings," Shannon paused to take a deep breath. "Clara is my maternal half-sister. The crazy thing is, we were so shocked to learn this we never even had a chance to talk about it. I was busy setting up appointments in the city while she prepared childcare. And on the way back, we were shocked to discover I have a half-brother. Just as everything was sinking in, Clara was not only one of my best friends but also my sister. Bullets suddenly were flying in the air! And we are rolling down into the ravine."

Tears were streaming down her face as she whispered, "Because of my recklessness, one of my best friends, *my sister*, was almost killed before we even had a chance to be sisters. I need to be physically close to Clara while she recovers. Well, if she'll let me. She must be so mad."

Joel reached over to take her hand. "Shan, Clara's getting better. She isn't angry with you or blaming you for the accident. Chances are, she's also missing her sister."

"How would you know?"

"I know Clara too. Maybe not as well or as long as you, but I know she loves you. She's tolerated your OCD enough to let you stay with her over the summer. If she saw that kitchen, she would never let you live it down." He gestured toward the mess with a big grin.

And as he hoped, she looked over and chuckled, wiping the tears from her face.

"Who is your brother?"

When Shannon answered, Joel's face paled.

Clara never heard her cell ringing. It seemed only minutes later when Clara heard her name being called, unaware it had been three hours since she closed her eyes.

"Clara! What the hell are you doing on the steps? Did you fall?" Devan Mancuso was standing at the bottom of the stairs looking up.

"No, I am just resting a minute," Clara answered, disorientated.

"Yeah? Just resting? Do you always sleep on the stairs?" Devan asked as he slowly lifted her into his arms.

He was carrying her into the family room as Connor stormed through the front door. "Clara! What happened?"

"I'm alright, Connor. Why are you here?" Clara could not conceal her annoyance as Devan slowly lowered into her chair.

"You didn't answer your phone," Connor explained. He looked toward his cousin, not understanding why she would be in his arms. "Did she fall? Where was she?"

"Connor, I told you, I'm alright. I was just taking a quick rest. And honestly, I am insulted that you immediately think I fell. What if I was in the bathroom or something? You expect me to always answer on the first ring? I must have fallen into a deep sleep because I didn't hear my cell. You shouldn't have bothered Devan," Clara argued.

Despite having the hearing aid and cochlear implant, she wasn't always guaranteed to hear when she was sleeping soundly. "Shouldn't you be in the middle of surgery or something?"

"No, I kept my schedule light in case there was an emergency like this one," he answered. "And I didn't immediately call him. It's been three hours!"

"Why didn't you wait until he called you back?"

"She was sleeping on the stairs when I came in." Devan felt the detail was paramount.

"Devan!" Clara yelled defensively.

"Clara, why were you on the stairs? Everything you need is down here." Connor had squatted down, resting his hand on her knee.

"I wanted to get one of my mother's journals to read," she answered, forgetting she never told him about them.

"Your mother's journals?"

"Hey, if everything is alright here, I'm taking off," Devan stated. He wasn't in the mood to watch them get all mushy together.

After Devan left, Connor lifted Clara into his arms before sitting in the recliner with her on his lap. "You have your mother's journals?"

"Yeah, Rob brought them over the evening you came home, when we were arguing."

"You never told me about them," he stated.

Clara shrugged as she wondered why herself. "I don't know why I didn't. I guess I just wanted something private of my mother's, which is stupid because it's not like you'd want to read them."

"Probably not. What does your mother write about?" Connor was curious if his brother was in them.

"Oh, you know, typical teenage girl's dreams, heartaches, and crushes," she answered. "She only uses initials and never mentions anyone by name, so it's been a challenge trying to figure out who everyone is."

"Yeah?" He thought about the time she received them. It was roughly the time her nightmares started to get worse. The journals were probably a triggering point in her behavior and added to his theory she saw something all those years before. "Does she write throughout her adulthood?"

"No, only through high school. Rob found them in my room, hidden away. He found them when they were tearing down a wall. I enjoyed reading them, but it made me worry." Clara paused as she reached for his hand.

Connor remained silent, as he always did, as she placed her palm against his. It was a familiar gesture from when she was younger. He knew Clara was debating something. He remained quiet, waiting and wondering what she was going to say.

"Reading them has made me more aware of how much she lost at an early age. Her brother and her parents, the choices she had to make, and the choices made for her. It made me miss her and sad to lose her so soon. Everyone close to me also dies young. It's like a family curse," she whispered. "I thought if I pushed you away, you would leave me before something happened to you. Instead, it was Shannon."

Connor knew Clara had anxiety, but he was shocked it was over his safety. And to realize they were working through this just days before her accident and what happened to Shannon. What horrible timing!

"Clara, what are you afraid is going to happen?"

"The shadow will get you," Clara answered as a tear fell. "I realize it sounds stupid, especially saying it out loud. When I was young, I hid from it in your treehouse. Something would wake me in the night. I don't know what it was. Looking back, I would have thought it was a dream. Someone hidden in the shadows would lead me out of my room and protect me from Evil. I would look out the window of the treehouse and see him looking for me in my room. Until now, I wondered if it was my mother's way of looking out for me, leading me in my dreams."

Connor cringed as he realized she was no longer talking about a child's perception of dreams but an actual person. "Clara, who is the shadow?"

"No idea. I know who he is in my dreams. I think I follow him into the light, and he turns in my direction. I don't know if he sees me. I always know who he is, but it fades. I don't remember it when I wake up," Clara whispered. "There's one journal that made my dreams so vivid. I would dream of following him around. It was always so real. It's like I'm cursed. Anyone close to me is at risk. The accident would never have happened if I hadn't been driving her car. Now, I've lost Shannon."

"Oh, sweetheart," Connor pulled her in for a close hug, "I forgot you were pretty out of it right after the accident. You don't remember us talking about it? You weren't the one to bring it on her. Shannon was the target, not you. Only you were injured in the accident. She's under protection as a witness. Her boss sent one of his guys after her. You were driving her car. He was aiming for the driver of her car, expecting it to be her."

Clara pulled back to look closely at his face. "How do you know this?"

"They caught the man who shot you," he explained, hoping to keep it to a minimum. But she continued to look at him in question. "When Lila was transporting Shannon to radiology for a CT scan, Devan and the ex-boyfriend followed. Shannon was agitated and concerned for you. He somehow followed and attempted to take her out. Instead, *he* was taken out. A code blue was called while I was preparing for your surgery. The ex-boyfriend decided to place her into protective custody."

"Ex-boyfriend? Joel? Why didn't Devan?" Clara asked.

"It wasn't his case. Besides, they broke up back when you had the incident with Felicia Thompson on the porch," he answered, hoping to avoid the details.

"They broke up a month before? Where was she staying if she wasn't with him?"

Connor simply raised an eyebrow as he tilted his head with a slight shrug. "I would rather not gossip about your friends."

Her green eyes remained on his brown as she quickly assessed what she knew. "So she stayed at the farm, not the first time. The farm was as much of a safe haven for her as it was for me."

He groaned inward as he realized he would have to spell it out for her. "Devan wasn't surprised she was staying at the farm; Lila was."

Clara was quiet, momentarily processing what he said and what he meant. "You are saying Lila wasn't aware Shannon was staying there because she stays at Dallas'? That's not shocking news. You've been staying here. Chase has been staying at Rachel's. So what if Lila stayed over at his place? What's the big deal if Shannon stays at the farm with Rob? It wouldn't be the first time."

"Rob and Shannon have been together before?" Connor was shocked.

Clara chuckled as she shrugged. "I am not sure the extent of what went on between them, but they have always been close."

"And you are alright with this?"

"Why would I care? I have you." She smiled, leaning in to kiss him. When she pulled back, her eyes twinkled. "So if you kept your day light, do you have to return to work?"

"Just to pick up the kids. Josh is busy with some paperwork," Connor chuckled, liking where the conversation was heading as he leaned down to kiss her.

Then the doorbell rang. Connor groaned out loud while Clara giggled, forgetting about the earlier invite.

Connor was surprised to see his brother when he opened the front door.

"Connor, what are you doing at home? I thought you were returning to work today," Matt commented, stepping around him.

"I live here," he answered in a quiet tone. "What are you doing here?"

"So, you didn't go to work?"

"I did. I kept my schedule light in case of emergencies like today," Connor explained. Clearly puzzled, he asked again, "Matt, why are you here?"

"Emergencies? What happened? Is Clara alright?" Matt turned to see Clara struggling to stand up from her chair. "Clara, are you alright? What happened?"

"I am getting annoyed. Connor, what the hell? It was not an emergency! I fell asleep and didn't hear my cell ringing. It wasn't next to me." She shrugged as she limped with her quad cane towards the kitchen. "Connor overreacted."

"I did not! You were not responding for three hours, Clara. And you promised me you wouldn't be on the stairs alone," he called after her before turning to his brother. "Why are you here?"

"Clara invited me over this morning," Matt answered honestly.

"Why?"

"Not sure. It could be about the interviews set up, the wills, don't know yet," Matt speculated as the brothers followed her into the kitchen.

"Matt, would you like some coffee or anything? Connor, shouldn't you be at work?" Clara asked as she started to prepare the coffee.

"Clara, should you be up and about like this? Why don't you sit down while I make the coffee," Matt suggested, attempting to take over the task.

Connor, without a word, simply sat down at the table to watch the dynamics between the two. He continued to be curious about their interaction. No way he was returning to work. Connor pulled out his cell to send a text to Josh.

"Matt, of course, I should be up and about. It's the only way to get stronger. Please, have a seat. You drink your coffee black, right?" Clara asked, slowly making her way around. Noticing Connor was staying, she prepared three mugs.

When she finally sat, the men looked at her, waiting to learn about the meeting. Clara took a cautious sip from her coffee and pulled a cookie from the container on the table. She looked up to see both blue and brown eyes on her.

She smiled before she began, "Matt, I appreciate you stopping over on a busy day; I really do. What do you know about my mother being pregnant during her senior year of high school?"

Connor was shocked by the question. He had mentally listed the reasons for the invite, but this was not one.

Matt, on the other hand, while not shocked by the question, was more surprised by the person asking.

"How did you come by this information?" Matt asked.

"My mother's journals," she whispered, watching his reaction.

"Right, the journals," Matt's voice was quiet as he leaned back in his chair. "I forgot about them. She always had a composition book in middle school, constantly writing in it. I thought she would be a writer."

"Have you ever read them?"

"No, as far as I know, she always kept them away from prying eyes. I don't even know if Beth was ever allowed to read them," he commented, referring to Rachel's mother, Susannah's lifelong best friend. "What does she write about?"

It wasn't so much the question but the way he asked, Clara thought. He wants to know if her mother wrote about him. Again, she wondered about her mother's true feelings for the man across from her.

"She wrote about life. The first few were simply everyday things, what she did with who. Her opinions and feelings about whatever happened that day. As she started high school, her entries became more secretive. She had a code name for most people. I wasn't able to decipher beyond her brother and Beth. Until I read the journal, I never knew anything about her brother. She never really talked much about her childhood when I was young."

"Well, she did have some issues with her parents, especially after her brother's death, but her father had a heart attack and a massive stroke shortly after. It crushed your mother. In a short time, she went from a young girl raised to be a lady of leisure to ruling a household and business. Except she was never properly trained," Matt answered sadly.

"But you know about the pregnancy?" Clara pushed.

"Yes," he admitted. He looked around the table while he debated what to share. He wondered what the hell was the point of keeping the secrets now. The past is the past, and nothing will change it. He sipped his coffee before he answered.

"You know your mother and I grew up in homes next to each other. Looking back, I realize it was intentional. I didn't know it then. Our parents had encouraged us to be together, and we were, more or less, betrothed. It was a way for our fathers to secure their estates and combine resources. I would inherit the Emerson House, while her brother would inherit the Hawks House.

"When he died unexpectedly, your grandfather became bitter and angry. The day after he buried his son, Graham Hawks made it clear the arrangement was off. Your mother was no longer allowed to date me; forget us getting married. Susannah was to inherit her family house. I tried to fight it with my father, suggesting we live in the Hawks House while Connor inherited the Emerson House. I would still assist in the family businesses and study law. But my father demanded that I keep my distance from Susannah. We could still be friends, but never alone together. I wasn't sure if he thought maybe your grandfather would come around. Hell, we needed to finish high school and college before seriously discussing marriage."

Matt was quiet momentarily as he thought about the situation for the first time in years. He had been able to push the painful memories into a dark vault. He learned dwelling on the past was counterproductive.

"Her father set me up to be the bad guy. He *never* discussed his decision with her. I'm sitting outside trying to understand what my own father just demanded from me. I didn't even realize they had previously orchestrated us together only to cut us apart. I thought it was our decision, our dreams all along. Then your mother comes along. She's still upset about her brother's death and seeking me out for comfort. She had no clue our fathers were splitting us up. She believed I was breaking up with her on the worst week of her life. She kept her distance. Probably easier that way. But eventually, she learned the truth."

Matt stood up to walk around the kitchen and stopped to look out the back window as he debated what to share. *But she had already read the journals*, he reminded himself. *Clara already knows the worst*. He turned back, leaning against the counter as he continued.

"We gradually renewed our friendship. By senior year, I would usually drive her and Beth to school. One day, Beth was home sick with the flu or something. When we pulled into the parking lot, your mother opened her door to throw up. Then she closed her door and leaned back into her seat. Figuring she had Beth's flu, I offered to drive her home. She let out this harsh hollow laugh before turning towards me and announcing, 'I'm not sick, just pregnant.'"

Clara and Connor remained silent as they watched Matt deal with his conflicting emotions as he debated what to share. He returned to the table and sat down with renewed sadness.

"I was immediately upset that she would give herself to someone when we never did more than share an occasional kiss and hold hands. I had to remind myself there was a huge difference between fourteen and seventeen. If I were seeing other girls, why wouldn't she be seeing other guys? It's not like we were attached at the hip anymore. I asked, pretty harshly, who the hell the father was. I was so ready to punch him out for not taking precautions, the stupid prick.

"Instead, she denied knowing how or who. She thought maybe she was too drunk one night at a party because she had no recollection of the event." Matt was quiet again. Realizing his mug was empty, he retrieved the coffee pot to refill everyone's mug.

When he continued, Matt was across the kitchen. "I was about to ask her what she would do, but instead she asked me what I thought she should do. I mentioned the two guys she was casually seeing, but she didn't believe it was either of them based on how they acted around her.

"So, long story short, she and I skipped school that day. I drove her to a clinic I knew. Far enough away to keep her confidentiality but close enough to be back home by early evening. They gave her resources while she debated what to do. She never considered the easy way out. She said she could never live with herself. Towards the end of her pregnancy, she left home, lived in the city until the baby was born, and gave it up for adoption before she returned home."

Matt returned to the table to sit.

"And you never figured out who the father was? Were you able to narrow it down?" Clara questioned.

"I tried initially, but she would deny it," Matt answered before sipping his coffee. "I even talked with them, the guys I suspected, but both described platonic relationships. In the end, I suspected it was your father."

Clara was quiet as she wondered who the two guys were in the journal. Her mother did write about other guys. She had assumed one was Matt and the other was her father. Somehow, she never understood how her father won her mother's affection. Maybe that wasn't the case. Perhaps he was just the only one left. But he wasn't the father of the child given up for adoption.

"So, she wasn't your child?" Clara asked.

"No, she was not," Matt answered sadly, shaking his head.

"You two were never together until after she married my dad?"

"Why do you think we were ever together?" Matt challenged.

"Josh told me," she admitted.

Connor, quiet throughout the discussion, started coughing as he was drinking his coffee.

Both ignored him as Matt's eyes narrowed, studying her face.

Clara explained, "I would never have thought about it until he told me. He was a bit drunk, I suppose. He said that part of his fascination with me was that I was the product of the cause of his parent's divorce. He later learned his mother was likely exaggerating."

Matt could not contain the shock of his ex-wife telling their son about his infidelities, leading to a possible illegitimate child. "He told you all of this?"

"Yeah, he and I had a few drinks together," she glanced toward Connor before continuing, "He's a great kid. You are undoubtedly proud of him, despite his rebellion of going to medical school instead of law."

"I am proud of him, always have been. He's a bright kid. How did he come to realize his mother was exaggerating?"

"He did believe it when he was younger. Apparently, as I grew older and moved to the city, Josh figured you would have made more attempts to stay in contact with me. That was his first clue. Over the years, he realized Connor and his mother talked about me during family meals. Each updating the other about my life. Josh didn't think you would have remained on the sidelines. His theory was confirmed when I moved back, and you allowed Connor to date me."

Matt didn't know what to think about his son and Susi's daughter discussing their affair. He was partly embarrassed his son was the one to broach the topic. He didn't understand why the issue even needed to come up—ancient history.

Clara was quiet for a minute, studying Matt's face. Noting the sadness, she wanted to quickly explain her reason for bringing this up, not to have him beat himself up over the past.

"I'm asking about the baby because I found her," Clara announced.

"You found her? How? Your mother did a closed adoption in the city," Matt questioned.

Clara briefly explained about Shannon having the DNA tests for the whole group before she concluded, "Shannon and I are maternal half-sisters. The results arrived the week of the shooting. We had gone into the city to open up her file to determine who her biological father was. Instead, we found a biological paternal half-brother of hers."

When both men were looking at her in question, she whispered the answer for the first time since she heard the news. "It was Jason."

"Jason? Your Jason? He is Shannon's half-brother? How the hell did you figure this out?" Matt's eyes widened, not who he expected.

"He was adopted. His adoptive parents were killed in a car accident when he was young. When he came of age, he received papers. He had been quietly investigating his family tree. Jason had already taken the DNA test, but it only works if others also take it. There weren't any hits until Shannon's test results. As it turns out, my mother and Jason's biological mother used the same clinic and law firm. Both had similar reports of an unknown father. Shannon and I believed the circumstances were similar."

Speechless, Matt leaned back in shock. *Shannon Doyle is Susannah's child?*

Connor was leaning onto the table as he watched the two discuss personal details. When he glanced at his watch, he realized the late hour. He needed to pick the kids up soon. He watched as Matt leaned back in shock, momentarily speechless.

Connor stood up and walked to the refrigerator to pull out a beer to place in front of his brother. "Listen, I'm going to go get Reese and Hailey. While I'm gone, I've got the oven preheating. Matt, stay for dinner. We have one of Cook's pre-made casseroles of chicken and rice."

Matt didn't say a word as he sipped from the beer. He watched his brother kiss Clara's head, pausing to ask about her pain pills. Clara nodded as she looked up, rewarded with a kiss. He waited until Connor left the house before he spoke.

"You thought I was the father of both Shannon and Jason?" he asked sadly.

"At first, I thought maybe you were Shannon's father. I didn't know she was related to Jay. My mother's family believed a child out of wedlock was unacceptable; I know this. Her parents would never have accepted this child, regardless of who the father was. I had just read about her pregnancy a day or two before I learned about Shannon. I thought it wouldn't be so bad learning you were the father. You're a great guy. Who wouldn't be proud to have you for a dad? But I had my doubts when I learned about Jay. And hours later, the accident happened. Shannon and I didn't have the opportunity to discuss this," she quietly explained. "I don't know who was in more shock."

Matt was quiet as he continued to process the information. When the oven was preheated, he motioned for Clara to remain seated as he placed the dish into the oven.

Matt retrieved another beer. He remained in front of the fridge as he sipped, looking over pictures scattered of Clara with her children and her friends. He noted a photo of her with Dallas. Dallas' legal father, Zacariah Thompson, was not his biological father. Carl Gibson was, a fact recently made public.

He sighed again, remembering the conversation with Susannah after she announced her engagement. Matt tried to talk her out of it. She was adamant about going through with it, stating she and Gibson understood each other, but she never went into detail. Now he wondered if Susannah and Gibson both knew about the other's child, each unable to claim. He sipped again before he turned away to join Clara at the table.

"I can see the resemblance in her face. You both have her green eyes and similar facial features. You are a splitting image of your mom, except for your curly hair. But isn't Shannon your age?" Matt asked with skepticism.

"We thought so, but her original birth certificate was off by a year. Her birthday is in January, and mine's in December. She was already almost a full year older. She was pretty pissed, learning she was a year older but has decided to keep it mum," she answered. "We were too shocked to discuss this before the shooting."

"Why do you keep calling it the shooting?" Matt wondered.

"The shooting caused the accident," Clara explained. "If the tires had not been shot, the accident would not have happened. Hell, I might have been able to prevent the accident if my arm didn't give out on me or if we had been on a different stretch of the road. But they don't call that curve a killer for nothing."

"No, they don't," he agreed. "I'm sure you know of previous accidents at that spot."

"Yeah, my original prom date had an accident at that same spot the week of the prom. He was lucky the car that hit him had sent him into the ditch, not the ravine," Clara answered.

"I hadn't heard about that one," Matt answered.

"He was tapped from behind by an overly anxious idiot that should have known better. Luckily he only suffered a broken leg with minor bruising. Tell me about the others."

"There were many, most people too drunk to make the sharp turn or icy conditions," Matt paused, but decided she was bound to hear sooner than later. "That's the same spot where your uncle was killed. Except for the bullets, the accident was similar to yours. The driver lost control of the car. He missed the turn, went down the ravine, hit the same tree, and bounced as the car rolled further down. I'm fairly sure the car stopped in the same spot as yours. Fortunately, your car had better safety features."

"Very similar," she whispered, thinking of the irony. "I'm surprised no one mentioned earlier."

"Oh, it has been talked about, or I wouldn't have brought it up," Matt clarified. "You haven't mingled among the town elders since the accident. Only the older generations remember it. Many people were concerned the first weekend, waiting for your outcome. It didn't help that Shannon had disappeared. The details of the shooting aren't public knowledge. That, itself, is very surprising. Nothing seems to stay secret for long in this town."

"Well, both accidents were caused by outside factors. I can see why many saw the similarities," Clara agreed.

"What do you mean?"

"My mother wrote about her brother's car being sabotaged," Clara answered as he heard the front door open.

"Momma? I'm home!" They could hear the little boy yelling.

Matt wasn't able to inquire further.

Before Clara could stand up, her children surrounded her in the kitchen. Connor was standing in the doorway watching the reunion. He realized it would be a long night when he noted a second beer in front of Matt.

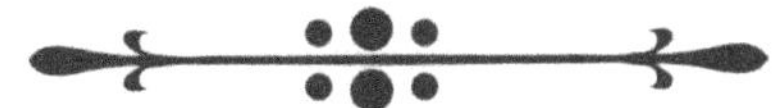

9 surprises

Chase Foxwood was usually easygoing. He thrived on challenges, especially when renovating a house that was centuries old. But the current puzzle was agitating him. He had what he once believed were the original house plans but learned the hard way the plans in his possession were only about a hundred years old. It didn't account for the original plans or the changes before the previous turn of the century. He retraced his steps as he knocked on the wall in the upstairs back hall. He continued back into the first room.

Rob was watching, intrigued. He followed his cousin into the room. "What are you doing?"

"I'm missing about ten square feet. The dimensions aren't adding up. This house is so ancient the original plans aren't even the original. I noticed the numbers weren't adding up last week, but now, it's pissing me off. I can't even think about tonight," he explained with frustration as he turned around to retrace his steps, knocking on the wall. Without realizing it, his hand was higher up. When the hollow sound echoed into the room, his gray eyes met his cousin's steel blue.

Rob's eyes widened in surprise as they studied the wall. He pulled out a small flashlight to examine it from top to bottom. No signs of a possible hidden doorway. Rob turned around to explore the whole room. The closet was obviously added years, if not a century, after the original build.

"Maybe we're going about this wrong," Rob stated as he walked from the room to the neighboring room. Chase followed behind as Rob explained his thoughts. "You notice how most closets are the length of the wall? But not Clara's closet. It's the smallest one; surprised we didn't notice it before."

He entered the closet and turned on the light as they examined the walls. "Not only is this closet smaller, but the entrance is also near the window instead of the hall."

Chase nodded in agreement as he pointed his flashlight up toward the ceiling, tracing down the wall. He noticed a slight gap, barely visible to the naked eye. When he pushed, it moved inward like a door.

Both cousins stared into a dark room leading to a hidden staircase.

"Damn! These old houses are insane! Secret passages with hidden doors? Where the hell does it go?" Chase yelled with excitement.

"The stories of secret passages aren't that uncommon in houses this old. It kept the servants hidden while they did their jobs. Let's check them out!" Rob suggested. He used the light from his cell phone to navigate the stairs going up.

"It's getting late. I need to get going, clean up for date night," Chase mumbled before following inside once the door was propped open.

Rachel was enjoying the simplicity of working during the day, then returning to her family home in the evening. She had recently started to improve her culinary skills by preparing various dishes each night for Chase. Rachel found the task of planning, shopping, and preparing relieved her anxiety. It gave her something to focus on when she was home alone.

Tonight, she planned a romantic dinner with chicken cordon bleu. Initially, she worried the dish would be too complicated, but it was within her skillset.

The doorbell rang as she put the final touches on the dining room table. She paused to wonder as she glanced at the clock. It wasn't Chase. *He had already sent a text with his estimated time home, nor would he ring the bell*, she thought as she went to answer the front door. Chase had his key.

When she opened the door, she was speechless.

Max Kauffman, her old personal trainer from the city, was standing on her porch, partially turned away as he looked over his shoulder at his surroundings. Hearing the door open, he turned with a smile.

She looks stunning, he thought.

"Hey, baby, you look great!" He took the opportunity to step towards her for a hug. He knew his visit caught her off guard, just as he had planned. During the hug, he viewed the grand foyer behind her. *Damn, this place is enormous*, Max thought, careful to contain his excitement.

"Max, what are you doing here?" Rachel finally found her voice as she unconsciously stepped away from him.

"Rach, I'm here for the job interview I told you about during our last conversation. I wanted to check this town out. Give us a better chance. I'm staying at a bed and breakfast just outside of town, but it looks like you have plenty of room here," Max declared. He had booked a few nights at what he believed she would consider a romantic getaway. He planned to invite her to stay with him. Max was shocked at the apparent family money. *This may call for something more permanent than a fling challenge*, he debated within himself.

"Max, you cannot stay here. I don't remember you telling me about this," Rachel admitted.

"Rachel, baby, I know. I wanted to surprise you. I'm taking you out to dinner tonight," Max quickly announced. He intended to bring her to his bed and breakfast afterward, knowing he would first need to get the setting just right.

"I can't. I already have plans for tonight," Rachel answered, wondering how long before Chase would be here. He would not like finding Max here at the house, hell, not even in town.

"Baby, are you going to just leave me to myself? Alone in this small town? You know that would be dangerous," he declared as he gently touched her cheek, almost leaning in to kiss her but feeling her shift her weight away from him.

"Max, I already have plans. You can't simply drop in unannounced and expect me to be free. You're lucky I'm even home," Rachel stated, the irritation in her voice evident.

"Rachel, that's not very hospitable," Max declared in his soft charming voice as he smiled with a slight raise of his eyebrows. "I came all this way to surprise you. I've missed you, and you won't let me take you to dinner?"

"Max, nothing has changed just because I returned home. I've never sat home alone at night waiting for someone to make plans for me, here or in the city. Why would you think I would be here alone with no plans now? It's insulting," she stated as she kept her body firmly at the doorway.

Max read her body language. *She has no intent to invite me in*, he realized with disappointment. He also knew she would not be giving in to the dinner plans; good thing the restaurant didn't require reservations. Max stepped back and sighed with his hands up in compromise.

"You are right. Someone as beautiful as you would already have dinner plans this late into the day. My bad, it's already after six in the evening. We can discuss dinner another time. Meet me for drinks instead."

Rachel sighed as she nodded, accepting his apology. While shocked by his visit, she thought it was sweet he would want to surprise her. After all, he did drive quite a distance. It was the least she could do.

"Alright, I could probably have a drink later in the evening. We can meet at Memories," Rachel quickly gave him the address. A few moments later, she watched him walk towards the sidewalk to his rental car before she closed and locked the door. Before she turned around, Rachel heard a voice behind her.

"What the hell is he doing here, so far from the city?"

Startled, Rachel jumped. When she turned around, Chase stood at the doorway from the kitchen. Once the door was closed, he pulled himself away and slowly walked towards her. He leaned down to kiss her, hands on her hips, allowing the kiss to linger before he pulled back.

"Did you just schedule a date for tonight after our dinner date? Rachel MacKenzie, I am shocked! Shannon would do that," Chase declared as he leaned down to kiss her again.

Rachel inwardly groaned, the unasked question answered. Chase heard the whole conversation. Without thinking, she answered on the defensive. "What are you talking about? Shannon doesn't date multiple guys. Why are you all always on her case?"

Chase sighed; of course, Rachel would focus on the frequent slander of their friend. "Hey, I love Shannon, but she's always had a guy or two at her side. She doesn't like to be alone and usually isn't for long."

"So, what people have been saying about her and Rob, is that true?" She looked up into his gray-blue eyes. He was relieved she didn't pull away as he tightened his hold on her.

"I don't know how together they may or may not have been. Rob doesn't talk about it, and I don't ask. If they wanted me to know, they would tell me," he explained before kissing her forehead while she expressed her opinion.

"Just because Shannon was staying at the farm doesn't mean things were going on between them," she continued to defend her friend's reputation.

"Yeah, well, like I said, I don't know the details. I only know I have seen Shannon leave his room wearing only a nightie," Chase admitted, keeping it simple.

"You don't know for a fact if they've slept together?" Rachel stepped back when she made the following comment. "You practically live here, and we haven't really gone there yet."

"True. But let me ask you, would you be wearing that lovely blue nightie while sitting at the breakfast table with Rob?"

"Of course not! That wouldn't be proper!" Rachel was immediately appalled at the idea.

Chase was pleased with her answer as she had been at the breakfast table in his presence, but he still needed to navigate the discussion carefully. He didn't want her to see his jealous side. He's learned from Rob's mistakes.

"So, since I am here often, including the nights, would you say we are a couple? Or just friends?"

"A couple," she answered without hesitation.

Chase paused to smile before continuing. "And if I were to walk into the kitchen one morning to see you sitting at the breakfast table with Rob wearing only that nightie, what would I be thinking? It doesn't matter what actually happened, it's the assumption."

Rachel sighed as she crossed her arms. After a moment, she agreed. "Stupid assumptions people make. So we still don't know if they've actually been together as a couple, nor does it matter. It's not anyone's business."

"It's the small town mentality." Chase laughed at the look on her face before turning the topic back, "So you are going to meet with Max tonight for drinks?"

"Chase, what was I supposed to do? He's here in town for a job interview. He doesn't know anyone. I thought it would be a nice gesture for us all to hang out with him and introduce him to the town," she quietly explained.

Chase looked at her as he wondered, not for the first time, *how she could still be so naïve at her age. Why would a guy like him even want a job in this small town? Hadn't she processed that yet?*

"Rach, why is it your responsibility to show him around? Did you invite him to interview here?" He paused for a moment, continuing after she shook her head. "Then why does it fall on you to entertain him?"

"Chase, I'm just being hospitable," she answered.

"Hospitable, yeah, sure. I'm surprised you didn't invite Max to stay here," he commented.

"That would not be proper. I need to check on dinner. Are you hungry?" Rachel announced as she walked towards the kitchen.

"For once, I am relieved you are so proper," Chase called out after her.

After dinner, Clara and the children went into the family room to allow the brothers to talk freely without her presence. Connor remained silent as he listened to Matt's reaction to the news of the journals surfacing before describing Susannah's changed behavior leading up to her pregnancy. She had become withdrawn and easily spooked, just as Clara had been over the summer.

"You have no idea who the father is?" Connor asked with skepticism.

"I said I didn't, didn't I?" Matt answered, irritated.

Connor admitted, "I wasn't sure if you were choosing not to clue in Clara. You're protective of her."

"If I had any idea who the bastard was, I would have sought him out and killed him myself. I thought she didn't tell me because she was protecting the guy. Believed it was Gibson when she announced their engagement. Now I hear there were two. That can't be a coincidence. She was roofied and raped. I am so furious right now," he announced, his voice was low but shook with anger.

Connor was impressed with Matt's ability to control his rage, but he also thought of Clara. Granted, she was a generation younger than her mother, but too many similarities existed for this to be a coincidence. But where to begin, Connor wondered before asking, "Matt, when you were in high school, there were a lot of parties out in the woods, right?"

"Of course. Dad made it clear he was to never hear about me being there, so I avoided them," he answered.

"There have always been parties with alcohol. How else would he have known? In my day, there was an incident of a few girls found left alone in the woods, unable to recall details of the evening before. They were taken to the hospital with confirmation of drugs in their system and evidence of sex. They couldn't collect any DNA evidence because he used protection."

"How did I not hear about this?"

"You already left home to live in the city. Joe Mancuso confided in me. His dad was a deputy at the time. He warned me away from those parties whenever he thought I planned to go. There had been an investigation but never any arrests." He paused. "Never anything like that in your time?"

"I honestly don't know what went on at those parties. Personally, I don't see the appeal. I never had trouble getting a girl to sleep with me. I could never understand the purpose of drugging someone to make her willing. But as we learned in psych class, it's more about control, not sex. Why? What are you thinking?" Matt wondered.

"I know you weren't there when Eric was arrested. After he admitted to drugging Clara, Eric said he was doing me a favor. He said, 'each and every time, she went right back to you. Each and every time.'" Connor paused, replaying the scene in his head.

"Joshua told me about the arrest. He was there, but not this part. What did Eric mean?"

"That's what concerns me. How many times has he drugged Clara? I know he was drugging her coffee, but why also her drink when she's out? Isn't that excessive? And was this just since she returned home, or was it also during their high school years?" Connor continued to give details of Clara's prom, and a few other times Clara was rattled. "And now I'm wondering about the theater."

"What about it? She was one of the first ones out after the explosion," Matt stated as he studied his brother's face. He tilted his head. "You aren't seriously suggesting Eric caused the explosion, are you?"

"Not sure if I'd go that far, though, I wouldn't be surprised. I suppose Eric could have been messing with things, not understanding the severity of the reaction. His friend's family owned the restaurant," Connor stated thoughtfully.

"But I, like many others in town, was there immediately after the explosion. They believed Clara was in the bathroom. She was conscious but dazed. Hell, who wouldn't be? She was walking and talking, but she made no sense," Connor kept his voice low. "I stayed with her all night and into the next morning. She had a concussion but no internal bleeding and no neurological signs. Beth and Rachel arrived in the late morning. They had been out of town but returned when they heard of the explosion, stopping at the theater, waiting with the Foxwoods to hear about Lila. Beth was the one to sign Clara out of the hospital. She brought her back to her house until her father arrived."

Connor paused as he mentally replayed the horrible night. He had been playing with his beer bottle, rolling it in his hands as he remembered the next part. "The morning after her discharge, Clara was out on her porch. I went over to ask how she was feeling. Clara said she was fine and didn't remember much about it. She waited for Rachel and her mother to pick her up to visit Lila. Clara was giving me details she had learned secondhand. She was surprised when I told her I was there with her the whole time, from when the firefighter carried her out until the Mackenzies arrived. Clara had absolutely no memory of me or the explosion."

He paused to sip his beer while Matt commented, "I thought her memory loss was due to the concussion."

"Yes, it could have been. Sounds plausible. Granted, they didn't do any significant blood testing. I wouldn't have thought otherwise until Eric's comment, 'Each and every time.' After they loaded her up in the ambulance with me beside her, Eric was the next one pulled out of the rubble. He was also conscious. I later learned he had a similar concussion diagnosis. He remembered every detail of the incident. Eric immediately spotted her getting into the ambulance. She saw him and waved while I sat beside her holding her other hand," Connor shared. "How does he remember everything while she doesn't remember a thing? It sounds horrible to say the explosion was likely a blessing in disguise."

Eric was getting fed up with the stupid ankle monitor. Three months after the ridiculous arrest, even the frequent sneaking out to visit the bars was getting old. He missed his old life. He never thought he'd miss getting up each day for work. But the job was amazingly better when Clara returned home and started to work with him. He never imagined she'd move back.

Eric paused in the doorway of his room to listen. Confident his disguise was perfect, he looked back into his room. The music was loud enough to appear he was sulking in his room but not enough to be disturbed. Eric cautiously navigated the backstairs and out of the house. As he slipped out the door, he decided his first stop was to see his love.

During the walk, Eric thought of ways to surprise his love. A romantic getaway would be the best. He could decorate the cabin with flowers, have music in the background and a fire burning in the fireplace. He'd have to talk to the family chef about preparing a lovely meal.

Matt was silent, lost in his thoughts as the brothers processed the new information. His cell alerted him to a text. He pulled out his phone and sighed when he realized how late it was. His wife, Talia, was asking when he would be home.

After replying, Matt stated, "We've certainly opened many cans of worms tonight. Do you really believe Eric has been drugging Clara all this time? During high school and now? In her coffee and drinks?"

"Well, not when she lived in the city for the last twelve years. I don't think their paths crossed. But I can think of three times she wasn't herself when we ran into each other, literally by accident," Connor held up a finger as he listed the times, "The theater explosion, the prom, and the girls' night out. I would never have thought anything of it, just that she's ridiculously accident-prone, given the number of times I used to carry her home from the park before I graduated high school. Those incidents occasionally included Eric, but usually it was his friend Danny Thompson."

Matt was about to stand but leaned back at the name. "Danny Thompson? As in bailing Foxwood out of jail after a bar fight over Clara, that Danny Thompson?"

"Now are you are seeing the pattern, Counselor?" Connor responded. "Thompson's grandparents owned the restaurant next to the theater, right?"

"Yeah," Matt answered thoughtfully. "But this is all circumstantial. Alarming when you think about his violent history. I'm amazed Lee didn't cut off that friendship. But the explosion was ruled a freak accident. Eric was too young to be involved with the drugging when you were in school. But doesn't Danny have an older brother that has been arrested for drug dealing a few towns over?"

"Yeah, but it doesn't explain the incidents from your time," Connor stated.

"Maybe not, but there are some deep connections," Matt answered. "Now that you mentioned the Thompson family, it reminds me of how I knew about the clinic. There was a rumor, Sarah Thompson, now Black, was pregnant in high school. She was on the wild side and had a child in high school, which didn't tame her. She suddenly drifted into her shell after leaving town for a few months. One of the guys casually mentioned she probably went away to have her baby. I dismissed it because she already had a child at home, so why would she not want to keep this one?"

"Really? Hmm, that is interesting," Connor agreed. "Sarah's a quiet, respectable nurse. She's very good with patients. Interestingly, Sarah has dark blond hair and sky-blue eyes. Are you saying she left town for a few months? Do you think she was pregnant? Gave the baby up?"

At that moment, little Hailey entered the room. Matt watched with amusement as she went straight to Connor, pulling on his pants to climb into his lap. Once settled, Hailey flashed her sky-blue eyes at him as she blew him a kiss before falling asleep.

"Damn, it's getting late. I need to get these kids to bed. Clara probably passed out on the sofa with Reese." Connor stood up, holding the young toddler up on his shoulder.

Matt followed him into the family room. His initial intent had been to leave. Instead, he was distracted by the sight of Clara sound asleep with her son snuggled in close. He nodded quietly as his brother first carried up the little girl.

After Connor returned a few minutes later for the boy, Matt reached for the blanket thrown over the back of the sofa. He gently covered Clara up as he touched her hair, bending down to kiss her forehead as he whispered, "Sleep tight, kiddo."

Clara may have been sound asleep earlier, but was now partially awake but not stirring. With her hearing aids still in place, she was vaguely aware of her surroundings. She felt the blanket over her and the familiar kiss on her forehead. But this time, she heard the words as she felt the warmth of his breath in her ear, "Sleep tight, kiddo."

Her eyes immediately opened to familiar blue eyes.

    SHADOWS OF THE PAST

unexpected night out

Rachel and Chase were the first to arrive at Memories. They already had a drink when Rob and Lila entered from the back entrance.

"There's the happy couple," Rob announced but stopped when Chase looked with a slight shake of the head.

The exchange was not lost on Lila. *Was Chase expecting to propose*, she wondered as she greeted her friend with a hug.

Rob was about to ask what happened, or didn't happen, when he saw the man from the Korean restaurant in the city enter the front door. *Ahh*, Rob thought. *Damn, shame!* He didn't see that coming.

Chase remained silent, watching Rachel introduce Max to Lila, then again when Dallas arrived. While he was confident in his relationship with Rachel, he was worried about the unexpected appearance of this guy. *Why would he come here for an interview? Or is it simply an interview to mask the real pursuit of winning her over, completing a conquest? Did he have any intention of actually relocating here?* He felt slightly panicked at the thought that maybe Max was in love with her. Chase remained at the bar with his beer, watching Max's eyes following Rachel mingling among the crowd.

Max was disappointed when he entered the place to see Rachel surrounded by friends. His previous thoughts were confirmed when he felt Chase's annoyance. *She had been lying to me about her status with the guy.* Hell, Chase was probably in the house when he stopped in, and since there was no ring on her finger, he was still in the running.

Lila sat with her friend, inquiring about the apparent guest of honor. "How do you know Max?"

"I met him almost two years ago when I joined the gym. We've been friends. He is in town for a couple of days for a job interview at the new YMCA when it opens up this winter," Rachel patiently explained.

"Does he have family in the area?"

Rachel laughed. "I highly doubt it. He's always bragged about being born and bred in the city. Never mentioned family here."

Lila turned towards her friend with concern. Clara was usually the one that could get through her dense naivete. "Does he really have an interview tomorrow, or is he just saying that?"

"Why would someone lie about that?" Rachel was shocked at the suggestion.

"I don't know. Maybe Max does have the interview, but no intention of actually moving here. Maybe he's simply using that as an excuse to visit you," Lila cautiously answered. The look on her friend's face made her further explain, "This visit may just be another attempt at marking his bedpost."

"Lila! You are not suggesting he wants to sleep with me," Rachel gasped as she finally understood. "That's a little excessive, don't you think? Why would anyone go to this extreme to simply sleep with me?"

"Rach, I love you like a sister, I really do. But you are very dense when it comes to the male species. The guy is over there talking about the nightlife in the city. Why would he ever consider moving here? Max would be bored out of his mind. The only explanation is you are the one to escape his bed. He likely just wants to sleep with you and then move on. You are a challenge that has been defying him since you both met," Lila rudely explained.

"I don't understand why a guy would do that. It's not true," Rachel defended the visitor.

"Rachel, guys are pigs. No need to explain further," Lila squeezed her friend's hand before stepping away.

"Hey, pretty lady, why are you frowning?" Chase asked, suddenly at Rachel's side.

Rachel's blue eyes followed Lila as she walked away. *Max just wants to sleep with me? How does Lila know that?* When she felt Chase's hand on her shoulder, she looked up into his gray-blue eyes as he repeated the question. She simply shrugged as she tried to comprehend Lila's comments. She could not even focus on what Chase was saying.

"Lila seems to think she knows guys. She says guys are pigs. That Max is only here to sleep with me. He has no intention of moving here," Rachel blurted out.

Chase laughed at the idea of his sweet little cousin bluntly explaining the true intentions of Max Kauffman. "Yeah, she's right. He is."

Rachel's eyes sought out the visitor across the room. Max must have felt her eyes on him, for he turned his head towards her and winked. She blushed as she looked away, causing Chase to chuckle again. *Yeah, she really has no idea.*

"Hey, Chase, Rachel, have either of you," Dallas had been approaching the couple but stopped mid-question, feeling as if he were intruding on a private moment. Lila had mentioned she thought they would make an announcement tonight, which didn't seem to be on the agenda. "Am I interrupting something?"

"Dallas, is it true guys are pigs?" Rachel asked the unexpected question.

Dallas paused for a moment, looking between the two. Chase remained silent with a slight smile, his eyebrows raised in question as if encouraging the truth.

"Well, uh, yeah. It's true. Guys, in general, are pigs. It's not one of our favorable traits, but some of us have the potential to grow out of it."

Rachel sighed loudly in frustration as she walked away.

"Chase, I am sorry for interrupting an *obviously* weird conversation," Dallas slowly commented as they watched her storm off delicately, as only Rachel could.

Chase simply laughed. "Oh, don't be. She's having difficulty processing what my favorite little cousin has stated as fact."

"Lila says guys are pigs?" Dallas asked in confusion, wondering if there was a hidden problem in their relationship, feeling his insecurities slightly surface.

"I don't think she was implying you and I are pigs, though, I wouldn't be surprised if she still believes Rob is. She's trying to explain that Madmax over there is only in town this week to get Rachel into bed with him," Chase explained.

Dallas was suddenly relieved. Good, no hidden issues. "Hell yeah, I think that's a given. The way he looks at her and the nasty looks he gives you. You're obviously in his path. I'd be cautious if I were you. If you intend to make your move, you better do it soon and be obvious about it."

He slapped Chase's shoulder before he walked away.

Matt was no sooner stepping back from Clara when she sat up, wincing in pain as she stared into his blue eyes. Somehow something triggered a memory.

"Clara, I didn't mean to wake you up," he stated, realizing she looked shocked.

"No, I was already awake, just not stirring yet. Matt, did you used to tuck me in when I was little?" Clara asked softly.

Matt tilted his head in wonder before he answered, "Yes. Your mother would ask me to check on you before I left."

"I remember," Clara whispered as her green eyes met his blue.

Matt remained silent, wondering what exactly she did remember: the time she walked in on her mother, snuggled up to him on the sofa in the parlor, the time she walked into her mother's room while they were both asleep as she crawled into bed next to her mother. Shit, the times he carried her to bed? He shook his head at the foolishness of his youth. His father had been correct. Matt had been playing with fire.

Both turned when Connor returned to the family room with a chuckle. "Man, the little guy was fighting it. Trying to convince me it was morning and he could stay up."

Connor stopped when he realized Clara was awake, looking like she'd seen a ghost; what did he miss? Before Connor could say anything, his brother was saying goodnight.

A moment later, Connor was locking the door behind him. He told Clara he'd help her up the stairs once he locked up and turned off the lights. She nodded as she remained on the sofa, digging up memories from when she was a child.

Walking to his SUV, Matt was distracted by his thoughts. He paused when he saw movement in the shadows. "Who's there?"

A moment later, Clara's father, Carl Gibson, stepped into the light.

"What the hell are you doing here? You have no right to be here. You need to stay away from her, you hear me?"

"What are you whining about? Clara invited me here. What the hell are you doing, hiding in the shadows, you loser?" Matt yelled back as he stepped from his vehicle.

While he was surprised to find Gibson hiding outside Clara's place, he expected the punch. Matt knew exactly where the security cameras were. Hell, he even knew the swings the stupid fuck would take. It was as if he was suddenly decades younger as the same fight was replayed again.

This time, he wouldn't take the bait. Matt allowed the first swing of Carl's fist to his jaw before he stepped back to avoid the second. But the third swing made contact with his left forearm as he blocked it before stepping in to deliver his own. The instant his fist made contact, Matt lost all control of his anger. He started to swing with both fists in rapid succession.

Neither Matt nor Carl was aware of the blue flashing lights of a deputy's car as the fists continued to swing. Seconds later, the driveway was crowded as Joe Mancuso and his partner, Walker, struggled to pull the men apart. Devan, already near by since he stayed in the other duplex next door to assist with the security, suddenly pushed Matt back as he stepped between the two. An instant later, Connor was also assisting with pulling his brother back towards the porch.

Even after the two were physically separated, the accusations continued.

"You killed my wife! She'd still be alive today if you hadn't meddled in our lives," Carl yelled over Walker's shoulder.

"I didn't go searching! She walked right into my arms. She was going to leave you! You were cheating on her before you two even tied the knot. What makes you think she would continue to put up with your crap?" Matt yelled back just as Devan gave him a good shove toward the porch.

Sheriff Mancuso suddenly appeared between the men as the shouts and insults flew around him. He sighed as he looked between them, then signaled to his deputies to handcuff them both.

The second Matt was turned, his eyes connected with Clara's. He was instantly quiet and ashamed. She remained silently on the porch, watching. *Shit, does she place me on the same low level of scum as her father?*

When Clara's eyes met Matt's, a memory was triggered from shortly before her mother disappeared:

> Her mother was packing suitcases. Clara secretly watched from the doorway before she quietly entered the room. A moment later, her mother turned around and screamed when she realized she wasn't alone.

'Clara Noelle! Why are you sneaking up on me like that? When did you get home?'

'Just now. Are you going somewhere?'

'No, babygirl. I'm packing up for a surprise vacation,' her mother said as she lifted bathing suits to show her daughter. One was obviously for Clara. 'It's a surprise. You can't tell anyone.'

'Is Daddy going with us?' Clara asked as she looked into the suitcase. It was full of both her and her mother's clothing.

'No,' her mother answered without any further explanation.

Clara knew then, as she did now, her mother had lied. She intended to leave her father. Or rather, her mother arranged to have her father served divorce papers while they were out of town. He would be removed from the Hawks House. That was the afternoon before she disappeared.

Returning to the present, Clara watched silently as her mother's husband and lover were each escorted into different vehicles. She listened as the sheriff spoke with Connor.

"Connor, these two have had bad chemistry since high school. I'm simply taking them back to the station until they cool down. You're more than welcome to follow while everything is properly sorted out. We'll let the good neighbors get back to their evening," Sheriff Mancuso looked up as he finished. "Sorry for all the chaos, Clara."

The sheriff turned around as he talked with his son and nephew.

Connor finally seemed to realize Clara was standing on the porch. He escorted her back into the house and toward the sofa. When she wouldn't sit down, he worried she believed her father's accusations, that Matt had direct involvement with her mother's death.

"Clara, please, I need to follow them down to the station and help sort this out. Do you want me to carry you up the stairs, or will you remain on the sofa until I return?"

"Connor, I am alright, go. I don't need you to carry me or tuck me in. Go deal with your brother. We'll be alright here," she caressed his cheek to reassure him.

Connor paused before turning as he studied her face, trying to figure out what she was thinking.

"Connor, go!" Clara repeated in a calm voice as she grabbed him, steadying herself as she pulled up on her tippy toes to kiss his cheek. "Go! Don't worry about me."

He nodded and kissed her. "Alright, I'm going. I'll lock the door behind me. Get some rest."

When Connor was out of the house, she whispered, "Rest? Yeah, right."

Clara reached for her cell and pulled up a contact.

Connor had already pulled away when Eric stepped from the shrubs. He was excited he had arrived in time to witness the altercation. Wait until he informed his father they had Susannah's killer in custody. It should lighten his mood. Father had been so irritable lately. The younger man started his return home but decided to stop in at The Lantern on the way.

Still overly confident, Eric didn't realize he was followed.

The evening was fairly young, by Max's standards anyway, when Chase informed Rachel he was heading out. Knowing his concerns were validated, Chase decided he wouldn't force her to leave. He was leaving regardless; he had a busy day ahead of him.

"Do you want a ride home, or are you sticking around?"

Rachel innocently smiled up at him, oblivious of the tension between Chase and Max, regardless of Lila's earlier comments. "I'm ready. Let me say goodbye."

As they made their way around, Chase paused without a word when Rachel stopped at Max, squeezing his arm.

"Max, good luck with your interview tomorrow. Have a good night."

"Rachel, baby, you are leaving so soon?" Max pulled her in for a hug as he whispered, "Stay with me for another round, and I'll see you home tonight."

"No, I have work tomorrow," she slowly answered as she stepped back. For the first time, she was uncomfortable with his closeness. Rachel turned toward Chase as she reached for his hand without further explanation.

Lila and Dallas exchanged looks as they observed the newcomer's behavior while making rounds for goodnights. Rob followed them into the parking lot. Believing his sister was riding home with him, he announced he'd wait for her by his truck.

Lila first looked up at Dallas, signaling she would be a moment before following her brother to clarify her evening plans. She reached for his arm before reaching his truck. "Rob, I'm not going home with you. I'm going with Dallas."

"What? Why the hell would you want to do that?" Rob turned towards her, his anger and annoyance were evident.

"I am going home with him because I love him. I want to spend the night with him," Lila bluntly explained. "You need to bring your tone down a few notches. I am with Dallas Thompson; got that? Nothing you say or do will change that, so let's drop the attitude and accept it. Both of our lives will be so much easier."

Lila turned and walked away without waiting for him to argue or anchor her beside him.

Dallas had been leaning against the passenger door, patiently waiting. He opened her door when she turned towards him with a purposeful stride.

Shocked by her sudden boldness, Rob remained still as he watched her walk away, leaving to spend the night with the town asshole.

Lila watched her older brother as the vehicle pulled away. She felt a sudden lightness; the weight of carrying the secret was gone. Lila was finally liberated from her brother's tight hold. Not a physical grip but more a mental and emotional one after feeling forced to keep her true relationship hidden all these years.

She was ready to tell her parents and face any consequences. Lila was so happy, she waved to Rob.

As he pulled from the parking space, Dallas observed the change. "Lila, how many guns does he own?"

Lila laughed as she reached for his hand. "Dal, he's not going to come after you. I promise."

"I don't know. I'd feel safer if all his hunting rifles were locked up for the next five years," Dallas stated as he read a text. "Is it alright if we stop at Clara's?"

When Dallas pulled up in front of her house, Clara opened the front door. "Dallas, Lila, I am so sorry to call you so late, but I didn't know what to do. Matt Emerson was over for dinner, and Dad was outside waiting for him when he left. They were both arrested!"

After explaining further, Dallas agreed to take her to the sheriff's department while Lila remained with the children.

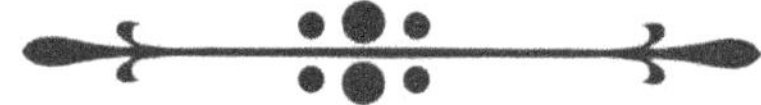

many questions, no answers

Connor was getting restless, waiting with his cousin at the front desk. Sheriff Mancuso was behind the desk, quietly reviewing the security footage outside Clara's home.

"Sheriff?" Connor called out. When he came closer, he continued, "My brother didn't kill Clara's mother."

"Connor, I didn't arrest him. I've only detained them. Those two have never gotten along, not even in high school. There was no way either would peacefully walk away. I brought them both down here to keep the peace in the neighborhood and prevent a potentially severe altercation," the sheriff explained.

"Am I correct to assume your brother was invited to Clara's?" When he received the expected nod, the sheriff continued, "I was just confirming from the security cameras that Carl was lurking in the shadows an hour before Matt left the house. A cruiser was nearby to monitor the situation the moment we knew of his presence. Initially, we thought it was Eric. When we realized it was her father, we became suspicious when he didn't go to the door. I figured he knew who was inside and meant to keep a polite distance."

Connor gave the sheriff a dubious look. "Polite distance? Are we talking about Carl Gibson?"

Sheriff Mancuso chuckled, "You never know. Carl could have mellowed with age. I thought your brother did, but he proved me wrong. The riff between them has always been violent. I'm honestly surprised it has taken this long."

Before Connor could respond, the door opened. The front entrance had a small foyer with two sets of double doors to protect against the elements. Everyone turned to see the new arrivals. No one was more shocked than Connor was to see Clara walking in with her good arm on Dallas's.

Connor rushed to her side. "Clara, what are you doing here? I thought you were going to stay home."

Clara looked up into his panicked brown eyes. She placed a hand on his arm and squeezed. "Connor, I came to talk to him."

"Clara, I promise you, Matt had nothing to do with your mother's disappearance," he blurted out. Connor worried she would believe her father, regardless of their distance in recent years. If her father thought it, why wouldn't she? There was no way their relationship would survive the accusations.

Clara smiled as she touched his arm to reassure him. "I know, Connor. I know Matt had nothing to do with her death."

The sheriff had no intention of broaching the disappearance and death of Susannah Gibson. However, he had to inquire further if someone had made such bold statements.

"Clara, how do you know Matt Emerson didn't do it?"

"Wrong color eyes," Clara dismissed before changing the subject to the true nature of her visit. "Sheriff, my brother and I want a moment with our father. I want to know why he was hanging around outside my home."

That was the million-dollar question, the sheriff thought. Everyone wanted to know why Carl Gibson, the man lying low without a current address, was hiding in the shrubs late into the evening. He thought, *what the hell, why not?* He glanced over at his son, obviously reading his mind.

Joe shrugged in agreement.

"Clara, I'll let Joe take you two to see your father. We brought them in for disturbing the peace; formal charges have not been made at this time," the sheriff explained with a gesture toward the locked gate.

"Thank you, Sheriff Mancuso. I appreciate this," Clara said as she slowly followed the deputy.

Dallas paused for a moment. "Sheriff, who decides the charges?"

"It's Clara's home, so she decides if she wants to press charges for trespassing. Mr. Emerson was punched first as a guest on her property, so he decides if he wants to press assault charges," the sheriff explained. Both knew Clara would never have charges pressed against her father.

Once Clara and Dallas had gone through, Sheriff Mancuso turned towards Connor. "What does she mean Matt has the wrong eye color?"

"I've always speculated she saw something the night her mother disappeared. Her behavior that morning, she was terrified," Connor explained. "Clara has nightmares but claims not to remember them in the morning. She doesn't talk about it."

"Why didn't you tell me?" Tony Mancuso demanded.

"I did. I called you that morning, remember?" Connor reminded him of the morning twenty years before when he found Clara outside alone, the morning her mother first went missing.

Carl was pacing the small room. One of the walls was half-covered with a double mirror, and the short time alone allowed his rarely-seen temper to dissipate. While calmer, Carl was still furious at the idea of Matthew Emerson hanging out with his daughter.

Usually a confident man, his wife's lover mentally tormented him. It always caused him to doubt his abilities to please his wife, especially when Susannah turned to the other man for comfort on her darkest days. It never dawned on him that his wife had only followed his lead.

In his attempt to keep only a positive front for his wife, Carl turned towards the bottle and others for comfort.

Unfortunately, that was when Felicia Thompson could reel him in with ease. He could not release the hook Felicia had in him since their school days. Carl and Susannah both made the mistake of turning to their old flames during the rocky roads of their marriage. Rarely did they ever seek comfort in each other.

Carl paused in his pacing when the door opened. He leaned back into the wall when his daughter entered, followed by his son. The last two people he expected to see in this place. Carl leaned onto the table as he spoke.

"Clara, why are you here? You should be home resting. Dallas, please take her home."

Dallas kept silent as he remained near the closed door. His sole purpose was to support his sister. The man before him never publicly acknowledged him, nor did he know him. Dallas simply leaned into the wall with his arms crossing his chest as he shrugged.

"Hello, Dad. How's it going? Been a while, don't you think? It's been so long; I didn't think you cared anymore," Clara announced, gesturing with uncharacteristic drama.

She slowly paced the room length, similar to himself just a few moments before. But after a couple of paces, the continuous ache in her leg progressed to throbbing pain. Clara tried not to grimace as she leaned into the table.

"Why are you here?" Carl repeated.

Looking between the children, he was surprised to see the subtle similarities. *Why had I not seen this before*, he wondered. While Clara favored her mother's appearance, Clara and Dallas had similar mannerisms. Clara did not have her mother's reserved personality. She had his easygoing, take-it-one-day-at-a-time outlook on life. Granted, it was not enough to confirm both were his children, but he could see something else he couldn't describe.

Carl had been laced with doubt regarding the paternity of both children, which kept him from getting close to either as they grew older. Felicia often added fuel to the fire. To his surprise, his wife was the one that assured him the boy was his. *How could you possibly know?* Carl had asked in disbelief. *The boy has your eyes*, she answered after spending the morning at the park. Clara could not have been more than two at the time. But Susannah didn't stress it since they weren't married at the time of the conception. She did have issues when he expressed doubt about Clara. Susannah was always hurt by the accusations, causing the riff to open further.

"To see you, of course. You are the one hanging out at my place. I figured you wanted to see me," Clara quietly answered with forced cheerfulness, arms across her chest. She waited a moment in silence before she continued, "Or were you not there for me? Were you following Matt?"

Carl winced at the familiarity with which she said the name. "Why was he even there? He has no business seeing you! You're not his!"

"I'm not his what?" Clara asked in a chillingly soft tone.

"I don't like you around him. He's never brought anything but pain to our family," Carl answered.

It suddenly dawned on him she may not know about the affairs. Clara was only nine at the time of her mother's disappearance. He was always annoyed Clara idolized her mother without ever seeing her faults, while his always seemed to be put on display.

"Well, that may be a problem, he is my lawyer, and he's Connor's brother! Of course, I'll be hanging around him," Clara answered sarcastically.

"Why do you even need a lawyer?"

"To handle my legal affairs, including settling my mother's and husband's estates," Clara paused to study his face. What were her father's issues with Matt? Or was she reading something else? "You know what?

I'm done giving you information. It's your turn to talk. Why were you at my house?"

"I don't like you hanging around the Emerson boys," Carl quietly responded. To Clara's surprise, he sounded like a father talking to his teenage daughter.

"I've always hung out with Connor, ever since I was a child," she answered. "What is your issue with him?"

"The younger one is too old for you," he stated as if it were the most obvious.

"When I was a child, there was never anything inappropriate. Connor was always a friend that looked out for me. Nothing romantic ever happened until this summer. I'm almost thirty, and he's thirty-eight; he's not that much older than me," Clara dismissed.

"You don't think it's odd that he's always followed you around? Why would a teenager want to hang out with a young girl? They're only after your money," he argued. "I'm trying to protect you from them. I'm trying to keep you and the money safe."

"What money?" Clara demanded with a harsh laugh. When he didn't respond, she almost yelled, "There is no money!"

"How did you pay for college?" Carl asked as if that was all the proof.

"I worked my ass off for the grants and will be paying off my student loans for the next thirty years," she answered. "I always had jobs when I was a teenager and on campus. How else would I have any money?"

Carl wondered about the accuracy of the information given to him years ago. Could his cousin have been wrong? Could Graham Hawks truly have lost the money without anyone's knowledge? Susannah also denied there was any significant money whenever he started his excessive spending. Or did the women just not know? The old man was suddenly incapacitated towards the end. He may not have had time to instruct Susannah properly before he died.

"Matt killed your mother," Carl yelled out.

"No, he didn't," Clara quickly dismissed with a wave of her hand.

"How would you know? You were a child when your mother disappeared," he argued.

"I was there that night. He wasn't," Clara's answer was automatic. "You weren't there either. Where were you? You accuse people of doing things; how would you know if you weren't there? Why? Why weren't you home that night?"

Dallas pulled away from the wall; *what the hell is happening here?* he wondered. *Does Clara know who killed her mother? Did she see it?* He looked towards the double glass mirror, hoping the sheriff was listening.

"Clara, sweetheart, you were not home that night. You were staying at a friend's house, probably Rachel's," Carl clarified. It always bothered him that she arrived home before he did that morning.

Clara was shaking her head as a buried memory surfaced. She whispered, "No, I was there. It was a last-minute change. I don't remember why, but I stayed home with Mom. We had dinner together and planned what flowers to plant the next day. We read Little Women together. I was there."

Carl's face paled as he looked between his son and daughter. *Was Clara truly there that night? Does she know what happened to her mother? It had to be Matt Emerson. If it weren't him, then who?* Carl slowly sat down in the chair at the thought of the danger she could have been in if she were, in fact, home that night. *Why didn't she tell him sooner? More importantly, why wasn't he home? Did the bitch pull him into her web on purpose?*

Clara remained silent as she fought the tears. She was determined to keep her control. "You have not attempted to be a part of my life. I've reached out many times, and you've ignored me. I'm done. Don't come near my children or me. Dallas can speak for himself."

She slowly turned to leave. Dallas opened the door as Clara stepped through with an obvious antalgic gait. She fought to keep from wincing with every step. But once she was in the hallway, Clara leaned into the wall for support and lost her battle with the tears. She felt Dallas's arms around her as she cried. Her father wasn't at her house to see her; He was too preoccupied with Matt, her mother's lover, to concern himself with his daughter and grandchildren.

Sheriff Mancuso had allowed both Devan and Connor behind the double mirror. He studied Connor's face during the comments about the money and the accusation that his brother killed Susannah Gibson twenty years ago. Still, Connor kept his thoughts to himself and his facial expression neutral. *I'll have to pay Clara another visit,* he thought.

When Clara and Dallas left, the men watched Carl pick up the chair beside him and throw it across the small room. Connor flinched when the chair hit the double mirror, expecting it to shatter. He was surprised at Carl's temper tonight. The man was always known as an easygoing charismatic guy.

"Connor, why don't you go talk to your brother and see if he wants to press charges," the sheriff instructed.

Connor nodded as he went into the other room.

Matt was playing chess on his cell phone as he pondered what he had learned earlier. He found himself thinking of Susi, their highs and lows through the years. Matt wasn't sure he could handle learning the circumstances of her death, knowing what he did about her burial site. He was trying to push his emotions back into the locked box that kept his sanity when Connor opened the door.

Both brothers looked at each other for a long moment before Connor spoke, "Sheriff Mancuso is letting you go. No charges against you. Are you pressing charges on him?"

"For what?"

"Assault."

Matt sighed as he thought of the pleasure of having Carl arrested and serving time. It likely wouldn't ease his pain and would definitely cause Clara further upset. He stood up and shook his head. Connor opened the door for his brother. When Matt turned into the small hallway, he was surprised to see Clara as Dallas attempted to comfort her. He felt bad about upsetting her.

"Matt, give me a minute before I take you home," Connor stated as he walked toward Clara. "Clara?"

Clara turned toward Connor, struggling and wincing with every step. She remained silent when her eyes met his.

"Sweetheart, I need to take Matt home. The sheriff wants to know if you want to press charges." Connor wasn't surprised when she shrugged a no. "Dallas, can you take her home? I'll be there in a few minutes."

Clara, still not talking, simply nodded as he kissed her forehead before returning to Matt's side. While she watched him leave, she saw Matt watching sadly from behind.

Connor was quiet while he drove his brother home. When he parked the car in the driveway, he finally asked, "Does Clara have money from the Hawks' family estate?"

Matt shrugged. "Susi's father and grandfather had a way with money. They knew how to save and invest. I have no idea of the details."

"Really? How is that possible?" Connor wondered.

"I don't know. Susi and I never talked about money. It's likely invested and placed in trusts. The old man didn't properly prepare his daughter for it. It was his son he was grooming to take over the business. Susi's will wouldn't have surfaced until now. I'll have to ask Dad about it," he paused as he was half out the door, "why are you asking? Did Clara ask about it?"

Connor didn't want to stir up more conflict between Matt and Carl. "Just wondering. When you say they had a way with money, do you mean like we have money?"

Matt chuckled harshly before he answered, "Dad never talks about other people's money, but Grandma once commented that the Emerson's Estate was pocket change compared to the Hawks' Estate."

Matt looked at his brother for a moment, knowing Carl had brought up the topic. Instead of commenting further, he decided he'd look into it. He would have thought if there was money, Susi's spouse would have been aware, but not have access to it. Matt apologized for his part in the trouble and thanked his brother for the ride. He'd have Josh drop him off in the morning to pick up his vehicle.

Dallas assisted Clara as she slowly ascended the steps up her porch and unlocked the door. Once inside, she went to the recliner to sit, almost collapsing. After getting drinks, Dallas sat at the end of the sofa where his wife was sleeping soundly.

"Anything you want to talk about?" Dallas wondered.

"I don't know, what is there to say? I feel like everyone in that generation has been hiding something for years. Your mother brought up money that afternoon out on my porch. I have no idea what she's talking about. I do not know of it. I don't understand how they both think there is any money. Do you?"

"I only know she's always been fascinated about living in the Hawks House. Even that doesn't make much sense," he answered.

"Do you think it could be a family thing, like the third child of the third child that lost out to the house generations ago?" Clara theorized.

"I doubt it. Her family isn't originally from this area," he speculated.

"How old is your mother?"

"I don't know. I think she graduated the same year as your dad," Dallas responded.

"Dad was a few years older than my mom. I bet that's it!" Clara almost shouted. Her brother simply raised his eyebrows in question. "I bet your mother was dating my uncle in high school."

Dallas' eyes narrowed in question. "What uncle?"

"My mother's older brother was killed in an accident just after he graduated from high school. He was to inherit the house and all. My mother has journals. She talked about her brother and his girlfriend.

Initially, it was implied they were unofficially engaged and would marry once he graduated college, but he broke it off before he was killed," she explained. "He caught her with someone else."

"That still doesn't explain why she believes she has the right to live there. I'm married to Lila, but I don't expect to inherit the Foxwood Farm or anything from it," he dismissed.

"Well, it's the only thing that makes sense," Clara quietly stated as she followed through with the idea. Felicia Thompson reattached herself to her former boyfriend once her mother was out of the picture, expecting to be allowed into the house. *Was it simply the anticipated grandeur of living in one of the nicest houses in town with the perceived status it brought?* Because Felicia was his mother, Clara didn't verbalize her thoughts.

Dallas was also silently pondering the reasons for his mother's behavior and infatuation with all things Clara and the Hawks House when he heard footsteps on the front porch. He stood up as the door opened. When Connor stepped inside, he woke Lila up before saying his goodbyes.

Clara scooted forward in her seat. "Thanks for coming over tonight. I really appreciate it."

"Anytime," Dallas answered as he escorted Lila out the door.

After they left, Connor assisted Clara up the steps. He waited at each of the children's doors as she kissed them good night. As she limped out of the room, he asked her when she last took her pain medicine.

Clara simply shrugged. "I don't know. Don't worry about it."

He watched as she headed into the bathroom in preparation for bed. He followed her in, and when his eyes met hers in the mirror, Clara turned around before he could speak.

"Connor, I just need to get off my feet. Once I'm in bed, it'll be fine. I don't want a drug-induced sleep."

12

new day, new questions

Clara was sitting at the top of the slide, watching everyone on the playground. She didn't know why she climbed so high as she sat at the top, her hands holding on tight. She wanted to go down but didn't know how, so she sat and waited.

"Everyone looks so small from up here," she thought as she looked over at the kids on the swings. The older kids were playing basketball on the courts. She saw Connor playing with his cousin. When the cousin, she could never remember his name, said something, they both turned to look in her direction.

She waved.

She watched as he tossed the ball before walking towards the slide. When he was closer, Connor called up to her, "Clara, what are you doing up so high?"

"I'm going to slide," she called down.

"Alright, I'll wait for you down here," Connor answered. After a few minutes, he asked her when she would go down.

"I don't know how," Clara admitted with sadness.

"Want me to help?"

"Do you know how to slide?" she asked.

"Yeah, I do. Give me a minute," he told her.

"Where did you go, Connor?" she called out nervously.

"I'm right here, Clara," he said from behind her. He was standing on the top rung of the ladder.

"Oh no!" she whispered, crying.

Connor was sitting on the landing behind her. "What's wrong?"

"Now you're stuck up here with me," she cried.

Connor chuckled as he placed an arm around her waist. "It's alright, Clara. I'm going to slide with you. Hang on, alright? Are you ready?"

"No," she answered honestly.

"We'll be alright, I promise. It'll be fun. I'd never do something that would hurt you," he promised as he pushed off.

She screamed the whole way down the long slide with her hands holding tight onto his arms. When they reached the bottom, they laughed as they stood up. When he looked down at her face, he realized Clara was covered in dirt with streaks down her face from her tears, and blood was streaking from her mouth.

Connor squatted down in front of her and looked closely at her face. "Clara what's happened to your face?"

"Why? Is it ugly?" Clara asked, bringing her hands up to her face. Her cheek was sore, and her lip felt bigger than usual. Her hands felt wet. When she looked down, she gasped, "I bleed!"

"Yeah, Clara, you look like you were in a fight. What happened?" he asked with concern.

Tears returned as she described her struggle up the ladder that made her ugly. She had made the mistake of looking down and lost her footing, causing her face to hit the ladder. When the hiccups started, Connor looked around the park with concern. Who did she come to the park with? No one seemed to be watching her, nor did he see anyone she would likely be with.

When his friends joined them, Anthony's older brother, Joe, asked if everything was alright.

"I don't know who brought her here. Her mother would never allow her to be at the park alone. She's only three," Connor answered. "Clara, who came with you to the park?"

"Connor, her face is bleeding," the cousin stated, making her cry again.

"Clara, are you hurt?" Joe asked, squatting down in front of her.

"No, I not hurt. I ugly," she sobbed, scaring him.

Connor chuckled as he hugged her. "Clara, you aren't ugly. Dirty and bloody, but still beautiful."

The teenager used the bottom of his t-shirt to wipe the blood before offering her a piggyback ride home.

Clara opened her eyes just before dawn. She rolled over onto her back, feeling Connor still asleep beside her. Her hand slowly caressed his chest, playing with his hair. She slowly brought herself up and straddled him, leaning down on one hand, wincing from the pain as she lowered herself and shifted weight. Clara leaned down to kiss his neck, his ear. When she reached his lips, his hands were on her back as he kissed her. She felt him say something but continued to move slowly.

After the unexpected lovemaking, Connor lay in the dark as Clara cuddled close. He listened to her breathing as she returned to sleep. Her heartbeat slowly returned to normal as it beat against his chest. Her hair tickled his chin and chest. His hands gently caressed her backside with an occasional massage when he felt a knot, easing up on the pressure when she quietly moaned in her sleep. Connor had thought to get up. The children would likely be awake soon.

Instead, he fell back asleep.

It seemed only a few moments passed when Connor's eyes opened again, surprised by the daylight. He could hear the children talking as they were apparently walking away from their room.

"We should just let them sleep. I can make breakfast," Reese was saying.

He heard the little girl say a few words he couldn't understand, but Reese reported, "Yeah, we can make French toast; Uncle Rob showed me how."

Shit, Connor thought as he hurried out of bed.

An hour later, newly showered Clara slowly entered the kitchen, pausing at the sight before her. Connor and her children were busy preparing French toast with fruit.

"Mama!" The young girl was the first to see her mother.

"Mommy, we made breakfast," Reese announced as the children ran to her.

"This looks great! I am starving," Clara said as she was escorted to her chair.

Everyone lingered at the breakfast table until little Hailey became restless, wanting out of her booster seat. Before Connor could start, Clara motioned for him to remain sitting while she went to retrieve a washcloth to clean up the toddler and then Reese before they were each excused. They could hear them making their way to the family room.

When Clara started to clear the table, Connor pulled her down on his lap.

"Thank you for breakfast. I almost feel bad about not being a good cook. I can't get over how good your cooking is when you grew up with a professional chef. It's crazy!" Clara commented. Her eyes watched his hand casually caress her legs.

"You slept well last night," he commented with a grin. "I was pleasantly surprised by the wake-up activity."

"I'm sorry," Clara blushed, "I was too forward."

"Oh, you don't ever have to apologize for waking me up like that," he whispered between kisses to her neck. "I wasn't expecting you'd be ready for that, not with the pain."

"I had a dream, but I'm not sure if it was a memory or not," she explained. "Either way, it reminded me how long we've known each other and how close we've always been. How much love I have for you. I've always been in love with you, even when I was a child."

"Oh? Tell me the dream." Connor was intrigued.

"I was sitting on the slide at the playground, the tall one. I just sat up there looking around, watching everyone, and you came over from the basketball court," she shared.

Connor chuckled. "Yeah, that did happen. You were about three. We had no idea how you got to the park at first. We later learned you wandered alone. You climbed the ladder to the taller slide because you'd never been allowed. Once you were up there, you didn't know how to slide down. I'm surprised you remember that."

"One of my first memories," Clara's voice was soft. "It's the first time you called me beautiful. When I woke up, I watched you sleeping beside me. Connor, you've literally been here for me my whole life. I don't remember why I was at the park alone, do you?"

She felt him nod before he spoke, "Your grandmother was watching you. The two of you laid down to take a nap. You woke up before her and went to the park. You said you were letting her rest. We were worried so Joe called his dad from the park. He was at your house before we got there."

"She died in her sleep, didn't she? If I had called for help, she could have been saved," her voice was sad.

Connor was already shaking his head. "No, not true. Even if you knew how to call someone, it wouldn't have mattered. It was later confirmed she passed shortly after you both laid down. She was gone before you woke up. She passed peacefully beside her little pride and joy."

"Pride and joy?"

"Your grandmother never stopped grieving after Aaron died. I'm sure it was the same for your grandfather. But he became an angry, bitter man while she withered. Your grandfather ruled the household, I suspect without any input from her. There were drastic changes. Shortly after, your grandfather had his heart attack, then a stroke, and not long after, he broke his hip because of his stubbornness. She was beside him through it all. Even though there was a nurse around the clock, she assisted with his care. But when you were born, the light returned to her eyes. She doted on you.

"I remember being on the porch, everyone hanging out. You would be on her lap and turn her head so you could see her face. I realized later, you were reading her lips, but we didn't know you were hearing impaired. And according to Sylvia Hawks, you were the perfect well-behaved little girl. We all know she had to be senile because you were constantly into trouble," Connor teased.

"I was not!" Clara defended herself as she tried to stand up.

But Connor pulled her in close for a hug. "I love you, Clara. I'll get the kids to daycare and myself to work. Will you please remain off the stairs today?"

"I will try," she promised. "Rachel and Lila are coming over with lunch."

Rachel was excited to have the afternoon off. The school year had started hectic with the accident a week before it began. She would pick up salads before meeting with Lila for a girls' lunch at Clara's house. It had been a while since it was just the girls. Too bad Shannon couldn't be there. She thought it was horrible for Shannon to do everything right and still get into trouble with her previous boss.

Parking on Main Street, Rachel was lost in her thoughts as she slowly walked towards the door.

"Rachel! Perfect timing! Are you skipping class?"

Rachel looked over, surprised to see Max walking towards her on the sidewalk. "Max, hello. How did the interview go?"

Max stepped over to give her an easy hug. "I got the job. The offer was too good to turn down. It's perfect timing to run into you here. You're going to join me as I celebrate."

Rachel could only stare at him and wonder. *Is he really moving here?* She smiled but shook her head.

"Max, that's great. Congratulations, it doesn't surprise me you were offered the job, but seriously? Are you planning to move here? You hate the small-town vibe."

Smiling, Max studied her beautiful face. He loved listening to her talk. Her voice was so soothing. He could picture himself returning home every evening to her large mansion. Max had since learned Rachel could easily have servants, but her mother had declined the services. He would certainly encourage it.

Max closed the space between them.

"Rachel, what's not to love? The offer was unbelievable! And the small town grows on you, you know? Besides, you're here. What more could I ever need?"

Rachel froze, not prepared for such physical contact, or she would have stepped back. Max appeared to advance towards her in slow motion. She still could not process what he was doing, even as he did it. His arms went around her low back as he pulled her in tight against him; his lips were on hers.

Max was delighted when she didn't pull away, encouraging him to deepen the kiss. While one hand pulled her in closer, the other hand was in her hair.

"What the hell do you think you are doing?" Chase's voice was suddenly heard behind her.

"Oh, hey man, how's it going?" Max asked as he grabbed Rachel's hand, keeping her from stepping further back. He loved pushing the boundaries and setting off her boyfriend's temper. He grinned as she blushed further.

"She's congratulating me on a successful interview. It looks like I'll be moving here after all."

Chase stepped between them, gently pushing her back behind him. "You have no business kissing her. Stay the hell away from her."

Rachel was immediately standing between them. Her back was to Max, placing a hand on Chase's chest to prevent him from swinging his fist. She didn't see Max's face, grinning and raising his eyebrows, further baiting him. "Chase, stop. You don't speak for me. I can speak for myself."

"Is that what you want? Kissing Max, here on the sidewalk for all the town to see? You don't need to say anything more," Chase stepped back with his hands fisted at this side. The hurt was evident on his face. "I'll stop to get my things when you aren't home and leave your key on the table. It'll give you time to decide which one of us you want. I can't guarantee I'll still be waiting."

Rachel tried to grab his arm as he walked away. "Chase? Stop a minute, please."

Chase continued to walk away. When she turned around, Max had already gone inside the restaurant. He was confident she would join him, already ordering her drink. Rachel remained on the sidewalk, watching Chase drive off.

"Rachel, what's going on?"

She turned to see Lila walking up behind her. She had been driving towards Clara's when she saw her cousin storming away from Rachel.

"Lila, I have no idea," Rachel admitted. She could not process the last five minutes.

Twenty minutes later, Clara opened the door to her friends. Sitting at the dining room table, Lila and Clara talked about simple things, curious about Rachel's quietness.

"Rach, what's wrong?" Clara finally asked.

"I think I messed up. When I stopped to pick up the salads, I ran into Max. Chase came out of nowhere and started to get all possessive. When I told him to stop, he just walked away. I think we broke up," she answered, unaware her details were too general.

Lila and Clara exchanged looks.

"I'm missing something. Max who?" Clara asked.

Rachel realized she did not have an opportunity to update her on the previous evening. She sighed before giving the details.

"Chase just came up when you were talking to Max?" Clara asked, attempting to clarify the details. When her friend nodded, she asked, "What, exactly, were you two talking about?"

Rachel sighed again, moving her fork around her salad. "He told me he was offered the job and was moving here. Max invited me to join him for lunch to celebrate."

Clara's eyes narrowed. "And?"

Rachel looked up at Clara first and then at Lila. "And what?"

"What else happened?" Clara waited a moment before continuing, "Chase suddenly starts a fight with Max because you two were talking? That sounds like Rob, not Chase. Were you two touching? Hugging?"

Rachel sighed again before she slowly nodded. "He was kissing me."

Clara's eyebrows were raised at the phrase used, kissing, not kissed. It implied more than a peck. "Did you respond to the kiss? Encourage it?"

"Clara, I wasn't expecting it! One minute he's talking to me. The next, he's pulling me in, and his tongue is in my mouth. Before I had a chance to react, Chase was suddenly standing between us, demanding Max stays away from me. I told him not to speak for me. He then asked if I wanted Max and walked away before I could even answer him," Rachel explained, tears threatening to fall.

"Wow! Max kissed you on the sidewalk, and you were kissing him back?" Lila asked to clarify. Without voicing it, she sided with her cousin.

"Well, yeah, I can see why Chase would have been upset," Clara commented.

"What do you mean?"

"Before this, did you consider yourself to be his girlfriend?" Lila asked.

"Yes, of course. Chase's practically living with me," Rachel answered. Her friends already knew he slept in a separate room.

Clara subtly raised her hand at Lila, gesturing she would explain. "How would you feel if you walked into the restaurant and saw Chase kissing the server?"

Rachel's blue eyes were suddenly big in shock. "Why would Chase even consider doing that?"

"Why indeed? That is exactly how Chase felt. How did he even know Max?" Clara asked with confusion. She had obviously been out of the loop.

Rachel gave the account of her last evening in the city with Chase and Rob. She explained how Max unexpectedly showed up at her house. Her monologue ended with a vague description of the gathering at Memories.

"So, you scheduled a date with Max later in the evening after a dinner date with Chase?" Lila exclaimed. She suddenly understood her cousin's mood the previous night. "Do you like Max?"

"I never really thought about it," Rachel shrugged.

"Rachel, who do you see yourself with, say, ten years from now? Max or Chase?" Clara asked. "And if you don't see yourself with either one, that's ok," Clara inserted.

Lila nodded, debating sharing what she knew. "Rachel, I shouldn't tell you this, but Chase pulled out his mother's engagement ring earlier this week."

"What?" Rachel was shocked.

"Rob and I thought that was why you two were inviting us to Memories last night, to celebrate your engagement," she explained.

"But he didn't propose! Why didn't he?" Rachel asked, totally not understanding.

Lila looked over at Clara in disbelief.

"Rach, think about it. You are preparing for a romantic evening with Chase. He's preparing to ask you to marry him and spend the rest of your lives together. But when Chase arrives, he overhears you making plans with another guy the same evening. Chase probably figured you weren't ready for the next step he was proposing," she explained, pun intended.

"But I didn't even know he was going to propose," Rachel answered softly.

Lila and Clara exchanged another look before Clara reached across the table to squeeze her hand. "Do it. Close your eyes, relax, and simply see yourself. Now advance ten years from now."

Rachel felt silly sitting there with her eyes closed. They used to play this game when they were kids, but she never admitted it out loud; it was always Chase. Every single guy she dated was always compared to him. He kept her standards high. If a guy didn't open the door, she lost interest. If he was too forceful, there wasn't another date. It was the main reason for her "no men in her loft rule," and why she always stayed out of theirs. She did not want to be in a position where she could not safely get herself out.

She opened her eyes, her blue looking into the green. "I have always seen myself with Chase. Even in high school."

"There you go. So, what do you want to do about it?" Lila asked.

"I don't know what to do. I never know how to act or what guys are thinking. But with Chase, I can always relax and be myself. Lila, you are probably right. Max just wants to sleep with me," she sighed sadly. She had considered him a friend.

"I told you that last year when I first met him," Clara argued. "Rachel, you have always limited your intimacy with guys. Is it because you want your wedding night to be special?"

"I honestly don't know anymore. I just wanted my future husband to be the one and only with whom I shared that level of intimacy with. It was something my grandmother seemed to have drilled into me. It's old-fashioned, I know. As I grew older, I would suddenly feel awkward if a guy started getting too touchy-feely. I don't even know what to do with a guy, it's embarrassing," Rachel whispered.

Lila gently touched her friend's shoulder. "Rachel, any time with a guy should be special. It's better when you both care about each other, more magical. And if he feels the same about you, he'll be patient. If he doesn't, he's not worth it."

Rachel looked between her friends, both nodding in agreement. "What should I do?"

"You finish your salad and go find him, and tell him how you feel about him," Clara suggested. "Or just leave the salad and go."

"I don't know what to do if he wants to, you know," she stated as she blushed slightly.

"He's likely very aware of that. If you trust him, Chase will only do what you're comfortable with. You have to communicate that. He's not going to expect you to be an expert. Besides, exploring each other is half the fun," Lila explained.

Sheriff Mancuso was drained from the previous late night. He felt as if he'd not had any sleep in a week! Relieved all was quiet within the department, he sat at his desk, reading over the reports from the previous day. He quietly groaned with annoyance when he came to the incident between Matt Emerson and Carl Gibson. For years, he thought the two men had finally let go of the riff between them over Susannah. But since her remains were found last summer, Tony needed to review everything known about the days before the disappearance.

For the first time, he learned of a witness to her disappearance, possibly even her death. Did little Clara actually witness it? And why didn't the sheriff's department investigate further back then? Tony had only been a deputy at the time. Reaching for his mug, Tony realized it was empty. *Definitely need a refill before reviewing the file.* He planned to spend the afternoon listing those he needed to reinterview.

As he came out of his small office, his brown eyes met the sharp blue of Lee Howell. The unexpected sight of the mayor answered his earlier question: Lee was the prosecuting attorney at the time. Did he instruct the sheriff to stop the investigation twenty years ago? Lee always had a misguided understanding of his responsibility, initially as the DA and now as the Mayor. He always acted as if he had the power to control things. *But what does he need to control?*

Interesting, he would be here today after the incident outside Clara's home last night.

"Sheriff, perfect timing. I have a few questions for you," the mayor announced across the department's lobby. Everyone's heads turned.

A moment later, the sheriff and mayor both sat in his small but comfortable office. Tony decided he would wait to hear what Lee wanted. Expecting it to be regarding the mayor's son, Eric, currently on house arrest pending trial for drugging Clara the previous summer. And yet, he wasn't entirely caught off guard by the question.

"I heard there's been a development in Susannah's murder. Have formal charges finally been filed?"

The Sheriff's eyes narrowed as he returned his mug to his desk without drinking. "What new developments?"

"Matthew Emerson is accused of murdering Susannah. The town is talking about it." Lee's blue eyes almost sparkled with the announcement.

"Lee, what are you talking about?" Tony decided to play dumb. His sons had assured him the incident the previous night was not the talk of the town. The current town focus was on the soon-to-be-opened YMCA, with speculation of a young man from the city being hired for the position of the lead personal trainer. Sadly, the murder of Susannah Gibson was considered old news.

"Last night, you arrested both Matthew and Carl. What further progress has been made?"

"You aren't the DA anymore; I have no reason to update you on the investigation," the sheriff reminded him.

"I'm the mayor! Of course, I have the right to know. When you think about it, it's not surprising, is it? The guy was always chasing after her, even after she married." Lee's eyes narrowed when the man before him remained silent. "He often followed her when she went into the city. He just couldn't let her go. You didn't seriously release Matthew already?"

With uncharacteristic restlessness, Lee stood up and paced the small office. "Tony, I can't believe you are protecting Matthew Emerson! He murdered the heir to the Hawks Estate! How can you possibly just let this go? Everyone knew they were seeing each other. She tries to break it off with him, and he won't let her go. Why aren't you doing your job?"

"Lee, if I made an arrest every time accusations were made without any evidence to back it up, the judge would have my ass for wasting his time and everyone else's. As a former district attorney, you know this." Tony Mancuso leaned back in his chair, studying the other man. Always dressed immaculately, Lee seemed slightly disheveled, with his dress shirt slightly pulled from the waist. Of course, having your only child suspected of murder could make the most put-together person disheveled.

But Lee wasn't even broaching the concerns of Eric's pending trial. "How do you know about the fight anyway?"

"Who doesn't know about it? It's all everyone is talking about: the fight on Prospect where both Matthew and Carl are throwing fists! The sheriff and his whole department were needed to break it up and restore order! Both men were dragged to the station in handcuffs! Good God, Tony, are you telling me you're gullible enough to simply let such accusations go unchecked? Do we need to bring another sheriff to town?"

Tony remained silent during the outburst and watched as the mayor stormed out of his office. Contrary to the mayor's statement, Matt and Susannah's affair was not public knowledge. *If it had been, Dan Emerson would have snipped it. Did Lee Howell have personal knowledge because neighbors see things from next door? Or did he have more personal knowledge of Susannah? Lee has always had a wandering eye. Not speculation, he was often seen cuddling close to someone, not his wife, around town. It couldn't be that simple.*

But what other reason for such an odd reaction to the incident last night? Tony's eyes remained on the doorway in case the mayor returned. *Carl was kind of a cousin of Lee's. Lee was married to Matt's aunt, so they were all kind of kin of sorts. The town rumor at the time of the marriage was that Lee needed access to more money since his father continued to control the Howell Estate. He kept a tight leash, or so most thought. The elder, Leander, a pharmacist, was forced into retirement a while back. Some speculated there wasn't much money, especially compared to the Emerson estate.*

Or the Hawks Estate, a small voice in his head speculated.

Tony remembered his father saying no one had money like the Hawks did. Which raised the question, where is the money? Clara didn't seem to know about it as the heiress to the Hawks Estate. Who does?

Playing devil's advocate, Tony needed to present all sides to his theory. He listed everything in his notebook: his theories, his thoughts, and what he remembered. Then, he made a list of people to interview. To keep the information contained, he decided this investigation would be kept old school with eyes only! No copies, no email files, and especially no dictation.

Kathleen, Lee's second wife, could have provided inside knowledge of Matt and Susannah's affair. She was shrewd enough to want to cause trouble for others in the family. Tony wrote her name on the list. Next, he wrote the most obvious: Lee had blue eyes. Beside it, he wrote, 'the right shade?'

13
unexpected events

Chase was annoyed with the knock on the door. He wasn't going to bother answering it, but when the noise persisted, he finally opened the door. He was shocked to see Rachel, but remained silent.

"It's you," Rachel quietly announced.

"Yes, it's me. I live here," Chase answered with irritation.

Rachel felt panic, hands twisting as she remembered what her friends said, "Tell him what you feel, or how else will he ever know?" Rachel took a deep breath before she slowly exhaled.

When she looked up into his gray-blue eyes, she smiled. "It's you that I want to kiss, no one else. What I meant earlier was that I wanted to be the one to tell him to stop touching and kissing me. I wanted to be the one to speak for myself. It's you that I want beside me."

Chase's eyes narrowed as he watched her blush, her baby-blue eyes looking directly into his. He remained where he was, not saying a word.

Not discouraged by his lack of response, Rachel boldly stepped forward. She willed herself to relax and did what she always dreamed of doing: she placed her palms on his chest, rubbed her hands up towards his shoulders, and pulled him down to kiss him. Her friends were right; he would take over.

Chase's breath caught when her tongue began to mate with his. He felt her body press against his. He had a moment to think, closing the door and stepping her back into the door. He pulled back a moment, touching her cheek, trying to catch his breath before she pulled him down to kiss his neck.

"Rachel, we need to stop," he gasped.

"Why?" she wondered, her hands caressing his shoulders, slowly down his chest. He's always been so strong, she thought, filling out more since that night in the woods. Rachel looked into his eyes as her hands played with the buttons on his shirt.

"I won't be able to control myself if you continue like this," he honestly admitted as he stepped further back.

"Chase, I trust you. I love you. I have always loved you. I want to be with you: today, tomorrow, and ten years from now. If you want me just today, then alright. We stop now." She lowered her hands, but her eyes remained on his. "But if you want me beyond today, tomorrow, and next week, then I trust you."

Rachel leaned back into the door as she watched his eyes. A grin slowly appeared as he processed what she was saying. He stepped closer, hands up on the door, and only his lips touched her as he kissed her slowly on the forehead, lips, cheek, and neck. He nibbled on her ear, watching her respond to his simple touch. He slowly leaned his body into hers, allowing her to feel his response.

Chase was surprised she didn't try to pull away or stiffen, her normal response when he was getting too close for her comfort.

"Are you sure?"

After Rachel left her friends, Clara asked Lila, "How are things going with you and Dallas?"

"Good," she answered with a smile.

Clara waited to see if Lila would expand but decided, what the hell. "Lila, how in the world did you and Dallas end up together? I think it's great, we're sisters-in-law, but the fact that you two were able to give it a shot and keep it a secret, it floors me."

Lila shrugged and debated opening the vault kept tight over the years while they walked into the family room. Once they were both sitting, she sighed; *what the hell?* "You remember the night the theater exploded?"

"Not really," Clara quietly admitted with a shrug. She never really talked about that night, not because she had nightmares but because she truly didn't have memories firsthand. She only remembered what others told her. Never did she share with anyone about the gap in her memory. Clara assumed it was due to the concussion.

"I do know we were there. I stopped in the bathroom. You went into the theater. Then I woke up in the Taylor House the next afternoon."

Clara was silent as she remembered the shock of waking up without any memories of the explosion, trapped underneath all the rubble. When she later told Connor about it, she was shocked to learn he had been at her side from when the firefighters brought her to the ambulance until when Rachel and her mother brought her home. Try as she did, Clara had no memory of it.

"Yeah, you were one of the first ones out. I was so worried about you," Lila paused as she looked down at her hands, "I can't believe we've never talked about this before now. When I walked into the theater, there were a few others already sitting down but on the right side, further away from the sharing wall of the theater. We were to be sitting on the left side. As it turned out, Dallas was already sitting at his seat."

Lila smiled, remembering the innocent joy of seeing him already sitting near their seats. "He asked me if Rob knew where I was. I laughed and said, of course, he dropped us off before going to pick up Shannon. We kept the conversation simple. He joked about hoping the lights dimmed before Rob joined us but cheered when I mentioned you were already there. I remember feeling slightly disappointed that he was more interested in you than me. He later told me you were siblings. He swore me to secrecy."

I dropped something, I don't know what, maybe my water bottle. I stood up to retrieve it, and suddenly the wall was blowing up. Somehow, he was immediately on me. He grabbed me and pushed me down towards the floor. We were shielded some by the seats, but Dallas used his body to protect me. It all happened so fast. One second I was standing, and then I was flat on my back with his arms protectively over our heads while he lay on top of me." Lila sipped from her drink a moment before she continued.

"It seemed as if the sky was literally falling on us. Happening so fast, and yet it seemed as if time had stopped. When the roof and everything stopped falling, we couldn't see a damn thing. Dallas slowly lifted his head and asked if I was alright." Lila smiled sadly as she remembered looking up to see a mere shadow of his head and feeling the weight of his body on hers. "He had gently touched my face. I remember hearing him wince in pain as he apologized if he hurt me as he shifted his weight. I didn't know until later some debris fell onto him, fracturing his ribs and cutting into his back."

Clara remained quiet, listening to her friend describe her nightmare of being trapped inside the collapsed building and the screaming sounds of another teenager. Apparently, Sam Black was walking down the left aisle when the explosion happened. His injuries were fatal, but it took him about an hour to die.

Tears fell as Lila quietly described the anguish of being trapped without help. She and Dallas both tried to stop his bleeding. "He was awake until the end and even joked about finally talking with the hottest girl in high school. But we could hear his wheezing and struggles to breathe. We thought he had a concussion. There was bleeding from minor cuts. We didn't know about internal bleeding. Dallas had removed his jacket to help keep him warm. Sammy's head was in my lap, and I held his hand when he slowly faded out. It wasn't until after we were out that I remembered Sam was Dallas' cousin. But when he died, I was the one who lost it. I became hysterical, crying as I held him in my arms." Lila's gaze was distant as she retold the story with silent tears streaking her face.

"But Dallas somehow kept his cool. He later told me he probably would have been the same, but he was too concerned about me," she laughed harshly.

Lila was quiet as she struggled to keep her emotions controlled as they started to slip from the vault from so long ago. She silently debated how much to share. "After that night, I had horrible nightmares, but I couldn't bring myself to talk about it."

To Clara's shock, Lila explained about her drug addiction. "It started slowly. Just a little something to take the edge off. Relax me, you know? And amazingly, it gave me the courage to come out of my comfort zone and seek thrills. I went to Dallas' place. Do you remember the vacant house that was on the edge of town? Interestingly, if you went into the woods behind it and walked in the proper direction, you would come out on Foxwood land. I went there alone to see Dallas."

Lila had been nervous as she slowly stepped up towards the porch. It was still early evening, but being in the valley surrounded by mountains, the fading light gave the impression it was later in the day. Initially, the house appeared empty. However, the moment her foot touched the porch, a group of stoners surrounded her.

'Well, well, well! Look what the cat dragged in! Does the golden boy know his baby sister is out here? All alone? You are either very brave or foolish,' the one called Slater commented as his dirty hand touched her face.

Lila froze with fear as she heard her brother's voice in her head, telling her vile things about these boys. She had recently learned Rob had exaggerated his warnings but quickly found herself second-guessing her decision to ignore them.

A sharp voice was heard before the hand could stroke her cheek. 'Hands off her, now!'

Lila was relieved to hear Dallas' voice, but her gray-blue eyes remained on bloodshot eyes before her as Slater appeared to debate his next action. His pupils were pinpoint. Amused, he dropped his hand but remained within a foot of the petite little sister of the town's golden boy.

Unspoken fear kept Lila fixed in her spot, her eyes staring at Slater. Dallas was suddenly between them, standing protectively with his back to her. The other delinquents had stepped back at the harshness of his tone but remained to watch as the two strongest-minded residents silently challenged the other.

'Ears aren't working today, Slater? Hands off her! Back away. Your hands are always off her, is that understood?' Dallas instructed as he looked among the group before his eyes settled again on the one before him.

'You and her, hmm? You are seriously stupid to be hooking up with her. Her brother gets wind of this, he'll have this house knocked down and all of us in the ground,' Slater warned. When Dallas didn't comment, he simply smiled, almost making him look handsome, before he stepped back and disappeared inside the house.

Dallas had remained silent, waiting for everyone to leave. Once alone on the porch, he turned around, momentarily distracted by her eyes as she smiled up at him.

'What the hell are you doing here?' Dallas had demanded. But before she could answer, he had taken her hand to lead her off the porch. They needed to be a safe distance from prying eyes and ears into the shadows of the treeline. When Dallas stopped and turned towards her, he repeated his question.

"My nerves were frayed by that point. It had been weeks since the explosion, and I hardly had a night's rest. I always felt relaxed and safe when I saw Dallas in the hallways at school or around town. Suddenly, he wasn't around anymore, and my anxiety grew. But my fears and anxiety dropped when I stood before him that night. I boldly stepped forward, touched his chest, and told him I had come to see him. I stood up on my tiptoes to kiss his lips." She grinned at the memory.

"It wasn't our first kiss. He kissed me when we were alone that night, trying to keep me calm and distracted. It worked. But when we were alone in the woods, Dallas was shocked. He pulled back. I was hurt and accused him of not meaning what he said and being a jerk. I started to walk away. He grabbed my hand again to stop me from walking further into the woods. He told me he was worried about my safety and that I should never come alone to the house. It wasn't safe.

"Being only fourteen at the time and sheltered, I didn't quite grasp what he was getting at," Lila stared absently as she remembered. "I asked him why he wasn't around at school anymore. He simply shrugged and said he quit. It wasn't like anyone cared anyway. I told him I cared. And that he should finish school and continue his dream of leaving town to better himself.

"Long story short, I promised not to look for him unexpectedly at the house, and Dallas was to return to school."

"He was the one that gave you the drugs?" Clara asked, shocked. She had not been aware either had been into drugs back then.

"No, it wasn't him. Dallas never touched the stuff. He was aware I was doing them and helped me," Lila answered with a shake of her head. "That's the short version."

"And you two have been together all this time?" Clara confirmed, still shocked the secret was kept so well. She had recently learned from Dallas that the explosion was a catalyst that literally sparked their relationship, but not the details.

"Not really," Lila laughed. "Back then, I thought of us as a couple, and maybe we were. We shared things we never shared with others. Dallas looked out for me. I always looked forward to seeing him, even if it was a glimpse in the hall or at the diner where he worked. Dallas has always been a perfect gentleman around me. Back then, we would hold hands or cuddle together at night. He never pushed for anything beyond kissing.”

“We kept in touch when he left to join the army. When we met up for a weekend my first year in college,” she grinned, “that’s when things started heating up. And the rest is history.”

Connor arrived home in the late afternoon with the children just as Lila said goodbye.

“We have plenty of steaks to grill for dinner. Lila, call Dallas and join us tonight,” he invited.

“We already have plans. I need to get on; I’m already late. I still need to stop at the store first,” she said, hugging her friends.

After Lila made her small purchase at the store, she grabbed her bag and hurried to her car. As she was opening the door, she heard her name. When she turned, Slater was standing beside her. He was almost as tall as Dallas but bulkier. While handsome wasn’t the word to describe the man before her, he wasn’t ugly. His outgoing personality pulled people towards him. Lila kept her distance because he had a mean streak if he felt wronged.

“Lila Foxwood, how are you? I’m surprised we haven’t run into each other before. Let’s go for a drink,” he suggested, stepping in to hug her.

“Slater? How are you? What have you been up to?” Lila studied him. He was no longer the town’s dirtbag that lurked in the shadows. In high school, he had the connections and provided anything needed to party or to chill.

Currently, his eyes were clear: gone were the dark bags under his eyes. A sign he no longer touched the drugs. His dark hair was professionally trimmed, his face cleanly shaved, and his clothes were casual dressy. His skin was clean and clear. When he wasn’t smiling, he looked angry and unapproachable. But the minute he laughed, his face relaxed, displaying his easygoing personality.

"Returned home a few months ago. I'm now the district attorney," he answered. His blue eyes twinkled with his smile as he continued. "I owe you for everything you did for me when we were kids. If it weren't for you, I'd be dead now."

"I didn't do anything. You were the one that went back to school and completed all the hard work, including law school," Lila answered proudly.

"You were the only one that believed in me and encouraged me to follow my true path. You gave me the tools," Slater responded, squeezing her shoulder. His hand slowly trailed down her arm. When he saw her eyes lower to his hand, he felt her tense slightly with a step back, just as she did when they were younger. *Some things never change*, he thought.

"Slater, I'm with Dallas," Lila announced.

"I heard. I can't believe you two lasted this long! I would have expected the golden boy would have killed him by now," he laughed. "Let's go have a drink. A gesture of gratitude for your support."

"I can't; I'm running late. I am proud of you. All your hard work has paid off. It's great seeing you again."

"Another time, right? And, of course, bring Dallas," Slater suggested, opening her car door. He watched as she pulled away, pulling out his cell to send a text as she drove out of town.

Clara and the children followed Connor outside onto the deck as he started up the grill. She slowly sat in a chair to supervise the children playing in the yard. She considered purchasing a sandbox or swing set as she watched them chase each other. Hearing the door open, she turned to see Connor coming out with a glass of iced tea. He sat beside her, content with holding her hand.

Both turned towards the yard when Hailey started to cry.

The little girl had fallen on the ground, her knee scraping on something sharp, tearing open the skin. Reese was helping her onto her feet, guiding her towards the steps as Connor came down. He picked her up and carried her over to her mother, gently placing her on her lap. He kneeled to assess the damage.

"Do you want me to get the first aid kit?" Reese volunteered, looking over his shoulder.

"That would be great, thanks, Buddy."

Reese was back a moment later. Connor quickly looked over the contents, opening a septic wipe as he gently cleansed the wound.

Hailey screamed, attempting to pull away as Clara held her with her right arm.

"Do you want me to get your staple gun?" the boy offered.

Connor was surprised by the size of the gash but remained calm as he declined. "Hailey, this only needs a bandaid. What color do you want?"

"Lellow," she hiccupped.

He placed a large yellow one on her knee. "All better?"

"Hiss!" Hailey demanded. After he kissed it, Connor looked up into her blue eyes questioningly. "Mama hiss."

Connor gently slid her down her mother's lap, lifting her feet over her head to allow Clara to kiss the knee. When she was settled in her mother's lap, the toddler smiled as she stated, "Butte."

He rubbed her hair as he chuckled, asking Reese to show him where she fell. Connor wanted to remove all the sharp objects from the yard, curious to know what it was.

"What is all the racket going on out here?" Devan asked from his deck.

"Hailey had a fall out in the yard and cut her knee. Connor has decided the staple gun is unnecessary, " Clara said.

"That's always good to hear," Devan answered as both turned towards Connor.

Connor and Reese were stepping back up onto the deck. He instructed the boy to remain off the grass until he completed a yard sweep. He quietly showed Clara and Devan the pieces of a broken bottle.

Without a discussion, Devan pulled a napkin from his pocket. He would send the glass to the lab to analyze. It may not be anything.

Clara motioned for her daughter to stand up as she led the children into the house to wash up for dinner as Connor invited his cousin to dinner. She left the men, sensing they had something to discuss. Part of her wanted to hear it, but the other part was too exhausted to care.

As they were finishing dinner, Clara reached for her cell, noting the call was from Dallas. She had initially intended to let it run to voicemail, not a big talker on the phone, but she answered anyway.

"Hi, Dallas."

"How long ago did Lila leave?" he asked without greeting.

"She left about two hours ago. Why? Dallas, what's wrong?" Clara held her phone away from her ear to allow Connor and Devan to hear.

"That's about the time I received her text that she was on her way home. I tried calling her, but it went straight to voicemail. Still not hearing from her, I started back towards town and found her car. It's sitting here on the shoulder with two flat tires," Dallas explained.

Devan reached for the phone, rising to go into the kitchen to talk. "Dallas, where exactly are you?" He paused and then said, "Wait for us. Help is on the way. Don't go into the woods. We are on our way to you."

Devan returned the phone to Clara as he instructed Connor and called the Mancusos.

Without a word, Devan returned home, and Connor ran upstairs to change his clothes. When he returned, Clara was waiting for him at the doorway. She followed him outside. "Clara, please. I need you to stay inside and lock the doors. Don't go anywhere. I need to know you are safe."

"Connor, if she's lost in the woods, I want to help," Clara began but stopped. Once the words were out, she realized her statement was stupid. First, Lila never got lost in the woods. She was raised inside them and knew her way around as well as how to get out again. And second, what exactly would she even be able to do to help find her? *She could barely walk as it was!*

Connor had opened the back of his SUV. Unbeknownst to her, he kept an emergency backpack with hiking boots and a medicine kit. He was one of many volunteers from around the county that gathered together to either look for the lost or to assist with the hurt in the federal park. He was already removing his shoes and donning his hiking boots.

Without lacing them, he stood up, hands on Clara's shoulders. He faced her, making sure there was no question she understood him. "You are not in a position to run around in the woods. We don't know what happened or if someone is with her. I need you to stay safe and locked inside. Call Rachel, have her stay with you, then call Rob and Chase. They'll help us."

"But what about Dallas? Someone should be with him while everyone is searching for her," Clara began as Connor grabbed his bag and headed towards Devan's vehicle, but Devan cut her off.

"Dallas won't be sitting anywhere. Top tracker in the county. He'll be leading us. It sounds more like she's not alone; if we don't get there fast enough, he'll start without us," Devan explained.

"Ok. I promise. I'm going inside and locking up. I'll make the calls." She reached for Connor's hand. "Both of you, be careful."

Once inside with the doors locked, Clara called Rachel's cell. She did not see the shadow shifting across the street.

"Hello, you have reached Rachel's phone. She is naked and unable to talk right now," a male voice answered. Clara could hear her friend's voice in the background.

"Chase? Is that you?"

"Yeah," he answered, about to make a sarcastic comment about who else it would be, but she rushed through.

"Chase, Dallas just called. Lila didn't make it home this afternoon. He found her car along the side of the road with two flat tires. The guys are all meeting up to start a search," Clara began.

Chase was grabbing clothes from the floor. He motioned for Rachel to dress.

"Where are they meeting?"

"Call either Connor or Devan. They are heading there now. Do you have either number?"

"I have both. Listen, Rachel is going to be driving to your place. If she doesn't arrive within the next twenty minutes, you call me." Chase quickly glanced at his watch as he hung up to call Devan. Once he had the information, he called Rob. "Someone's missing in the woods. A team is forming. Meet me at the truck in three."

As soon as he heard confirmation, Chase hung up. He finished dressing as he instructed Rachel. "Lila is missing. I have no details, but a team is forming. I want you to call me on your cell once you are in your car. You drive directly to Clara's. Do not stop for anyone, agreed?"

Rachel's eyes were big with worry as many questions raced through her head. Chase grabbed her hand as they both headed down the steps.

"Want me to drive?" Rob asked without a greeting.

"I'll drive. I know where we are going." Chase answered as he kissed Rachel, eyes following her as she ran to her car. Once they were both in his truck, he answered his Bluetooth. "Rachel?"

"Yes," her voice answered as she followed his truck down the driveway. She turned toward town, watching in her rearview mirror as the truck turned in the other direction. She listened in silence as she heard Rob's voice.

"Are you going to tell me why you're so rattled?" Chase remained quiet as his cousin continued, "I know it's not Rachel. Clara is still under lock and key. Don't tell me it's Lila."

Chase simply looked over as Rob exploded. "That bastard allowed her to get lost in the woods? Lila doesn't get lost in the woods. What the hell are you not telling me?"

"All I know is Dallas found her car with two flat tires and her cell smashed up with footprints leading into the woods. Rob, you need to contain your temper. I can't have you shooting off at him when all our time and effort needs to be focused on finding her. Do you hear me? I won't have you hindering the search." Chase looked over as he saw the other vehicles parked along the side of the road. "Rachel, honey, are you still there?"

"Yeah, I'm in town. Three blocks before I get to Clara's. Go, find her," she instructed before turning off the phone.

A minute later, Rachel pulled into the driveway. Reaching across the seat for her purse, she saw movement in her mirror. Looking over her shoulder, Rachel debated if she in fact, saw something or if Chase had caused her to fear the wind blowing in the shrubs. Playing it safe, she called Clara.

"Rachel? Where are you?"

"I'm here in your driveway," Rachel stated as she saw Clara look out the window before opening the door. Once she saw her friend at the doorway, Rachel ran up to the porch.

"Who else is here?"

"Me and the kids," Clara stated as she relocked the door. The friends each told the other what they knew and speculated. As they headed into the family room, Clara's eyes caught something.

"Rachel, let me see your hand."

"So, he popped the question? That's great!" Clara first admired the ring recently placed on her finger before the friends hugged.

"I totally forgot," Rachel admitted, shoving her blonde hair from her face. "Chase has me so freaked out. I know this isn't the time or place, but will you be my maid of honor?"

Before she could answer, both were startled by a sudden knocking on the door.

Rachel went to the window. "That's weird. It's Matt and Talia."

Not so weird, Clara thought as she opened the door. "Matt? What are you doing here?"

"Connor called me and explained everything that was going on. He wanted me to check in with you," he said, stepping aside to allow the woman with him to enter the house first.

Clara nodded her head as her eyes turned toward the woman beside him. Matt's eyes followed, turning to his wife. "Oh yeah, I keep forgetting you two have not met. Clara, my wife, Talia. Talia, Clara."

"Clara, I'm sorry for the circumstances but pleased to meet you," Talia stated as she held up a covered cake. "I don't mean to intrude! I asked Matt to bring me along. I brought cake, it's not much, but chocolate always helps to calm me."

Clara smiled as she gestured towards the kitchen with both women following, as well as the children.

Matt immediately locked the door and walked to the kitchen without another word. He went out into the garage and back again. Down into the basement, returning within a few minutes.

Everyone was sitting around the table when Clara asked, "Matt, what are you not telling me?"

His blue eyes looked into her green, *so much like her mother's*, he thought before answering. "Just like I said, Connor called. He asked that I check in on you. Make sure no one else has been here." He paused a moment, looking between both Clara and Rachel before continuing. "The security cameras caught movement. Connor wanted to be sure it wasn't someone hiding out front in the shrubs."

"Yes, I think there was," Rachel nodded agreement.

All eyes turned to her.

"Was it anyone you know?" Matt asked.

"Why would it be someone I know?"

Rachel paused to think things through. Lila was taken, literally, from the road. Everyone goes to look for her leaving Clara alone and vulnerable. Eric is still out on bail. *Shoot*, Rachel thought.

"Honestly, I wasn't even sure. I was pretty spooked driving here by myself. When I pulled into the driveway, I thought I saw movement in the rearview mirror. When I turned to look back, I might have seen someone walking along the sidewalk. I can't be sure exactly what I saw. I blinked, and no one was there."

"It's alright. It may have been someone just walking by. Not unusual this time of day," Matt assured her.

After Rachel and Talia assisted Clara with cleaning up the kitchen, she slowly negotiated the steps to put the children in bed. Talia sliced up the cake and made coffee while Matt continued to survey the windows.

"Matt, you need to relax. You're going to make Clara nervous," she told her husband.

"Matt, do you believe this is all connected somehow?" Rachel asked.

His eyes looked toward his wife before answering. "No idea. It just seems to be a lot of coincidences lately. We're here simply to keep you two company until they find her."

"And Rachel, I have been dying to ask when you got that engagement ring?" Talia asked.

Lila's head was killing her. Her first thought was she had too much to drink the evening before. But she realized her hands were bound behind her when she tried to touch her head. *What the hell?*

Her eyes flew open. *Where the hell am I?*

Lila felt a moment of panic when she discovered she was sitting on the ground deep in the woods, leaning against a tree. She immediately searched her thoughts.

She had lunch with Clara and Rachel. She left to go home to Dallas but had a flat. She remembered standing beside the car, looking at the flat tires as she started to call Dallas when another vehicle pulled up behind her. There were two guys. One had stepped out to look over the flats, realizing she had two. He attempted to assure her all was well and offered to fix them. When Lila tried to call Dallas, the man slapped the cell from her hand, and his friendliness disappeared.

That's when Lila ran into the woods. She made it to the trees, but that's all she remembered.

She assessed her body for possible injuries: rolled her shoulders, and turned her head. Lila winced at the pain in the back of her head. She tried to release her hands and worked on the knots with her fingers. The material was soft, and she was surprised she could break free. Lila pulled what appeared to be a bandana onto her lap before working on her ankle restraints.

Within minutes, Lila was free. Unsure where she was, obviously in the park, surrounded by trees, she closed her eyes to listen. She heard the birds, the soft rustling of the leaves as a breeze blew through, and the water flowing. She was near the river, hearing the fast flow of the rapids, suggesting further up the mountainside.

With a better idea of where she was, she flexed her knees, about to stand but heard leaves crunching as if someone were walking. The sounds suggested he was getting closer, so Lila remained still.

A moment later, a shadow appeared. When he was close enough, his foot tapped hers.

"Bitch, you awake?"

Lila had a split second to think which would be better: asleep or awake? Then she heard the unmistakable sound of the safety being removed from a gun. *Awake it is.*

"What do you want with me?" she quietly asked, keeping her tone neutral.

"I want to know who killed my brother," the man demanded.

Lila's brows lowered in confusion; who was this guy? She studied him in the dark when the man kicked her again. He wore jeans with a flannel over a t-shirt, an appropriate enough outfit for these woods, but the shoes gave away a sense of city man. He was bound to slip if he went too fast over rough terrain.

"I don't know who you are, let alone your brother," Lila honestly answered.

Realizing it was dark, the man activated the light on his cell, exposing his face.

Lila's eyes squinted as she studied the man who held her captive, stocky build of medium height with dark eyes and crew-cut hair. No recognition.

"Now that I see your face, it only confirms I have never seen you. And I still don't know who your brother is."

"Yes, you do. You were there when my brother was shot and killed in August. Was it the stupid cop or the bartender?" As his eyes watched her, he saw her eyes widen with recollection.

Scenes from the horrible night when her friends were in the accident flew through Lila's mind. At the time, she thought it was just that, a horrible accident. She transported Shannon on a stretcher to radiology to confirm no significant injuries. Initially, the escorts of both Devan and Joel annoyed and irritated her. Lila did not know the true cause of the tension or the accident. She hadn't even known the other guy was Shannon's ex-boyfriend. When they entered the small room, Lila suddenly found herself pushed down to the ground as Devan stood before her. She heard the gunshots but couldn't see anything from her place on the floor.

When Lila looked up again, there was a man on the ground, bleeding, Devan and Joel standing over him with their guns drawn. Shannon sat on the stretcher with her hands on Joel's back as she looked over his shoulder. He had used his body to shield Shannon while Devan protected her. Who fired the killing shot, Lila did not know, nor did she ask.

"What makes you think I know anything about that?"

"You were there when my brother was killed," he repeated; it wasn't a question.

The man was getting agitated. The afternoon was not going as planned. She was supposed to be a helpless female with a flat tire on the side of the road. She should have been happy to have two men pull over in the middle of nowhere to assist. Instead, the stupid bitch was on the phone calling someone. When he pulled the phone away, she *actually* ran towards the woods. *Who does that?*

He and his cousin had to chase after the girl. When they caught up to her, his cousin went to get something from the car but instead drove off. He called and said something about hiding the car. They were supposed to meet at another location. Instead, he lost touch with his cousin because of the crap cell service in these damn woods.

After hiking along a makeshift trail with the girl on his shoulders for what felt like hours, he had to admit, he wasn't sure if he was walking in circles or almost to the peak of the damn mountain! After he secured the girl, he spent another hour searching for bars to allow a call to go through to his cousin.

He honestly didn't know if his cousin had abandoned him or not. His cousin was the one who grew up in these damn woods, not him. But he also had been clear, he would not get caught.

Regardless, he needed to get the information. His assignment was to find Shannon Doyle's location. His cousin had confirmed the woman in front of him was her best friend and a witness to his brother's death. When this was over, he would go after his brother's murderer and get his revenge.

When he heard movements from behind, he pivoted quickly in that direction.

Lila heard it, too. It sounded like a small tree branch snapping as someone or something stepped over it. She knew it wouldn't be anyone looking for her, the footsteps were too loud. Dallas would never be so noisy. Then she heard the steps as if they galloped away. *Definitely a deer*, she thought. Lila watched her captor panic as he turned toward the sound.

Lila kept her movements slow as she stood and slowly eased away from him to avoid making any sounds. His night vision was likely momentarily impaired after flashing a light in his face.

Without another thought, Lila turned and ran.

"Come back here, bitch, or I will shoot," the man yelled. He held up his gun and fired in her direction.

With only a moment to react, Lila needed to think fast. Uphill or down? She chose the more challenging path uphill, listening to the sounds of the river flowing to keep her track somewhat parallel to prevent getting lost. She half expected a gunshot to hit her in the back. She continued up, hoping he wasn't a weekend warrior. Lila voted for speed over caution, very aware the sound of her movements was giving away her location.

· · · ·

Evil's earlier pleasure at seeing the men drive away quickly hardened to exasperation when, not even a half hour later, a car soon pulled into the driveway! When he heard the women's voices, he realized it was just the quiet one. He could easily wait them out. He was already inside. He just needed to wait. But his mood quickly shifted to rage when he realized he wouldn't have fun.

As Evil listened to the conversation, he knew it wouldn't be a short visit. The visitors' intent was clear, they meant to stay until the situation was resolved. A girl was taken? And it wasn't his doing. Who the hell was messing with his town? Without wasting any more of his time, Evil quietly exited the home before fading further into the shadows.

As he entered the alley behind The Lantern, Evil was surprised to see the boy was out again. Hmm, what is he up to? He watched a moment before following him inside.

At the sound of the gunshot, everyone came to a sudden stop.

"That's definitely not a hunting rifle," Chase needlessly commented as everyone's pace quickened after a slight change in direction.

"She probably got away from him, so he's shooting warning shots," Devan commented, mainly because it made sense but also to assure Dallas and Rob that Lila would be alright. He needed everyone to be calm and focused.

"How can you be so sure?" Dallas asked quietly.

"He doesn't want her dead, not yet anyway. He had a reason to take her," he answered. Devan didn't say out loud what the various reasons could be. "He probably doesn't realize he took the one woman that knows these woods better than most."

"He's right; Lila grew up in these woods. She knows her way around and how to find her way out again," Chase agreed. But if it had been Rachel, *she would never find her way out alone*, he thought grimly.

Lila's pace was slowing as she continued her climb. The sharp pain in her side was not helping. Seeking shelter, she hid behind a large tree, squeezing her side as she fought to control her heavy breathing. *Dear God, I will start running with Dallas if I make it out of this alive!*

Closing her eyes, Lila focused on taking slower, deeper breaths. Once her breathing was better, she tuned in to her surroundings. She was still close to the river. She reminded herself she was married to the number one tracker in the county. Dallas will find me. I just need to stay alive until he does.

Lila continued cautiously toward the sound of the rapids, hoping the roars of the water would deafen her loud breathing. Every noise she made appeared to echo into the dark, rapidly cooling night, giving away her location.

She knew where she was, more or less. It helped with her pep talk. *I've got this! I'll be alright as long as I remain hidden until Dallas arrives.* A part of her brain asked pessimistically, *how would he even know to look?* And even if he did, where would he know to start?

Lila fought the panic growing inside. *Stop it! He'll know if you're late. He will find the car. Dallas will find you. He loves you.*

When she heard the next round of gunshots, she turned to look over her shoulder, causing her to misstep with sudden pain in her right leg as she started sliding down the steep hill. The thundering of the waterfall below masked her screams.

     SHADOWS OF THE PAST

The man was frustrated, loudly cussing his dead brother for screwing up a simple assignment and cursing his cousin for abandoning him. He bent down with his arms on his thighs to catch his breath but shot up suddenly when he heard a noise ahead.

He was totally out of his comfort zone and had no idea of the animals in his immediate area. The man slowly advanced when he heard the leaves crunch.

"You won't be able to get away, bitch! You better come back before you get lost!"

He heard her footsteps again. *It sounds like she's running*, he thought. He lifted his gun to fire in her direction, continuing toward the sounds.

A moment later, he heard footsteps behind him. He turned, expecting to face the girl trying to sneak up on him. He froze in shock at the silhouette of a man emerging from the shadows. He lowered his gun when he recognized the bartender.

"What business do you have here?" Devan asked, keeping his gun out of sight behind his back.

"Nothing you need to concern yourself with," the man answered.

He turned when he felt another presence to his right. He inwardly groaned as he realized it was the ranger. *Damn it!* Can't he ever catch a break? First, he's related to a bunch of idiots that can't complete a simple assignment. The bitch runs away, and now he's being hounded by a bartender and park ranger. *It sounded like the beginning of a bad joke,* he thought tangibly.

His cousin had cautioned him not to underestimate the ranger. He served in the military and had a mean streak if the right buttons were pushed. "I suggest you both turn around and head back to town."

"That's not going to happen," Devan quietly stated. "Where is Lila?"

"As I said, my business with the girl has nothing to do with you, gentlemen. Please, just turn around and walk out of here," the man replied, silently debating which to take out first before continuing his hunt.

"You think you can outgun us? I am an FBI agent," Devan announced before he gestured toward the others. "Over there is her boyfriend, her brother, and her cousin. I happen to know for a fact they're all excellent shooters. Take down any one of us, and the others will get you before you even turn your arm to the next. Might as well give it up now," Devan instructed. His voice was surprisingly mild.

Shit, he thought. *A fucking FBI agent?* How did his cousin not know this? He lives in this town and knows all the players. He even works in the damn prosecutor's office. The man quickly debated his options. The agent wasn't wrong. He could easily take one or two down but not all four. If he aimed at the agent, he was in for life *if* he survived the night.

He didn't want to go back to prison.

The man pulled up his gun to aim, but before he could squeeze the trigger, he felt a sharp pain in his right arm as his gun flew to the ground.

Devan immediately advanced with his gun still aimed at the kidnapper. He quickly retrieved the weapon from the ground as he called Connor over.

Dallas was already running up the hill, shouting, "Lila? Lila, it's safe to come out."

Dallas paused at the sight of a newly torn shrub. To block out the visual distractions, he closed his eyes. He heard the chatter of the others behind him, the flow of the water falling to the river below, and there! He heard it. The faint sound of ground giving away as something, or someone, slid down the mountainside.

Opening his eyes, they instantly spotted the footprints in the dirt. Hurrying along, fear built up as he mentally acknowledged the location getting dangerously close to the edge, overlooking the river. Dallas cautiously made his way close with his headlamp shining down the steep slope. At his feet, a new path was leading toward the water. At the bottom, he could see Lila holding on to a root. Her feet were already touching the water, the fast rapids pulling her in.

"Lila! Hold on, baby. I'm coming down! Just hold on!" Dallas shouted as he dropped his backpack to pull out the rope.

Without waiting for the others to catch up, he expertly tied one end around himself before anchoring the other to a tree. Normally, he would not have rushed, but there was no time! He needed to save Lila before it was too late. Once her body submerged in the water, saving her would take a miracle. And the chilled October temperatures shortened the time further.

Since Rob was guarding the asshole while Connor acted as the doctor, Chase followed Dallas. Devan was calling in their location. His headlamp shined over the backpack on the ground next to the rope. Chase looked up in time to see Dallas for a split second before he jumped over the edge of the cliff.

Lila cried out, more from panic than pain, as she slid further down the rocky hillside. She tried to break her fall and almost succeeded. But the momentum was too great! She was quickly plummeting toward the water. The loud roaring of the rapids kept her from hearing anything but the fast pounding of her heart.

Lila focused her energy on avoiding the water by reaching for a tree branch. She was confident that once her body went under, the chances of surviving the frigid night would be slim to zero. Just as her feet touched the water, she secured her grip on a branch, slowing her fall. Lila tried to ease herself up, but the pull of the water on her feet was stronger.

The rapids won out and jerked her under.

The icy water immediately shocked her system, momentarily numbing her mind and body. Lila's fatigued body was further sucked down toward her inevitable death. The burning in her lungs forced her into action. *This couldn't be the end.* No, not when she was finally able to live her life out in the open. She had to resist the urge to give in and fight for her life, or this will be it!

Motivated by the tightness in her chest, Lila started to propel her way toward the air.

Chase cautiously looked over the edge, just in time to see Dallas' headlamp as he reached the bottom of the hill. He could hear him shouting, "Lila! Hold on, baby! Hold on!"

And he disappeared into the rapids.

"Damn it! Devan! Over here!" Chase yelled as he also dropped his backpack to pull out his rope. After swiftly anchoring himself, Devan appeared just as he was about to start down the hill. Chase quickly relayed the obvious plan before following Dallas down the hillside.

Dallas quickly repelled down the steep hill, silently praying the rope was properly secured and someone knew where he was. There was no time! He needed to get to Lila before she was pulled under and tugged down the river. She wouldn't survive long in the cold water. He kept his eye on the spot where she went into the water. Once he was close enough, Dallas leaped!

His light did not fail! Dallas saw her immediately. Her bright auburn hair floated around her, the only source of color. He wrapped his long legs around her waist, hoping she was still conscious to hold on as he used his arms to pull them up on the rope.

When they broke the surface, Dallas was relieved to see Chase, also tied, start to pull on his rope, bringing them both towards the bank. When he was close enough, Dallas pushed Lila up toward her cousin. Together, they pulled Lila onto the wet slippery bank before Dallas climbed out.

The sounds of Lila coughing were music to his ears.

Exhausted, Dallas lay beside her as he moved the wet hair from her face. He kissed her forehead as he closed his eyes to give her a quick hug.

"Baby, we need to get you back up the hill."

"Wait, here's an extra rope. Let's get her tied in, just in case," Chase instructed, reaching for a third rope just tossed down.

He felt slightly awkward after watching an intense loving moment between Dallas and his cousin. But one thing he knew, all concerns he previously had for the guy were gone. Dallas truly loved Lila. It was obvious in his actions, stupid as they were. Chase wasn't sure if Rob could be convinced, but he wasn't here to see it.

"Dal, I'm numb. I can't feel my legs. No way I can climb," Lila acknowledged.

"Baby, don't worry, we got you," Dallas assured her.

Rachel immediately grabbed her phone when it rang. "Chase?"

"We got her. Lila's going to be alright. We need to hike back and get her to the hospital. Stay there, and I'll swing by to pick you up," she heard over the phone.

"You found her? Is she alright?" Rachel confirmed.

"She broke her leg and fell into the river but she will be alright," Chase repeated.

"That's terrible! She fell into the river?" Rachel was horrified. "The water temperature is too cold this time of year."

"Rach, I promise you, Lila is awake and alert. We're carrying her out in a portable stretcher. I'll call you when I get back to the truck."

"Be safe hiking in the dark. Chase, I love you!" Rachel ended the call.

"They found her! She's going to be alright!" Rachel announced as she answered her ringing cell without looking at the caller ID. "Hello?"

"Hey, baby, I'm here. Let me in," a male voice replied.

Rachel looked down at her caller ID. *Darn it*, she thought. She wasn't in the mood to deal with Max.

"Max, I'm not home. I'm at a friend's," she explained. She turned to see everyone in the room looking at her. She stepped into the dining room.

"Rachel, I'm not going to ask again. Open the damn door," he demanded.

Rachel wasn't sure, but she thought he sounded drunk. "Max, I just told you, I am not home. You best continue to your hotel room."

"Stop lying, bitch! I can see you moving around in there. Stop the game playing and open the damn door! I am going to make you glad you did, I promise," he attempted to sound assuring, oblivious to his callous tone.

Rachel hit the mute button as she stepped back into the family room. "Max says he's on my porch, and someone is inside my house!"

"It's not your house; he's at mine. My housekeeper is calling on my cell." Matt stepped closer to show her the security screen of an intruder on his porch. "Is this the famous Max?"

Rachel looked down at the cell, horrified as the situation sank in. "Yes, that's him. What should I do?"

"Nothing. The sheriff's department has already been notified," Matt answered.

The cousin sighed as he sat in his home office. With a drink in his hand, he listened to the chatter of the first responders on the radio. Slater shook his head, thinking about the mess. Never in a million years did he expect the situation from the city to flow over into his small town. He'd hoped to have left the criminal life behind when he secured the position. He dreamed of returning home with a good job to shove in his mother's face.

She never seemed to have the time or the temperament to care for him when he was a child. But when she learned he had climbed out of the hellhole he called childhood, she was instantly clinging to false happy memories. She sought him out, trying hard to attach herself to his money and prestige as if the town would forget her past; living from one boyfriend's home to another. He knew small towns didn't work that way.

Nothing was ever forgotten, and few secrets were ever fully kept.

Holding his breath, Slater listened to the reports of shots fired. And he cussed with the announcement that the idiot was only wounded. He wasn't able to breathe until he learned she was safe. *Damn it*, Slater thought in anger. Why didn't Lila just go with him for a drink? His ability to protect her was slipping.

Max Kauffman's annoyance was progressing to seriously pissed off. His pounding headache kept him from processing his current situation. Max could not understand why he was arrested and left alone for hours in this confining room. Leaning onto the table, he cradled his head onto his arms.

After what seemed like hours, Max heard the door open. Looking up, he assessed the man before him, obviously older and dressed in what he had recently learned was business casual. Without a word, the man closed the door behind him and stood on the other side of the table.

"Who the hell are you? My court-appointed lawyer?" his tone displayed his irritation.

"No, I'm Matthew Emerson, the owner of the home you were trespassing on," Matt patiently explained. He and the sheriff had been in the next room watching Max, debating how to handle the situation. Matt suspected there was more going on than just a drunken late evening visit.

"What the hell are you talking about? I was at Rachel's house," Max confidently answered with an irritated tone.

"No, you were clearly at my house," Matt answered, reaching for his cell to pull up a video. He held it up for the other man to watch as he narrated, "What you are watching is my security footage from last night. My porch you are standing on, my front door you were pounding on, and that was my housekeeper you saw moving around behind the covered windows. She's an intelligent woman and didn't open the door. It isn't common for us to receive belligerent visitors after midnight. Hell, not common during the daytime either."

"So, you decide to hide behind a woman? Too afraid to open the door yourself?"

"Not at all. I wasn't home, just as Rachel was not home. Tell me, why were you expecting her to open the door?"

"My relationship with Rachel is no one's business but our own," Max stated defensively. "Are you sure it wasn't her house? All she had to do was let me inside. She could have avoided this whole thing."

"I'm confident that's my house," Matt replied. "And because it's my house you were trying to break into, this does not involve her. I have known Rachel MacKenzie her whole life. I know for a fact she's not one to accept late-night gentlemen callers, especially one so indiscreet."

Matt was silent as he studied the man before him. Chase was right. He was slime. Clara, to his amusement, didn't have anything positive to add either.

"What the hell did she tell you about us?" the younger man demanded.

"There is no 'us' between you and her. She's quite shocked and appalled about the whole situation. She doesn't like your excessive attention toward her," Matt answered.

"My attention is not excessive!" Max almost shouted.

"Forget you were at the wrong house for a moment, shall we? You drop in unannounced at her house, as late as it was, in your condition? Yeah, it's excessive and unwanted. Her words, not mine," Matt clarified. "But let's get to the point, shall we? You were extremely intoxicated, but your rental car was not in the area. It's still parked on Main St., in front of The Lantern. We know you were dropped off. The headlights of a car were shown on the security video. Who dropped you off?"

"What? What are you talking about?"

Matt could see the situation finally clicked in the other man's eyes. He continued, "A few facts you may not be aware of, one of Rachel's close friends has a stalker. He's even drugged her. Another of her close friends was kidnapped last evening. The common theory is the person that dropped you off last night was purposefully pulling the already stretched-thin sheriff's department away to give the stalker better access to an innocent woman. Everyone is debating whether you know your role or the severity of the situation. The general consensus is that you are simply the pawn, manipulated by the stalker."

Max leaned forward to slap his hands on the table, and shouted, "Wait a minute! I have no idea what you are talking about! I have nothing to do with a stalker or kidnapping! Hell, I don't even know Rachel's friends. I don't live here! I've only been visiting while I interviewed for a job yesterday."

When Matt raised his eyebrow in question, Max took a deep breath before explaining his actions calmly. "I was offered the job yesterday. I admit I started celebrating earlier than appropriate. I was just trying to get to know the people of this town, getting an idea of places to live. Toward the night's end, I wanted to see the person who made all this happen. Rachel is a beautiful woman. I've known her for almost two years in the city. We often hung out before she moved. Her commitment to her family is one of the many things that have attracted me to her. I wanted to see her, end the day right."

"End the day right? By stopping in at her place unannounced and intoxicated? Tell me, how well do you know our Rachel? It doesn't sound like you know her at all. As it is, I can understand you aren't familiar with the town. A city boy, the bigger houses must all look alike to you. You weren't even at the correct house. If you walked, which no one believes, you walked past her house and two more before getting to mine."

Matt paused to allow the information to sink in before continuing. "If it were me, I wouldn't be happy if someone deliberately dropped me off at the wrong house. Someone else facilitated the scene. That person knew whoever would be at the house would call the sheriff's department, especially in light of recent events. Sounds like a pawn to me."

Matt paced quietly in the small room. When he continued, he shifted the topic. "My wife has assured me if charges are pressed, your job offer will be recanted."

Max's eyes narrowed. *Who the hell does this asshole think he is? Does he honestly think he can dictate events in my life?* Before he could censor his thoughts, he bluntly asked, "Who the hell is your wife?"

"Talia Emerson, she was present at your interview yesterday," Matt's voice was chilled.

Max's eyes widened, the shock was obvious on his face. Before he could filter his response, he blurted out, "Talia's your wife? She's kind of young for you, isn't she?"

"She doesn't agree," Matt shrugged confidently.

It was the one insecurity he didn't like to discuss. Though, fourteen years in, Matt was becoming more confident his third marriage would be his last. "She was with me last night when we were notified of someone trying to break into our home. Talia was concerned about the safety of our children."

He paused to let the information register before he continued quietly. "The sheriff has informed me it's my decision to press charges. If you really want to relocate to our town, I suggest you tell me now, who dropped you off."

"Why you? It should be Rachel, and I know she won't press charges," Max stated confidently with a smile as he leaned back in his seat, crossing his arms.

"Maybe, maybe not, if you were actually at her place. But you weren't," Matt repeated slowly. "You were arrested at my house. My children awakened from sleep last night while you were resisting arrest. At this point, Rachel has nothing to do with this."

Matt paused, ready to nail in the final detail. "Her fiance has requested I pass along to you that if you decide to relocate here and are stupid enough to drop in after hours, intoxicated or not, charges will be pressed."

"What? Rachel is engaged? To who? When the hell did this happen?" Max slammed his hands on the table as he shot up to his feet. His anger was obvious.

"Don't know the details," Matt shrugged as he contained his pleasure in ruffling the man before him. "So, have you decided yet? Tell me who dropped you off."

A few minutes later, Matt stepped out into the small hall. The sheriff and his wife quickly joined him.

"You were right, Matt. I can't believe Eric's been getting out all this time. Damn." Tony made a mental list of things needing to get done. "So, what are you both deciding?"

Matt looked down at Talia, slightly shaking her head. Keeping his eyes on his wife when he spoke, "We won't be pressing charges this time, Tony. But I would be curious to know if his drink was spiked. According to Rachel, the guy's behavior last night was not typical. Even Clara says he's usually more discreet."

The sheriff nodded in agreement before returning to his office.

"Thanks, Matt." Talia stepped closer to her husband for a hug. Not being one for public displays of affection, she was pleasantly surprised when his arms came around her for a tight squeeze. "He really is the best candidate for the position. I'll keep my eye on him to make sure he stays in line."

"Keep your eyes at a distance. I don't trust him, and I sure as hell don't like him," Matt stated as his eyes glanced toward the closed door.

Talia smiled into his chest, pleased he was keeping his jealousy streak contained. When she leaned up on her toes to kiss his cheek, she whispered, "Matt, you know I wouldn't step out on you. He's not worth it. Besides, he's too young."

Matt had leaned down to accept the kiss, pausing momentarily at the last comment before quietly answering. "Too young? He's closer to your age than I am."

She simply reached up to cradle his face as she kissed him. "Don't start down that road."

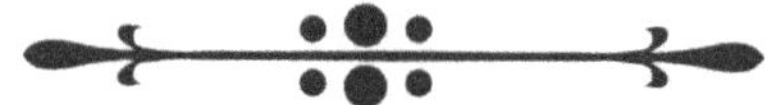

misdirection

Eugene Slater was up and out of his place early, as usual. But instead of going to his office, he went directly to the hospital. His first order of business was to prevent his cousin from talking. For years he was able to hide the connection to his father's family and he would do anything for that to continue. The last thing he needed was for the town to learn his relation to the guy arrested for kidnapping the previous day.

He approached the room, stopping to inform the guard he was the DA. The guard waved him in. He smiled, surprised how easy it was.

When Slater entered the room, he slowly approached the sleeping figure in the bed. He debated ending the situation but knew it would cause more trouble than it was worth. Lila was alive, so he would allow his cousin to continue breathing, for now, anyway.

"What are you doing here?" the cousin whispered from the bed in panic. He knew what happened when situations went wrong. And technically, his actions yesterday were not the issue. Getting caught was.

"Just checking in. Boss wants to know why you went off script," Slater lied. "You were only supposed to find Shannon Doyle's location, not kidnap Lila Foxwood. Now I have to do serious damage control."

"What was I supposed to do? I need to know who killed my brother," he answered angrily. "The stupid bitch didn't even know anything."

"The instructions were to follow her and find out where her friend is hiding," Slater responded quietly. "Not get revenge! Hell, there were easier and more efficient ways to do that anyway."

"Boss learned she's close to the city. He called me off yesterday morning," the man answered. "Sounds to me like you aren't so connected after all. Boss told me I could do what I wanted with Lila. As the DA, you need to get the charges dropped."

"Not happening," Slater answered firmly, crossing his arms. "You abducted her, brought her onto federal land, and shot at a federal agent. It's out of my jurisdiction. The Feds are taking the lead on this. As it is, the phone found on you has connected you to the Boss. They already know you're just another one of his thugs. If I were your lawyer, I'd advise you to cooperate when they ask questions and leave my name out. I'll get you a lawyer to assist with keeping your time to a minimum."

"Why would I do that?"

"Regardless of what you say or do, you were caught. You can serve hard time or relocate with protection," Slater looked around him before lowering his voice. "If my name is mentioned, I will see to it your only option is serving the hard time after you snitched details leading to the Boss' arrest."

A few minutes later, Slater was out into the hall. He took a moment to simply breathe. It had been a bad idea getting involved with all this, not that he had a choice. In the city a year ago, he learned of the investigation while working in the DA's office. Keeping tabs on the police department had been tricky. Wanting to warn the Boss without showing his hand was challenging.

Until he realized Shannon Doyle worked at the company. The stupid bitch got what she deserved. He, on the other hand, only used her once. He lied and told the Boss one of his accountants, Shannon, was leaking information to the police. He had no idea, at the time, who the undercover detective was. And since he was able to warn the Boss, Slater was rewarded. He couldn't get greedy, but he did hint she had returned to her hometown when the Boss ordered a hit on her. Not his fault his cousins were so incompetent! Messing up an easy assignment! Not only did he cause her to go underground, he potentially alerted the detective, Joel Montgomery, of the mole in the police department.

And somehow, miracles happened. An opportunity to return home with a prestigious position. He would do what he needed to do to remain in his position.

Slater slowly made his way toward Lila's room. While he wasn't surprised to find Dallas at her bedside, he was disappointed. Unbeknownst to Lila, her presence during high school caused a strain between the two friends. Her influence positively impacted both of the men's lives when they were at turning points. But Slater's influence harmed Lila's.

"How's she doing?"

Dallas turned in his seat. When he realized who it was, he slowly stood up and stepped out into the hall. Struggling to control his temper, Dallas kept his voice low.

"What the hell are you doing here?"

"Dallas, you can't still be mad at me for something that happened, what, fifteen years ago? Let it go, man," Slater dismissed. "I heard what happened. Just wanted to stop in and see that she's alright."

"She's sleeping, but I'm sure she doesn't want to see you," Dallas stated as he stepped forward. "You keep away from her."

"Dallas, she's always been an independent person. She made her own choices back then, and I'm sure now. She was happy to see me when we bumped into each other earlier," Slater shrugged.

Devan had been on the phone with his boss, just hanging up as he entered the ICU area. He wanted to check in on Lila and bring Dallas breakfast.

As he turned the corner, he was startled to see Dallas, normally easy-tempered, starting to grab the district attorney. Devan rushed forward, pulling his friend back as he threw the first punch.

"Let me go!" Dallas yelled in anger as his fist only met air. He shoved at his friend, attempting to step around.

"Hey Dallas, knock it off," Devan yelled, pushing back.

"I mean it, Slater, you stay away," Dallas yelled over Devan's shoulder as he pushed again, entering Lila's room.

Devan turned to ensure the other guy was walking away before returning to his friend. "What the hell are you doing? Trying to get yourself arrested? You keep pushing a guy like that around, you'll be wearing metal bracelets."

Dallas let out a harsh chuckle. "Yeah, right. Stupid weasel knows better."

"What's going on?" Devan asked after he retrieved the bag and coffee at the nurses' station.

"I don't trust him around Lila." Dallas struggled to control his anger.

"Alright," Devan stated. "Tell me. What happened?"

"What makes you think anything happened?"

"You are the one that never loses his cool when another guy approaches your girl," Devan started. "Either Foxwood has been rubbing off on you, or something happened. So, tell me, what's this all about?"

"Devan, it's not my story to share," he answered as his eyes shifted to Lila, asleep nearby.

Devan turned towards Lila before he looked back with raised eyebrows in question. "You never know, just talking about it could help you keep your temper next time you see him."

Dallas sighed again before nodding in agreement. He pulled the chairs back away from Lila so she wouldn't overhear. "What do you know about how Lila and I met?"

"Is that a trick question? You both were born and raised here."

"You know what I mean," Dallas stated before clarifying, "The events that led to us seeing each other?"

"Nothing. I just know your family doesn't get along with hers," Devan honestly admitted as he sat down, handing him the coffee.

Dallas waited a minute before giving a short version of the night the movie theater exploded, being trapped with Lila as his cousin slowly died before being rescued. He explained how he and Slater became friends, describing the abandoned house where all the delinquents crashed. Without overstepping Lila's trust, he talked more about his demons from the horrible night, leading Devan to speculate about hers.

"I suspected she was on something one night when she came looking for me at the house, but Slater saw her first. Nothing happened that night. I made it clear to her that she wasn't ever to come looking for me without first giving me a heads-up. I also warned him to stay away from her."

Dallas paused for a moment, eyes looking over at Lila. "Eventually, things simmered down. Slater stopped referring to her as the golden girl when she started tutoring him in school. Stupid me, I never paid attention to the extra cash he had around. He was dealing, not really sure of his connections. One night I was late getting home from work. Lila was higher than a kite on a horrible paranoid trip, standing out on the ledge of the third floor."

Devan's eyes grew wide in shock as he looked over toward Lila. Never in a million years would he have suspected the All-American girl to have a drug history.

"Somehow, I was able to talk her down off the ledge. She was pretty sick after that. I've never seen anyone puke so much in my life. I kept my eye on her through the night. The next morning, I had a serious talk with Slater. He admitted he gave her something to take her edge off, not realizing the dose would be too much for her, stupid idiot.

"Anyway, she miraculously quits the drug habit while I'm limiting her presence at the house. And yet, somehow, Slater developed this crazy infatuation with her. One day while Lila's tutoring him I catch him trying to make a move on her. I walked in unexpectedly as she was, literally, shoving him away and yelling no. I picked him up and shoved him across the room." Dallas' affection was obvious as he watched Lila sleep.

Devan whistled softly. "That's pretty heavy. How old were you guys? Did she seek help?"

"She was fourteen, fifteen, and we were sixteen, seventeen," Dallas answered softly. "We were so ridiculously young. She was naïve. I was stupid. She grew up fast. Somehow, the drug issue faded. Instead of coming to my place, we met at hers. I would sneak into her room at night."

Both were quiet as Devan processed the information before saying, "It's amazing."

"What is?"

"That Rob didn't kill you back then. And that the DA not only did drugs but also dealt drugs in a high school that he barely attended," Devan answered.

"His history isn't really common knowledge. No one would notice or care about a year with low attendance and grades. Lila helped him get back on track. Slater's never been arrested. He was always able to make himself scarce, except that night. And Rob would have been well in his rights to kill me, but he had distractions of his own that year," Dallas dismissed.

"I need to get going," Devan stated as he stood up. He wanted to check in on the prisoner, hoping to ask some questions. He planned to do a deep dive into the backgrounds of both the prisoner and the DA. Things were adding up wrong.

Rob had a late start to his usual routine of ensuring the livestock was being adequately cared for. He had debated taking his favorite horse out for a ride but wasn't sure if his mood would allow it. Rob didn't want to take his anger out on the stallion. When his chores were completed, he realized it was exactly what he needed.

As he rode, Rob purposely kept his mind from the events of the night before. His thoughts went to Clara when they rode on the same trail the previous spring. He had enjoyed watching her re-explore the world around her and thought back to when they were younger.

He had always enjoyed her company. He had been aware of her crush on him when she was young. After the disappearance of her mother, Clara was at the farm more. Rob smiled, remembering her tagging along beside him, helping with his chores. By the time she was in high school, he had realized he wasn't the only one that noticed Clara blossoming into a beautiful woman. Instead of making a move on her, Rob remained one of her best friends and protectors. He wondered if he had played things differently then, if it would have made a difference in the outcome now.

After he returned to the stables, Rob brushed his horse as his mind turned to the evening before. He had been so pissed at Dallas for allowing his sister to be taken. He was relieved she was safe, but now his anger was directed at Lila.

Why the hell would she marry the damn bastard? What the hell could Lila even see in Dallas Thompson? Her whole life, she was warned to stay away from him. Dallas and his friends were never up to any good. The stupid cousin Danny was the worst of the lot!

Rob sighed in frustration, unable to wrap his head around the fact that his little sister was legally married to the damn bastard.

When he returned to the house, Rob made himself a drink. He didn't care that it was early in the day nor that it broke his rule of avoiding the hard stuff. His eye caught the pile of mail. Normally, he dealt with it immediately, dropping the junk into the recycle bin next to the desk, and organizing the bills for business or personal before paying them. Instead, piles of various sized envelopes, postcards, and magazines seemed to have multiplied each day through the last few weeks.

Rob remained standing, sipping his whiskey, as he began the long overdue annoyance of sorting. Within minutes, the simple task was soothing his temper when he came across the oversized envelope from the DNA tests. Rob smiled as he recalled the evening when the whole gang hung out on the back porch, drinking and hanging, just like old times.

After refilling his glass, he returned to his desk. He sipped deeply before opening the envelope. A few moments later, he was at his computer, following the instructions to create his account and read over his results.

Less than ten minutes later, Rob's world as he knew it fell out from under him. *What the fuck? No, it can't be right.* He stood from the desk but glanced down at the screen.

"No fucking way! This can't be correct! I need to step away from this. It's just a gimmick to con people out of their money," Rob growled as he refilled his glass.

The intake of more alcohol had a negative effect. Instead of soothing his already ill-tempered mood, it fed the storm. Rob was teetering on the line of control. Everyone was well aware that once his temper was out of hand, he had trouble reining it back before serious damage was done.

Damn it! He repeated as he roamed through the house. In the kitchen, the pile of dishes in the sink caught his attention. Thinking the menial task would calm him as he remembered the house needed a good cleaning before his parents returned home.

Rob reached down to place the ceramic bowl into the dishwasher when the voice in his head stated, *but they aren't MY parents, are they?*

Instead of being placed on the top rack, the bowl sailed through the air and crashed into the wall.

Within minutes, the sink and cabinets were emptied. Shattered glass and ceramics of various sizes blanketed the floor. Rob was no longer capable of any rationalized thinking. Ignoring the crunch under his feet, he paced the kitchen. He mentally listed the changes this brought.

He couldn't be alone now. But for every person that came to his mind, Rob listed grievances against them. His father and mother were the worst, the lies. His mother had an affair with a Thompson! His sister married a Thompson! And his cousin, shit, Rob's knees buckled, causing him to lean onto the counter. Chase wasn't even his cousin!

But Clara? Not his Clara, she had never hurt him like the others, he thought as he once again refilled his drink.

. . . .

Evil remained in the shadows, watching as the stupid fool of a boy descended the two flights of stairs from his slut's third-floor apartment. It still surprised him the boy had such a considerable appetite for women. According to his watch, the halfwit has been out of the house for over four hours.

He'd had enough of the kid ruining his plans. "This has been going on long enough. If he thinks he's old enough to handle family obligations and life's stress, let's see how he deals with losing his slut," Evil chuckled maliciously.

He waited a few minutes before retracing the boy's steps upstairs. When Evil arrived at her door, he knocked quietly. He didn't want the bitch across the hall to hear him. He was pleased when the door opened a few seconds later. The boy's slut was standing in only a robe with her hair all messed up.

"What do you want?" the girl asked with annoyance.

"Is that any way to answer the door? Let me in before anyone sees us," Evil answered in his usual polite calmness.

Without a word, she stepped back, making the biggest mistake of her life.

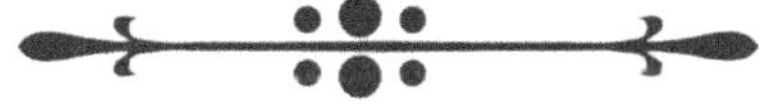

18 rough night

Clara's pain was the worst since being discharged from the hospital. Her limp was more pronounced when she stumbled to the counter, debating the sleepytime tea. Her hand hovered over the canister, she had flashbacks from last summer of the weird and vivid dreams of chasing after Evil in the shadows of the night after she drank the tea. *Was that what she wanted now?* But the dreams were a result of reading her mother's journals.

Her eyes shifted from the tea to the bottle of pain medicine. She wasn't looking for drugs to relieve her pain, just relaxation after a stressful couple of days. Clara was confident her pain would ease up with a restful night's sleep. *The tea*, she decided.

Leaning onto the counter, her mind wandered while waiting for the kettle to boil. Clara realized she hadn't had her tea since before the accident. The recent late nights were weighing on her. The unexpected visit from her father. *Well, that wasn't a visit, was it?* He followed Matt. She sighed sadly at the thought of her father's anger and bitterness having a higher priority than his only daughter.

Clara had been recovering at home for over a week. It had been about a month since the accident. Her recovery was starting to slip. She needed to take better care of herself so she could return to work, and her life. *I will be in control when I wake up in the morning,* she vowed as the tooting from the kettle brought her back to the moment.

Wincing in pain as she crossed the room, she placed her tea on the table before sitting too quickly on the kitchen chair. Immediately, her eyes filled with tears at the extreme pain on her left side as she cried out. After a few minutes, which felt like hours, the pain started to subside.

As she sipped her tea, she debated settling on the sofa or heading upstairs. With her current pain levels, Clara wasn't sure she could make the climb up a flight of stairs. She had no idea when Connor would be home. She thought about texting him, but her cell was on the counter. She sighed in frustration as the width of her kitchen seemed to double since her last trek across.

Connor had been up late the night before, being on the search and rescue team, then assisting in Lila's surgery to repair her broken leg in the early hours. She wasn't even sure if he had slept before starting his shift.

Sipping again, Clara paused as she lowered her mug to the table. Did she hear something? Was it a bump? Something falling? She couldn't wait to have the cochlear implant for the right ear. Hearing so well in one ear still impeded her ability to determine where sounds originated. Sipping her tea, Clara returned to her debate, up to bed or the sofa.

There it is again! Was the noise coming from upstairs? Clara sighed again. The decision was made, upstairs to check on the children. Every once in a while, Hailey would wake up and wander. The result of putting a toddler in a bed instead of a crib when they moved.

It never crossed her mind that someone else could be in the house.

As Clara stood, she heard the sound again. This time, she was confident it was coming from behind her. Turning back, she paused a moment as she stared at the door leading to the garage. Was the doorknob moving?

The sudden pounding on the front door caused her to jump.

Lila slowly stirred. She felt weird. Her limbs were too heavy to move. She felt a slight panic as she opened her eyes. Dallas was sitting beside her, leaning down onto the bed with his head on his arms, sleeping. She tried to lift her hand to his head, to touch his face as she remembered him jumping into the cold water after her.

He loves me, she thought with a sleepy smile before falling back asleep.

Dallas sat up when he felt the squeeze in his hand. "Lila? Hey, baby, are you awake?"

He watched her face as he talked. Connor had explained Lila would be in and out of it with very brief moments of clarity. Keeping one hand in hers, Dallas reached over to brush her hair from her face. He felt another slight squeeze as he continued to talk. He assured her she was safe, explained the surgery to her and ended by saying he loved her before kissing her forehead. He leaned back in his chair to watch her sleep with her hand in his.

When he glanced up at the door, Dallas realized Lila's parents were standing in the doorway, watching him. *Shit*, he thought, wondering how long they had been standing there. Ignoring his discomfort and embarrassment, he rarely displayed his affection in front of others, Dallas took a deep breath as he prepared himself to talk with them.

Allison Foxwood's eyes widened with surprise at seeing Dallas Thompson beside her daughter. As she watched his affection for Lila, she grabbed her husband's wrist. She didn't want to interrupt when her daughter's eyes opened briefly. Her eyes were still cloudy from the drugs but the love they showed for Dallas Thompson was obvious and shocking.

When did this happen? How long have they been together? Rob had left a message early in the morning, but they couldn't connect with him, each leaving messages in the ongoing game of telephone tag. Instead, Chase had filled them in with a few details.

The most shocking was her daughter's secret marriage. Lila never seemed to show interest in dating, let alone having a serious relationship. *Understandably, Lila had kept them all in the dark*, Allison thought.

Like mother, like daughter, she sighed, *to keep the most important details of one's life a secret from the rest of the world and family.* Her eyes met the blue-greens of the man before her as she finally accepted the most shocking news, the individual Lila chose to marry. Dallas Thompson was the last man Allison ever expected to join the Foxwood family.

Allison smiled as the younger man stood up. She noted his discomfort and embarrassment, but Dallas continued towards the door.

"Mrs. Foxwood, Mr. Foxwood, I'm sure Lila will be happy to see you both when she wakes up." Dallas reached his hand out to shake as he addressed them.

Allison gave her husband a warning look to behave. They had discussed it during the drive back to town. She was pleased he kept in line with what they agreed on: don't ask for details, just be supportive. Time will provide answers to the many questions.

"Dallas, how is she?" Allison hurried to her daughter's side.

"She's been in and out. She's opened her eyes briefly, but that's to be expected." Dallas provided a quick summary of her status. "Can I get either of you something to drink? Water or coffee?"

"No, thank you," Allison answered looking away from Lila to Dallas. Her eyes noted the wrinkled scrubs, the disheveled hair, and the dark circles under his eyes. She recalled Chase's account of the rescue. Dallas had jumped into the cold river to rescue her baby before he carried her up the steep rocky hill, shivering in his wet clothes.

"Dallas, have you been at the hospital this whole time?"

"Yes, ma'am," he answered. He remembered instructions provided by a lawyer years previously, never providing more information than was asked.

Allison smiled gently. "Dallas, we can sit with Lila if you want to head home for a quick shower and change of clothes. Get some rest."

Dallas felt a moment of panic at the idea of not being able to remain beside Lila. He refused to be wedged out of her life. He looked between the older couple, debating the line of being respectful but determined while he held his place beside his wife. Mitch had stepped over to Lila's other side, gently touching her hair before looking between his wife and the younger man.

"Dallas, I'm not trying to push you away. I simply mean we can rotate sitting with her. It was only a suggestion. We'll be happy to sit with you both," Allison clarified after seeing the panic in his eyes. *Hell, she thought, he's probably terrified of them after being raised to hate the Foxwoods.* She was well aware of the issues and generations of family hatred over the years.

Allison understood why Lila kept her relationship with the family's sworn enemy a secret. If she had to choose between her daughter's happiness or some stupid Foxwood family feud, Lila's happiness would always win.

"No, ma'am. I mean, I can step out for a few minutes while you sit with her." Without thinking about it, he stepped back beside his wife to kiss her forehead before nodding a quick goodbye.

"Dallas?"

"Yes, ma'am?" He turned at the doorway.

"You don't need to be so formal. It's Allison and Mitch. Welcome to the family," Allison welcomed as she leaned up to kiss his cheek.

Too embarrassed to say anything, Dallas stepped back, nodding to them both before mumbling about being back within the hour.

Once he was gone, Allison sat beside her daughter. When she looked toward her husband, he looked as if he were about to make a rude comment.

"Mitch, don't start. Lila might hear you. It won't help her recovery if she senses your dislike. Remember what we agreed on," she quietly reminded.

"I didn't agree on anything," he started but stopped when she gave him another look.

The couple remained in uncomfortable silence as they sat with their daughter.

Clara's heart almost popped out of her chest when the doorknob to the garage started turning. She looked back and forth between the pounding from the front door and the side door leading to the garage.

"Clara? Open up! It's me!" Rob was yelling between the pounds.

Clara looked back at the garage door one last time before limping to the front window to peek out. Sure enough, Rob was standing on the porch, holding the screen door open with his body as he started to pound again.

She quickly unlocked the door and peeked out, leaning into the doorframe. She wasn't sure how much longer she could remain on her feet. "Rob? I was just about to head up to bed."

"Clara, please, I need to talk. You are the only one I can talk to," Rob declared with unusual desperation, squeezing inside through the small space.

She had no choice but to step back, studying him. Rob was really not taking well to the announcement of Lila and Dallas' marriage.

Rob closed the door behind him before his steel blue eyes looked down into her green with such intensity Clara felt awkward. As he leaned down, she could smell the alcohol on his breath.

Shit, Clara thought, the last thing she needed was Connor returning home to find her with a drunk Rob. While Connor had been surprisingly supportive of their friendship, she didn't want to cause any unnecessary friction. Rob had a negative reputation when drinking the hard stuff. And a confrontation with an overtired Connor would not end well.

Expecting the kiss to be a simple peck on her forehead or cheek, Clara was not prepared for the kiss on her lips, let alone his lips lingering. She attempted to step back, but his hands pulled her in for a tight hug.

"Clara, you are my best friend, you know that? You have always been here for me," Rob whispered as he rested his forehead on hers. "I love you."

"Rob, you are drunk. You shouldn't even be driving. Let's get you some coffee," Clara suggested, stepping back but not quickly enough. Rob grabbed her right hand to gently pull her towards him as he leaned back into the door. He smiled tenderly.

Clara shrugged her arm out of his hand. "Don't. You know better. You need to be gone before Connor gets home."

"He's not home? That's the best news I've heard all day," he declared as his smile grew wider, and he shook his eyebrows suggestively.

"Don't, Rob! Please don't go there." Her discomfort was evident as she backed away from him, limping into the kitchen. Clara eyed her cell on the counter as she hit the button to start the coffee already prepared for the next morning.

The concern over the sounds from the garage was forgotten as she reached for her cell to text Chase. Maybe he could pick up his cousin and get him home safely.

Rob reluctantly followed Clara into the kitchen, oblivious to her antalgic gait. He sat at the table to watch the most beautiful girl in town. Her bare feet showed off her dark purple toenails; her jeans were snug over her tight calves. His eyes slowly moved up to her perfectly round ass. He always wanted to rest his hands over her perfect ass. He sighed as she turned around. His eyes continued to her chest as he fantasized about taking each of her bare breasts into his mouth.

Shit, Rob thought when he felt his body respond to his fantasy, he needed to gain control of himself.

"Rob, do you want to talk about it?" Clara asked, her cell tossed back onto the counter.

"Are you going to stay all the way over there?"

"Yes, you're making me uncomfortable," Clara admitted, leaning back onto the counter to unload her weight from her painful left leg.

"Clara, sorry. I shouldn't have kissed you." Rob paused for a moment. "You are right, I have been drinking. I'm a little drunk."

When Clara's eyebrows went up in question, he clarified with a harsh chuckle. "Alright, a lot drunk. Come sit down, get off your leg. I promise I won't touch you."

"Rob, it's more than that," Clara started to say but stopped when she realized she wasn't sure why she felt so off. Anxious, maybe? She's never felt anxious around Rob. Pissed off, yes, but never anxious.

"Please come sit down. I'll be my normal gentlemanly self," Rob promised as he crossed his chest, like the girls did when they were young.

It took her a moment to realize the few steps across the kitchen seemed too much effort. She cautiously stepped forward. Her legs both suddenly felt like noodles. When Clara tried to move her leg forward, the pain was too much.

"Clara, let me help you," Rob offered when she wobbled. He went to her side to relieve her weight from her bad leg. He placed his arm around her waist, more or less carried her to the table.

Clara nodded her thanks as he gently lowered her down in the chair. He pulled the remainder of tea closer and asked if she needed anything else.

This is the Rob I like, she thought. The helpful, kind and caring man.

Rob returned to his seat and grabbed an apple from the fruit bowl on the table. Suddenly starving, he realized he had not eaten all day. As he chewed, he studied his friend. She looked paler than the last visit. "Let me carry you up to bed."

"I don't think so. You drunk in my bedroom is not something I want to deal with tonight. Connor is expected home soon. If I can't make the stairs, he'll carry me," Clara stated firmly.

"I'm sorry, Clara. I wasn't hitting on you. I get you're tired and it's late. I don't want you to ever be uncomfortable around me. You're my best friend, you know that? Next to my family, you know me better than anyone. The last thing I need is to screw up our friendship." Rob's voice was soft. He continued to study her as he bit into the apple.

Clara eyed him carefully as she finished her tea. "Why aren't you at the hospital? Aren't your parents here?"

"I don't want to see them. I can't believe the lies everyone has been telling me. Lila has been sneaking around with that stupid bastard, God only knows for how long, and actually married him? I mean what the hell. And my parents? Shit," Rob mumbled before taking another bite.

As he chewed, he watched her wince in pain when she shifted in the chair. "Your leg is really hurting you. Why aren't you resting it?"

"I'm exhausted," she admitted, fighting to keep her eyes open. "I was heading to bed but someone was at the door."

Rob sighed at her sarcasm. "Sorry. It's stupid and inappropriate of me to drop in so late. I best be off before your guy returns."

He started to stand but Clara reached for his arm. "Rob, I'm sorry. I'm exhausted. My body is feeling so heavy. A lot has been happening these last few nights. As tired as I am and as annoyed as Connor will be when he gets home, neither of us want you driving in your condition."

Clara's eyes narrowed as she tried to focus. "What about your parents?"

"You remember that DNA test Shannon wanted us all to take?"

Clara nodded.

Rob looked into her tense green eyes and thought she's the only one that always gave her undivided attention when he talked. He always felt a special bond with her, not realizing in the past she was compensating for being hearing impaired and needed to read his lips. Regardless, it gave him a sense of importance and made him feel as if she really cared about what he said. Rob looked away when his jeans continued to tighten around him. To distract himself, he looked down at his apple as he talked.

"I just opened mine today." He glanced over briefly, seeing her nod again. "I think I received it the afternoon of your accident. I saw no need to rush, I had no doubt of my family. But damn it, it was not what I was expecting. I have a half-sister! Lila is only my maternal half-sister!"

Rob pounded on the table, causing Clara to flinch. "Clara, I'm sorry. I didn't mean to upset you."

"Ok, tell me," she suggested quietly, struggling to focused on him.

"My father isn't the man I thought he was. I mean my biological father isn't my mother's husband. It's fuckin Zachariah Thompson!" Rob shouted. "Can you believe that shit? My birthdate is twelve months after my parents' wedding date. My mother was sleeping around with the fucking bastard behind my father's back! Then, she passed me off as his legitimate child!"

Unable to contain his anger, Rob stood up during the explanation and paced, struggling to control his temper.

Clara was slow to process what he was saying. Once she did, she was shocked. Absolutely shocked. She never imagined such a thing. Not only was his biological father not Mitch Foxwood, it was his sworn enemy! *Damn*, she thought, *no wonder he's been drinking*.

The smell of the coffee shifted her attention back to the immediate goal, sobering up Rob before Connor returned home. Clara slowly stood up, pausing to test the weight on her left leg and limped across the kitchen. She struggled to complete the simple task of pouring coffee, unaware it spilled. Her eyes were unable to focus.

Clara stopped when she felt him standing close behind her, one hand on either side of the counter. She tried to sidestep but he closed in tighter as a voice whispered in her ear, "Love, I need you right now. I need you more than I've ever needed anyone. I want to take care of you. Let me take care of you."

"Stop," Clara shouted, pushing herself past strong arms. She suddenly felt as if she were fighting to stay afloat as the exhaustion pulled her under. "You aren't acting like yourself. This isn't you."

Clara turned and leaned back into the counter, using both her hands to hold herself up. She winced from the pain in her left shoulder. Her blurred vision attempted to focus on a blurry blue blob on the floor of the kitchen. *What the hell is that*, she wondered.

"Hey, love, what the hell? Why are you always resisting me? We are meant for each other. I have always been there for you, always. Why are you fighting this? Stop. It'll be so easy. All you have to do is relax and just let it happen!"

Clara was slow to place the voice. It echoed around her head as the familiar face came closer. His anger caused his normally soft blue eyes to shift a violent blue. His hand came up to caress the side of her face.

"Don't, don't touch me," Clara tried to shout but could barely hear her voice. *Something is wrong*, Clara thought as she looked to the blue blob on the floor. There was a red puddle next to it.

Her eyes flew back to the man before her. Her body, too heavy for her legs to hold up, she appeared to melt towards the floor.

Oh no, her drugged mind finally understood. *Someone else is in the house*, she thought.

Clara felt strong arms grab her as her eyes finally focused. A chill ran through her body like a cold blanket as she stared at Rob's unconscious body on the floor before she blacked out.

· · · ·

As he exited out of the worn down building, Evil felt refreshed and surprisingly satisfied. It had been too long since he felt one's heart beat cease in his bare hands. In his good mood, he was tempted to walk over to see his babydoll but he knew she wouldn't be alone. Those damn friends were always close by, especially since the accident. Evil couldn't really fault them, he too wanted to be continuously at her side.

Maybe tomorrow, he thought as he cut into the alley behind the building. He paused only for a moment to toss a cloth into the dumpster before heading home. He was confident he had removed all his DNA from the scene.

Devan was relieved to finally be heading home. The previous late night and early morning left him exhausted. He could not believe how easy it was to get Lila's kidnapper to cave to the questions. He was willing to explain everything in exchange for protection. He was the brother of the man responsible for bringing counterfeit twenties into town. The same man who shot Shannon's car, causing the accident and almost killing both her and Clara. But, his answers seemed too rehearsed. He was hiding important details, Devan was sure of it. He just needed to ask the right questions, he thought as he turned on to the street behind Connor.

Connor was exhausted. He wanted nothing more than to crawl in bed beside Clara. He would actually sleep a full eight hours tonight, he was that tired. But the moment he pulled into the driveway, his body tensed.

What the hell, he thought, discovering the front door was ajar.

Connor slowly walked up the steps, unaware his cousin had pulled into the neighboring driveway, also aware of the opened door.

"Clara?" Connor called out as he stepped through the door. Nothing appeared out of place. Seeing the kitchen light on, he headed back. The sight of the kitchen stopped him in his tracks.

The table laid on its side with the fruit bowl upside down on the floor. The apples and pears were thrown around. A banana was apparently stepped on, covered in what appeared to be blood splatter. A broken mug was in pieces in a brown pool on the floor. His eyes followed up to the counter, another pool of black liquid dripped over the edge next to the coffee pot, sitting suspiciously on the counter next to the coffee maker.

When he saw a small black circle piece lying on the floor, Connor slumped into the doorway. Clara's kanso. The receiver that attached to her cochlear implant. He knew she was in trouble. Clara would never willingly leave it recklessly on the floor, he thought as his world shattered around him.

"Connor? What's going on?" Devan called out as Connor fell into the frame of the door. When he looked into the kitchen, Devan grabbed his arm to prevent him from entering as he reached for his cell.

"Clara?" Connor whispered before he turned toward the stairs and yelled, "Shit! Clara? Clara?"

Connor flew up the stairs, too terrified to think. When he arrived at the first room, he saw Hailey snuggled up on her side with her favorite baby doll. *Ok, she's alright*, he told himself as she shifted in her sleep. He hurried to the next room. The young boy was sprawled out across his bed. Connor stepped forward to gently touch his hair, to assure himself the boy, too, was safe and asleep in his bed. Just like his sister.

Am I overreacting? Yeah, I must be. She may have leaned too heavily onto the table. It's old and tipped over, he justified the scene downstairs. *She's probably too proud to call me and crawled up the stairs on her own*, Connor thought as he walked across the hall.

But Connor knew before he turned on the light, Clara's bed would be empty. She never slept in total darkness alone and he didn't sense her presence. He stared at the bed as he stepped back into the hall. When his back touched the opposite wall, he slid down to the floor.

Fuck, Evil finally got her.

Bored and restless, Shannon emptied her closet, all of the clothes were piled onto the bed with her shoes on the floor next to the dresser. She tried on each article of clothing, studied herself in the full length mirror before debating the level of joy it brought her.

Not feeling it, she stripped off the outfit before donning another. Within an hour, more clothes laid on the floor to be discarded than hung in the closet.

In only her underwear, she reorganized the closet as she remembered all her friends laughing at her excessive OCD. Shannon was always the most organized in the group. She had a physiological need to have everything in its place, properly sorted: play clothes, leisure, professional, then formal wear from left to right. Within each section, clothes were sectioned with similar articles of clothing together with tops, bottoms then dresses, short then long, and then light to dark.

When she was finished, Shannon smiled at the perfectly organized space. Until her eyes shifted to the pile of clothes tossed into the corner. Feeling a crazy panic, she realized, not for the first time, her friends were right. She had a disease and needed help. Quickly scooping the clothes onto the bed, she organized them into similar piles before placing them into a garbage bag to be donated.

With the task completed, Shannon decided enough was done for the night. She could tackle the drawers in the morning. Feeling relaxed, she prepared for bed. As she fell asleep, her thoughts went to her friends. She hoped everyone was well and Clara was quickly recovering.

19 *gone*

Devan assisted Connor down the stairs. He had already called his uncle, who was to notify his boss and cousins. They were on their way to assess the scene in the kitchen. Just as Connor sat down on the sofa, he heard a vehicle pull into the driveway.

Excellent response time, Devan thought as he went to the door at the bottom of the staircase. The front door was still open. He didn't want anyone touching anything until forensics was able to process the house. Turning on the light, Devan opened the door, surprised to see Chase and Rachel heading up the drive.

"What are you two doing here this late?" Devan glanced at his watch.

"Shit, am I too late? I tried to get here sooner but," Chase simply shrugged. It had been a tense couple of days. "What did he do?"

"Let's try this again, why are you two here?" Devan repeated.

Chase's eyes narrowed at Devan's tone and body language. Very similar to when he was in agent mode.

"Clara texted me about, I don't know, forty minutes ago. Said Rob stopped in, drunk, and wanted me to take him home. I'm not leaving Rachel alone at night with all the crap that's been going on lately."

"Rob was here? Drunk? His truck isn't here. He wasn't at Memories. Could he have been at The Lantern and walked over from there?" Devan asked, pulling out his cell to text his cousin, instructing him to look for Rob's truck. "Hold on a second."

Others had arrived. Devan stepped out onto the porch to give instructions before he returned back inside. He motioned for Chase to continue.

"No idea. I haven't seen him all day. You saw how he was last night, even I couldn't calm him down," Chase answered.

"Why? What the hell happened last night?" Connor asked from the sofa.

Devan went into the family room as he talked, the others followed. "That's right, you went into the ER while the rest of us were out in the waiting room. A nurse had stepped forward with the clipboard, requesting the next of kin to please fill out Lila's personal information. Rob came forward but Dallas beat him to it. He grabbed the clipboard, already had her medical card out. Announced he was her husband. The two are married! And since it was a military ID, it was very clear the wedding was legal and before his discharge from the military. Rob lost it."

"That's an understatement. I've never seen him so furious. It took three of us to pull him away from Dallas. The nurse was nice enough to allow Dallas in the back to fill out the paperwork while Rob was escorted out. He wouldn't even talk to me. Accused me and everyone else of knowing this and keeping it from him," Chase further explained.

"Married? Lila and Dallas? For what, four or five years?" Connor clarified, looking at Rachel. "Damn, you girls know how to keep a secret."

"We didn't know about the marriage until this past summer. Lila swore us to secrecy. She was really concerned about Rob and her father's reaction," Rachel defended, feeling uncomfortable with everyone's eyes on hers. Never able to lie, Rachel didn't want to speak further.

"Oh, I get that. After seeing his reaction last night, Lila was smart," Devan agreed. He looked over at Chase. "You're also a Foxwood. My understanding is the hostilities are from generations of family disputes."

Chase simply shrugged. "My dad told me years ago, he didn't know the original cause. Called it the local version of the Hatfield-McCoy war. He said it wasn't worth it to get involved. He had no issues with the current family members and suggested I consider the same."

"What about Rob and your uncle?" Devan wondered.

"My dad was vague. Something about my uncle and Dallas' dad fighting over a woman. Goes back to middle school, if not when they all played in the sandbox," Chase answered. "What the hell does this have to do with what's going on now? Why are you and half of the sheriff's department here? Where's Clara?"

"We don't know," Connor answered miserably. He was still on the sofa.

"What do you mean you don't know?" Rachel looked over in confusion.

"Clara isn't here and there are signs of a struggle," Devan answered quietly. He gave the few details he knew: no Clara, kids alone upstairs, and Rob currently nowhere to be found.

"Wait a minute, are you suggesting Rob did something to Clara?" Rachel demanded. She looked back and forth between Devan and Connor. They knew him the least. But when she glanced at Chase, she realized he was also thinking it. "Chase, he's your cousin. He may want to beat Dallas senselessly and has had several fights with anyone named Thompson but he would never hurt Clara!"

Both Devan and Connor waited for Chase to respond. It took him a moment to gather his thoughts. Reaching for Rachel's hand before he spoke, "Rachel is right about his history of fights. Rob's issues were always with other guys. Women, in general, he's always adored. And Clara the most. He and Clara have always been tight."

"What do you mean by tight?" Devan asked.

"You know, they each always had the other's back. They were close, confided in each other. Rob was protective of her," Chase struggled to explain.

"Protective of her? How?"

"He made her feel safe," Connor simply stated.

Devan and Chase both looked questioningly at him.

"What are you talking about?"

"Clara has insecurities and fear that exacerbated when her mother went missing. She would avoid being alone in her house. She never trusted attention from anyone not already in her close group of friends. After her mother was gone in the spring and I left town for college that fall, that's when she started spending more time at the farm," Connor explained, looking over at Rachel.

She nodded in agreement. "It's true. In retrospect, her mother was the anchor in the family. If she weren't home, Clara would come over to our house before she disappeared. Rob was initially the big brother type, very protective."

"By middle school, Clara was helping with the chores around the farm," Chase continued, "Rob taught her how to ride and care for the horses. Heck, he even taught her how to drive the tractor and the other farm equipment."

"Tell me about their relationship in high school," Devan asked. "When did they start dating and what broke them up?"

Both Chase and Rachel shook their heads while Chase answered, "They were never a couple, at least not in the sense everyone defines a couple. By high school, their bond may have had a flirty tone but never physical. Strictly platonic relationship."

Devan noted Rachel nodded in agreement. He tried to keep his thoughts professional but he knew Rob's reputation as a player, even back in high school. "Was Rob's relationship with Shannon also platonic?"

Rachel's eyes widened in surprise at the question. "Why are you asking that? What does Shannon even have to do with tonight?"

Chase, Devan noted, remained silent. He did give a look with a subtle raise of his eyebrows as he tilted his head slightly towards his girlfriend. The message was clear, he wouldn't expand on the topic in her presence. Regardless, he asked anyway, "Chase?"

"I would be speculating about any relationship, romantic or physical, Rob had with anyone. We never discussed details. He has never been like that. I can only say with confidence, he and Clara never had a physical relationship," he answered, totally uncomfortable with the turn of topic.

"Because he told you?" Devan pushed.

"I don't know. Maybe he did but more because he was the most protective of Clara. He was always familiar with her schedule, knew where she was and with whom. They always clicked, more or less. Not to say she was a pushover, acting as a damsel in distress. Clara would put Rob in his place when he overstepped his boundaries of friendship. I don't mean physically but telling her what she could or couldn't do, trying to make decisions for her. Rob has always adored Clara," Chase declared. "And he's always respected her. With Shannon, they had a different bond for different reasons. You would need to ask him."

"Chase is right," Connor agreed. "I've seen their interaction together, both back then and now. Clara trusts Rob and cares for him. I walked in on them when they were having a screaming match. Don't need to go into details but she was crying and he was devastated. I even had a beer with him afterwards, you were there, Devan. He wouldn't hurt her."

"Devan?"

He turned to see Jack Ruddy standing at the doorway. Devan's immediate supervisor was ordinary-looking, with average height, average weight, and average looks. Nothing about him ever stood out in a crowd of strangers, making Jack perfect for overseeing a team of undercover agents. His most current assignment of blending in with a small town was not the easiest for others but to him, it was child's play. He silently motioned Devan over. After talking quietly in the kitchen, Devan returned with the other agent.

"Everyone, this is my boss, Special Agent in charge Jack Ruddy," Devan announced then proceeded to introduce everyone. Then he asked one last question, "You all agreed Rob would never hurt Clara, but what about after he's touched the hard stuff?"

Connor raised his eyebrows at the question but remained silent. He's never seen the guy drink more than a couple of beers. Until now, he never gave it a thought.

Rachel also remained quiet.

"What exactly are you implying?" Chase asked quietly, he could feel his temper raise. He'd had enough of these questions. While he wanted to help find Clara, he didn't want to be the one to implicate his cousin. He and Rob were raised as brothers.

"Rob's truck isn't anywhere in town, at least not on the streets or parking lots. Nor is it at home. When the deputy checked the house, the kitchen was a mess," Agent Ruddy explained. He pulled up pictures on his cell phone to show.

"Someone broke into the house," Chase demanded.

"No, one of the workers reported Mr. Foxwood's mood was on edge throughout the day. He was seen drinking and later emptied the cabinets by throwing everything at the wall," he reported.

"Something else must have happened after last night," Chase speculated. "Yeah, the guy has a temper. His fuse is quick to explode followed by relative calm. He would not have been able to hold on to his anger from last night all through the day. If he had, there would have been a trail in his wake. Something else happened."

"Sir?"

Everyone turned to look at the tech standing in the doorway, he was wearing blue booties over his shoes and gloves on his hands. He spoke after receiving a nod from the boss. "The preliminary test confirms the dark liquid on the counter is coffee; the brown liquid is tea and the blood on the floor is from a male."

Connor leaned back relieved. It wasn't her blood. Was it Rob's? If so, then who else was here. No way in hell could she have moved his body, not in her current condition.

"Where's Eric?"

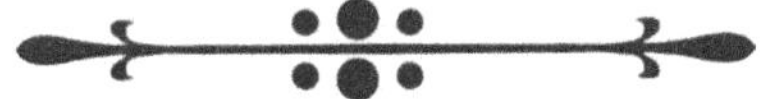

worst nightmare come true

*R*ob *dreamt of Clara. They had taken the high trail up towards the lake, tied up the horses when they stopped to eat the simple lunch he prepared. He looked adoringly into her bright green eyes and laughed when she suggested they go for a swim.*

He watched as she skipped to the edge of the lake, stripped off her shorts and blouse, then executed a perfect dive wearing only her matching red bra and panties.

"What are you waiting for?" Clara called out. "The water is perfect."

"It's too cold," he replied.

"No, it won't be if you join me. I'll heat you right up," she responded, throwing her bra out towards him. "Come on, you know you want to."

"I have a headache," he stated as the lacey bra landed on his foot.

When he tried to stand, his body wouldn't move. But the next moment, Rob was sitting on the bank of the lake with his legs dangling in the water. The weight of the water held him down. He looked out as Clara was floating further away on her back.

The icy chill brought him out of his dream. *Oh shit*, Rob thought, initially thinking he had wet his bed as he dreamed of Clara. Damn, she never lets me get her in my dreams either, he realized for the first time in his life.

When he opened his eyes, Rob was surprised to discover he was sitting inside his truck, which was rapidly filling with icy water. *What the hell*, he wondered through his pounding headache. Shivering, he tried to bring his hands up to the wetness on the side of his face. But he couldn't move.

Looking down, Rob was slow to process, his hands were pinned down beside him by the seat belt.

What the fuck is going on? How the hell did I get here? Rob began to panic, the water level at his upper chest. He kicked his feet, but the movement wasn't enough to free his hands.

The full moon provided enough light for him to see his truck had settled in the shallow part of a lake. The surface appeared to be just above the truck. When he turned his head, steel blue eyes in the rearview mirror caught his attention.

"This is how it ends? At the bottom of some random lake, practically in my back yard? Will anyone know what happened to me? Will anyone even care?" Rob's voice whispered, the water already to his chin. "Maybe it's just as well."

Resigned to the inevitable, Rob closed his eyes and focused on his breathing. As he relaxed, his mind wandered and his thoughts shifted to Clara.

Rob's eyes shot open in alarm as he yelled, "Clara? Clara?"

Hours later, Connor was still sitting on the sofa, numb, as his mind went over any and all horrible scenarios Clara could be enduring at this very moment. He really didn't need an active imagination, he worked too many hours in the ER of the Trauma Center in the city. Humans were horrible to other humans, accidentally, maliciously, recklessly.

Stop, Clara's a strong, resourceful person. Don't borrow trouble, he heard his grandmother's voice in his head.

To shift his focus, Connor returned his attention to what the others were discussing around him.

"Sir, you need to see this," a voice said.

Everyone gathered around as the agent played the surveillance videos from the day before on a laptop. After Eric's arrest, Connor had multiple cameras covering each of the doors leading to the outside. The agent narrated as he altered the speed. They first watched a man doing something to Lila's tires. In fast forward, they watched the events from the day when Lila went missing. He slowed it down as a shadow emerged later in the evening. When Rachel's car pulled into the driveway, it faded into the shrubs. It continued fast again but slowed two hours before Clara returned home the next evening. The same shadow appeared as it walked along the edge of the yard, fading behind the garage. Clara was dropped off by Chase in the fast forwarding and the babysitter left soon after. The speed slows down again when Foxwood pulls into the driveway and she opens the door after peeking out the window. Less than a half hour later, a person dressed in dark clothes comes out of the front door carrying Rob over his shoulder.

Everyone cringed when he dropped the unconscious Rob into the bed of his truck like a sack of potatoes before returning back inside. A moment later, the person returns. Clara, also unconscious, is being carried in the arms of the shadow.

"The shadow just dumps him in the back but is gentle with her," an agent sums up.

"You all keep talking about a shadow," Connor states. He was standing at the doorway leading into the dining room. "Who the hell is the damn shadow?"

Everyone was quiet as they looked at him in confusion before Connor realized he needed to give her history. "Clara is convinced her mother was taken and killed by a shadow. Are you now telling me she was taken by this same shadow? While her children were upstairs sleeping?"

The horror on his face was evident as he realized the similarities: same age, same time of day, same room of the house and even children sleeping upstairs. *Why wasn't I home yet?*

"What are you talking about?" Jack asked.

"A shadow was in her house?" Chase repeated. It was the way he said it that caused everyone to turn to him. He and Rachel had remained as the investigation continued.

"Yeah, that's how she always described it. When she was young, Clara talked about a shadow that came out of the walls, only at night when all was dark. That's the real reason she never liked the house," Connor explained. "As an adult, she only talked about it as a memory of a recurring dream she had as a child but she rarely discusses it. She was a little drunk the last time she mentioned it. Still, she never sleeps alone in the dark, never."

"A shadow," Chase repeated, this time dragging it out, as if it answered an unspoken question. "Yeah, that makes sense. It probably would seem that way. She couldn't hear and she was young."

"Chase, what the hell are you talking about?" Devan asked before anyone else could.

"A few days back, Rob and I discovered a secret door in Clara's room. Did she ever tell you about it?" Chase looked over to Rachel, who was shaking her head.

"A secret door? Where did it go?" Jack asked before Rachel could.

"No idea. It was time to close up for the night, so we were going to check it out the next day, but that didn't happen," he shrugged.

"You find a secret door in Clara's childhood home and you never mention it or even tell me about it?" Rachel accused.

"It was the same day as your date with Madmax. The next day, Rob was late for work and I was too pissed off by lunchtime to work. That same night, we were all out searching for Lila. Neither Rob nor I worked yesterday. I was at the hospital," Chase explained. "It seems like months but it was just, what, three days ago?"

In the early hours, Lila opened her eyes again. Instead of Dallas, her parents sat on either side of her bed. Each was holding one of her hands. Her mother's eyes were red, as if she'd been crying. Her father also looked very upset.

Oh no, Lila thought, *they heard about me and Dallas*. To avoid the pending confrontation, she closed her eyes until she fell back asleep.

Hours later, she opened her eyes again. Lila was relieved to see Dallas beside her.

"Welcome back, Sleeping Beauty. I was beginning to think you would never wake up," Dallas stated as he pulled her hand up to kiss. "How are you feeling?"

"Dal, my parents are here! They are so upset, I don't know what to say," Lila blurted out.

He looked at her closely, she seemed more alert this time, but her parents said she never woke up while they sat with her. Maybe she heard them talking. "Of course they're upset. Everything that has been going on these last few days, the waiting is the worst."

"Waiting? What do you mean? What waiting?"

"Lila, what are you talking about?"

"My parents! They know about us! I saw my mother crying, she looked so distraught," she answered sadly. Lila knew the day would come, forcing her to choose between her family or the man she loved.

"Lila, baby, no it's not that. Well, they do know we're married. Your mother seems to be handling it fine, but that's not what's going on. Rob and Clara are missing."

"What? What do you mean missing?" Lila tried to sit up but stopped when she felt pain in her leg.

"Just that. Connor returned home last night. There was evidence of a struggle in the kitchen, no Clara and both Reese and Hailey asleep in their beds." Dallas continued to give the modified version. She didn't need to know the details.

"The children were sleeping the whole time? How horrible! Who do they think it was?"

"No idea. Everyone keeps describing the person as a shadow. Connor seems to think it's the same shadow Clara saw when she was young. He says she often talked about a shadow in the house and thinks that's who killed her mother," Dallas explained. "The last Chase has reported, he was taking the FBI to her Hawks House to search."

• • • •

Evil paced his large study in an attempt to control his anger. He was furious! Absolutely furious, as he returned to his desk to replay the surveillance videos. He was able to monitor the damn investigation from his hidden cameras inside his babydoll's home.

"The stupid boy is too much like his mother, constantly ruining everything! I give him firm instructions and what does he do? The disrespect!" Evil thought.

His hard work all these years could potentially go down the drain. Everything had been in place. Evil was ready for his final move. He was prepared for the last phase of his plan, just in time for the deadline, December twenty-fifth. Over thirty years it took for him to get to this place. He was so close and the damn boy had to shove his way in and ruin it all.

But fortunately, Evil was always a step ahead with backup plans for the backup plans, he chuckled harshly. "If the boy was not going to be respectful, he would simply have to pay the consequences. Everything was in place for the boy to go down. All his DNA and finger prints were at his slut's apartment." He looked at his watch, "Shit."

"Maybe I can use it to my advantage. The stupid agents will likely be here soon, looking for the boy, no doubt." His ridiculous infatuation with the girl was common knowledge. Evil was confident he knew where the boy had taken her. The boy was lazy and didn't think well on his feet, and wouldn't even attempt to find something of his own. Hell, he didn't have the money or

the common sense. Evil already confirmed the boy didn't bring her up to his suite of rooms. That only left one other place.

Glancing at the clock, Evil wondered how long before they would arrive. He needed to be here when they did and set them in the right direction. "Hmm, maybe this could work out after all," he thought. Get the kid out of the way once and for all.

The quiet knock refueled his anger. "Damn it! What part of no interruptions is everyone having trouble understanding?" Evil closed his eyes to take a few calming breaths before calling out in his calm voice, "Come in."

"Honey, what are you still doing? It's late." His wife stood in the doorway. Without waiting for an answer, she strolled towards him. Her long silk robe was open, revealing a new bright blue teddy. The built-in push-up bra made it seem like her large breasts were actually perky.

Evil quickly pulled up the screen saver on his computer, smiling encouragingly to his wife. "It wouldn't hurt to have an alibi," he thought. Relax for a few hours, make her useful until the idiots stop in for questioning. Once they are gone, he can send his wife to sleep and head out to the cabin. "That has to be where he went. The boy will be dealt with once and for all."

His plans would finally be complete. He'd finally have his revenge on the damn Hawks empire and take control of the Trusts. And his babydoll would finally be his in every sense.

Evil's blue eyes watched his wife as she did her ridiculous dance. He leaned back in his chair with a smile. And when he was running the trust, he would no longer have need for the foolish woman before him. He was still undecided on how to get rid of her. It had to be something new.

She smiled back, believing her presence with her new lingerie brought on his arousal. When he remained sitting in the chair, opening his pants, the years of marriage told her what he was expecting. As she lowered herself to her knees, he closed his eyes as he visualized his sweet babydoll's mouth once again bringing him pleasure.

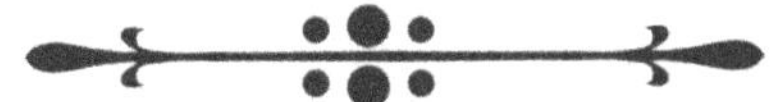

21
an easy explanation

It was late when they pulled the SUV into the driveway of the Hawks House. The headlights were off as the bright moonlight guided them. While they parked near the backdoor, no one saw the curtain move slightly from the third story window as the squatter peeked down.

"I feel weird being here without Clara, don't you?" Rachel whispered to Chase.

"Not at all. This is just another work site. Rach, I'm not leaving you out here on your own," Chase explained as he met up with the others on the back porch.

Chase unlocked the back door and turned on the lights, leading Devan, Jack, and Rachel inside . They each looked around with curiosity.

"This is the mud room. The kitchen is straight through here. We haven't touched the kitchen yet," Chase explained as he opened a box to retrieve flashlights. He checked the batteries as he handed each one out.

"Why not?" Jack asked. "Hell, it's not too bad as it is. Granted the appliances need to be replaced and the colors are certainly outdated."

"Rob and I are hesitant to make any real changes to the layout. We've only completed upgrades, like the plumbing and the electric. This house is a historical landmark with years of history," he declared, touching the original woodwork of the staircase. "It was beautifully planned and artistically designed. The craftsmanship is absolutely crazy."

Chase stopped talking as the others all stared back at him.

"I see you love your profession, Chase," Devan commented. "But why haven't you closed up any walls?"

"Honestly, I'm not sure. Rob seems to think Clara will later regret having strangers living in her family home. This house is two hundred and fifty years old. Whenever we pulled out family heirlooms, she was always in awe of the history. He knows her better than I do. He believes Clara will want to one day return here. We've been working to upgrade the wiring and pipes, give her time to change her mind," Chase shrugged.

"Connor says Clara never liked the kitchen," Devan stated.

"No, she's never been a serious cook either," Rachel stated. "After her mother disappeared, she would rarely be found in one. At my house, or even the farm, she avoids cooking. I just figured it was because she and her mother always cooked together. "

Devan looked over at Jack. He made a mental note to have forensics pull up the kitchen floor. Maybe they would find a clue or something to explain Susannah Gibson's death.

Everyone followed Chase up the backstairs and down the hall. When he entered the bedroom, Rachel paused as she looked around the room she had not seen in years. She glanced out the window and smiled before she followed the others towards the closet as Chase explained.

"The blueprints and the physical measurements were not adding up. It was driving me crazy trying to find the missing space," he explained, switching on the closet light.

The others watched in fascination as Chase pushed on the wall, revealing a staircase. "Like I said before, we didn't have time to check it out. It has obviously been used in recent years."

Chase started down the steps, Rachel was close behind. She was relieved the space wasn't covered in cobwebs.

Devan followed next but stopped on the fourth step. Looking back up, he watched his boss play with the door. The frequent movement of the door caused the irritating squeak similar to hands on a chalkboard.

"It's kind of noisy, don't you think? How could anyone sleep through that?" Jack wondered.

"Well, no one has lived here in, what, twelve years," Devan looked down at Rachel for confirmation.

"Correct, her father moved away with his girlfriend the day after our graduation. Clara went to college. Besides, she can't hear without her hearing aids," Rachel explained.

"Really? Nothing?" Jack asked.

Chase came to a stop on the landing he believed was the first floor. There was a door on either side before the stairs continued down to, most likely, the lower level. He cautiously pulled on the door handle but nothing happened. He tried the handle on the other side, likewise, nothing, not even a slight shift in the door. He pointed his flashlight around the doorway.

"Not really. Back then, we could all be talking and singing to loud music without waking her up but if you touched her bed or changed the lighting, Clara was immediately awake," Rachel confirmed, watching Chase attempting to open the door.

Chase nodded in agreement.

"Were you there at the slumber parties, Chase?" Devan teased.

"Not really. If the girls were at the farm, then kind of yeah. But the girls were always in Lila's room or the sunroom. Rob and I never slept in the same room with them, " Chase answered. He reached out for Rachel's hand to assist her down the next flight of narrow steps. "These doors must have been sealed shut on the other side. This one likely opens into the bathroom off the mudroom and the other into a back room. We are leaving the main floor and are now heading down to the lower level."

"I can't believe we never knew this was here!" Rachel exclaimed. "Do you think my house has hidden passages as well?"

Chase was busy checking each step as they descended. Many of the steps were repaired sometime in the last half of the century. He was surprised the lights were holding up. "Probably."

When they arrived at the next landing, he again checked the doors. As before, the door didn't budge. He flashed his light around the door again. "We are in the lower level. Do you want to continue?"

"Absolutely. I want to know where these stairs go and who would have access," Jack stated. He also realized they would need to clear the house, to assure Clara wasn't hidden away somewhere inside her own house.

The last flight seemed longer as it narrowed. The hall, for lack of a better word, brought them into a large room. Chase's flashlight showed a naked light bulb hanging in the middle of the ceiling. He turned it on. "Definitely recently used. These light bulbs came out approximately five years ago."

Chase remained quiet as he studied the layout. It was more of a widening of the previous tunnel than an actual room. He walked to the south, flashed his light down the tunnel. Then it dawned on him, "Son of a bitch."

Jack turned his flashlight onto Chase. "What? What do you see?"

"Nothing really, just speculating. These tunnels must connect the four houses together," Chase stated as he looked at Rachel. He could tell by her expression, she already figured it out. *She may be naïve*, he thought, *but she's never been stupid.* "Back in the day, all these homes had servants. The hidden passages were probably made to keep the servants hidden as they completed their jobs."

"Many of the servants were married to each other. The tunnels probably allowed the servants to move around between homes without being seen. A butler from my house might have been married to the head cook at Clara's and their child could have been the stable boy at Eric's," Rachel explained. Chase again nodded in agreement.

"Really?" Devan wondered in fascination. "How was it determined where the family lived?"

"Not really sure. Could be the position that provided the better quarters or the availability. My mother once said a home could have as many as twenty-five employees. Some lived elsewhere in town, not all lived here," she explained quietly.

"You don't have any servants?" Devan asked.

"No. Well, I do have the landscapers, as Clara's did. The excessive staff became less and less as modern conveniences became available. When my grandfather became head of the Taylor House, he did away with the live-in staff. He kept a maid, a cook, and the landscaper. There's a story about the servants spying on the businesses of the other houses." Rachel smiled at Devan when she was finished.

Jack had been taking pictures with his cell. When he was finished, he addressed the group. "I can only imagine the fascinating history we've yet to uncover, but how does this help find Rob and Clara?"

"Not sure if it has any connection to tonight's events but it does provide an explanation to Clara's interpretation of a shadow emerging from the wall. She was not imagining it. Someone was literally in her house," Chase stated. When Rachel stepped closer to him, he placed his arm around her. "The south end of the tunnel leads to the Emerson House. The tunnel to Clara's house shows fairly recent usage. We can keep going to confirm the tunnel goes to the Howell House and ends at the Taylor House."

Both Devan and Jack nodded, gesturing for Chase to lead the group. They followed the tunnel and found another smaller tunnel to the right before it continued.

Chase was consulting his cell, monitoring the distance from the previous smaller tunnel. "The distance suggests this most likely leads to the Howell House."

Staying in the entrance, he flashed his light. He was curious to see if there were any simplified alarms in place. Seeing nothing but darkness, Chase stepped back. He continued further down the main tunnel, figuring the next turn would lead to the Taylor House. When they turned around to retrace their steps, Chase motioned he wanted to check the other direction, to confirm the exits were only leading to the main houses.

When he arrived at the south tunnel, Chase confirmed it led to the Emerson House. He flashed his light around the corner into the darkness, but instead of finding another empty hallway, his light stopped at a flowered luggage set. "Damn."

"Chase, step back. Take Rachel back to Clara's," Devan instructed as he pulled out his cell. "Damn it. I don't have any reception this far down. We need to head back up and call in the rest of the team. We have to quietly have the forensics team assess all this while we clear the Hawks House."

Jack was finished taking pictures as he backed out of the narrow tunnel. His eyebrows narrowed in question. As an outsider, he once again felt out of the loop. Even Rachel seemed to understand the significance of the luggage set as she stared at it with tears in her eyes.

Chase first looked at Devan before he answered, "Clara's mother disappeared when she was nine years old. No one ever looked for her, not even entertained the possibility of foul play. That's because her luggage set was missing as well as much of her clothes. Her husband reported his wife had a history of leaving town for days with her lover."

Unbeknown to everyone in town, Carl Gibson had been secretly living on the third floor of the Hawks House. Over the years, he would return when he was between lady friends or hiding from Felicia. As far as he was concerned, he was still the legal spouse of Susannah Hawks. He had every reason to be there.

A simple man, he didn't need an elaborate lifestyle or place to stay. A simple bed with a roof and four walls, running water and enough light to find his way around was always enough for him. Why pay rent somewhere when he still had access to his marriage bed?

That was until last spring when Clara started the renovations and the furniture was getting moved into storage. Fortunately, the third floor wasn't touched yet.

Carl panicked when the young Foxwood showed up with the damn FBI. He still could not believe he didn't know the damn bartender was an agent. He thought for sure they were here for his arrest.

Until he saw Rachel.

Then he was intrigued. Never in his wildest imagination did he believe the stories he heard as a child were true. The four mansions were all connected. How could his cousin not have told him? Lee had to have known. He slowly descended to the second floor, cautiously going to the back of the house.

He stopped in horror, looking at the entrance to a secret passage that came out from Clara's closet. *The bastard, all these years!* Carl realized he was being used. He returned back up to his space on the third floor. He quickly retrieved his few belongings, then exited out of one of the many side doors.

Keeping in the shadows, he returned to his truck, which he kept parked a few blocks down towards Main Street.

early morning check

22

Whyen the doorbell rang at six in the morning, Lee Howell was in bed beside his wife, already awake.

"What the hell?" he almost yelled, pushing the covers back. He silently debated simply donning his bathrobe or getting dressed. He went with the third option. *Always plan C*, he thought, walking naked to his dresser. He pulled out a pair of flannel pajama bottoms.

When the doorbell rang again, his wife sat straight up. The covers fell from her chest, revealing her bare breasts. "Lee, is that the doorbell?"

"Yes, Kathleen. At this hour, it better be important." Lee pulled up his pants as he headed towards the stairs. He knew they would stop ringing once they saw a light come on. "Damn it. They better not wake up Father."

He paused to watch his wife stand naked beside the bed looking around before she reached for her silk robe. "Kathleen, for the love of God, put some clothes on."

"It's six in the morning. If someone wants to drop in unexpectedly this early, they aren't going to be shocked to see me not properly dressed," she declared.

"Good point," he agreed as he left the room.

When he opened the door, Lee found the sheriff, his nephew, the agent, his son Anthony, and another man standing on his porch. "Gentlemen, it's kind of early for a visit, don't you think?"

"Good morning, Lee. Sorry to be dragging you out of bed. Is Eric home?" Sheriff Mancuso asked.

"Of course, he is, you idiot," Kathleen Howell answered, stepping up beside her husband. "You are the ones that placed that stupid ankle monitor on him. He can't even step onto the curb out front without you sending one of your morons to check on him."

"Mrs. Howell, my apologies but I'm sure your husband is well aware of the condition of your son's bail. We do not ever need a reason to stop in to assure his location. The sooner we see him and ask him a few questions, the sooner we will be on our way," the sheriff explained.

"What kind of questions?" Lee asked. When no one answered, he explained, "I am his attorney. I have the right to be present whenever he's questioned."

"Mom, Dad, what's going on?" a voice was heard from inside the house.

Lee's eyes grew wide at the sound of his son's voice, it was only for a split second before he turned to look behind him. When he looked back towards the group, his expression read, *I told you so.*

"Sweetheart, the Sheriff woke us all up because he has nothing better to do during the night," Kathleen's voice was rude and defensive.

"Kathleen, dear," Lee was quick to cut his wife off as he touched her arm, "please head back to the kitchen to get our coffee started. Eric and I will join you shortly."

To Devan's surprise, Kathleen simply nodded her head and left without another word. He'd known her his whole life and never seen the outspoken woman act passive. He was trying to determine what was staged and why, because Lee was not surprised by the early morning visit, but was Kathleen in the dark about her son's activities? Was she unaware Eric had been leaving the house, breaking the conditions of his bail?

"Eric, can you please step out here on the porch? Anthony is going to change the battery on your monitor while Special Agent Ruddy asks you some questions," the Sheriff instructed.

Devan's eyes followed Lee's movements to monitor his behavior and reaction. They had two cases to solve, but the disappearance of Clara and Rob was more urgent than finding Susannah's killer. Devan was suspicious that Lee had something to do with his neighbor's death, regardless of the limited evidence and the luggage set hidden near the Emerson House.

But the involvement of Clara's disappearance, he wasn't sure. Eric made more sense. Devan believed Rob was simply in the wrong place at the wrong time. Hopefully, to Clara's benefit.

Eric, wearing a pair of old sweat pants and a faded t-shirt, walked barefooted onto the porch. He sat in the nearest wicker chair. He didn't say a word as Anthony squatted down. He had a specific tool to replace the batteries and the small SD chip. When he was finished, Anthony stood up and moved to the side.

"Eric, when was the last time you had contact with Clara O'Reilly?" Jack asked.

"When these guys arrested me," he answered as if it were the most obvious answer to a stupid question. "Why? Is she saying something about me?"

"Eric," Lee cautioned, drawing out his son's name with a warning expression on his face. "Don't say anything more than the answers to their questions."

"Why? She's missing me, isn't she?" Eric asked, ignoring his father's advice as he looked around the group standing before him. "Is she alright?"

"She was taken last night," Jack stated. "I assume you were here?"

Eric leaned forward as if to stand but Anthony placed a hand firmly on his shoulder, keeping him in his seat. "Why the hell aren't you looking for her? Rob Foxwood is probably behind this."

"Why do you say that?"

"He's always been jealous of our relationship. Always trying to get her to break it off with me. But Clara always stood her ground and told him to back off," Eric reported.

Devan and Jack kept their comments to themselves as they walked away from the house. Once they were in the car, they shared a look but remained quiet. Each deep in thought. Once they were in the temporary FBI office, the conference room of the Sheriff's department, Devan finally spoke. "That was interesting."

"Lee seemed genuinely surprised to see his son, don't you think? His wife, not at all. She really believed Eric was in his room all night," Jack commented. "And like both Chase and Anthony predicted, he brought up Rob."

"Yeah, he did," Devan answered thoughtfully. "Lee didn't seem surprised by anything except his son's presence in the house. I just don't understand his connection. It makes no sense. I get a weird vibe between the father and son. I don't think they really get along."

"The whole family is a bit off. I agree, Lee knows more than he's letting on. Eric appears to be living a fictional relationship with Clara. He's genuinely the real deal," Jack turned towards his subordinate, handing him a fresh mug of coffee. "How are you related to them?"

Devan sighed, "Not related. I am second cousins with Connor, our mothers are first cousins. Connor is first cousins with Eric. His father, Dan, is Kathleen's older brother. I am not related to Eric in any way, shape or form. There were occasions when the Emerson family had parties or gatherings which included both sides."

"So, not related, a cousin's cousin. Got it," Jack chuckled at the younger man's obvious annoyance. He sipped his coffee in silence for a moment, thinking back to the search of the Hawks House after returning from the tunnels. It looked obviously lived in. "Who do you think was hanging out on the third floor of the Hawks House?"

"We know it wasn't Eric with Clara, that would have been too easy. But one person seems to not have a current address, it's probably Carl Gibson," Devan speculated. "Makes the most sense. He's Clara's father and lived in that house almost twenty years. He would have the keys. The electricity and water have been left on all this time."

"How does an abandoned house still have running water and electricity? Who's paying these bills?" Jack asked with suspicion.

Devan struggled to explain what he barely understood. "I'm not really sure. My understanding is there's a trust that pays for the general maintenance and any upgrades of the home."

"And the utilities?" Jack wondered.

"Included, as well as staff and landscapers." Devan nodded.

"But if the owner has been missing for twenty years, who oversees it? Clara or the husband? Companies change hands or go under, who oversees the process? I find it hard to believe the paperwork doesn't exist." Jack was on the verge of an idea which could pan out to a lead.

But then they were interrupted by a knock. "Sir, we have pictures of the items in the suitcase."

Jack turned toward the agent at the door then motioned for the pictures to be placed on the desk. Together, the agents looked at each picture while the younger one explained, "The large bag appears to be packed for a woman and young girl for a vacation to warm climate, such as the beach. The small bag has toiletries for them. They were neatly packed and organized. The other two bags were packed hurriedly without any effort to coordinate outfits for season or event. Interestingly, there were a few maternity items. While the items were folded, there wasn't the same organization as the other two bags. The clothes in the large bag were organized together by outfits with an equal number of days for both child and adult, enough for approximately a week. The second set of bags were folded differently and organized by type and color. All the tops folded and packed together, all the bottoms, etcetera. And, not really sure if this means anything, but no shoes. The smaller of the two bags was full of lingerie and other undergarments for a woman."

"Interesting, sounds like the mother was planning a trip with her daughter," Jack concluded. "Do we know if the mother was pregnant?"

"No evidence suggesting it," Devan answered. He thought back to the incident between Carl and Matt. There were some truths to the accusations. Susannah was rumored to have a lover. Could a pregnancy have been the catalyst for her to leave her spouse? Carl was well known for his not so secret romantic liaisons with many women.

"And what about the kitchen?" Devan asked.

"Preliminary tests on the floor suggests significant bleach was used to clean up only part of the kitchen. When we pulled up the tiles, we found traces of blood." He placed the pictures from the kitchen on the table. The first showed the section of the floor cleaned with bleach, the glowing light suggesting a clean up near the table. The next picture showed the removal of tiles and the large glowing of light where the blood seeped through the tiles. "This looks like a primary crime scene. The samples of the blood were sent to the lab."

Lee thought the police would never leave. He walked back into the kitchen, expecting his son to follow, but when he reached the doorway he was pulled in by his father.

"What the hell is everyone doing here at this ungodly hour?" the old man demanded.

"Apparently Clara Gibson is missing. They seemed to think Eric had something to do with it," Lee answered.

"Hmmm," Leander snorted before he sipped his coffee. "Back in the day, the Sheriff's people knew how to treat the people running this town. You are the mayor, for crying out loud. They shouldn't be calling and asking stupid questions. And so what if the young boy has his girl up in his room. There's no crime in it. They're both consenting adults."

"Eric has Clara up in his room now?" Lee paused to look at his father before replacing the coffee pot.

"I don't know if she's up there now. Hell, I don't keep track of that boy's activities. He's always sneaking one in or out through the back entrance. The fun of the youth," the older man sighed.

"I just don't understand her appeal. He can do so much better," Kathleen stated as she sipped her coffee. She glanced at the clock, annoyed all over again at the earliness of the hour. Her father-in-law was likely to expect her to cook his breakfast instead of waiting for the cook to arrive.

"Clara Gibson is a fine looking woman. I would be chasing after her myself if I thought I could get away with it," Leander chuckled, "as a youngster, I thought she looked like her great-grandmother but damn when she returned back, I thought she was Susannah. The women in that house have always been very fine."

Lee silently agreed. It was too early in the day to get his wife started on the flaws of the other women. Both men ignored the woman's obvious bitterness as the younger man listened to his father commemorate the women of the Hawks House.

Upstairs, Eric was quick to pack his small bag before he slipped back outside. Keeping out of the lighted areas, he jogged toward the park. He was relieved that everything was previously set up. He had convinced his friend Danny to loan his motorcycle. Unable to contain his excitement, Eric began to hum as he drove up the hill towards the cabin.

Everything was going as planned, including the *surprise* visit from the sheriff's department. He couldn't wait to return to his love.

Eric didn't see the headlights following behind him.

23

nightmares

Clara dreamed of riding with Rob in his truck. She looked over and smiled as the seventeen year old version of Rob started to sing "We will Rock You" with Queen on the radio. Always at ease in his presence, she leaned back and closed her eyes. His deep voice had a lullaby effect. Clara smiled when the chorus was interrupted with his cursing at a vehicle ahead of them moving too slow. The driver ahead was unsure which right turn he wanted to make. As the truck ascended up the hills, she could smell the outdoors. Actually, it smelled more like wetness.

When Clara opened her eyes again, she was surprised to find the truck was parked beside a large lake. She could no longer feel the humming of the engine. The seat was suddenly smaller. Her leg was touching his as his arm came up on the back of the seat. His fingers softly stroked her shoulder while the other hand rested tenderly on her knee, as if testing the waters. Classical music surrounded them.

When their eyes met, her stomach tensed in anticipation of the long overdue kiss. Clara was nervous. Her heart was pounding in her chest. She saw love and passion in his eyes as he whispered, "You are so beautiful, my love."

His hand gently touched her face as he leaned in to kiss her. She closed her eyes, feeling his tongue touch her lips. His other hand was rubbing her thigh, slow long strokes from her knee up towards her hip. As he stroked, his hand continued toward her ass and squeezed. He groaned softly as he pulled her in closer.

"We are finally together. No one will stop us this time," he said as he kissed her again. His lips lingered on hers before moving towards her neck. "I will take care of you."

"Should we be doing this here," Clara started to ask, feeling an unexplained emotion as her body tensed. She felt his lips pause on her neck.

"Shh, it's alright. I promise, you'll feel so good," he whispered as his lips continued to nibble on her neck.

Distracted by movement in the back of the truck, Clara tried to turn her head but his hand on her neck held firm. "What's in the back of the truck?"

"Just the trash," he answered as his hand slid under her sweater. She could feel his clammy hand against her skin.

Clara pulled back in alarm, suddenly feeling nauseous. "You want to do this here? Now? With trash in the back?"

When he pulled back, he stared at her a moment before nodding. "You are right. Our first time should not be in the truck. It should be in a soft bed surrounded by flowers and candlelight. This is just a little foreplay before I take care of the trash."

Movement again caught her attention. As she looked out the back window, a red hand print suddenly appeared. Clara jumped back in her seat, startled. She looked over at him and then back out the window. The print appeared to be bleeding as her vision blurred. "What is that? What is happening?"

"Shh, my love, everything will be ok. Just relax and let me touch you," he whispered. His lips were back on her neck, both hands were under her sweater in search of her breasts. Instead, he touched her surgical incision, she flinched as she cried out in pain.

"Oww," Clara pushed away with a scream.

Rob's face suddenly appeared at the back window.

The fear in his steel blue eyes sent shivers down her spine. His pale face seemed to be outlined by blood. When his eyes met hers, his mouth moved as she read his lips, "Run, Clara, run!"

When Clara looked back to the person beside her, his eyes were the wrong shade of blue. And when he smiled, the dimples winked at her as he announced, "I'll take care of it. I'll be right back, love. I just need to take out the trash."

Clara's eyes were suddenly open. It's alright, only a dream she thought, looking around in the dark before she closed her eyes again. A weird one. While she was willing to admit she had many dreams involving Rob, it had been years. They never made out in his truck. Well, they never made out, period. But the sense of everything feeling so real with a slight fuzzy feel was leaving her unsettled. *It's that stupid sleepy time tea*, Clara thought with a sigh. She tried to clear her mind so she could get a few more hours of sleep.

Lying on her back, Clara could feel Connor breathing beside her. He was on his left side, his hand resting on her stomach. Clara brought her hand up to his, gently rubbing as she thought about Lila.

She looked so pale and fragile in the hospital bed, she thought. Clara hated leaving Dallas alone while they waited for the Foxwoods to arrive. Rob had been so pissed the previous night…

Clara's eyes popped open again as she remembered Rob's face peering into the back window of the truck. Damn, that was so real. He had blood all over his face and hair. And the bleeding hand print on the window, talk about creepy! Why would Rob tell her to run?

As she pondered the weirdness of her dream, her mind drifted to another scene. One of her mother's bloody face mouthing for her to run.

It played again with the steel blue eyes…each time, she turned to see violent blue eyes…

The growing chills in her spine caused Clara's hand to stop moving. *Something was off.*

Shit, everything was off, she clarified.

The person beside her was neither Rob nor Connor. The odor was wrong. Rob smelled of the outdoors and horses with occasional sawdust. And Connor always had a masculine odor, similar to aftershave. Each had the strong hands of a worker. Rob's had more calluses but Connor's had more hair on the back of his wrists. The hand on her stomach did not feel strong…

Sudden bright light turned on in the room, momentarily blinding Clara. Without thinking, she jumped into a partial sit, slowed by the pain in her pelvis. When she looked up, she stifled a scream as she read the lips of the man beside her.

"Good morning, love. Did you sleep well?"

In the late morning, Rachel was again standing in the doorway of her mother's bedroom, debating what to do when she heard knocking on the wall. She followed the sound to the back room where she found Chase, simply staring at the wall.

"Chase, what's going on?"

Without turning around, he sighed in frustration. "The carpenters back then really knew how to design the damn secret passageways. It has to be here somewhere. This is the only spot on this floor that has missing space but I can't find the door.

"With everything going on, why do you have to find it right now?"

"We can't sleep another night in this house if we can't keep all the doors locked. And we won't know if all the doors are lock if we can't find them!" Chase began knocking on the wall again.

"Have you considered going in through the Hawks House? It could be easier," Rachel suggested.

"Can't, the house is currently off limits. They have the kitchen blocked off. Tiles removed. I think they found the place where Clara's mother was killed." Chase had glanced over at her before knocking again on the wall, but turned back when he heard a gasp.

"Crime scene? They found where Susannah was killed?" Rachel had taken a step back as she placed her hand over her heart. "I can't believe this is happening! Worst, Clara's mother was killed twenty years ago and no one thought to report her missing!"

She started to pace with anxious energy, her tone bordering hysteria. "When they discovered her remains last spring, I thought Susannah was out of her house somewhere, maybe she was a victim of being in the wrong place at the wrong time or something. But now they're discovering she was killed inside her house? The only place she called home? Isn't that suppose to be the one place we should be safe? Inside her own home? And now they discover the crime scene? Susannah was killed in her kitchen? By who? With what? The butler with a candlestick?"

Chase was momentarily shocked at her sarcastic references from the popular board game but he couldn't help himself when he replied, "More likely by the lover with a vase."

"The lover with a vase? Why do you say that?" Rachel studied her fiance, a man she'd known her whole life. "Chase, what do you know?"

Chase paused in his knocking and faced Rachel. "Strictly speculation. Have you ever listened to what Clara said about the last night with her mother? Clara spent the evening with her mother. They made dinner together, cleaned up the kitchen. Clara placed the cornflower blue tablecloth on the table, in a vase she's not seen since after placing the freshly cut flowers in it. Her mother's remains were found in the cornflower blue tablecloth. And after finding the luggage set last night, I bet the rumors we heard back then are true."

"That Susannah was pregnant with her lover's child?" Rachel whispered.

"She was pregnant?" Chase stopped knocking on the wall and fully turned around to face her.

"She was but she miscarried. I think it made her wake up to the realization she was in a loveless marriage while her heart belonged to someone else. She was planning a trip at the end of the school year. While she was gone, Clara's father was going to be served papers for a divorce."

"You aren't speculating," Chase commented after studying her face. "How do you know this?"

"I'm putting all the pieces together now. Clara told me back then about a trip she was taking with her mother, made me promise not to tell Lila or Shannon. For some reason, it was to be a surprise. But now, I understand. Susannah was temporarily leaving the house under the disguise of a vacation with Clara while papers were to be served. I was eavesdropping on my mother and Susannah talking," Rachel admitted. "She was crying, upset about losing the baby. The way they talked, it wasn't Carl's baby."

"Who was the lover?" Chase asked.

"Not sure. I've heard rumors it was Matt Emerson. But he didn't live in town back then, so I don't know," Rachel admitted, unaware tears were falling.

Chase pulled her in close toward his chest. "Rach, I didn't mean to upset you."

"I can't believe I didn't put it all together before now. But seeing the luggage set and the secret passages last night, hearing about the kitchen, everything now makes sense." Rachel was quiet for a few minutes before she finally admitted, "And there's more. I can't believe I didn't put this together sooner."

Rachel stepped away to look around the room. Growing up, it had been Gigi's sitting room. One wall was covered with shelves of pictures and various mementos. Memories from her childhood with her grandmother flashed through mind.

Chase returned to knocking on the wall but stopped when she walked out to the next room.

Chase silently followed. He remained at the doorway while Rachel went into the closet. He was about to explain she was on the wrong wall when he heard the unmistakable sound of a sliding door opening.

"How did you know?" Chase was pulling out his cell to use as a flashlight. He pointed the light down towards the staircase, surprised to see shoe prints in the dust.

"This space never made sense. It used to frustrate my grandmother. She often ask who would create such a small useless space?" Rachel's voice was sad as she reached for his hand. "I think he killed my mother too."

24
wrong, all wrong

When Clara opened her eyes, she was surprised to see her father sitting on the edge of the bed. He smiled tenderly as he touched her cheek, moving a curl. "Good afternoon, princess. I was beginning to think you'd sleep the whole day away. It's well past noon."

"Daddy? What's going on?" Clara asked sleepily, feeling like a young child, her vision blurry as she fell back to sleep.

Carl walked out into the main room of the cabin. "What the hell did you give her? She's out again. She can't seem to stay awake."

"Stop worrying, she's alright," the other man answered reassuringly. Lee wasn't positive what, if anything, the boy had been giving her. He was confident the reaction of multiple drugs in her system wouldn't be too severe, temporarily, anyway. Lee gestured out towards the porch as he handed over a beer. "Felicia isn't going to be following you up here, is she?"

"Hell no. I haven't seen her since last spring. Besides, Felicia's still confined to her place. Her reckless attack on Clara last summer backfired when she fell off the porch and broke her hip," Carl reported as he sipped from his beer.

The conversation continued as the men sipped from their beer outside on the simple porch, overlooking the mountains. The cool, late morning air was hinting at the autumn season. The older cousin patiently waited as he sipped from his beer. He loved the old cabin. He was relieved years ago when his wife declared it too simple and rustic for her taste. She didn't like the idea of having to prepare simple meals. The whole concept "off the radar" was lost on her. It gave him the privacy and space he needed, especially when he was with others.

Lee gave out an unexpected chuckle at the silliness of it all, looking over his bottle as he sipped. He glanced at his watch, trying to guess the time before the drugs would take effect.

"I don't understand what she and her mother see in the damn Emerson boys," Carl was saying, unaware of the slight slur of his words. "They always think they're so smooth and in control. He could have had any girl in town or even the city but the stupid bastard tried to take my girl?"

Lee leaned forward to grab the bottle before it fell from Carl's unclenched hand and broke.

"I didn't understand what she saw in him either but let's get one thing straight, she's my girl," Lee announced as he stood up from the chair. It never dawned on him the sleeping figure was still mourning the loss of his wife while he, himself, saw the mother and daughter as one and the same girl, his girl. She would lead him to the reward in the end.

Lee stepped through the open door, back into the cabin. The main room was too dim for him to see his son as a poker stick swung on his head.

"Stupid Fuck! She's mine! MINE, MINE, MINE!" Eric yelled at the collapsed body in front of him. He tossed the weapon back towards the fireplace, giving his father one last kick. He brought his tied wrists to his mouth to pull off the restraints. "You stupid fuck!"

Eric continued to yell as he walked around the small cabin. *His perfectly laid plans were now ruined!*

"It's alright," Eric said aloud, trying to reassure himself. "We just need a new plan. I'll just pack up and bring you back to town. No one will think to look for us at my house. It's already been searched. No one in the house ever goes up to my floor. We'll be able to continue our lives together."

Relieved to have a new plan, Eric went to the kitchen to repack the bag. His extensive temper tantrum once again caused him to lose control of the situation. He didn't think to check on Clara until after he packed up his father's truck. When he turned on the light to the bedroom, Eric howled at the sight of the empty bed.

When Clara opened her eyes again, she slowly sat up and slid to the edge of the bed. She faced the window covered with an ugly brown curtain. *Where am I?* Slowly standing, her bare feet stepped cautiously on the floor. She winced slightly when she felt the slight vibration of the floorboard underneath. *Damn it! I don't want to be making any noise.*

Being hearing impaired, Clara was always cautious about being too noisy. She was probably seven or eight years old when she learned that just because she couldn't hear what she was doing, doesn't mean others around her couldn't. When she reached the dusty drapes, she pulled them back.

Surprised to see a simple door doubling as a window, Clara smiled in awe at the exquisite scene surrounding her. Not aware a haze was inhibiting her thinking, she stepped outside. *It's beautiful here, the colors are so vivid*, she thought as she inhaled the crisp smell of autumn. Looking up, she smiled at the psychedelic sky, oblivious to her bare feet trudging through the dried leaves. This dream is so much better she thought as she merged into the kaleidoscope of colors.

Clara never heard the frantic calling of her name.

Her eyes were pulled to the different shapes and hues surrounding her. The extensive combination of drugs in her system masked the pain she'd been suffering. Feeling better than she had in weeks, Clara breathed in deep the chilly air of the mountains as she slowly disappeared further into the forest.

Getting a late start to his work day, Matt stood at the window of his kitchen with his coffee, tuning out the sound of his sons playing in the yard. His wife was in the mud room attempting to organize it. She was forever losing the battle of organization, in the mud room of all places, with four boys constantly in and out. Each was always dumping a pair of shoes, a muddy stained sweatshirt or simply a dirt trail through the room. He could hear her voice but ignored her words. He could not forget the dream from the night before.

Susi was lying beside him, surrounding him with her voice as she touched his body. It seemed so real, like he was once again a young man with his forbidden lover. After the love making, he had propped himself on his forearms while he kissed her neck.

All so damn real, he thought again as he inwardly cringed and remembered how the dream ended. When he looked down at her beautiful face, the green eyes of Clara Noelle stared back at him with a satisfied smile.

What the hell is going on with me? I have never thought of her in that way. That's Susi's daughter, for crying out loud. She's my little brother's girlfriend, young enough to be my daughter. Hell, she was only a few years older than his oldest son.

Distracted, Matt pulled out his cell phone when it chimed. "Matt Emerson."

"Dad? I need help," Josh's scared voice answered.

"Joshua? What's wrong?" Matt's mind immediately cleared.

"She's dead!" The words were whispered over the phone.

Matt's blood turned cold as he stumbled back towards the table, unsure if his legs would buckle beneath him while his mind immediately went to the worst.

"What? Who?" Matt struggled to keep himself in the present as his mind went into overdrive, seeing Clara's body lying lifeless on a bed.

"My friend, Shiloh. I came to her place this morning and she's dead on the floor." Josh's voice caught as his blue eyes remained fixed on the young girl's vacant green eyes.

"You found her? Did you call 911?" He heard his father ask over the phone.

"She's dead, Dad. Did you hear me?" Josh's panic was evident in his voice.

"Joshua, listen to me. Are you at her place? I am calling the sheriff right now. Stay where you are. I am on my way. Do not talk to anyone," Matt continued to reassure his son as he reached for the house phone to call the sheriff's personal number.

Josh remained on the floor, leaning against the wall with his cell at his ear. He could hear his father's voice. He had no concept of time as people suddenly appeared into the room. His blue eyes were locked on Shiloh's empty green eyes.

"Joshua? Hey, buddy, come on, let's get you out of here." Devan was suddenly beside him, pulling him up onto his feet and out of the tiny studio apartment into the hall.

Devan had been sitting beside his uncle when the call was received. Despite having an already full day ahead of him after a busy night, he came along with his boss. Devan doubted there was a connection with this woman's death to Clara's disappearance but she was employed at the nursing home. Therefore, also connected to Eric.

"She's dead!" Josh whispered as his eyes were pulled away from hers.

Devan gently guided the younger man down to the top step as he sat beside him. "What happened?"

"She's dead! She asked me last night to come over today. She was alive yesterday. She was alive and now she's dead," Josh gasped. He leaned over to rest his head on his knees.

"Is she your girlfriend?" Devan inquired. The kid seemed to have a new girlfriend every week.

"Joshua!" Matt yelled, running up the steps. He remained standing on the steps when he reached his son. "What happened?"

"She's dead, Dad!" His voice cracked as he whispered.

Matt looked over at Devan in question.

"No idea yet. I pulled him out of the room. The others are processing the scene," Devan answered.

"I called the sheriff. Why are you here?" Matt quietly asked.

"Do you know Shiloh Prentiss?" Devan asked, ignoring the question.

"Are you here as an agent or family?"

"With everything going on right now, the FBI is taking the lead on this," Devan stated.

"Everything going on? Has something happened since Lila Foxwood's kidnapping?" Matt asked.

Devan narrowed his eyes to look over the older brother of his cousin Connor. They weren't technically related, but they had always been friendly enough. He was surprised Connor hadn't already talked to his brother today. "Clara and Rob Foxwood were taken from her home last night."

"What? How?" Matt asked.

"We don't really know much right now," Devan kept his answers vague. While they had more information than twelve hours ago, they still had nothing to help find Clara and Foxwood.

"Eric?"

"Not sure," Devan shrugged, noting the look on Josh's face.

"Listen, I need to ask a few questions and then you can take Josh home," Devan stated as his boss came out into the hall. Standing up, he made the introductions.

Jack, remembering why he placed Devan undercover, gave him a slight nod to take the lead with the questions.

"Josh, tell me what happened," Devan asked.

"I don't know. She told me last night to come over today. I did and now she's dead," Josh answered.

"What's your relationship with her?"

"Friends. We went to high school together. She's a receptionist at the nursing home," he answered quietly.

"Why did she ask you to come over?"

"She asked me to come over last night. We were both at The Lantern. I had a few drinks. She's been trying to get into nursing school. I was going to help her with the scholarship application," Josh explained as he wiped away a tear.

"Tell me what happened this morning," Devan instructed.

"I knocked on the door. It wasn't latched closed so it opened. I walked in. She was lying there when I came in."

"The door was unlocked?"

Josh simply nodded.

"Did you touch her?" When the younger man shook his head, Devan asked, "How did you know she was dead?"

"Her eyes," Josh whispered. He lowered his face into his hands, struggling to maintain his control.

Devan nodded understanding. He looked at his boss for a moment, ignoring Matt's intense stare. He knew the lawyer in him wanted to talk with his son alone but he asked the next question, "Josh, did you have sex with Shiloh?"

"Not last night. Not since high school," he answered absently. "I think she was seeing Eric."

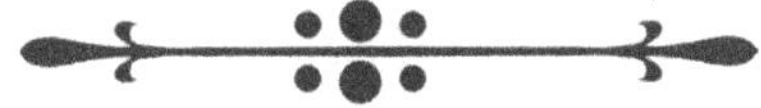

awake and alive

Clara walked along a narrow path. Everything seemed off, as her dreams often do. Her surroundings were familiar, but she wasn't sure why or how. The sky was a violet gray color with occasional patches of blue where the sun attempted to shine through. The brightness of the leaves in various autumn colors distracted her from her original task.

On the ground, Clara could feel the crunching of the leaves under her bare feet as she walked over them. It never dawned on her that she couldn't hear the sounds of the birds or the wind blowing through the leaves.

She's never hearing impaired in her dreams.

As Clara continued to look up towards the trees, she twirled around in circles. The various colors moved, similar to a kaleidoscope, she could hear a symphony playing from the bright colors as they swirled around. She chuckled as she thought how much Rob would love this!

"No he wouldn't," she laughed. She attempted to use a deep voice to mimic him. "He would be telling me to hurry up, damn it."

"Oh, Rob!" Clara stopped in mid-twirl.

"Shit, Rob! I need to find Rob," she whispered. She stumbled on the uneven terrain and landed in a pile of wet smelly leaves. Clara, still not feeling any pain, struggled to pull herself back up onto her feet.

The fall reminded her of the immediate goal: to save Rob.

She had to get to Rob. Clara couldn't remember why but that she needed to get to the lake and find him. *Were they meeting?* Her brain seemed to chant *save Rob, save Rob.* Clara believed once she found him, she would be safe and he would help get her home.

"Wait a minute," she paused in her step. "Why do I need him to be safe or to get home? I am a strong, independent woman. I can get myself home. This is my dream and I can control it. Why am I dreaming about Rob being my hero?"

"But you are the hero," a voice told her. "You need to go back to the lake and save him."

"Save him from what?" Clara whispered fearfully.

In her distraction, she stumbled when her bare foot stepped onto a sharp tree root. Not feeling the pain from the cut, she continued forward. Oblivious to her loss of balance, Clara lost her footing again and she tumbled down the hillside. During her slide, she had flashbacks of the accident, the car playing ping pong with the trees. And Rob's face popping up from the back of the truck.

When her body stopped at the bottom, Clara was already passed out.

Rob woke up to the October chill in the late afternoon with his face up towards the cloudy sky. His clothes were still damp from his late night swim. Leaning up on his elbows, he surveyed his surroundings in daylight. His eyes paused seeing the tire marks from his truck before it was pushed into the lake. Rob closed his eyes, trying to remember the night before.

He was at Clara's house but he woke up in his truck with the water filling in. He was alone in the truck, right? Did he leave an unconscious

Clara behind while he swam to the shore? Horrified, Rob leaped to his feet.

The sudden movement caused the pounding in his head to increase. *Damn it, the headache is killing me*, he thought as he closed his eyes to recall his struggle from the seatbelt the night before. *Clara wasn't beside me*, he remembered. *It was just me. The stupid bastard is too infatuated to kill her, right?*

"Shit, you need to get your lazy ass moving and find her already, Foxwood."

Visions of looking through a blood soaked rear truck window suddenly flashed through his mind. Seeing Clara struggle haunted him as he leaned into the lake to drink the cool water. Rob believed the headache was from a hangover, he had no idea of the blood or bump on his head.

After a moment, Rob looked around, then up into the sky. Once he determined the position of the sun in the overcast sky, he headed northwest away from the lake. Without any awareness of time, he followed a path with a slight incline up the mountain. He paused when he saw something in the shrubbery ahead.

"Clara?" Rob called out, breaking into a run.

Feeling a slight shake of her shoulder, Clara stirred, wincing in pain as she opened her eyes. Familiar steel blue eyes looked down at her. She smiled weakly and said his name. She could see his lips moving but couldn't hear him, nor could she focus to read his lips.

"I can't hear you, your face is blurry," Clara commented. She tried to sit, but it was too painful.

Relieved to see Clara, Rob squatted down beside her. The trained paramedic in him quickly assessed the bloody sweater, gently lifting it up, he leaned back in shock. "Shit, your side is bleeding. You have a huge gash."

He pulled off his mostly dried flannel shirt, still wearing a t-shirt underneath. Using it as a compression dressing, Rob wrapped the sleeves around her body. As he was reaching around her, he felt Clara giving him a hug.

"I'm so happy to see you, Rob. Have you been out here long? Your face is red. Why is it so red?" Clara's words slurred.

Rob leaned back after tying the improvised dressing in place. "It'll have to do for now."

When he looked into her eyes, he was confident she was under the influence of something. *She's never been this touchy feely with me*, he thought as she gently caressed his cheek. He looked down at her feet and visibly shuddered at the pain she must be feeling with the cuts. He quickly removed his work boots. Without thinking, he looked at her face, allowed her to read his lips as he explained what he was doing. He attempted to protect her feet with his socks.

Once his boots were back on, Rob stood up and reached out his hand. Clara grabbed it, needing the assistance to stand. And together the pair staggered down the hill.

no answers to more questions

It was early evening when the two city detectives stepped into the small county sheriff's department. They had hoped to catch the sheriff before he left work. Expecting a typical small town law enforcement building to be nearly vacant this time on a Friday, both Andy Sanders and Jim Walters were surprised to find the front lobby as busy as a city department on a Saturday night.

"Can I help you?" Maggie Adders, the receptionist asked. Initially annoyed at being asked to work overtime, the unexpected activities in town made for an interesting day.

"We are looking for the Sheriff, is he here?" the younger detective asked.

"He is but with all the excitement, I don't think he'll have time," the older woman explained with a glance at the phone lines. "He's currently on the phone."

"What's going on?" Jim, the older detective, asked.

"What isn't going on?" the talkative receptionist wondered. "We have a young girl murdered, a cold case warming up, and a kidnapping! We haven't had this much activity since, well, I guess that's the point.

We don't usually get this much commotion in our small town, let alone at the same time. One would think we were in the inner city!"

"Kidnapping and a murder?" the older detective's eyes squinted in question. "Who?"

"Our very own Clara Gibson! Would you believe right out of her own home? Just like her mother years ago. It's creepy how similar the cases are," Maggie answered.

"Clara Gibson O'Reilly?" Andy's eyebrows shot up in surprise.

Maggie nodded thoughtfully. "Yeah, I keep forgetting her married name. I didn't know her husband. She never came home for a visit while she was married. Her grandfather must be turning over in his grave at the idea of his granddaughter running away from town to elope with a commoner. And now she's met the same fate as her mother."

"Clara's dead?" Andy felt a flash of panic at the idea of failing to save the young mother.

"Oh, no, it was someone else that's been found dead. A younger woman." Maggie's eyes looked around the room before she lowered her voice. "Who she was, isn't really important. It's who she's involved with that's crucial! The sons of the pillars of the community! Both Lee Howell and Matt Emerson's sons. Can you believe it?"

"No, I can't," Jim stated, his eyes met his partners. The two people they came to talk with.

"It's really sad, she was hoping to start college after the holidays to be a nurse," Maggie reported.

"Did you know her well?" Andy asked.

"Not really. I went to school with her grandmother, she lives a few miles out of town with her no good fourth husband," the receptionist answered. Margaret Adders had been born and raised in the small town, she never lived beyond the five mile radius of where she currently sat. She had gone to the local community college after graduation, married her high school sweetheart, and raised her children locally. When her youngest started school, she started to work part time at the sheriff's department. She was surprised to find that she actually enjoyed the work. She, like many other town's people, had been to the city for short visits but never traveled beyond the state lines. And why would one need to? Her hometown was a hot tourist site for the nearby federal park and lakes. She lived where people came for vacation, all seasons of the year. "But you can just ask anyone. No one can keep a secret in this small town."

"No secrets?" Jim asked suspiciously. He knew the reputation of small towns.

"Hardly! People don't need to close their blinds to hide what they are doing inside, when the wrong truck is parked in the driveway," she answered absently with a glance at the phone lines, noting the sheriff was off the phone.

Before she could further comment, Tony Mancuso stepped out from his office. He paused when his eyes met those of the city detectives. They had previously met when the detectives gave notification of Jason O'Reilly's death last spring. *Not surprised*, he thought. Not with everything going on right now. Not believing in coincidences, he wondered how the current events in his town were connected with the murder from last winter in the city.

"Sheriff, I have been telling these gentlemen you're busy," Maggie started to say but stopped, flabbergasted when the sheriff waved them back.

A few minutes later, all three men were sitting in his office before Tony started, "To what do I owe this visit?"

"Sheriff, we understand you are busy but we have a theory we want to further explore regarding Jason O'Reilly's death," Detective Walters explained. "We think Jason O'Reilly was killed to help lure Clara, a young mother, back to her small hometown."

"Well, that is certainly an interesting theory," Tony stated as his suspicions were confirmed. Without giving away any suspects of his own, he asked, "Who are you looking at?"

Jim had been an officer of the law as long as the sheriff, he recognized the man's attempt to hide his own theories. Is he already working a similar angle for her disappearance or is it something else? Must be something big with the presence of the federal agents in town. Curious to see how the sheriff would play it, the detective answered cautiously, "Please understand, the individuals we want to talk with are people of interest, not suspects of Jason O'Reilly's death."

"I understand. I do have to wonder why you came here first and not to their homes for questioning," he admitted.

"We want to be respectful of your jurisdiction and get your take before speaking with them. Both are respected people in your town with frequent trips to the city," Andy started. He paused as the sheriff seemed to agree, without the names spoken out loud. "You know who we're talking about?"

"I'd be purely speculating, but seeing you two here now makes me question the odd timing. Clara moved back home after her husband disappeared. Likely someone removed him from the picture to prompt her return. And I would bet a month's salary, if I were a betting man, that those *people of interest* grew up in homes next door to Clara's," the Sheriff paused to mentally organize his thoughts.

Clara, like her mother, was a common topic of interest in town. Men fought for her attention. Granted, the attentions were subtle when each woman was young but similar disappearances at the exact same age? Same men as her mother or was it the younger generation? "You want to speak with a Howell and an Emerson, yes?"

Shocked he was correct, both the detectives were impressed the sheriff was able to theorize and narrow down the suspects so quickly. The older man spoke first, "You have suspected this? How long?"

"I honestly just started to mull this around in the last few days. The cold case was not even a case until the remains were found last spring and the list of suspects narrowed just hours ago," Tony simply shrugged before explaining. "Before I go any further, I think it's best to pull in Agent Ruddy."

Less than thirty minutes later, Jack Ruddy, the sheriff, and the city detectives were all caught up on each of their prospective cases before the agent wanted clarification. "Who exactly are you expecting to talk with?"

"Leander Howell III and Matthew Emerson," Andy answered. "Do you know where they are?"

After receiving a nod from the agent, the sheriff answered, "Matt is likely home with his family. Lee was home early this morning but that was over twelve hours ago, anything's possible now. Do you want me to call them in or give you directions to their houses?"

Carl Gibson was slow to stir. When he finally opened his eyes, he was shocked to find himself sitting on the porch of the old cabin while the sun set over the mountains. As he stared out over the porch rail, his mind began to clear as he remembered why he came out. He had followed the stupid kid to the cabin. When his cousin arrived almost immediately after, Carl went to sit with his daughter while father and son argued in the living room.

"What the hell are you doing bringing her here? The place will be swarming with those damn FBI agents! I don't want them here! I've told you before, this is my place. You need to get your own," the older man had whispered harshly. "I want you out of here!"

"Fine! Give me a few minutes to get our stuff together," the younger one had answered.

"No, she stays. You leave," Lee responded.

"I am not leaving her here with you. I won't have her subjected to your vile ways," Eric had shouted before Carl heard the sound of a face being slapped. He heard further wrestling before Lee announced, "You will not touch a hair on her, you understand. She's not yours! She never was. It's best that you get over this infatuation."

When Carl had first stepped out of the bedroom, Clara was sleeping soundly but didn't seem any worse for wear, he was relieved to see the younger man restrained. Carl was wrong to think Eric's interest in Clara had been anything but innocent over the years. He had been silently relieved when Susannah refused to consider matching the pair when they were kids, stating their daughter should be allowed to choose her future partner.

Carl had believed, at the time, Susannah was referring to her own "matching" as a child. She didn't even mention Eric being an only child and sole heir to the Howell House. His cousin did. Lee said the young couple could live in the Hawks House while their future children would have both houses. It seemed like an innocent conversation at the time.

Looking back, he felt the growing sense of doom as he once again replayed many scenes from the past in his head. Each time, Carl came to the same conclusion, Lee really was evil, just as everyone used to say when they were kids: *the E in his middle name stands for Evil*. He's the one that offered to pay for the private investigator to find Susannah. Of course the PI never found her, because Lee probably never hired one! Lee's the one that killed his wife! And now the stupid kid has actually kidnapped Clara!

After all these years, Carl finally understood what was happening to his wife when she was alive. The realization, the horror! He staggered back, as if kicked in the gut. Susannah was drugged! All that time, Lee Evil drugged her and touched her without her consent. And then Lee Evil killed her!

But why was I so blind all this time?

Carl's eyes immediately fell on the beer bottle resting on the porch rail.

Carl slowly stood up, wondering what was in his system as he reached for the unfinished bottle. He sniffed the bottle, then he broke it on the rail. Sure enough, there was a slight white residue on the inside of the bottle.

Drugs! Whenever he had doubts or concerns, the stupid bastard drugged me, just like Lee drugged poor Susannah. It would have been easy as the son of a pharmacist with the greenhouse in the back. Uncle Leander was known within the family for growing his own stuff.

Carl needed to find Lee Evil before Clara fell into the same fate as her mother.

Devan was looking over the crime scene photos when his cell chimed a text. He pulled it out distractedly reading the message. *Not encrypted at all*, he thought as he pushed the call button.

"What's going on?"

"Devan, are you available to come over to Rachel's house?" Chase asked.

Devan looked around his house filled with FBI agents. The walls of his office upstairs were covered with pictures relating to missing people and murder scenes. One half of his dining room was devoted to finding Foxwood and Clara with the other half to the recent death of the young girl found that morning. His living room wall had recent pictures believed to be related to Susannah's disappearance and death. To say he had a lot on his plate was an understatement.

"Is it urgent? Something related to Clara's kidnapping?"

"It's important but not an emergency. I doubt it's related to Clara's current situation. More of a new cold case. It can wait," Chase decided. As he talked, his eyes scanned Elizabeth MacKenzie's bedroom, stopping at a photo of a man, very familiar.

"Chase, what's going on?" Devan asked over the phone.

"I would rather not say over the phone. When you come over, I'll show you and let you decide the importance."

Devan was about to agree to stop in but paused to read a text from his boss. *What now*, he wondered before he returned to the call. "Chase, there's something I need to check out. Will you be at Rachel's?"

"With all this going on, hell no!" he answered as he closed the bedroom door, returning to Rachel's room. "We are going to be staying at my place. When you have time, text me. We'll either be at the hospital or at the farm. I'll meet you at her house. It might be less creepy if it's during the day anyway."

Devan paused as his overworked brain processed the conversation. Knowing Chase, he likely searched the Taylor House for the hidden passages and found something. And the recent death of Elizabeth Mackenzie could mean her death was not from natural causes. Another hidden homicide, the victim was the director of nursing at the nursing home. And her house was conveniently next to the Howell House. "Shit! Did Rachel put it together?"

"We have our theories. But Devan, she remembers things from twenty years ago. Things that wouldn't mean anything to a child but," Chase paused.

"But not over the phone," Devan agreed. "I don't know how long before I get back to you."

Chase hung up his cell. Remaining in the doorway, he watched as Rachel quickly but efficiently packed her bags. When she was finished, they carried everything out to his truck. He was relieved the driveway was on the side of the house opposite Howell House. It would be more difficult to monitor Rachel's coming and going.

"Chase, what about my car? I'm going to need it to get to work," Rachel argued.

"Right now, I'll be driving you. I don't want you going anywhere by yourself." He reached over for her hand and squeezed it before bringing it up to kiss. "Sweetheart, I promise, we'll get through this."

"Smells like it's going to rain," Rob heard Clara say as he reached for her hand to pull her up the steep incline.

"I hope not. We won't get far in the cold wet dark," Rob answered. He tilted his head up to the darkening sky and realized she was right.

Not much time before the sky opens up. Looking around, he attempted to gauge where exactly they were in the damn forest to determine the best direction to go. Rob knew better than to ignore her sense of smell. Clara was well known in the group for having the nose of a bloodhound. If she smelled rain, they needed shelter fast. That's when he spotted the large boulder ahead. *That would have to do*, he thought as he looked back.

Clara's eyes followed Rob's as he pointed ahead and nodded, answering the slight squeeze in her hand with a squeeze of her own as she allowed him to lead her up the hill.

After he settled her on the ground in the shallow cave, Rob motioned he would be back. A bit of time passed before he returned with large branches to cover the opening to further shelter them from the weather and assist with hiding. While he didn't actually see the perpetrator, he believed it to be Eric. He knew the family had an old mountain cabin somewhere nearby.

In the last of the evening light, Rob turned to face Clara as he spoke, "You doing alright?"

Clara nodded. "In the morning, you should head out. I'll never make it back."

Rob didn't have the heart to admit he wouldn't either. He was too dehydrated and weak but he didn't want her to give up hope. Instead, he responded, "We're both tired. After we get some sleep, we'll be better refreshed to head towards town in the morning."

"Rob, there's no way I can walk the distance back, not now after the accident. My leg and pelvis are killing me. It takes us hours on a horse to reach this area, it'll take me weeks to cover the distance," Clara admitted.

"You know where we are?" Rob was impressed.

"Of course, Rachel is the one without a sense of direction. Rob, I grew up in the area, the same as you. Just because I was gone a few years, doesn't mean I don't remember my way around the woods. Well, I could if I wasn't in so much pain." Clara leaned back against the boulder, wincing slightly as she shifted her weight, trying to find a less painful position. She leaned into his side for warmth. She was unaware the heat of his body was actually from a fever setting in.

Just as he was unaware the coolness of her body was from shock.

"Here comes the rain," he heard her mumble with the sudden downpour.

"Yup, never underestimate the power of Clara's nose," Rob mumbled, knowing his comment went unheard as he placed his arm around her. He sighed in contentment, leaning down to kiss her head before falling into a deep sleep.

In town, Connor was pacing in the family room. He had called off work and stayed home with Reese and Hailey during the day. Feeling paranoid, the children remained at his side the whole time. Many offered to stay with them but he declined the assistance. When they slept, he remained in the hall between their rooms.

How could Clara have been taken from her own place? Even with someone in the same room with her, how did this happen? Connor could not stop comparing the similarities of Clara's disappearance to her mother's: children upstairs asleep, suddenly gone, perhaps from the kitchen each time and a shadow.

But what about the differences? Clara's mother was rumored to have a lover, even his brother claimed Susannah was seeing someone other than himself. Clara didn't have another lover besides him, did she? Her mother also left town unexpectedly for days and weeks at a time, leaving the young child to stay with friends. Clara didn't do that.

And most importantly, someone else was with Clara, also taken. If they make it out alive, Connor decided, he will owe Foxwood big time.

If? Connor slid down the wall of the young girl's room. *I need to keep it positive. When she and Foxwood return home, everything will change. We won't be staying here anymore, that's for sure.* He leaned over to her small bookshelf in the shape of a dollhouse and pulled out a book. He sadly smiled as he remembered Clara reading this book to the kids. Throughout the summer, Hailey insisted on this book being read, "Harvey the Harvester." Such a simple story.

Replacing the book, Connor went into the boy's room. Again he sat down next to the bookshelf, this one shaped like a barn, and studied the books. Reese had a significantly less number of books compared to his sister. That's when he remembered the conversation he overheard, when the boy asked Hailey where the book came from.

Unable to relax his thoughts, Connor pulled out the biggest book: "Mother Goose's Collection of Nursery Rhymes" and started to read.

An hour later, Connor was awakened by small hands lifting his head and placing a pillow underneath, followed by a tiny blanket placed over his arms.

"Hailey, why aren't you sleeping?"

"NaNa flay bo na-na," Hailey whispered, touching his hair, similar to when he tucked the young girl in bed earlier in the night. When he nodded agreement, the young girl settled down beside him with her own pillow and blanket.

Before dawn, Connor woke up covered with three toddler size blankets and both Hailey and Reese sprawled out on either side of him.

Connor couldn't face another day in Clara's home without any news. Nor could he set foot in the kitchen to prepare a simple meal. He packed day bags for each child and loaded them into his SUV. They would spend the day at his loft.

Not wanting to deal with people in general, he stopped at the Tim Hortons drive thru for breakfast before taking the children to his place.

When they arrived, they set up a blanket for a picnic. While they ate, he pulled out his tablet, and together, each child picked out colors for new bedding and clothes.

Connor wasn't giving up on Clara returning home safe and sound, of course not. He was giving up on the place she called home since the spring. Too many odd instances occurred at that house. When she returned home, he would personally change all the locks and reset the code for the alarm, as well as the garage door.

In the meantime, he was distracting everyone with online marathon shopping. Once they arrived at his place, he realized his loft wasn't properly suited for young children. What bachelor pad is? What started as shopping for the basic childproof safety gadgets, turned into an excessive spree that would have brought his previous girlfriends to tears of joy. Connor sighed at the irony. Clara was the only one that ever resisted such excessive shopping, while the other women complained he didn't shop enough.

He smiled down at Reese and Hailey on either side of him and chuckled at the fun they were having. Clara was always resistant to Connor's attempt to splurge on her but her children had no such qualms. By lunch time, he had purchased each child two separate bedroom sets complete with bedding and enough clothes to fill the closets at each the loft and lake house. Winter was coming, they would need the warmer clothes anyway.

After completing the latest purchase of clothes, the children were becoming restless. And no wonder, Connor thought with a quick glance at this watch. It was already half past noon.

"Shopping is hard work! I'm starving, Connor," Reese announced, his sister agreed. The children followed him into the kitchen as he decided what to make for lunch. "How come we don't do that shopping more often?"

"Your mother doesn't like me spending money and spoiling everyone," he explained while pulling out the makings for homemade mac-n-cheese. He pulled up stools to allow the children to help.

"What's not to like? I like it when you buy us stuff," the preschooler announced. "The clothes shopping isn't as much fun as the toys, but the bedroom set was fun! I can't believe you got me bunk beds! Wait until I tell Sawyer, he'll be able to spend the night!"

"This heavy shopping isn't going to happen often, Reese. Your mother is an independent woman, always has been. She believes in paying her way. If she wants something, she works for it and earns it. She wants both you and Hailey to do the same," Connor explained as the children each took turns grating the cheese in the shredder.

"Why?"

"When you work hard for what you need, you have a better appreciation for what you have. If you spend your whole life having everything handed to you, you won't have any respect for your things or others. Your mother wants both of you to be independent when you grow up."

"So if Mommy was here right now, we wouldn't have been shopping online?"

"No," Connor admitted.

"Will she be unhappy with me if I let you buy me those things?"

"No, your mother will not be upset with either of you," he clarified. *She will be upset with me*, he thought with a smile. "But, if we are all staying together in different houses, you and your sister need a place to sleep, right? And winter is coming."

"Winter is coming! That means we'll also need snow clothes and toys. Connor, after lunch, we need to do more shopping!" Reese stated happily.

After lunch, the shopping continued, progressing to outdoor toys and playhouses. Instead of actually purchasing the items, he decided to place them on a wish list. He needed to save something for their birthdays and Christmas, didn't he?

After putting the children into his own bed, Connor found himself once again restless as he waited for a word, anything about Clara. He sent another text to his cousin, Devan, asking if there was an update. Tossing his phone onto the counter, he sighed in frustration.

He found himself standing at the large window in the front of his loft overlooking Main Street, watching as others in town continued about their lives. People were being dropped off and others were dashing quickly through the rain.

Connor sighed again as he thought of Clara. *Where are you, Sweetheart? Are you somewhere dry out of the rainstorm? Is Foxwood keeping you safe? Or were you two separated?* His forehead touched the glass, hundreds of worst case scenarios were going through his mind.

A few blocks over, Matt wasn't surprised to open his front door to the Sheriff, but he was surprised to see the detectives from the city. He remained silent, waiting for one of the other men to speak first.

"Matt, who is it?" his wife called from behind. Talia reached for her husband's hand as she greeted the sheriff. They had just finished cleaning up the kitchen from dinner but still had plenty of cake left.

She sensed her husband's hesitation and concern. Were they here for Josh, her stepson? Or was the visit about Clara? Talia was well aware of her husband's infatuation with the young girl's mother, though it was long before her time. She refused to believe Matt had anything to do with either woman's disappearance.

"Talia, I am sorry to be stopping in so late on a Friday evening unannounced. Matt, we have a few questions for you," Tony explained.

"In my study," Matt responded, stepping back. He knew his wife was about to offer coffee, he sighed, not wanting them in the house any longer than was necessary.

"I'm sure a pot of hot coffee will help you all, especially if you're working late into the night in this horrible weather," Talia offered, quickly dismissing herself.

"Dad, when are you going to help me with my homework?"

Everyone turned to see a boy close to his teen years standing on the landing of the grand staircase looking down into the large formal foyer.

"Alex, we'll only be a few minutes of your father's time," the Sheriff answered.

Matt nodded in agreement when his son dramatically sighed and turned back up the steps to his room. He felt an odd sense of pride at his second son wishing to tackle his assignments on a non-school night. *He's going to be successful*, he thought tangibly, while leading the men into his study.

Matt closed the door, then gestured toward the sitting area of his large study. He remained silent as the introductions were made. He was relieved it had nothing to do with the death of the girl that morning. While he didn't believe his son killed the unfortunate girl, he wasn't sure what kind of evidence was found that could make Josh a suspect or even be cause for reasonable doubt.

"How old is your son?" Detective Sanders asked, attempting to ease the tension in the room.

"Alex is twelve," Matt answered. He debated a moment before expanding on the topic, understanding the purpose of the question. "He's very goal oriented and focused. He has plans for the weekend and wants to get his assignments out of the way."

"Is he your only son?" The other detective asked.

"He's my second of four sons," Matt answered, continuing without a pause. "Why are you gentlemen here? It isn't to inquire about my family, the sheriff could have spared you the time or even a simple search would have provided you with the information."

The two city detectives shared a glance before the younger detective asked the next question, "What was your relationship with Jason O'Reilly?"

"Strictly business. He was hired to look over the Trusts," Matt answered, not sure what this was about. He briefly explained the nature of the Trusts of the four houses in town.

"Didn't you think he would have a conflict of interest with his wife being attached to the homes?"

"Not at all. At first, I didn't even know who his wife was, let alone that he was married. I found out when I went to his office. He had a picture of her on his desk," he admitted. He didn't mention the fact the single picture first looked like his Susi before he saw it up close.

"Clara O'Reilly grew up in the house next to yours, did she not? You weren't invited to her wedding?" the older detective asked.

Matt first looked over at the sheriff before he turned back to the detective. "Yes, I grew up in the house next to hers. But I moved to the city for college before she was born. I only had the occasional contact with her as a child when I came home to visit the family. I was told after the fact that she was married. I believe she eloped. As it was, she had yet to receive the key to her family home."

"What do you mean, receive the key?" the older detective asked.

"It's simply the term used," Matt shrugged. "There are two ways the house is legally handed down to the next generation, either by a parent signing the house and Trust over to the next in line, often the first child, or with the death of the current heir. In Clara's case, it had been declared years ago that her mother willingly left town. Neither Clara or her husband would be able to properly access the accounts. As it was, Jason only had access to the bookkeeping, not the money."

"Why did you hire him specifically?"

"My law firm already had his company on retainer. My father assigned oversight of the Trusts to me. I requested a forensic accountant and he was recommended," Matt stated.

"When was the last time you saw him?"

"We met a few times after the initial meeting but corresponded by email or phone mainly," Matt paused a moment in thought. "I would have to say it's been over two years since we last met face to face."

"You didn't think it was odd when you hadn't heard from him for several months?"

"No, his company sent an email about the reassignment to another accountant," Matt explained as he looked around the group. "Before you ask, no, I didn't think anything of it. It happens. People leave the company, get transferred out to another location or change positions within the company. It's no different than having another doctor see you at your next appointment."

Before the next question was asked, there was a soft knock on the door as it opened. Matt was immediately on his feet. Knowing Talia, he was expecting her to have the tea cart with coffee and likely the leftover cake. She could never resist being a hostess.

Quietly, she pushed the cart towards her husband and discreetly left without a word. Matt contained his amusement when he looked down at the cart. *Talk about meeting halfway*, he thought. Talia had arranged a pot of hot coffee with the cream and sugar. Instead of mugs, she had placed to-go cups with lids.

"Gentlemen, what would you like in your coffee?" Matt looked around the room. He quickly prepared the coffees as requested and passed out a piece of cake to everyone before sitting back down. "Where were we?"

"What is your relationship to Leander Howell?"

"Which one?" Matt wondered.

"Excuse me?" Detective Sanders asked.

"There's currently three Leander Howells living in that house: Leander Howell, Jr., Lee E. Howell the third and L. Eric Howell the fourth," Matt explained with a hint of an amused smile.

The older detective detected the sarcastic tone while his partner clarified, "The third."

"I wouldn't call it a relationship. His second wife is my father's younger sister," he explained.

"Doesn't that make him your uncle?" Sanders clarified, noticing the man visibly wince.

"Uncle is too respectful of a title," Matt replied as cautiously as he could. "I prefer to avoid any misunderstandings that may even hint at a relationship. He's married to my father's sister."

"Second wife? What happened to the first? Is he divorced?" Sanders asked.

"My understanding is she died due to an undiagnosed medical condition. Lee was several years ahead of me in school. I believe he met his wife in college. When they moved back here, I was in middle school. Honestly, I don't even know the full story. Just that Kathleen married him afterwards." Matt thought it was an interesting question as he was confident the first wife was still in the picture when his aunt's relationship started. At the time, Matt was relieved it had distracted his father's attention from his own activities.

Andy nodded, mentally noting to look into the cause of death.

The sheriff had remained quiet, eating his cake as the city detectives asked the questions. He was already thinking about the many deaths in Lee's wake. His first wife's death had been suspicious but ultimately ruled natural causes. His mother had died fairly young of cardiac arrest, believed to have an undiagnosed congenital heart defect. His sister died before her ninth birthday from a tragic sledding accident.

"What was Mrs. O'Reilly's relationship with Mr. Howell?"

"I honestly couldn't answer that. Clara grew up in the house next to his. His son, the fourth, who goes by Eric, is roughly her age so I assume they went to school together. Eric hired her at the nursing home when she moved back to town."

"Eric hired her? Did she reach out to him first?" Detective Walters asked. They had the phone records indicating Eric initiated the first contact by phone but she could have reached out first in person or sent in her resume.

Matt sat back in his seat. The shock was obvious on his face as he appeared to process the information. Where was this leading? Did they believe Eric had something to do with Jason's death? Did Eric kill to facilitate her move back home, closer to him?

"I honestly don't know who contacted who first. My family owns the nursing facility. I oversee the legal and financial aspects. I don't do the hiring," Matt stated distractedly.

"When did you learn Mrs. O'Reilly was moving back to town and would be working at the nursing home?"

Matt's blue eyes met the sheriff's brown as he mentally reviewed the previous spring's calendar. "I saw Clara for the first time since she was a child at Beth MacKenzie's funeral, but we didn't talk. She kept to her close circle of friends. She did talk with Eric then but I have no clue what they discussed. Shortly after, Eric informed me we needed to contract a physical therapist until a new one was hired. I approved the contract, but he didn't mention Clara."

"When did you learn she would be working at your place?" Sanders repeated when Matt paused.

"Probably the week before she moved. Tony's wife had me review the rental contract before signing. Clara was the tenant listed on the contract. I remember thinking it would be great to have Jason locally. I figured that was why he was no longer with the company."

"I understand she is currently involved with your brother?" Andy continued when Matt simply kept his eyes on his and nodded. "When did your brother learn Mrs. O'Reilly was returning?"

"I don't know. We didn't talk about it until after we learned her mother's remains were found a few weeks after she arrived back in town. Connor was the one who informed me it was Susannah," Matt answered sadly.

"Is that when you learned they were dating?"

"No, they weren't seeing each other yet. I wasn't aware of his interest in her at that point. I asked how she was doing, if she needed anything. We are talking about a close family friend. Her mother and I went to school together. I had only seen Clara around town. It was a couple of weeks after that when we were reacquainted at a fundraiser," Matt commented as he mentally reviewed the interaction between them.

"That's when I learned Connor was developing romantic feelings for her. I told him to stay away from her, she was still married. Connor said Clara was looking into a lawyer to start the divorce process," Matt reported as he stood up, attempting to hide his emotions. "Can I offer you gentlemen something stronger than the coffee?"

When everyone else declined, Matt poured himself a short glass of whiskey. He sipped before returning to his seat. "You don't think Connor had anything to do with Jason's death, do you?"

"Do you?" Jim asked. He didn't believe it, but was curious if the brother did. He already knew the younger brother had not been to the city within the time frame.

"No." Matt didn't even hesitate. "Hell, Tony, you are practically family!"

"Matt, relax, they don't have any evidence to suggest it," the sheriff quickly responded. He was having enough trouble accepting someone he knew was killing people in his town. But the killer being a Howell was an easy enough sell. They were one weird family. Influential, yes, but weird regardless.

"If you don't think Connor did it, then why are you talking to me?" Matt demanded.

"You are connected to the nursing home, as was Eric. You might have more insight," Andy explained.

"Connor is more connected than I am. Being there almost every day, he would have more insight." Matt's voice gave away to his agitation.

"Possibly but he's not really up to answering any questions right now," Tony stated.

Matt nodded in agreement before sipping his drink. "The last month has been rough for them."

"What do you mean?" Andy asked, looking at both Tony and Matt.

"Clara was involved in an accident. She's not even been home for two weeks and now she's missing. Her friend, also in the accident, was taken into protective custody," the sheriff answered.

"Yeah, we heard about that. Joel Montgomery is a detective from our district. What were her injuries?"

"Clara was shot in the arm and chest, suffered a broken arm, collar bone, pelvis, and leg. She underwent multiple surgeries. The last I saw her a couple of nights ago, she was slow on her feet, using a cane. Damn it, Tony, you don't have any word on her yet?" Matt asked as he stood up, feeling restless. He walked over to the other side of the room to glance out the window. All he could see was the dark forest.

"The FBI has taken point on that case. My department is taking the lead on the murder from this morning," Tony answered quietly. He wasn't even going to mention the missing luggage set found below the house they were all standing in.

"So, it's a confirmed murder?"

"Afraid so."

"Shiloh was seeing Eric?"

"Yes. Her neighbor confirmed he was there last night. The rain is coming down pretty hard," Tony commented as the wind blew the rain hard against the house.

"I would hate to be out in the woods right now," Matt mumbled. He turned suddenly. "Tony, you already searched the Howell House, correct? But what about the hunting cabin?"

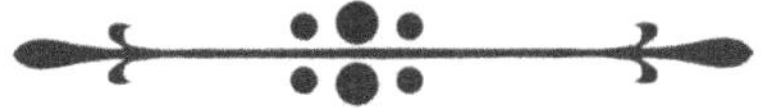

27 *a lead*

Clara snuggled in closer as she shivered in the cool air. Despite being tucked out of the pouring rain, she felt wet. She was unaware her sweater was soaked in blood, her wound hidden by the throbbing pain on her whole left side. She attempted to shift her weight, not aware the movement caused her to groan loudly.

A moment later, Clara was surprised to see the shrubbery moving in the darkness. Suddenly, a shadowy face appeared a split second before she felt a sharp prick in her arm.

Rob's eyes flew open at the sound of Clara's scream. Momentarily confused, he watched a shadow move beside Clara. Her continued screaming pulled him into action. Immediately on his feet, he tackled the shadow, forgetting they were on a steep spot on the hill.

Both Rob and the shadow fell into the pouring rain, sliding down the hill. When they landed, Rob was on the bottom and a familiar voice started yelling.

"Damn, bastard! You need to leave her alone, you hear me? She's not yours, she's mine," he yelled as they both began to throw punches.

Under normal circumstances, Rob would have pummeled the guy without breaking a sweat, but his current situation was far from normal.

Weak from dehydration with a pounding headache, he was lucky to be standing. Hell, he wasn't even sure what day it was.

Clara, painfully followed down the hill behind them and tried to shove him off Rob. But the shadow shrugged her off, sending her falling back.

She didn't see the gun nor hear it fire, but she smelled it! Terrified at the thought of Rob getting shot, Clara looked around for something to use as a weapon.

Rob pushed the gun away from his face as he fought to roll over to get the upper hand. During the roll, the gun went off again, narrowly missing its target. He pushed the gun out of the assailant's hand, but he was too weak to maintain control as they rolled again, sliding further down the hill. They landed with Rob again on the bottom, without the gun.

The shadow wrapped his hands tight around Rob's neck as he squeezed, causing Rob's vision to narrow as he thought it would be goodnight for sure.

But the sound of Clara screaming pulled Rob back into the fight. No way in hell was Rob going to lose. He would not leave her alone with him, especially knowing what he was capable of. Rob kicked his feet into the air, attempting to pull himself up into a sitting position.

Suddenly, the pressure was gone!

Clara swung hard with a tree branch. Screaming, she continued to swing at the shadow. Not able to hear Rob's shouts, she continued swinging until Rob's warm strong arms pulled her back away from the bleeding body.

Not wanting to stick around for round two, Rob grabbed the branch and threw it away as he struggled to pull Clara towards the treeline. Turning her around, he cradled her face as he talked, "Clara, we're ok, we are going to get out of here. I promise."

When her eyes met his, Clara shook her head, her voice filled with defeat. "I can't, it hurts too much. Everything's spinning. I'm fading. Just hide me somewhere."

"Hey, sweetheart, none of that loser talk. We got this," Rob whispered, wiping the tears from her face with his thumbs.

Clara shook her head sadly. "I can't. I'm not meant to survive this. Just go. The quicker you get away, the safer it'll be for you. I never meant to pull you into this mess."

Rob stared at her in confusion, *what the hell is she talking about? What mess?* "Clara, we'll get through this together. I promise, you'll be home soon with your kids and Connor."

Clara's eyes were on his, realizing she was able to make out his features and read his lips. The sun was rising. Bringing along hope at the start of a new day as her usual nighttime despair began to fade.

At the moment, Clara wasn't able to distinguish reality from fiction. Nor did she care. She only wanted to lie down and sleep.

Rob pulled her in for a quick hug, his eyes looked over her shoulder at the unconscious body. How the hell did he find us? He never figured the man to be a tracker, never.

When Rob reached for her good hand, he noted Clara's side was bleeding again. Damn it!

"We need to get out of here." Rob turned to lead her away from the small clearing. Looking towards the sky, he oriented himself as he altered the direction towards home.

Rob wasn't sure how long it was before Clara suddenly dropped to her knees. Pausing long enough to lift her up into his arms, before continuing. He never saw the excessive blood on her clothes. It was probably just as well because he would have panicked. His mind drifted back to the fun they had together, hiking and riding in the woods when they were kids.

The Sheriff was able to confirm the location of the cabin, and it was just before dawn when he and his deputies, along with the FBI started out into the mountains. The city detectives remained in town since this didn't involve their investigation.

"How did we not know about this place before?" Special Agent Jack Ruddy asked Devan from the passenger seat as they followed the sheriff's vehicle up an old muddy road.

"I never knew anything about it, not sure Uncle Tony did either. It appears to be off the grid, no electricity or running water. I think it was in the first Leander's name. Uncle Tony said Matt only knows of it because Kathleen, Lee's wife, complained that the getaway cabin wasn't even worth mentioning. She hated the simplicity of it. She wanted something more elaborate with servants but the Trust only covered servants for the large house," Devan explained as the old narrow road opened to a clearing.

After a final turn, a small simple cabin appeared, overlooking a great panoramic view. Parked in front was an old beat up car, newly washed from the storm the night before.

As everyone stepped from the vehicles, Jack gave instructions for some to surround the cabin as others were instructed to clear the surrounding area. He and Devan slowly advanced onto the porch, noting the broken beer bottle. Inside, they saw drops of blood on the floor and the surrounding mess, obvious signs of a struggle.

But the small cabin was empty.

Jack went to the door to bring in the forensic team as the sheriff reported the owner of the vehicle. "The car is registered to Shiloh, the girl found dead yesterday morning. What did you find inside?"

"Empty and signs of a struggle," Ruddy answered, wondering if there were any trained K-9s in the area. "No evidence either Clara or Rob were here."

"Clara was. I found a few curly hairs on the pillow in the bedroom," Devan announced from the doorway. He had already donned plastic gloves. He didn't mention the blond hairs on the other pillow or where his thoughts went but the grim tone in his voice betrayed him. The bed was obviously slept in by two people but the temperature on the bed was cool. Likely no one slept in it last night.

Jack looked back towards Devan. "How sure are you it's Clara's?"

"On a scale of 1 to 10, I'd say 9," he answered confidently. "We need to get a tracker up here."

Dallas was sitting with his wife as she slept. He had remained at her side throughout another long night. He could see her parents as they entered the ICU area just as his cell vibrated.

"Devan, did you find them?"

"Not yet. Listen, I really hate to pull you away from Lila but any chance you can meet me? We have a lead but it takes us into the mountains."

"Does Connor know?"

"What am I going to tell him? We don't have anything concrete yet," he answered.

"Alright, send me the coordinates. I'll give you a heads up on my ETA once I get to my vehicle," Dallas answered as his eyes met Allison's. He leaned down to kiss Lila's forehead before he faced his in-laws. "Please stay with her until I return. I need to head out."

Allison seemed to understand where he was going, her hand touched his arm as he stepped past her. "Dallas, please find them. Bring our boy back home."

Dallas only nodded before leaving the room.

"How do you know he's going to help with the search? Why would they even call him?" Mitch asked with irritation.

"He's a ranger at the park. Why wouldn't they call him?" Allison answered. "Chase said he was one of the best trackers in the county."

An hour later, around ten in the morning, Dallas was once again preparing to lead a group into the forest. The others quietly watched as he slowly walked the perimeter of the cabin to best determine where to enter into the woods.

"We'll start from here," he announced, tightening his pack around his shoulders.

"Why?" Jack asked. When everyone in the group looked at him, he explained, "I'm not judging, just curious why here and not the other spots."

"It's a direct line from the open back door and it's a newly made path," Dallas shrugged. He could never explain why he chose one path or the other. People would think he was crazy if he actually stated the truth. He usually went with his gut.

As he started onto the path, Devan, Jack, and Anthony followed. The sheriff was staying behind to help coordinate the search with another ranger. The other FBI agents were gathering evidence from the vehicle and the cabin, while a few others were setting up the mobile lab to confirm who was actually present and involved in the altercations. They were also researching the drugs found scattered throughout the cabin.

The group was quiet as they followed Dallas down a slow descent. Jack wasn't sure how the younger man knew when to turn right or left. He knew the hard rain from the previous night cleared the trails of footprints. So, how did Dallas know?

Anthony, worked with Dallas on a lot of rescue missions. He had seen him find many missing people, most before it was too late. He stopped asking questions a long time ago.

In the third hour, Dallas came to a stop. He gestured with his hand to wait as he climbed a short steep hill. Halfway up, he called down for one of them to come up with the camera. A few minutes later, Devan was at his side. "You pulled the short straw?"

"Not really," he answered, looking around. There was a pool of blood on the ground and smears of blood around the shallow cave. "Shit, one of them must be hurt."

"It's likely one or both fell somewhere. The rain washed the blood and the footprints away but over here, you can see the blood trail leads down this side of the hill. Clara walked down and Foxwood rolled or fell," Dallas explained absently as he cautiously started down the hill. "Clara's the one bleeding."

Devan had been taking pictures of the area with his cell phone. He returned it to his pocket before he followed, pausing at the last part. "How do you know it was her?"

"Smaller footprints around blood. She was still having pain walking the other day. It's not a stretch to know she would have trouble out here." Dallas' voice was void of emotion. "It's rough terrain for miles around. Only those in good shape have any business hiking in these areas. I don't think Foxwood chose the path. He knows they're being followed and they're in serious trouble. But he has a few things going for him. Look here, a syringe."

Devan looked where he pointed, pulled out his phone to snap a few shots before picking up the needle with a plastic bag.

"Like what?" Devan asked as he reached for a branch to assist in controlling his descent. "What does Foxwood have going for him?"

"He knows these woods, he knows how to survive out here and he's a stubborn son of a bitch. As long as Clara's beside him, he won't give up," Dallas answered as he started down the slope.

At the clearing below, Devan called for the others to join them while Dallas squatted down as he studied the surrounding area. There was another pool of blood and splatters all around. "There was an altercation here."

Dallas stood up as he pointed near the shrubs. "Sir? There's a tree branch over here with blood on it." Everyone looked to where he pointed when something else caught his eye. "I have a gun over here."

Dallas squatted down again as he looked over the ground. "The altercation happened early this morning after the storm. You can see the footprints. Two left together and the other went down that way."

"Which trail should we follow?" Jack wondered. "If Clara left with the assailant, Foxwood could be in trouble on his own."

Dallas stood up again as he closed his eyes a moment: *where are you, Clara? Show me which way you went.* When he opened his eyes, Dallas could see where the path was slightly disturbed. He headed in that direction as he answered, "Foxwood's an asshole, annoying and extremely condescending, but he would never leave Clara alone in the woods. Never. Foxwood left with her. If the other guy had her, nothing short of Rob's death would have kept him from following. He would have crawled if he had to."

They all looked around as Dallas did, not knowing what he was looking for. When he looked back before starting on the trail he paused. "What?"

"What are you looking for?" Devan asked.

"Just looking for a body. Foxwood isn't dead in the shrubs so he obviously went with Clara in this direction," Dallas explained with a gesture towards a barely made trail.

"He's right. Foxwood would never leave a woman in distress, especially one alone in the woods. He's always adored Clara. Foxwood knows the area as well as Dallas. He was probably finally able to choose the direction," Anthony agreed before following onto the newly made trail.

The agents had taken more pictures and placed the gun and branch in plastic bags before following the others. "How do you know he picked the direction?"

"Cause the sun was up and he's finally heading towards home," Dallas answered from the head of the pack.

Anthony was nodding in agreement.

Everyone was quiet as they quickly negotiated the narrow path. Dallas was now able to follow actual signs. It wasn't long before the path disappeared. He motioned for the others to take a break as he squatted down to survey the path. The footprints seemed to disappear without warning which made him wonder. Dallas reached over to move away a branch.

Under the shrubbery, his little sister was snuggled up next to his brother-in-law. Clara had blood all over her side as Rob held her protectively close to his chest. Both were pale, but breathing, Dallas realized as relief washed over him.

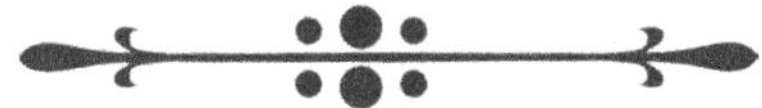

28
another long night

Connor had agreed to let Rachel and Chase stay with the children after he put them to bed. Once he was confident both Reese and Hailey were in good hands at his loft, he drove over to Clara's house. He needed to pick up a few more things.

Entering Clara's room, Connor looked around as he walked over to her side of the bed. Unable to keep still, he touched everything on her bedside table. Her hearing aid case, the picture of the children. He replaced it before opening the drawer.

On the top, was an old composition book. He pulled it out and debated reading it. When he opened it, a sheet of paper fell onto his lap. He picked it up, when he realized what it was, Connor slid down onto the floor, overcome with grief.

A letter addressed to him from Clara, in the case of her death:

Dear Connor,

If you are reading this, you're either being very snoopy, which I know to not be true, or I am gone. These last few months have taught me many things. First, life is short and can be taken without warning. And second, my love for you.

I have always felt an attachment to you, even when I was young. I remember so many moments together, the time you rescued me from the slide, the many times you carried me home, and most importantly, when you've always seemed to magically appear when I needed you the most.

I never told you, but the first time you knocked on my college dorm door, I was feeling overwhelmed and homesick. When I opened the door and saw your smiling face, I was finally able to breathe easy, knowing I was making the right decision for myself.

You are my rock. You have supported me throughout my life. Without you, I would have crumbled long ago. You were the light in my darkness that guided me through the tunnel full of shadows and fear. Even when I didn't know it, you were the calm in my storm. Thank you for always loving me, believing in me, and protecting me. I love you, Connor.

I wish we had more time together and I am sorry that it happened as it did. After everything you've done for me, I have one last thing to ask of you. Please take care of Reese and Hailey.

Take them far away from here. Please raise them away from Evil. Protect them from the harsh secrets of their grandparents. Show them, as you showed me, the love and light of the world. Let them know how much Jason and I loved them. Please, love them and treat them as if they were your own.

I am so sorry to ask so much of you but I can finally face Evil, knowing you are caring for my children. You have given me the strength, wisdom, and courage to see this through.

Connor, I wish I had spoken the words out loud, I love you. I always have. Please be safe and remember me with love.

Always yours,
Clara

Connor remained sitting on the floor oblivious to his surroundings as his world fell around him. He never heard the cell phone ringing, nor the calling of his name.

"Connor? Connor, are you up here?" Devan was suddenly standing over him. He was shocked by his appearance, grief evident on his face. "Connor, don't you have your cell on you?"

Connor was fading into his crumbling world, unable to process his cousins' words. He looked over at Devan, squatted down beside him. "What?"

"Hey Connor, Clara's alright, we found them!" Devan squeezed his shoulder. "Clara's at the hospital. I'm taking you to her."

Devan's eye caught the letter in his hand. He gently pulled it away, read over it quickly, thinking, *shit. After everything she's been through this year alone, of course Clara would write a damn goodbye letter.* Standing, Devan reached down for Connor's hand.

Connor studied the hand before reaching out to stand up. "You really found her? You actually saw her? She's alive? Is she hurt?"

The waiting room was getting crowded as Connor sat quietly beside his cousin. Devan had called Chase and Rachel, to inform them both Rob and Clara were found and being treated at the hospital. They agreed to remain at Connor's loft with the children.

During the short drive to the hospital, Devan had provided a rough overview of her injuries: many scratches and cuts, likely dehydration and loss of blood from a gunshot wound. Connor didn't take well to the news of Clara being shot again, but his cousin assured him the injury wasn't as severe as the previous ones. His thoughts came to a halt when Dr. Grayson Taylor came out of the emergency department.

Everyone stopped talking as they all stood up, waiting to hear what the doctor had to say.

Grayson looked around the room, he had initially planned to speak with Clara and Rob's family separately but realized that was not likely to happen. He looked at each person, able to place a name to most. He kept it simple. "They're both severely dehydrated. Rob has a concussion from a couple of hits to his head and has pneumonia. Clara's lost a lot of blood from a major laceration and a gunshot wound, both on her side. They both have many cuts and bruises. We'll need some time to complete our assessments, get them cleaned up, and into their rooms before you can see them."

As he stepped away, Connor followed him toward the door. "Grayson, let me back there, please. I need to see her."

Grayson studied his friend. *He looks terrible*, he thought to himself. "Connor, she's awake but fighting us. You don't want to see her like this."

"I've seen her unconscious, covered in blood, at death's door. If she's awake, then it can't be worse than before." He reached into his pocket to pull out a case. "I have her hearing aids. She can't hear without them. She may fight less if she can hear you, and if she sees me. Please, let me help."

Grayson lowered his voice, "Connor, she's been drugged. She's on something heavy and appears to be having strong hallucinations. We've already sent a sample of her blood to the lab. In the meantime, the FBI has informed me of drugs found. No name of the drug itself, but it appears to be homemade version of lysergic acid diethylamide.

"LSD? What the hell?" Connor was shocked as he followed Grayson through the emergency room.

After sunrise, Clara opened her eyes, startled to find herself, once again, in a hospital bed. She looked around in the dim light at the telemetry and the IV pole near her bed. Her vitals looked good. She tried to move but winced in pain from her whole left side.

What the hell happened?

She felt a touch on her hand, looking down, she realized it was Connor's. Her eyes nervously followed the hand up to his face. "Connor? What happened? Didn't I go home? Was it all a dream?"

Before answering, Connor reached for her hearing aids. He waited a moment for them to turn on before speaking. "Hey, beautiful. Yes, you were home. We don't really know what happened but you're safe and back with us."

"Where was I? What happened?" Clara demanded as she had a flashback of Rob touching her face and kissing her. She winced again in pain as she attempted to sit up. "Why am I hurting so much?"

"How much pain are you having?" Connor asked with concern. He still could not believe she was shot again. He debated allowing her anything more with all the drugs still metabolizing in her system.

"None if I don't move," she admitted. Clara shifted her weight a moment before wiggling her feet. She bent her knees slowly but she stopped when her pain worsened. "It feels like I broke my pelvis and was shot again."

Connor sighed as he realized she was smart enough to know what happened to her body. "Yeah, I guess you would know what that feels like."

"I was shot again?" she asked, alarmed. "Where? Who the hell shot me?"

"Like I said, we don't really have many details. We were hoping either you or Foxwood could tell us," he answered. Connor watched as her face clouded up as she appeared to be thinking. Does she not remember it? Her doctor seemed to think the drugs in her system were hallucinogenic, which immediately made everyone assume it was Eric. The questions remained, why did he take both her and Foxwood? Why not just leave him? Eric had to have known having Foxwood there would have been much more challenging.

As much as the guy got on his nerves, Foxwood was loyal to Clara. And for that, Connor would always be grateful to him. Of course, there was the nagging question he could not bring himself to ask out loud, why was Foxwood at her house so late in the evening in the first place?

"Rob? What did Rob have to do with this?" Clara closed her eyes, searching her memory. She could see him in her home, kissing her and letting his lips linger near hers. Good God! Was she kissing Rob? When? Why?

Connor watched her face as she appeared to be struggling with her emotions. He saw fear and panic mixed with confusion. He gently squeezed her hand to calm her but when her eyes met his, he saw panic. "Clara, you and Foxwood were both taken from your place. Dallas found you together out in the forest."

"We were taken? From my house?" This time Clara winced but ignored the pain when she sat up. "Where are Reese and Hailey?"

Connor scooted over to sit beside her on the bed, framing her face with his hands. "Clara, the children are good. Nothing happened to them. They weren't hurt."

"No? You wouldn't lie to me?" she accused as she studied his face. Something was off but she couldn't determine what it was.

"Clara, I would never lie to you, especially about the welfare of your children," he answered, deciding he wouldn't take offense.

"Where are they?" she demanded, watching him look at his watch.

"They're downstairs at daycare. Rachel dropped them off. I'll bring them up when you're ready to see them," he answered quietly as he reached over to remove a curl from her face before kissing her forehead.

"Rob and I were taken? We were found in the woods?" Clara whispered slowly.

As she said it, she saw glimpses of him holding her hand while she stumbled around the rough terrain. She could see the concern on his face as he pulled her close into his arms and held her…she remembered the feeling of comfort by the closeness of his body and the warmth as she leaned into his. But the images had a dream like quality, they didn't feel like a memory. She looked up into Connor's concerned brown eyes. He was holding something back, but she didn't know what. "What does Rob say happened?"

"He's still unconscious. Foxwood has pneumonia and a severe concussion. He's being closely monitored," Connor explained, reaching for her hand. He studied it, noting again, the lack of defensive wounds on her hands and forearms. Whereas Foxwood not only had extensive defensive wounds on his hands and arms, he also had extensive contusions throughout his body suggesting a major altercation.

Clara was somehow shot by an unregistered gun and had extensive cuts on her feet, likely from running on harsh terrain with only socks. *Foxwood's socks*, he reminded himself grumpily. *What the hell happened*, Connor wondered as he realized he couldn't stop obsessing about Clara alone with Foxwood. Why were they alone together so late into the night and how did they come to be so deep into the forest?

"You have to understand how it was back then," Allison Foxwood was sitting beside her daughter. Her eyes watched Lila's hand reach for Dallas'. Lila listened in silent shock to the news her brother recently learned. The dim light from the telemetry hid Allison's fear as she explained why she birthed a child from another man, not her lawful spouse.

Rob, resting barely three feet away in his bed, appeared to be sleeping. The light sounds of beeping from the monitors provided a constant reminder of the current events.

As he listened, Dallas wasn't sure who was more surprised by the information, he or Lila. But it certainly put everything from his childhood into better light. It explained so much.

"When we were all in elementary school, hell it could have been earlier, our parents arranged our lives and who we would be best partnered with." Allison let out a harsh chuckle. "We weren't really aware of it and likely would never have learned about it. Everyone was that sneaky, including the teachers. We had the same classes together, and were partners in labs and on group assignments. By middle school and early high school, we would be dating with the expectation of getting married after graduation. It didn't matter if it was high school or college. If anyone attempted to stray from the expected relationship, parents often dealt with it quickly.

"But then the accident happened. It created a domino effect that changed everything! That's when we learned how our parents had been arranging our marriages, hell, our whole lives. Apparently, it had been going on for generations," she stated quietly.

"What accident?" Lila asked in disbelief. She wondered if her parents had made arrangements for her, but was too terrified to ask. Somehow, it would have made her lose even more respect.

"A week after graduation, Aaron Hawks missed the turn on route 20. Ironically, very similar to Clara and Shannon's accident on Labor Day weekend. He and three other boys were killed. Felicia Gerwin, as well as three other girls, were suddenly without their expected mates. She was to marry Aaron. Her parents immediately began negotiations with Eli and Dianne Thompson." Allison paused for a moment as she remembered the argument with her parents. She looked up at Dallas when she continued, "I was originally expected to marry Zachariah Thompson."

The room was silent while she allowed the younger couple to digest the information. Dallas simply shook his head, Clara was right. His mother was originally expected to marry into the Hawks family. She was raised to believe she would one day be the lady of the Hawks House. What a shock it had to be, instead of moving into one of the most prestigious houses in town, she was being lowered to the third son of a farmer. He almost chuckled out loud at the cruelty and humor.

"That still doesn't explain how he fathered your child while you were legally wed to Dad," Lila stated harshly.

"Lila, I never pretended to be perfect! I had a difficult time letting go of Zac. He was my best friend and my first love! I loved him my whole life. How was I supposed to turn off my emotions? I couldn't. I continued to see him secretly until my wedding. Early in our marriage, your father and I had a fight. I don't even know how it started, probably something stupid and minor but it blew up horribly. We each said some hurtful things. Your dad admitted he only married me to get back at Zac. Said he didn't love me." Allison stood up to walk to the window in the dim light.

"I left him that night. Stormed out of the room and left the house as soon as I had a small bag packed. Zac was already living on his own in his house which was originally built for us. I stayed with him. Somehow, the secret was kept from my parents. But your dad came to see me. He even apologized. Ultimately, I agreed to return to him. Within weeks, we learned I was pregnant. We never discussed it." She shrugged sadly as she admitted, "I never really knew for sure, until now."

The younger couple remained quiet as Allison quietly left the room. No one was aware of Rob stirring slightly as he digested the news.

everything's different but nothing's changed

The next afternoon, Rob opened his eyes and answered to a soft knock on the door. He was surprised to see Devan and another man standing at the doorway.

"Hey, Rob, how are you feeling?" Devan inquired. He watched as the man before him simply shrugged with his eyes on his boss. He introduced the two before he continued, "We have some questions. Are you up to it?"

Rob shrugged his agreement before the agents sat down.

"What happened?" Devan started. He was curious to see where Foxwood would begin. Like Connor, he couldn't understand why he would be at Clara's home so late. They had learned, Rob had come across shocking news about his family and his biological father, which likely led to him drinking heavily.

But why go to Clara's? Why not to Chase?

"I don't even know where to begin," Rob admitted. So much had changed and yet nothing was different.

"Well, I have a good idea why you were upset and drinking but why go to Clara's?" the younger agent challenged, ignoring the warning look from his boss.

"Clara's one of my best friends," Rob chuckled harshly. "It's not like I had many options. Lila was in the hospital, guarded by that stupid fuck of a husband. Chase, well, I don't know. Maybe I didn't want to talk to him just yet. My mother is more of a mother than an aunt to him, I didn't want to ruin his relationship with her. Rachel is too close to Chase. He never allowed me to get very close to her anyway. Shannon is, God knows where and that leaves Clara. Aside from Chase, she's the closest one. Clara doesn't judge, only listens, which is really ironic. She's the one that's hearing impaired, but the best listener."

"I remember being in the kitchen telling her about my DNA results," Rob paused as he saw a flash of Clara lying passed out across the kitchen floor. He could only see someone in dark clothing kneeling down beside her. "Is she alright?"

"She will be," Agent Ruddy answered. "What happened in the kitchen?"

"I don't really know. I was sitting at the table and Clara was standing at the counter. The next thing I know, I'm on the floor with a horrible headache. I could barely keep my eyes open, but I saw Clara crumble to the floor," he stated distantly. He looked at Devan. "Was she drugged? She had to have been drugged cause there was something off about her."

"Like what?"

She never allowed me to get so close physically before, he thought, remembering the kiss. The feel of her lips as his lingered a bit while his hands started to explore her body under her sweater. He remembered his harsh laugh when she finally pushed him back. The fear in her eyes was what reigned him in. But when she turned to walk away, the unsteady limp reminded him of her recent physical injuries.

"Crap, she was probably on pain meds," Rob answered his own question. Devan gave a questioning look. "Nothing has ever happened between us. Not now or back in high school. When I showed up at her place, she opened the door and let me in without a thought. She's more or less always accepted me as I am. She's never tried to change me. I was so relieved to see her, I kissed her. I'm now realizing she likely had taken her pain meds and was slow to react."

"She's always been so easy to read and pulls back," Rob let out a harsh chuckle. "But that night, my drunken mind seemed to think I had a chance and pushed a bit further. She was slower to react but she set me straight. She shoved me away and told me Connor was on his way home."

Devan could feel his temper rising on Connor's behalf: the stupid ass actually made a move on her when she was vulnerable?

As if he could read his mind, Foxwood continued, "She didn't make a scene, but instead, put me in my place without so much as raising her voice. We went into the kitchen and talked while coffee brewed. She was texting on her cell, likely demanding Chase come get my sorry ass before her boyfriend returned home to kill me."

Rob was silent for a moment as he saw flashes of himself waking up in the back of his truck.

Devan noted the change in his expression and body language but remained quiet.

"Karma is a bitch, isn't it? I woke up in the back of my truck," he hesitated as he saw flashes of Clara struggling with someone in the cab before he blacked out again. He struggled to find the words to describe the scene.

"Next thing I remember, I was pinned down in my truck with the water flooding in. I was ready to call it quits, but images of Clara struggling against this guy in dark clothes kept surfacing in my mind."

The agents silently listened as Rob shared what he remembered from his time in the back of his truck. He kept to the facts, limiting the details of waking up trapped inside his sinking truck. He omitted his emotions of fear and panic, even acceptance of drowning, until he remembered Clara. He skipped over his feelings for her which gave him the motivation to free himself. When he woke up along the bank of the lake the next morning, Rob's focus was on finding Clara.

"It took me a while to get my bearings. It couldn't have been too far away that I saw Clara passed out on the hillside. She was still wearing the same sweater and jeans without socks. At first, she was so still, I thought she was dead," Rob's voice cracked. He looked down at his hands, the cuts were already healing. He reminded himself, Clara's alive, she's going to be alright. Or as alright as anyone can be after this.

"She had blood on her feet and her side, scratches on her face. I kneeled down to touch her face and her eyes opened. She smiled at me. Then, I heard her name being called. She couldn't hear a damn thing, didn't have her hearing aids on. I wasn't going to take any chances so I pulled her up and we hiked a bit until I could get us some coverage to hide. I wanted to be sure it was the good guys that found us, not the bad guys."

Devan only listened, while his boss took notes. Foxwood continued to describe how he removed his socks to provide some protection on Clara's bare feet. He described the climb up a steep hill, half carrying her as they stumbled into the shallow cave. He talked about how Clara would comment on the rain, explaining how she could smell but not hear it. He mentioned they both seemed to fall asleep, leaving out the details of being cuddled close. Regardless, Devan could see them both in the narrow spot, curled up together out of fear and need for warmth. Rob all protective with Clara scared and likely drugged. He could picture everything as the details were provided.

"I never imagined the bastard for a tracker. He's always so damn polished with the expensive shoes and manicured nails. Never in a million years would I have expected him to be able to find us. Never, especially with the heavy rain in the dark. We were well hidden and far away from the main trail. He should have never been able to find us in the dark, never. I was shocked to see him, covered in blood and mud. The look in his eyes, so deranged. I honestly thought I was done," Rob let out a harsh laugh. "But you know what they say, always know your opponent. There's always been something off about that guy!"

Rob talked about the struggle, falling down the steep hill as they wrestled. "Out of nowhere, I see a gun. Again, never even considered he owned one, let alone knew how to use it. Honestly, I'm surprised he didn't kill me. I was too dehydrated and weak, shit. I'm shocked a bullet didn't find me when it went off either time."

Rob was quiet as the scene played out in his mind. He heard Clara screaming in the background, felt the surprisingly strong grip around his neck as his vision blurred and darkened. And the sudden relief of pressure and flow of air when Clara swung a branch like a baseball bat at the damn bastard.

"Dehydrated and weak from not eating, you were still able to come out on top. I've seen you fight before. It's not really surprising you won against Eric, gun or no gun," Devan reassured. He was well aware of Foxwood's injuries but he still had yet to see the other guy.

Rob looked strangely at Devan and shook his head. "What the hell are you talking about?"

Devan looked at his boss before looking back at Foxwood. "What do you mean?"

"Why are you talking about Eric? It wasn't Eric out in the forest," Rob announced with certainty. When he realized both agents were looking at each other in confusion, he explained. "It was Lee Howell, the damn mayor. And as shocking as it is, I still didn't have the upper hand. Clara saved me."

Jack's eyes narrowed in question. "Clara?"

Foxwood saw Clara once again swinging the tree branch down on the prone body as she continued to beat him as if he were a pinata suddenly loose from its anchor. Shit, he realized for the first time, did she kill him? Rob never even thought to check for a pulse. He was too focused on getting her out of there. Rob looked between the agents. "What does Clara say happened?"

"We haven't talked with her yet. It's been reported she hasn't given any details," Jack answered. "But right now, we want to hear what you remember. Tell us how Clara saved you."

Rob was momentarily confused. Suddenly, he doubted the details as he remembered them. Were they really accurate? Shit, did Clara really kill the town mayor to save him? Looking at Devan with a shrug. "It's like I already said, Lee somehow found us in the dark. Well, it was just before daybreak, getting lighter as we fought. He grabbed me and we, more or less, wrestled down the hill. A gun appeared in his hand. We struggled as I tried to push it out of his hand. It went off, twice I think, before he dropped it. He had me pinned down on the ground, strangling me. And then he wasn't."

He paused for a moment, his hand to his throat. "Clara had a small tree branch and swung it at him like a baseball bat. It took me a moment to catch my breath before I could stop her. She kept swinging at him and he just laid there, not moving. Clara was hysterical at this point, yelling at him. I grabbed her and decided it was time to get out of dodge. I didn't even think to stop and check on him. We both needed medical attention. She was bleeding."

Everyone was quiet a moment before Rob looked over. "I can't believe she killed him. Is she really alright? She lost so much blood. I have no idea what it was from."

"She's going to be alright. Like you, she's dehydrated. Cuts on her feet but you gave her your socks. Her side opened up, probably from a tumble down the hillside. Her clavicle and pelvis refractured," Devan paused a moment.

"And? What? What aren't you telling me?" Rob demanded.

"Clara was shot. A bullet went through the knotted flannel around her waist. The material slowed it down but it still found its way into her side," Devan informed him. And just as he expected, Foxwood almost leaped from the bed as he sat up straight, swinging his legs over the edge.

"The wound itself is not bad. Like I said, the angle couldn't have been better planned, it went through the knotted material. It was superficial."

"Why the hell didn't she say anything? I would have carried her back," he declared, worry was evident on his face.

"Rob, she probably didn't even feel it. She had a significant amount of drugs in her system," Jack explained, "and there was no way you could have carried her back, lost and dehydrated."

Rob looked between the two. "I wasn't lost. I knew where we were. Hell, so did she. I just didn't have the strength. You thought the stupid bastard was Eric? You didn't find him yet, did you? If you give me a map, I could probably show you where we left him."

"We found the spot but no body," Devan explained.

"Really? How do you know you were in the right place?"

"We found the gun and the branch with the blood, hell we even saw the shallow cave you sheltered in but no body. As far as we could tell, the person walked off on his own," Jack answered.

"Lee walked off on his own? I doubt it. Clara was swinging at him pretty good. He had to have been seriously injured." Rob again looked between the two agents before his steel blue eyes settled on the older agent. "You're a tracker?"

"Me? A tracker," Jack chuckled. "Not at all. From what I hear, we had the best tracker in the county lead us straight to you two."

Rob looked over to Devan, his eyebrows wrinkled in confusion.

Devan couldn't keep the irony out of his voice. "Yes, Dallas assisted us. He led us from the cabin where, until before this conversation, we thought the two of you were held. Dallas found the small cave, the torn path down the hill and where you fought. He was able to read the scene and tell us what happened."

"Dallas led you guys?" Rob let out a harsh chuckle. "He only agreed to it so he could find Clara. If it were just me, he wouldn't have bothered."

"Rob, whatever went on between you two before this is over, Dallas had your back. He was the one that said you would never willingly leave

Clara alone or with someone dangerous. He always believed you'd keep her safe. And you did," Devan said.

Shortly after the agents left Rob's room, Devan received a text message from his Uncle Tony. "We seem to be looking for two people. The time of death for Shiloh is the same time the intruder carried Foxwood and Clara out to the truck. Eric could have killed the girl while Lee grabbed the two of them. Foxwood was nearly killed because he was in the wrong place at the wrong time. Both Eric and Lee were home when we showed up early the next morning."

• • • •

After struggling, Evil finally made his way inside. The first stop was the sink where he drank directly from the faucet. He was parched! The past week had been nothing but hell as he struggled to return to civilization. His original plan was to hide in his cabin to recover from his injuries. The cabin had been off the radar and was well stocked with non-perishable food and well water. He even had medicines and dressings.

But the place had been over run by the damn cops. The stupid boy! All the work and the years of planning, possibly down the drain. All because of the boy's stupid misplaced infatuation.

Instead, he stumbled home. But he couldn't deal with the idea of being so far from his babydoll. And honestly, the idea of spending another night next to his wife had become repulsive. He had no choice but to wait until dark to make his way here. He looked down at his muddy self.

He quickly removed his clothes to place everything into the washer. Then, he slowly ascended the stairs. He ran the water in the shower while he studied his injuries. Mostly bruises and shallow cuts, and the damn rib fractures. Nothing life threatening, he was confident, before stepping into the shower.

After the water ran cold, he stepped out and dried off. Wearing only a towel, he went back downstairs in search of food. He was famished. While the food was heating up, Evil debated the sleepy time tea. He knew the doctored tea would help him sleep and heal.

Not much time left before December 25th, less than three months! He needed to regain his strength and proceed with his plan.

Decision made, Evil finished his meal and brought the tea upstairs to bed.

After he drank, Evil slept blissfully in the clean fresh sheets for the first time since his babydoll went missing.

Connor was agitated at being away from Clara longer than he had anticipated. Using his hospital ID to enter the ICU and a wave at the extra security, his gait was purposeful in his excitement to see his girl. He came to a sudden stop at the nurse's station, Foxwood was sitting beside Clara on her bed, exactly where he wanted to be.

She was smiling while she looked up at Rob. He was holding her hand while she appeared to be shaking her head. Wishing he could read lips, Connor wondered what they were talking about. He reminded himself of the letter he read just before she was found. Clara had signed it 'always yours.'

Clara chose you, you idiot, not him. She doesn't like his jealous streak and she won't like yours either if she sees it, he warned himself. Connor debated continuing into the room but wanted to see what happened.

He grabbed a chart with Clara's latest blood results, pretending to be assessing her current status. When he looked up again, Foxwood was kissing her forehead as she appeared to be squeezing his hand. There was something different in her eyes when she looked at him, making him wonder, what the hell happened out there?

"Connor, are those Clara's latest blood tests?"

Connor turned to see Grayson Taylor standing beside him. He nodded and handed over the clipboard.

Dr. Taylor studied the labs before glancing up at his friend. "Looks like the drugs have metabolized out of her system. White blood cell count continues to be normal and her hemoglobin levels are improving. Let's go tell her the good news."

He kept the chart in his hand as they both headed towards her room. "Clara?"

Rob was already heading out of the room when the doctors entered. "Don't go too far, Rob. I'm heading into your room next."

Connor noted Clara's eyes watched Rob leave the room before she appeared to hesitantly nod at Grayson.

"Clara, is it alright if Connor stays while we talk?" Grayson asked as he reached for the hand sanitizer and rubbed his hands together.

"Of course, as long as I have the final say in any decision," Clara stated.

Grayson chuckled with a glance back at his friend. It surprised him when Connor stopped flirting and dating all the various female staff. And after seeing them together during her last admission, he knew. His buddy was head over heels in love with the woman before him. "Has he been bullying his way into your care?"

Before Clara could answer, he pulled out his stethoscope and listened to her chest. He asked her to sit up away from the pillows so he could listen to her lungs and assess her pain levels when she moved. Grayson remained silent when she waved Connor away when he stepped forward. He continued with the exam.

"The nurse reports you've not had any pain medicine yet today. How bad is it?"

"It's there only if I breathe deep, lift my left arm too high, or move my left leg," Clara answered dismissively.

"What about your feet?" Grayson asked while he gently removed the dressing. The deep lacerations and scratches were already scabbing over.

"They don't really hurt. I haven't been allowed out of bed yet. Can't you have them remove the catheter so I can start using the bathroom like a normal person?" Clara requested, avoiding Connor's eyes. "When will I be discharged?"

"Well, your labs look good, wounds show no sign of infection. We can have you moved out of the unit and onto the floor this afternoon," he announced as he wrote in her chart.

"Why onto the floor? Why can't I just be discharged?"

Grayson paused in his writing as his eyes met hers. "I think you need to be monitored a little longer."

"What exactly are you monitoring? My blood? What's wrong with it?"

"Your blood readings look good. Why the rush?"

"I would be more comfortable at home in my own bed with my children nearby. I don't like them seeing me in here all the time. Unless you're more concerned about my mental health. I could see a therapist as an outpatient," Clara shrugged slightly, stopping when a sharp pain raced across her left shoulder.

The facial grimacing was noted by both doctors but neither mentioned it.

"We don't even know if you can walk yet," Connor challenged.

The words were not even fully out of his mouth before Clara was already flipping the covers off and slowly scooting to the edge of the bed. She couldn't prevent the facial grimacing as she moved.

"Clara," Connor started as he watched her face. The simple movements were obviously causing her pain but he stopped when Grayson held up his hand. "You aren't seriously considering discharging today?"

Grayson shrugged as they both watched her reach down for her catheter bag before slowly standing up. Her nurse was suddenly beside her to assist with the short walk across the room to a chair.

"Is there a reason you don't want her home? Trouble in paradise?" Grayson questioned after they returned to the nurse's station.

"I don't think she's ready yet. She's been through so much these last few months," Connor shrugged, unable to find the correct words to express his concerns.

"I would have thought you'd want her away from Rob. But Connor, seriously, Clara's right. She'll be more comfortable at home. Her kids are there. You are there, right?" Grayson turned to step in front of him. "What's going on?"

"There's something off but I can't put my finger on it. She's not the same person. Whenever I touch her, there's fear and something else in her eyes," Connor paused a moment as he looked around them. Assured no one was close enough to listen, he continued, "I don't think I'm equipped to give her the help she needs."

Grayson studied his friend a moment before he answered, "You're right, Connor. She's different than she was last spring. Hell, forget what she went through during the spring and summer. Just the accident and the shooting would change anyone. I can't even begin to imagine the emotional strain of being kidnapped from her own home and being drugged. You know there will be some harsh moments ahead, night terrors and possibly even hallucinations. If she wants you with her, you'll both figure it out. Even more important, you'll be there for her as well as her children."

"But that's just the thing, why the hell would she want to return home to the scene of the crime? Wouldn't that be causing more issues? Don't you think it's weird she won't talk about it," Connor demanded.

"She claims she doesn't remember details but you're right, there could be some hidden anxiety returning to her place," Grayson allowed. "If that's your biggest concern, don't you have, what, four different residences you could be bringing her home to?"

When Connor remained quiet, Grayson continued, "Who is to say you need to return to her duplex. You have her mansion, your flat, and the lake house. All have advantages and plenty of space. If nothing else, you can keep the bastard guessing where she is until he's found. Hell, you have enough money to rent out another place if you find them all lacking or you can stay with family or friends. The point, Connor, is talk to her. Discuss where you both want to be and make it happen."

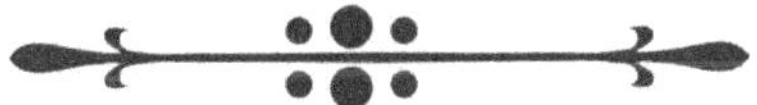

30

the arrest

Agents Jack and Devan pulled up outside the Howell house with a warrant for Leander Eric Howell IV's arrest. The current warrant only allowed search for his rooms, not the whole house. They weren't sure if he was home but they were giving agents enough time to cover the house, as well as the tunnel, to assure he didn't escape, if he was indeed home.

A few moments later, the door was opened by Kathleen Howell. She immediately showed her displeasure at seeing the agents on her porch. She outwardly groaned. "To what do I owe the displeasure?"

"Good day, Mrs. Howell. We would like to speak with your son," Jack answered.

Kathleen was tempted to slam the door in their faces but she was worried. She hadn't seen either her husband or son since Friday morning, before the weekend. When she tried to call Lee, his cell always went to his voicemail, as it did when he was off doing who knew what with his whores. Seeing the warrant, Kathleen had no choice but to simply step back with a gesture towards the grand staircase.

"Not sure of much anymore. His room is on the third floor, the first door on the left."

"Thank you, Mrs. Howell," Jack responded, following Devan up the stairs.

When Devan reached the bedroom door, he didn't even bother knocking. He opened the door and turned on the light. It was more a small apartment than a simple bedroom. They stepped into an entertainment room complete with large screen TV, large sofa, and small kitchenette in the corner. Without looking around, he continued toward the closed door.

Again, Devan turned on the light, surprised to find Eric actually in his bed. He walked over and immediately pulled him up to a sitting position, annoyed to find him naked.

"What the fuck?" Eric yelled as he tried to scoot back.

"Eric, get dressed. We are taking you down to the station," Devan patiently explained. He grabbed clothes from the nearby chair and tossed them into his lap as he read him his rights. "Do you understand these rights?"

"Son of a lawyer, of course I know my rights," Eric snarled as he stood to pull up his pants. "That damn maid will be fired for letting you all inside. She should have just come up for me instead of letting you idiots in. Wait until my dad hears about this."

"Honestly, Eric, I'm surprised your father isn't here. Where is he?" Devan asked, keeping him distracted as his boss walked around the room. He noted the guitar propped up in the corner of the room. He remembered Connor's comment about Billy Kingsley's death being from a guitar string to the throat. Devan made a mental note to have the agents entering bag and tag it, as well as any guitar string found in the room. If they were going to get Eric for the string of murders, they needed evidence connecting him to each victim. Employment and relationships alone would not convict him.

Jack noted the window facing the Hawks House gave a great view into the rooms of the second floor, if the blinds were open, but remembered Clara's room was on the other side. *But whose room was over here*, he wondered as he slowly walked around the room. He was disappointed to not see any traces of mud on the floor or even the shoes. Equally disappointing was no signs of blood or drugs anywhere. He stepped into the closet to look around.

When Jack returned, Eric was already dressed and standing up. He stepped back when he saw the handcuffs in Devan's hands. "Are those really necessary? And why are we doing this?"

"Eric, I just read you your rights. Of course, I'm going to handcuff you. It'll be my pleasure. You are under arrest for violating the conditions of your release on bail," Devan explained.

"What? How?" Eric demanded to know as they started toward the staircase.

Down in the foyer, his grandfather was standing with his mother. "Boy, just keep your mouth shut until your father arrives."

Devan was surprised Eric did just that. Not a word came from his mouth during the short trip to the station. Eric was escorted into the interview room and left alone. The agents went to the neighboring room to observe his behavior. This gave the others time to collect any forensics from his rooms to help build their case against him.

If nothing else, Eric was arrested for violation of the terms of his release on bail. Any type of drugs found in his private quarters was also considered a violation and promoted keeping him behind bars until his hearing.

They were both surprised by what was found.

Initial walk-through of Eric's rooms gave no significant evidence of Eric's involvement with Clara's kidnapping. But they had plenty of forensics from Shiloh's apartment and a witness. As they were preparing the interview, the younger agent was looking over pictures from Eric's rooms. Devan wasn't sure what he was looking for, but he had a gut feeling. He sent a text message to one of the agents still at the house before following Ruddy into the other room.

"It's about bloody time! Where the hell's my father?" Eric demanded when the agents entered the small room. "He'll have me out of here in no time, as well as your badges. You have no right to keep me here!"

"Actually, we do. Like I said, you were arrested in violation of the terms of your release on bail," Devan placed a copy of a photo of Eric sitting in The Lantern on the same evening of Shiloh's murder. "According to this photo, you violated the house arrest. This photo places you out of your house. We will be officially adding murder charges."

It was music to his ears, Eric thought excitedly as he fought to keep his face angry. So, he really did kill his old man? They could not have found Foxwood yet. Who would ever think to look for him in the lake? Eric was surprised they found his father already. Not many people knew about the stupid cabin, so off the grid.

Keeping with the charade, Eric asked, "Who's death?"

"Shiloh Prentiss," Jack answered. Both agents watched his reaction. The sheriff and his sons were watching from behind the double mirror.

"What? What the hell are you talking about?" Eric's face paled as he leaned back into his chair.

"Shiloh was found dead in her apartment early Friday morning. Her death has been ruled a homicide. We have many witnesses that put you with her the evening before, within the window of her death. This makes you the last to see her alive," Jack explained.

"She's dead? How? Why is this happening to me again?" Eric wondered out loud, totally perplexed.

"Why does what keep happening?" Devan was trying to gauge his involvement.

"Everyone keeps dying!" Eric howled, looking between the two agents. "Why? Why me?"

"Who else has died?" Jack inquired as he leaned forward onto the table.

"Billy, Tasha, Lauren. All worked at our nursing home and now they are dead. I didn't kill Shiloh or any of them!"

Eric fought to keep his composure. He wondered what kind of evidence they had and debated how to answer. If he admitted to being at her place, Shiloh was alive when he left, he was basically signing away his freedom for being out on his parole. It was an easier charge than murder.

But he didn't murder Shiloh or anyone else. His father's death was self-defense. Well, he did kill the stupid farmer, Eric admitted to himself as he laughed with glee in his mind.

"If you didn't kill Shiloh, who did?" The older agent asked.

"I want my lawyer. I'm not saying anything else until I talk with my dad." Eric finally remembered his grandfather's instructions.

"Yeah, about that, where is your dad? He's not been seen by anyone since we stopped at your house Friday morning. Any idea where he could be?"

"Check his cabin. He likes to go there to unwind and be off the grid," Eric answered honestly, leaning back into his chair, arms crossed.

"Yeah, we did and he wasn't there," Devan answered, noting a surprised expression, for just an instant. "We did find Shiloh's car."

"How the hell did her car get there?" Eric blurted out with mortification.

Shit, Eric thought as the pieces fell into place. Unable to control his anger, he stood up, slamming his hands onto the table. "Damn him, the damn bastard! He thinks he can go around killing everyone and leave me here locked up holding the bag? That stupid fuck wants to fight dirty? Damn it, I will fight him and come out on top! Again and again, every fucking time!"

Pacing the small room, Eric continued with his ranting.

Devan and Jack looked at each, surprised by his unexpected outburst. Did they have this all wrong? Foxwood did say it was the father in the woods. Could they have been in on it together? Or were they each acting alone. A scary thought, to think the town had two psychopaths roaming freely.

Worse, was the father framing his son?

"To be clear, you want to talk with us or wait for your lawyer?" Jack wanted to clarify before going any further.

"I still want a lawyer but not my father. I want my own damn lawyer," Eric demanded while he continued pacing in the small area behind his chair. Suddenly he stopped and turned to the older agent. "Please tell me, have you found Clara yet?"

The agents looked at each other before Devan answered, "Yes, we found both Clara and Rob late Saturday night."

"You found them both? Together? Really?" Eric appeared more shocked at them being together than anything. He wasn't aware of his slip until they answered him.

"We would love to tell you all about it but we'll have to wait until your lawyer arrives. Do you have anyone you want to call or do you want one appointed?"

"I need to call my mother," Eric answered miserably as he dropped into his chair.

In the conference room, currently the formal acting FBI office, Devan spoke first, "Something's not adding up. Eric was surprised about Shiloh's death, that Clara and Rob found together, and he was surprised we knew about the cabin."

"Yes, I noticed that too. Seems like he expected his father's body to be found if we knew about the cabin. Please tell me his mother isn't a lawyer," Jack stated as he grabbed a marker to start filling out the timeline of what they knew on the board.

"Well, I don't believe she sat for the bar but she did attend law school, not sure if she graduated. Her brother and father are lawyers, as well as her husband. She's bound to know a few good ones," Devan answered, informing him about her family money as well.

Daniel Emerson, father of both Matt and Connor, prayed for patience when he looked at the caller ID. He couldn't hold off his sister any longer. After the third ring, he hit the speaker button.

"Hello Kathleen."

"Daniel, we need your help! Eric has been arrested. You need to return home and help with his bail. I was his one phone call!" his sister's voice screeched over the line.

"What was he arrested for this time? Breaking the terms of his bail?" Dan tried to keep the impatience from his voice. He previously warned her of the consequences if Eric was stupid enough to sneak out and was caught. Getting back out on bail was next to impossible, short of charges being dropped or being ruled innocent by the jury.

His words were barely out when she started to cry, panic was evident in her voice. "Murder! They arrested him for the murder of his whore!"

Dan leaned forward, surprised by his sister's lack of composure, the charges and the harshness towards the deceased. He was already aware his grandson had found the body of Shiloh Prentiss. Matt had informed him of all the current events back in town, including Clara's disappearance. They had debated Joshua's need for a lawyer as well as the decision to remain out of the Howell affairs. He had just talked with Connor about Clara's status. What was going on in that town?

"Damn, Kath, he's been arrested for murder? I would think the house arrest with the ankle monitor would be enough proof of his innocence," he responded, unable to keep out the sarcasm.

Typical when talking with his sister, Dan knew she wasn't providing the whole story. He wasn't sure if it was on purpose or if she really didn't grasp the importance of all the details. "What exactly are you asking for?"

"I need you here to defend him, get him back out on bail!" Kathleen cried out over the phone.

"Kathleen, I've told you before, I'm not active in court trials. Eric will need someone with more experience, especially if they have enough proof the crime was committed while out on bail. If they have reason to arrest him, there's no way I can get him released on bail."

"You won't defend your nephew? Daniel, how can you be so cruel?"

"Don't you want the best lawyer? What does Lee say about all this?"

"I haven't seen him since Friday morning," she disclosed.

"You haven't seen your husband? Where is he? Don't you think it's too coincidental Lee's conveniently gone, leaving Eric holding the bag? His own son? Kathleen, you need to get out of that house. Find somewhere safe to stay!" Dan's bad feeling intensified.

"You don't think Lee killed the girl, do you?" she asked, mystified.

"I think there are too many recently found dead, all conveniently connected to Eric and the nursing home. A jury will see what they want to see unless they are shown something to make them think otherwise."

"Daniel, I'm going to need you to wire me more money from my trust. If you won't be his lawyer, I'm going to need someone who will! It'll be extremely expensive," she decided.

"Kath, you've drained all the money over the summer for Eric's bail and retainer. Can't you use the same lawyer?"

There was a moment of silence before he heard her whisper, "What are you talking about? We didn't need a retainer, Lee was his lawyer."

"Kathleen, you asked for over a million dollars, you said it was for bail and retaining a lawyer. Since Eric was obviously breaking the terms of the bail, the bail money is lost. You don't have any more money to take out at this time. We've been over this before. You can't withdraw beyond the set amount or you'll risk losing everything in the future!"

Wanting to pull his hair out, Dan leaned back, shaking his head in frustration. Kathleen never understood how to budget and he feared it was her husband doing the spending, not his sister.

After a heavy sigh, she agreed, "Alright. Then just send me the money from Eric's trust that Dad set up. It's for him and his defense anyway."

Dan was already shaking his head. As he suspected, she had allowed Lee to take control of the money. And likely, there wasn't any left.

"Kathleen, I don't have access to Eric's trust. Lee does. You requested he take control when Eric was a child. You signed the paperwork."

"No! Don't tell me that! Where's the money? What did he do with it? Daniel, where did he put the money?"

Before Dan could even think how to answer, he could hear her screaming over the line. Then he heard something bang and crash. Knowing his sister, he could visualize her tantrum. It wasn't pretty when she lost control. He cringed at the sound of glass shattering.

His first thought, if it was a window, then the house trust would pay for the repairs, anything else, Dan wasn't sure could be replaced unless they had insured everything. His next thought, what the hell did her husband spend all the money on?

"Please don't tell me my money is all gone," Kathleen whimpered.

"Kathleen, you need to pack a bag and get out of the house, now! I'll send you a list of lawyers to contact, but I'm warning you, it'll be expensive and coming out of your future earnings," Dan warned.

"You really think I'm in danger?" The surprise was evident in her tone.

"Ever wonder what happened to Lee's first wife? Wasn't it suspicious she died after her trust fund was emptied and you two were already seeing each other?"

"What are you talking about?"

"Lee's had access to an incredible amount of money over the years, haven't you ever wondered where it all went?" Daniel challenged.

"Lee has his own trust," Kathleen tried to defend but even she had to admit, she had concerns.

"Honestly, I don't think the Howell Trusts were ever as excessive as ours," he speculated. "Because if they were, why are you always accessing yours for everything?"

"You think Lee killed his first wife? Why? All he had to do was divorce her, like he said he was going to," Kathleen was quiet as she mentally reviewed everything since they started seeing each other years ago. She would only admit to herself, they actually started before his first marriage. They had been on and off through the years before finally getting married.

Her tears were already dry when she spoke again to her brother, "Daniel, thank you for helping. I really appreciate it."

Before he could respond, she hung up.

Lee was the killer, Kathleen concluded. *That damn bastard is killing people and letting our son take the blame. How do I fix this? How do I help Eric?*

And without another tear, she realized what needed to be done to prove her son's innocence.

 SHADOWS OF THE PAST

The afternoon was late when Connor pulled up to his lake house. Grayson was right, they had plenty of places to stay. He was relieved when Clara agreed without argument. He had informed Devan and Matt of the plans. And to his surprise, much of the clothes and toys ordered in the last week were due to be delivered today at the lake house.

Connor's previous idea to have each place set up in case they were to move unexpectedly was paying off. Naturally, Clara thought it was a waste of money. The children didn't have a big wardrobe, because they grew so fast.

After he pulled into the garage, he assisted her out of the vehicle first and then the children. After unlocking the door and turning off the alarm, Connor watched Clara slowly walk to the large picture window overlooking the lake. She remained there until he finished unpacking the SUV. She sat quietly on the stool looking into the kitchen as he reset the alarm and started to unpack the groceries.

"Connor, please don't be upset about this," Clara stated.

Connor turned from the refrigerator, and paused to look at her questioningly before grabbing more items. "Clara, I'm not upset. I want us all together, but most importantly, I want you all safe. I don't feel your place on Prospect is safe right now. I want to know how he got inside before we return there. We have a few places between us, we don't always have to stay at your place. I'm only suggesting we rotate around, leave him guessing where we are on any given night, that's all."

Clara chuckled. "Your bachelor pad isn't child proof. We can't keep moving around each night, it isn't practical. The children need their routine and favorite toys."

"We'll make it safe. I already ordered a bunch of safety supplies," he stepped around the large island so he could take her into his arms. "Sweetheart, we don't have to switch around every night. We can stay here a few nights. I'm off the hospital rotation this next week. I can work from home overseeing the residents at the nursing home. Please, let us do this for a few weeks until I know it's safe for you, Reese, and Hailey."

"And what about you?"

Connor pulled back to look at her. "What about me?"

"What about your safety?"

He paused a moment to assure the kids were not within hearing distance before he looked at her questioningly. "My safety isn't the issue."

"How can you say that? People around me are at risk. My mother and my husband have already been killed. Attempts to kill three of my best friends have been made. Connor, your being near me puts you at risk," Clara argued.

"So, what are you suggesting? You want to break up?" Connor had stepped back, he found himself sitting on a stool. He winced at the suggestion of breaking up. It was the last thing he wanted.

"I don't know what I'm suggesting. When I think about what could have happened to you, I'm paralyzed with fear. I don't want you to be trapped in your vehicle while it's driven into the lake or buried alive! The possibilities are killing me," she answered with grief as she ran her hand through her hair.

"How did you hear about that?" He wondered who was buried alive.

"Does it matter? It's a small town, something like that will never be kept quiet," she replied as she slowly stood up.

"Clara, come here." He stood up to lead her towards the sofa. He sat, pulling her down onto this lap before he continued.

"I know a little something about being paralyzed with fear. When you first arrived at the hospital after the accident, I didn't even recognize you! Half of your body was soaked in blood and covered in glass. The moment I realized it was you on the stretcher, struggling to breathe, my heart stopped because I didn't even know if I could save you. I was the only surgeon available. It was everything I could do to keep myself focused. But it is nothing compared to the panic I had when I came home to your place to find the mess in the kitchen. The signs of obvious struggle, the blood," His voice trailed off as he fought to compose himself. *Now isn't the time to fall apart*, he thought, trying to regroup.

"My intentions have been clear," Connor continued. He tightened his grip when she attempted to shift from his lap. "I love you. I want to be with you, here and now, as well as for the long haul. I don't care if it's legal or if there are more children, we can discuss all that when you're ready. But please stop pulling away from me whenever things start getting too serious. If you don't want to be with me, then tell me. Don't beat around the bush by pushing me away because you're concerned about me. I'm a big boy, I can handle rejection. It's not fair to me, you, or even the children if your feelings are not into us."

Clara remained silent as he talked, a tear slid down her cheek as she stared down at her hands.

Without a word, Connor scooted her off his lap and stood up.

"I'll let you rest. Let me know what you've decided."

He returned to the kitchen to finish unpacking the groceries before calling the children up to join him while he carried their bags and new packages upstairs to unpack.

Later that night, Connor remained in the doorway, watching Clara sit with her children. They were each arguing over which books she should read, the scene was similar to many previous evenings before her abduction, even before her accident. She calmly allowed them each to pick one and started reading.

After she tucked them each into bed, Connor entered the room to kiss each child goodnight before he followed her into their bedroom. He brushed his teeth before changing into his pajamas. He sat in the large overstuffed chair with his tablet while Clara prepared herself for bed. When she returned from the bathroom, she walked over to him and waited for him to look up from his reading.

"Connor, I can't even think about next year, next week, or even tomorrow. I can only take this one day at a time. The real reason I wanted to be discharged from the hospital was so you would sleep beside me tonight. I want the comfort and the familiarity of your arms around me when I sleep because you're the only one that keeps the darkest of shadows away at night."

Connor kept his eyes on hers as he stood up. "I guess that's as good as I'm going to get right now."

Clara nodded as his arms came around her and he kissed her forehead before she led him to the bed. Once they were settled in for the night, she was on her right side with her back up against his chest while his one arm cradling her head and the other cautiously draped over her side. His hand resting on her stomach. She placed her hand on his as she sighed in content.

"Connor?" Clara whispered. With her hearing aids removed, she was unable to hear but she could feel his body vibrate a 'hmm' before she continued, "I love you. I have always loved you and I always will, but I don't want you to be offended and hurt when I have another bone to pick with you tomorrow."

She could feel his body shake as if he were laughing. She felt his lips on her cheek and felt the whisper of his breath in her ear as he said words she couldn't hear. When she rolled onto her back, he leaned down to kiss her.

When she drifted off to sleep, he remained awake watching her sleep. His mind reviewed the earlier conversation: he shouldn't have been surprised by the comment of being trapped in a car after what happened to Rob, but buried alive?

Who was buried alive? Her mother was buried, but how would Clara know if she was alive at the time? What the hell happened that night, twenty years ago and how does she know?

• • • •

Evil sat up suddenly when he opened his eyes to the morning sun entering the windows. "Shit! What day is it? How long have I been asleep?" Feeling uncharacteristically paranoid, he quickly made his way through his morning routine.

So much to do today! He needed information.

And he cringed when he realized the muddy mess he left throughout. First task, clean up after yourself. Always. Then seek out the information you need. And figure out where to stay. Can't be staying here!

After his simple breakfast, Evil immediately went to work cleaning the kitchen. He found the simple task refreshing and tried to forgive himself of the appalling behavior of leaving the chaos throughout the house. But in his defense, he was injured.

Besides, the place would look great for her return.

Once he finished setting the first floor to rights, he took a break for lunch. Evil still had to the clean the second floor before he could give in to sleep again.

And during dinner, he realized he needed to figure out his next plan.

He returned upstairs to sleep for the night. And once his nighttime routine was complete, he settled into bed. Evil wondered what trouble the boy was currently in. He laughed out loud at his wife's probable reaction. And just as he was falling asleep, he wondered about his cousin.

It was a shame he had to burn the bridge with Carl. But that gave him an idea for his next step.

Lila paced her brother's hospital room, her agitation was apparent. She was furious with her mother, her father, and everyone else, for that matter. Why all the damn secrecy? And they wondered how she had the nerve to keep her marriage a secret.

"It's just crazy, Dallas! I can't believe everyone wants to just brush this under the rug and forget it happened," she stated in a loud whisper to avoid waking Rob. The only thing agreed on was rotating so he wouldn't be alone at the hospital, but Rob refused to see his parents. For once, she agreed with his all or nothing attitude.

"Lila, honey, you should sit down and elevate your leg. It's going to be killing you once the pain meds wear off," Dallas suggested without looking up from his game of solitaire on his phone.

"Dallas, how can you be so relaxed? How would you feel if you found out your father wasn't your biological father? That your mother cheated on your father?" Lila almost yelled.

Dallas sighed as he looked at his wife. "Well, I can speak from experience when I say the world will continue to turn. The sun will rise in the east tomorrow and the sun will set in the west. Life goes on. We can't control what the adults do. Nothing really changes, you and Rob are still who you were last week."

"But what does that mean? Will your dad claim Rob?" she wondered.

"He's not my dad," his response was automatic.

"Shit, Dal, I'm sorry! I don't mean to sound so insensitive. I forgot you literally do know what it's like," she turned toward the window. The hospital was shaped like the letter H with a parking lot in the front and in the back, allowing the building to semi-enclose the parking lots. When she looked outside into the night, she could see the entrance.

Lila paused to watch the scene below her.

Allison Foxwood sat on the bench outside of the main lobby as she pondered her life. She felt as if she'd aged decades since receiving the first call about Lila's kidnapping. It hadn't even been a full week, but it felt as if a year had dragged on. Staring out into the parking lot, the tears fell as she replayed the scene with her husband in her head.

After all they shared together for the last thirty-three years, their marriage was in trouble.

"Ally?"

She turned towards the familiar voice and felt her heart break again. "Zac?"

Zachariah Thompson walked toward her when he realized she was crying. He made a mental note of what he heard about her children. The girl had been taken but was found, likely to be discharged soon, if not already. The boy had also been taken with the Gibson girl. Well, woman and man, now, he had no doubt someone would clarify. But he thought all were going to be alright. Had someone taken a turn for the worst?

"Ally, is everyone alright? Your children? I thought they were alright." He cautiously sat beside her.

"Zac, I made a mistake so many years ago! I should have voiced my thoughts and desires back then. I have made a mess of everything. No one wants to talk to me," Allison sobbed.

She felt his familiar strong hands touch her, one on her knee and the other gently on her shoulder. She was well aware he spoke with such kindness to only a few. "Ally, baby, nothing can change what we had for each other. So many things were out of our control back then."

"This one was awful! Can you ever forgive me?" Allison pleaded as she looked into his familiar steel blue eyes. Yes, she could see so much of him in her son. How had she turned a blind eye to this? Did Mitch see what she saw?

"Ally, you've never done anything that warrants forgiveness," Zac answered. "Those weeks we had together were the best days of my life. I've never regretted it."

"Never?" Allison challenged. "The boy is yours. I never talked about it, not even with Mitch. He may have suspected but he never said a word. Oh, Zac, can you ever forgive me? I deprived you of knowing your son and allowed Mitch to raise him as his own. He raised your son to hate you. Rob knows now. My children will never forgive me."

She broke into another round of tears as he pulled her in close.

From the window above, Lila watched the scene below as she commented, "Think about it, did they ever break up? Have they been secretly seeing each other behind my father's back?"

"Lila, aren't you over thinking this? We should just let the adults be adults and live their lives. We can't change what happened over thirty years ago," Dallas responded as he joined her at the window.

"Dallas, do they look like things ended over thirty years ago?" she demanded as she pointed out the window.

Dallas's eyes followed her finger, looking down at the couple sitting on the bench kissing. "Or not. Damn!"

Lila immediately turned and started for the door but stopped when Dallas blocked the door with his body. "Sweetheart, what do you plan to do?"

"I am going to demand they stop right now! They're out there kissing for all the world to see! How could she keep this affair a secret for so long? How dare they judge while they have secrets of their own! Harmful secrets that involve others." Lila attempted to step around him.

Dallas side-stepped with her, reaching out to catch her as she buckled slightly from the pain in her leg.

"Lila, I know this is tough, but we don't know the whole story. You barging out there yelling at them will only fuel the gossip line. I know how much you hate that," he stepped closer to hug her, "we can only be there for the adults, support them, regardless of any mistakes they may make."

"Lila, Dallas is right. Leave them to sort this out on their own. Nothing we do or say will change the outcome," Rob commented from his bed.

"Rob, how long have you been awake? You should be resting," Lila pulled away from Dallas.

"Who could sleep with all your fussing," Rob answered quietly. He had remained silent when she had started her pacing and complaining about her parents. As much as it pained him, Dallas was right. Her going out and scolding them would not end well, especially once her temper flared. She was usually the peacemaker. "There's no reason for you to hang out here. You must want to be in your own bed. Please, Dallas, take my little sister home."

"Rob, I want to stay here with you. I don't want you to be alone. Dallas can go home," Lila started to say.

"No, he doesn't need to leave you here. Dallas wants to be with you. Lila, I am fine. Go home with your husband. Everything will still be as it is tomorrow. You missing a night's sleep isn't going to change a thing," Rob's voice was quiet but harsh.

Lila could hear the fatigue in his voice and immediately felt bad about keeping him awake with her whining. How horrible must this be for him. The last thing he needed was to hear it all from her. She stepped closer. "Are you sure you'll be alright?"

Rob nodded as he reached for her hand. "I might actually get some sleep without anyone in here watching me."

Lila squeezed his hand as she nodded her head in agreement and leaned down to kiss his cheek. "Call me any time, alright? I wrote everyone's cell on the pad next to the phone until you get yours replaced. I love you, Big Brother."

"I love you too, Little Sister," he answered quietly.

Dallas watched the siblings say goodnight. He reached out to shake hands before leading his wife to the wheelchair. The look on his face suggested she not refuse the ride downstairs.

They rode home in silence. Dallas reached for her hand as he drove. Once they were in bed, he laid on his side with his head propped up in his hand, listening quietly while Lila listed all the things that could happen between her parents.

"Dallas, I don't want my parents to get a divorce," she said tearfully.

Without saying a word, he pulled her in close as she cried for the first time since her abduction.

When Allison Foxwood walked into the house, only the porch light was on. Confident her spouse was sleeping, she quietly made her way to the bedroom. Without turning on the light, she went into the bathroom for a quick shower.

But when she returned to the bedroom, Mitch was sitting up in bed with the lights on. Allison came to a stop, still wrapped in only a towel. Her intent was to pull a nightie from the drawer and dress in the dark. Suddenly, she felt shy around her husband.

"I thought you were staying at the hospital with the kids," Mitch commented.

"Neither wanted me around," Allison admitted.

"Not surprising, is it?"

It wasn't so much what he said, but the tone that caused her to stop and turn while she was opening a drawer. "What do you mean?"

"What do you think I mean?" Mitch challenged.

"It's late, I just want to get some sleep." She grabbed a nightgown before returning into the bathroom. After she replaced the towel on the rack, Allison turned around to see her husband standing at the doorway.

"So this is how it's going to be? You're going to avoid me and push everything back under the rug again?"

"Do we need to talk about it now? For crying out loud, Mitch, it's midnight. The last few days have been extremely stressful. I just want to get some sleep. I promise, we can talk this to death in the morning," she answered, trying to side step around him.

"It's four-thirty. Morning is here. I'm starting the coffee before checking in on the animals," Mitch responded with his eyes on his wife's face. The panic was evident when she turned to consult the clock.

"It's four-thirty? Already?"

"Time flies when you're having fun. Were you two at the hospital this whole time or did you stop at his place before he dropped you off?" Mitch asked, still at the doorway.

"What are you insinuating?"

"You know damn well what I'm saying. You start kissing and feeling in front of the hospital, you don't think anyone will see it?" his voice was starting to raise.

"How do you know?" Allison's face paled.

"I was sitting in the parking lot. I thought you would need a ride home but that was at ten. Where have you been all night if you weren't with the kids?"

When she remained silent, Mitch had to ask, "Do you still love him?"

The tears on her face told him everything. And he knew from past experience, she needed to make the choice this time. "You have one week to decide. If you stay, you do not have any more contact with him."

"And if I leave?" her voice was soft.

"You'll be allowed here to see the children and any family events. I'm not going to stop you this time nor am I going to fight for you. If you stay, I need to know I can trust you. I don't want to be wondering every time you leave the farm if you're off fucking him instead of actually at a friend's or the damn grocery store for six hours!" Mitch tried to remain calm but he was yelling when he finished.

Taking a step back, he took a moment in an attempt to control his voice when he repeated, "You have the week to decide."

When he walked out of the room, Allison sat on the bed and cried.

Rachel woke up alone in Chase's bed. She reached over to touch his side, it was no longer warm. Meaning he was likely up for hours already. She smiled at staying on the farm again. Different now compared to last time. She was staying with Chase in his apartment over the stables. Smelling the coffee, she went out to the kitchen.

When her eyes met Chase, she came to a stop. "Chase, what's wrong?"

"Everything is changing," he admitted. He stood up to retrieve the coffeepot and another mug. "Normally, I wouldn't say anything, but if we stay here, you should probably know what's going on. Things are getting awkward around here real fast."

"Why?"

Ten minutes later, Rachel's eyes were wide as she attempted to absorb everything she just heard.

"Wait a minute, let me get this straight... Rob's biological father is Zacariah Thompson? Seriously? And Mitch was aware of this? Wow, Rob must be furious! He hates anything Thompson!" Rachel suddenly giggled out.

When Chase looked at her, she quickly covered her mouth.

"I'm sorry. It's not funny. It's just the true definition of irony. Danny Thompson is Rob's cousin. Wow!" Rachel was overcome with another fit of giggles.

"That's not the worst part," Chase continued, "apparently, Aunt Allison was seen kissing him and he dropped her off here at the farm. Not last night, but just before dawn."

"You don't honestly think they were doing it?" Rachel asked, obviously appalled.

"I have no idea, nor do I care what they were actually doing. The point is, she spent the night with the man and now Uncle Mitch has given her an ultimatum. She has a week to choose."

"Choose? Choose what? Between Mitch or Zac?" Rachel leaned back. "I'm impressed he's giving her a choice. I would have expected him to kick her out without any further ado."

Rachel studied his face a moment, sipping her coffee. Her blue eyes narrowed. "Your uncle told you all this?"

"Hell no! Uncle Mitch would never have such a conversion with me," Chase dismissed.

"Then how do you know all this? It's only seven in the morning," Rachel cringed. Not raised on a farm, her time to get up was actually mid morning to the Foxwoods. Since staying back on the farm, Chase was once again up early helping out.

Chase sighed with embarrassment before he finally admitted, "I was up when she was dropped off. They must have had their bedroom window open, I could hear them arguing."

"What do Rob and Lila know?" Rachel asked after a few minutes.

"As far as I know, just that. They were kissing in front of the hospital." Chase stood up to start breakfast. "I can't believe they were stupid enough to do that. They had to have known people would see them. And now everyone is talking about it, I'm sure."

"Are we going to continue staying here or head back to my place?"

"We need to meet Devan at your place but we aren't staying there until I'm confident we've found all the entrances and staircases."

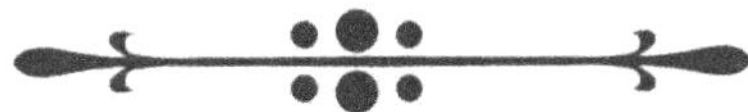

It was the third day at the lake house when Connor received the call from his cousin. Devan wanted to come out to get Clara's statement of events. He had mixed feelings, telling him he'd get back to him. Connor joined Clara on the deck while the children played.

"It's starting to get chilly out here. Are you warm enough?" he asked, placing his arm over her shoulder. She leaned into him as she nodded.

They sat in silence staring out into the lake, each in their own thoughts.

"Who were you talking to?"

"Devan. He wants to schedule a time to get your statement. He says Eric is still locked up. Apparently, they're waiting for some hotshot lawyer from the city," he explained.

"So, it's safe to return home?" Clara answered hopefully.

"I don't know about that," he answered as Hailey climbed into his lap. "Hailey, your hands are ice cold. You're turning into an icicle! Let's get you inside where it's warmer."

Once everyone was inside, she ushered the children into the bathroom. She changed the toddler's diaper before they each washed up. Once they were both lying down for their naps, Clara decided it was time to talk. She sat beside him on the sofa as he read from his never ending medical journals.

"Connor, what if we head back to town this afternoon. I want to stop in to see Rob," she responded.

Devan realized he'd never been inside the Taylor House as he pulled into the driveway. As he slowly ascended the steps to the back porch, Chase opened the door.

"Devan, thanks for making it out here," he greeted. "We have no idea the relevance, we'll let you decide."

Without a word, Rachel led the men up the back staircase to her mother's room. When she reached the door, she paused, feeling horrible about letting others into her mother's sanctuary. Taking a deep breath, she opened the door and stepped aside.

"Devan, I've never been in this room without my mother. The Friday before Labor Day, I was finally able to bring myself to start cleaning it out. I moved the bed over and found this."

Devan's eyes followed her pointed finger to a syringe lying on the rug. He used his phone to take pictures and pulled an evidence bag from his pocket as he asked questions, "Was your mother a diabetic or something else requiring her to give herself injections?"

"No," Rachel's voice was soft.

"Anything else different about this room?"

"I don't really know. But, Chase finally found the entrance to the hidden staircase," she motioned back towards the hall.

"I was able to narrow down the area, but Rachel found the door." Chase led the group to the room. When he opened the door, he used a flashlight to show the footprints in the dust. "We didn't dare wander inside until you were able to document any evidence of the bastard being here."

"Gotcha," Devan whispered, squatting down toward the footprint on the step. After taking pictures, he called for a forensics team. When he flashed the light down the steps, he was able to see the footprints all the way down.

Two days later, Clara was sitting on her sofa at her duplex wondering what happened and if she should be worried. Rob had been released from the hospital earlier in the day. Somehow, she had agreed to let him stay at her place. Before he arrived, she and Connor had another disagreement. Well, she couldn't really call it fighting or arguing, it was way too civil for that. She wasn't sure if they were taking a break or breaking up.

When they first arrived into town from the lake house, Clara asked if they could stop at her place for a few things. Connor agreed. During the ride back, they discussed the conditions of returning back to the duplex.

First, every single lock was to be changed, a task he would personally oversee. He made it clear, the basement and garage were included. Also, they would continue moving around ever so often without any pattern, limiting who knew the schedule. And they weren't moving suitcases and packing/unpacking with each move. Each place would be supplied with clothes and pantry items, a task Connor had already seen to. And finally, he wanted each place screened for surveillance equipment on a regular basis.

When Clara argued the rules, Connor remained silent as he leaned back in his seat with his arms crossed. At the end, he stated, "Those are the rules, take it or leave it."

He never stated what would happen if she chose 'leave it.'

After talking with Rachel, Clara realized she was the one being unrealistic. Her friend pointed out it was not only for her safety, but for the safety of both Reese and Hailey.

"Clara, I don't understand why you're being so stubborn about all this! I'm with Connor on each and every point! We have no idea how Eric got inside. Changing the locks is the least of it. Besides, Chase already has everything ready. We all need to be safe. Hell, Chase has me staying with him at the farm so I won't be alone at my house. Dallas has also set up an elaborate security system," Rachel said as she squeezed her hand.

"I don't understand why, I just know I don't want to be taken care of," Clara answered with a sigh. Once the words were out of her mouth, she knew she wasn't making any sense.

"Clara, after everything that's happened in the last year, why are you making an issue out of this? Connor ensuring your security is what partners do. It doesn't make you less independent. If anything, it should make you feel warm and loved!"

Instead, Clara felt anxious.

Rob returned inside after saying goodbye to his friends who helped him move his stuff to Clara's. He sat on the other end of the sofa, bringing Clara back to the present.

"Are you sure this will be alright?" Rob asked again.

"Of course, why wouldn't it? It's not like we don't have the room. I'm sorry you have to share the bathroom with the kids. You won't have much privacy," she answered as Rob seemed to dismiss the idea.

"What did Connor say when you told him?"

"I haven't told him," she admitted quietly, her eyes turned down to her hands.

Rob's eyebrows raised as he studied her face. "What's going on?"

"What do you mean?"

"What's going on between you and Connor?"

"I honestly don't know, right now," Clara sighed. "I guess you can say we're going through a rough patch."

"A rough patch? What does that even mean?"

Devan was shocked at Connor's appearance when he opened the door to his flat. He looked almost as bad as when Clara went missing.

His feet were bare, his wrinkled shirt was partially tucked and his hair was sticking up, as if he were constantly running his hands through it.

"What do you want? Did you get your statement from Clara yet?" Connor asked as he walked back to his recliner chair, detouring by the liquor cabinet to refill his glass.

Devan followed him in after closing the door. He also stopped to pour himself two fingers.

"Not yet. Honestly, I'm surprised to find you here. What's going on?"

"Hell if I know," Connor admitted before he downed the drink. "I think we may have broken up."

"Really? Why?" Devan asked. He'd seen Rob carrying in a few boxes before he arrived at Connor's. He wondered what really went on out in the woods between Rob and Clara. He felt Foxwood was keeping a few things to himself but they were able to confirm the attempt on his life. Divers found his truck in the lake earlier in the day. Word had not really gotten around yet about that. Only a matter of time.

"My fault, I guess. I started pushing. She wasn't ready and pushed back. She agreed to the terms I gave. Chase changed all the locks on the doors and the windows; You checked for bugs. Once we were settled in at the duplex, Clara found out I purchased her place and went off," Connor explained miserably.

"Yeah, well you did say she would be upset about it when you told her," Devan commented.

"I guess she would have if I had actually told her. We had everything together, Reese and I went to get groceries and check in at the nursing home. When we got back, she had the bills out all over the table. She had just hung up with your aunt," Connor paused as he refilled his glass, bringing the whole bottle back.

"You know, I've seen her temper before, but never like this. She had been harboring it all." Connor sipped his drink. "Today, she let me have it. She doesn't like decisions being made for her, I know that. She especially doesn't like being told what to do. Again, not new information. She told me I had no right to make changes in her place without her consent. I don't even know what she meant by that. All I did was pay her bills while she was in the hospital, was that so wrong? She agreed to the terms of returning back to the duplex. All the changes I made were with her consent."

"And you also purchased her home," Devan added.

"Except for that. I think she's trying to protect me by pushing me away," Connor speculated with dejection. "She actually said she didn't want me to be drowned in a truck or buried alive."

"Who was buried alive?" As he asked the question, Devan thought about all the ways people were killed. Tasha, the PT that went missing before Clara moved to town, was strangled and left dead in the woods off an infrequent path near Howell's cabin. Billy Kingsley, also strangled with something thin and sharp, was also left dead in the woods. Lauren, while also strangled, was thrown into a pond. And Shiloh was also strangled. The only body found in the last year that was buried, which surfaced only because of the spring storms, was Clara's mother. That was twenty years ago.

"What does Clara say about her mother's death?"

"She doesn't say anything," Connor answered, but his brown eyes were curious. Despite the intoxication, his brain was able to make the connection. "You think her mother was buried alive? How the hell would she even know that?"

Connor stood up to pace the room. "What are you not telling me? Shit, she really did see her mother's murder, didn't she?"

"I need to talk to her but she's been avoiding me," Devan started to say when his cell rang.

Clara sat restlessly, her bottom was getting sore but if she stood too much, her feet would hurt.

"Clara, tell me what happened," Rob encouraged.

"I was reviewing the bills. I wanted to make sure nothing was forgotten when I was in the hospital," she started. "But Connor already had it covered. He even changed all the accounts to autopay from his checking."

When she was quiet for a moment, Rob tilted his head in question. "Is that all?"

"He also purchased this place," she answered quietly.

"Wow, the guy sure knows how to take care of his girl," he started but stopped when she interrupted him with a near hysterical rant.

"I don't want to be taken care of! I'm not an invalid! I am capable of taking care of myself and my children. I don't need a man doing everything for me and making decisions about my life, where I sleep each night and what color I want my walls in the bathroom. If I want the walls smiley face yellow, then they should stay smiley face yellow. If the bathroom tub has paint splatters, don't you think he should, at the very least, ask me if I want it cleaned up?"

"Clara, seriously? This is what you two are arguing about? You were in the hospital for a few weeks. Instead of stressing you out about money, he paid the bills. He probably had every intention of switching everything over once you were back on your feet," Rob stated. No one was more surprised than he to be the one defending the actions of the good doctor. "But he probably heard the place was being put on the market. If Devan bought the place next door, why wouldn't he offer to buy yours? He probably intended to talk to you but you were in the accident. Don't be so hard on the guy."

"I thought you, of all people, would take my side," Clara stated harshly. She started to scoot forward to stand but stopped when he reached for her hand.

"Clara, nothing would make me happier than you giving the good doctor the boot, if that would make you happy." Rob squeezed her hand. "You don't seem too happy about it."

"He bought the place in my name," she explained miserably.

"Yeah? And? It's a nice gesture. Think of it as an investment," Rob suggested. "He's not implying you have to live here. He owns property and understands its value. You can always move out and live elsewhere."

"But it's too grand of a gesture! It's not like we're engaged or anything," she muttered.

And there, Rob thought, *is the issue.* He studied her a moment before he risked asking, "Do you want to be engaged? Is he pushing you into an engagement?"

"No," she sighed dramatically.

"No, what? You don't want to be engaged, or no, he's not pushing you?"

"He told me the first night I was out of the hospital what his intentions were. He's in for the long haul and that he loves me and the kids. He didn't care if we ever made it legal or if we had children together. Said we could decide all that another time." She was quiet for a moment. "He told me to decide if I wanted him around or not. And if I did, I was to stop pushing him away."

"Are you pushing him away?"

"I don't know. I worry about him getting hurt," she sniffed as a tear fell.

Rob looked around and reached over for a tissue from the end table. "Why? You think he can't handle you dumping him? Personally, I think he can handle it."

Clara let out a loud chuckle. "Funny. He said the exact same thing. No, I don't plan on dumping him! Or at least I hope I didn't. It's just so hard worrying about him. Every time I turn around, someone I care about is getting hurt or killed. My mom, Jason, Shannon, Lila, and even you."

"Clara, seriously? Are you really that worried about him? Your mom died twenty years ago. Your husband in another city. And as for Shannon, I thought that was about her old boss. It had nothing to do with you. You were the innocent bystander and the one that actually was hurt, not

Shannon. And that carried into Lila's kidnapping, none of that was your doing. And as for me," Rob paused as he scooted closer, "I am relieved I was here when the bastard came. Yes, I was at the wrong place at the wrong time, but we were able to save each other in the woods.

"And as for your doctor, he's crazy about you. But it's not the end of the world if you aren't crazy about him. You should tell him." Rob decided he had said enough.

"I can't believe he would get discharged from the hospital without telling any of us! Where the hell did he go? My parents haven't heard from him and neither has Chase." Lila was once again pacing in frustration as she cursed her brother. "We can't even call him because he has yet to buy another damn cell phone! Where the hell can he be?"

"Alright, thanks Devan," Dallas stated as he hung up his cell and returned back towards his wife, "Rob's at Clara's."

"What? Clara's? Why Clara's?" Lila demanded, wincing in pain from turning too fast.

Dallas knew better than to answer that. He saw how they were together, cuddled up in the shrubbery. Ironically, Rob's high fever was warming her, preventing her body from going into shock as she literally bled out. He knew the experience changed their relationship, something few would ever understand. Instead of attempting to explain, Dallas lifted his cell to call his sister.

"I am crazy about him! I love him, Rob. I really do. I don't even know what happened. One minute, we were having a simple discussion. I told him I didn't like him making decisions about my life or my children without me, and he tells me he just wanted to help out and take care of me. I lost it," she explained as her cell rang. "I lost my temper and started yelling at him. I was so angry, I don't even know what I said."

She reached for it, checking the caller ID before answering.

"Hi, Dallas," Clara answered as her eyes met Rob's. "Yeah, he's here."

Rob was shaking his head and holding up his hands, refusing to take her phone.

"Rob, Lila wants to talk to you. She's not done anything wrong. Seriously?" Clara returned to her brother on the phone. "Sorry, he's not taking any calls right now."

Rob watched as Clara continued to talk with her brother.

"Yeah, it's all good here, as much as it can be." She paused for a few seconds before she answered, "Sounds good. I should be up then. Have a good night."

After she hung up the phone, Clara stood up with a slight wince before she turned to Rob. "I'm heading to bed. I left sheets out on your bed upstairs and fresh towels in the closet. Help yourself to whatever you can find. And Dallas and Lila are stopping over tomorrow morning with breakfast."

"I will be sleeping. I can't believe you invited the guy over," Rob muttered.

"I didn't, he invited himself. Think of it as he's stopping in to see his favorite sister," Clara suggested. "Goodnight."

Rob stood up and gave her a hug as he commented, "Aren't you his only sibling?"

"Who knows with all the secrets in this town, there could be others out there. But I've no doubt, I'd be the favorite. Rob, are you going to be alright tonight?"

"Yeah, I guess. Clara, thanks."

"If you have trouble sleeping, come into my room. I have a large comfy chair if you don't want to be alone," she stated softly.

Rob nodded as she slowly ascended the steps. There was something off about Clara and her reaction to Connor's protectiveness. After everything she's been through in the last few months, the good doctor had every reason to be concerned and protective. Clara isn't the one that usually over reacts, he does.

Dallas hung up the phone as his eyes met Lila's.

"I can't believe he won't talk to me! He's staying at Clara's? Connor can't be too happy about this," Lila almost shouted, crossing her arms.

"Yeah, probably not," Dallas agreed. "I don't think he's staying there right now."

"What? Where is he? Is he back to work at the hospital?" She watched Dallas shake his head.

"All I know is what Devan told me, Rob is at Clara's and Connor's at his flat," Dallas answered.

"Why? Did they break up?" Lila wondered. "Why would Rob expect she could take care of him? I can actually walk better than she can. Why won't he stay here?"

Dallas hoped to hell he was able to keep his cringe internal. The idea of his first real home being plagued by Rob's presence didn't sit well with him but he answered honestly. "Maybe because I'm here. Maybe because you didn't extend the invite, but I don't think that's what this is about. I think it's more of a mutual need the two have to be with each other."

"You're taking this well. I thought you and Connor were friends."

"Yeah, well, we know better than anyone you can't fight who you fall in love with, sweetheart. We won't be able to solve anything tonight worrying over what is not in our control. Let's go to bed." Dallas reached over to kiss her.

. . . .

After the house was silent, Evil emerged from the darkness. He strolled into the dim room to her side of the bed. Quietly, he sat beside her as she rolled towards him. He smiled, believing she sensed his presence.

Gently touching her curls, his voice was soft, "I am so glad to see you made it back home safely. You had me worried when he had you tucked away at the cabin. I want so much more for you. But don't you worry. I have things in place and you won't have to worry about him much longer. Soon, we won't have to hide from the others. Sweet dreams, Babydoll, sweet dreams."

Clara felt the coldness as she pulled her arms under the covers after shifting. The sudden pain on her left side stopped her movements as she glanced across the room. She could see the shadow shifting in the chair. 'Baby, come to bed. It's late.'

The shadow shifted in her direction before standing up to join her in the bed. When he placed his arm around her, she placed her hand on his. She felt the wetness of his hand as she smelled the wet dampness of the lake. She sat up as the light came on, shocked to see Eric lying beside her.

'My love, it's alright! Let me take care of you,' he stated as she looked into his violet blue eyes.

Clara screamed as she tried to leave the bed.

'Baby? Wake up, you're having a bad dream,' Clara heard behind her. She turned to see the familiar sky blue eyes of her husband.

Clara leaned back on her pillow but her eyes caught the blood on the side of Jason's face. 'Jason, your head is bleeding.'

'It's nothing,' she heard Jason's voice as she studied the familiar features of his face.

'My love, wake up! Let me take care of you!'

Clara blinked as her husband's features shifted ever so slightly. Eric's face smiled back down as something clicked in her brain.

'No!' she screamed!

Clara opened her eyes as she caught herself from screaming out loud. She looked around her room to be sure shadows weren't lurking in the darkness. She slowly scooted out of the bed, peeking in on each child before she carefully descended the stairs. Pausing at the bottom of the stairs, her breath caught in her throat at the sight of Jason sleeping on the sofa.

Unaware of her painful limp, Clara sat and slowly laid herself down beside him. As his arm came around her, she could feel him scooting slightly to give her more room as her hand held his.

Rob had been vaguely aware of the foot steps above. He wasn't surprised when Clara came down the stairs. He never expected her to lay down beside him on the sofa but realized she was probably also having trouble sleeping…

The next morning, neither said a word about sleeping together on the sofa. Rob was already up when Clara started to stir.

As before, Clara's dreams of the past faded as the sun rose to a new day.

• • • •

Evil walked around the empty house debating what to do. His wounds were mostly healed, cuts were scabbed over, and the skin a palish yellow. His hair was the longest ever, even during his rebel days in high school. When he looked in the mirror, he was confident his own father would not recognize him. He finally had the perfect disguise!

But he still needed to get out of the house to access his cash and get an idea of what was going on in the world. Did they arrest the boy for murder? He giggled at the thought of the boy's mother panicking, struggling to get him released from jail. If not for murder, he should, at the least, be arrested for violating the terms of his bail. Shockingly, even the poor excuse for a sheriff should have figured it out sooner.

Looking out the back window from her bedroom, he pulled open a drawer. Evil allowed his fingers to linger among her silk panties and bras. He sighed as he thought about not sleeping in her bed the night before. He could wait another night or two.

Once Rachel was given the go ahead, she had a case of deja vu, standing in the doorway of her mother's room again with the vacuum cleaner and cleaning supplies beside her. She had to remind herself, her mother would not have any issues with the bathroom being clean. *That's where I shall start,* she decided.

Leaving the vacuum cleaner, Rachel made her way across the room. Within an hour, the bathroom was sparkling clean and she was once again standing at the doorway looking into her mother's room.

Where to start? Give the room a quick once over before tackling the closet and drawers? Without thinking, she reached for a shoe box on the shelf. As she was pulling it closer, the box slipped from her fingers and onto the floor. Expecting to find shoes, Rachel was surprised to find letters.

But not just any letters, she realized, reading the return address. They were letters from her father.

From prison.

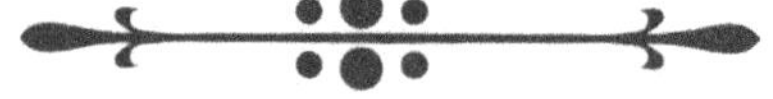

33 *not moving on*

On Thursday evening, a week after Clara returned to her duplex and kicked him out, Connor realized a trip to the store was necessary. His kitchen was lacking all the essentials for a pleasant meal. He was getting tired of takeout.

He wasn't even in the store for a full minute when he heard his name being called, "Connor! Connor!"

He turned towards the registers to see Reese running toward him with Hailey following in his wake. Connor squatted down to give them each a hug. When he stood up, the little girl remained in his arms. "Hey, guys! How are you doing?"

"Connor, where have you been? We have Uncle Rob with us. He's going to show us how to make fried chicken," the little boy announced.

"Fried chicken? That sounds delicious!" Connor looked over as Rob started outside with the grocery cart while Clara headed over. He noted her limp, but the coloring on her face was better. She still had the dark circles under her eyes, but her face lit up when she smiled at him. Without thinking, he leaned down to kiss her. "Clara, you're looking good."

"Mommy always looks good," Reese declared.

"You are right about that, Reese," Connor agreed.

"When are you going to come back home?" the little boy asked. But before Connor could answer he continued talking, "We are going to be planning my birthday party! I don't know where I want to have it! My friend Sawyer will be having his party in his backyard with a big bouncy house. My friend Joe's family lives on a farm near Uncle Rob and will be having a fall harvest with hayrides and a corn maze! Isn't that awesome? I don't even know what a corn maze is but I do love corn!"

Reese rambled, while Connor listened as they started walking towards the door. When he finally stopped talking, Connor asked, "Would you like me to take you guys one evening?"

"Yes, it would be awesome! Can Mommy come?"

"Absolutely," Connor agreed. "I thought his birthday was in December."

"It is. He has two months but his classroom has everyone's birthday posted. His is the next one after Sawyer's. He doesn't have a good concept of time," Clara explained as she took Reese's hand before heading out to the parking lot.

Once out in the chilly air, Connor watched as Rob finished loading the bags into the trunk. "You have the boyfriend driving and carrying groceries inside?"

Clara's eyes turned towards Connor. For once, she didn't take the bait and only shrugged when she answered, "Yes, his truck is at the bottom of the lake and my doctor hasn't cleared me to drive yet, so why not?"

When they reached the car, Connor shook Rob's hand before giving Hailey a hug and assisting her into the carseat. Then, he walked around to receive a hug from Reese. As Connor reached for Clara's door, he paused to ask, "I didn't overstep by offering to take them to the fall festival, did I?"

"Not at all. I know you aren't making false promises." Clara placed her hand on his chest. "I'm glad we ran into you. I miss you."

"Yeah? So, I don't have to worry about the boyfriend taking over?" Connor teased. Before she could take issue with his comment, he leaned down to whisper into her ear. "I love you."

Connor kissed her before opening her car door. He waited patiently while she slowly settled into her seat. He looked into the back window to wave back to the kids as he closed her door and watched them drive off.

As he pulled out of the lot, Rob looked over at Clara to assess her mood. "You alright?"

"Yeah, I am," Clara answered with a soft smile as she looked over at Rob. His facial expression triggered something, like a memory so close to the surface, if only she could retrieve it. She studied his profile as her mind searched for it. But Reese's comment interrupted her focus.

"Mommy, why does Connor call Uncle Rob your boyfriend?" the young boy wondered out loud.

Rob looked over with his eyebrows raised in question.

Clara burst out with unexpected laughter.

Lila was relieved when Dallas finally returned to work earlier that day. She had been surprised by the upgrade in the security system. The expense was unnecessary, but his response was that they would agree to disagree. Nothing was more important than her safety. Lila turned at the soft ding alerting her of a vehicle entering the property.

She reached for her cell and sighed. The security camera showed her parents slowly driving up to her house. She wasn't surprised by the unexpected visit. If anything, Lila was surprised it took this long. She'd been home from the hospital for a week.

Lila wasn't ready to face the music. Chase had caught her up on the ultimatum her father had given. Perhaps their visiting together meant they were staying together, she thought optimistically.

Dallas also received the alert of his in-laws arriving at his place. He was partly relieved their relationship was no longer hidden, but he felt uneasy having others in his home. Especially those not willing to acknowledge him when he was in high school.

He arrived home shortly after, entering the kitchen from the back door. Dallas paused at the doorway, feeling the tension in the room. No one was talking but everyone's eyes were on him. He momentarily wondered if he was walking in on something. Hell, the arguments he's been hearing about between Lila's parents were likely carrying over to Lila's unease.

She sat across the table from her parents with a cake in the center. Everyone had a mug of coffee and an untouched piece of cake before them. Dallas gestured for her to remain seated as he placed his bag and jacket on the hooks beside the door. He nodded a greeting to her parents before he leaned down to kiss Lila.

"Dallas, it's good seeing you again," Allison stated. "Would you like some cake?"

He first looked at his wife, she didn't seem to be holding onto any anger or resentment at the moment. He nodded agreement as he reached for the coffee pot to refill the mugs and pour some for himself.

Once he was seated, his mother-in-law started talking while Mitch seemed to watch his every move. Dallas felt like an animal in captivity while they silently waited for him to prove Mitch's point, that he was not worthy of Lila's affections.

"Lila, your father and I want to talk about your wedding. We have an account specifically for this. We've dreamed of planning it together with you," Allison stated with her eyes on Dallas.

Dallas realized from Lila's body language the topic had already been discussed prior to his arrival. Before he could respond, his wife did.

"Mom, I already told you. We don't need another wedding or a large reception. It's not necessary," Lila stated as she reached for Dallas' hand.

The gesture didn't go unnoticed as Mitch's eyes remained on the hands held together. He asked in a flat tone, "How, exactly, did you two meet?"

"Really, Dad? Why would you ask that? We grew up in the same town, went to the same school. There were barely eight hundred students in our school. How would we not know each other?" Lila answered.

"You never hung out in the same crowd. You weren't even in the same graduating class. I'm curious to know how this relationship developed," Mitch answered with a tone that sounded like he caught Dallas climbing into his daughter's window late at night.

"Mitch," Allison's voice warned.

"I don't think it's too big of a deal to answer. I want to know how long our daughter has been sneaking around behind our backs and why," Mitch honestly answered, missing the looks exchanged between the younger couple while he was looking at his wife.

After Dallas shrugged, Lila took a deep breath before she, for the second time in less than a month, talked about the night that changed her life. "It was the night the theater exploded."

Lila's voice had been quiet but the expressions on her parent's faces suggested she yelled. She allowed the statement to sink in before she continued, "I had gone into the theater to get our seats while Clara went into the bathroom. I had just sat down at my seat but stood up again to get my water bottle that rolled away. The next thing I knew, the walls were crumbling and Dallas was protectively over me, keeping the debris off me. He was injured. I wasn't. When the ceiling literally stopped falling, he and I were trapped along with his cousin Sam."

"Sam? Sam Black? Didn't he die?" Allison asked in confusion.

When Lila didn't answer, Dallas did. "Yes. He died about an hour after the explosion."

"Oh, honey! Why didn't you tell us?" She started to stand but Lila's tone stopped her.

"Tell you what? When I woke up in the hospital, the comments made were not very nice nor welcoming for discussion and explanation. Not once did either of you ask me about Dallas or Sam. Instead, you acted like he got what he deserved," she wiped a tear from her cheek as Dallas squeezed her hand, "he wasn't anything like you said. He was kind, thoughtful, and scared. He was a high school kid and he knew he wouldn't make it to see another sunrise. He put on a brave front while he and Dallas kept me calm. None of us mentioned the ongoing battles between our families. And not once did either of them breathe one inappropriate comment about the Foxwoods."

Lila paused as she fought to control her voice, "And when he died in my arms, Dallas kept me from freaking out. He kept me calm and talked with me even though it was his cousin that lay dead not even two feet away. When a passage was cleared, Dallas should have gone first since he was injured. Instead, he insisted I go before him. We started hanging out after that."

"You've been together since then?" Mitch asked in an accusing tone. "You were only fourteen years old! You had no business sleeping around with an older guy! And you had no business taking advantage of a young innocent girl."

Allison was about to intercept but paused just long enough to watch the younger man lean back, as if resigned to an expected death as her husband stood up while her daughter stepped between them.

"Isn't that just like you to assume the worst? I didn't say anything about sex! Our relationship was no more inappropriate than Rob's was with Clara. She wasn't even fourteen yet but you had no problem with Rob hanging out alone with her," Lila yelled back. "We were friends, close friends after that. He never once tried anything inappropriate until I was ready."

"Until you were ready?" Mitch repeated. Before he could continue, his wife was standing beside him with her hand on his arm.

"We kept in touch after he went into the army, we were both legal consenting adults when our paths crossed again. Dallas was hesitant to allow the relationship to grow, especially in secret. I was the one that wanted to keep it hidden," Lila told her parents. "He's never been anything but a gentleman. He's always treated me with love and kindness. And I will not let either of you come into his home and insult him, is that understood? You either accept him or don't bother coming here again."

"Lila, I love you. I've already accepted him," Allison started to say, "but you have to understand, you've thrown a lot at us in such a short time. Why didn't you tell us what happened that night?"

"It was too raw. I guess I thought you would have figured it out. The rescuer knew we were all together in a small space. Dallas was the next one out after me," Lila shrugged.

Allison and Mitch exchanged a look before he answered, "Once you were pulled out of the rubble, we followed the ambulance to the hospital. We never thought to ask for details. We were grateful you made it out alive."

Mitch walked around his wife to give his daughter a hug. He was already losing his son, he couldn't afford to also lose his daughter. "I just never thought anything good about him, since he was a Thompson. Rob never had anything good to say. And before you start, I realize he may have been biased."

After a few minutes, Allison tried again. "Dallas, don't you want to see your bride walking down the aisle in a beautiful white dress?"

Dallas inwardly sighed. He had seen his bride walk down the aisle towards him. Even though they eloped, they still had a small wedding album of their special day. He had a framed picture of his bride on his nightstand and a picture of them together on his desk.

"Mom, we've already been married long enough. I am no longer his bride, but his wife. We do not need or want another wedding," Lila answered.

"Do you always speak for him?" her father asked. He didn't want a pushover for a son-in-law.

"No, but he's wise enough to fight his own battles and let me fight mine," Lila fired a warning to her parents.

Allison had been silent as she studied again the man raised, mostly, by Zachariah Thompson. Until recently, she kept the details of her life with him to herself. Because she had despised Felicia Girwin Thompson, she never really had positive thoughts about the boy. She had allowed herself to believe the rumors, partly because she didn't allow herself to care either way. But now that she knew he was not Zac's son, but instead the child of Felicia Thompson and Carl Gibson. Damn, he was not what she would have expected. Because she was so intent on studying the younger man, looking for signs of her Zac in him, she missed the subtle change in the topic being discussed.

"Since you are hell bent against a wedding reception, the money is still yours. How about we give you two horses and a barn?" Mitch asked.

Dallas raised his eyebrows as he looked between Lila and her father.

Lila's eyes initially lit up, but narrowed in question. "Maybe, what's the catch?"

As Dallas and Lila later watched her parents drive away, he remained silent, studying her face.

Lila turned to go back into the house but stopped when her eyes met his. "What? Was it alright to agree to the horses?"

Dallas chuckled. "I have no problem with that. I guess I now see the family resemblance and how you learned to negotiate. Why didn't you ask them to dinner?"

"I figured you had enough of them. I know I did," Lila admitted. "He should never attempt to give a wedding gift with strings attached. And I'm not going to get involved between them and Rob. That's their battle, not mine."

The conversation in the vehicle leaving wasn't as pleasant.

34 small town fun

Running into Clara and the kids lifted Connor's mood. He decided to hit Memories for dinner when he realized Devan was working the bar. He gestured at an empty seat, next to his normal one. "Is this seat taken?"

"No," the stranger replied, watching Connor settle in. "I'm Max Kauffman. I'm relocating here, I'll be working at the new YMCA opening up in December."

"Right, my sister-in-law has been telling me about it. I'm Connor Emerson," he answered, shaking his hand. "How are you liking the town? It has to be a big change from the city."

"It certainly is," Max agreed. "I can't get over how little there is to do here! What do you do for fun around here?"

"We are close to the national park. It has all kinds of sports available year round, skiing, snowboarding, whitewater rafting, and hiking. I'm a volunteer on rescue missions when people get lost. I have a lake house close to the park. It's definitely a slower pace after living in the city but I like that," Connor answered before ordering his dinner.

He was curious about this guy. There had been so much stated about him, but not much positive. Talia did say he was perfect for the position but that was all. He smiled as he remembered Clara's comment, 'my mother raised me to not talk negatively about others.'

"That's an understatement! In the city, you have choices of restaurants, bars, nightclubs and even gyms. Here, there aren't many options." Max looked behind them as a group of women walked by.

"Hi, Connor!"

"Hello, Grace, how's it going?"

"Oh, it's going! We have a big birthday party happening this weekend. I don't know what I was thinking! We invited Sawyer's whole preschool class. I agreed to go all out with a huge jumping house in the backyard and everything!" Grace answered. She worked in the hospital with Connor.

Connor chuckled. "Yes, Reese was telling me about it. He's very excited."

"I hope you aren't working and can join your family on Saturday," Grace stated as she patted his arm.

"Oh, I wouldn't miss it. What can be more exciting than jumping around with a bunch of preschoolers high on sugar?" Connor speculated as his other neighbor chuckled. "I haven't been in one since Cole Denver's party."

"Isn't that when Bear fell out, broke his arm?" the neighbor, Adam Johnson, asked.

Connor nodded as Grace groaned out loud. "Hopefully Bear is working this weekend."

"There's always something going on," Connor stated as he turned back to Max.

"That's right," Adam agreed. "There's the Fall Festival every Friday, Saturday, and Sunday during the fall months. Games and activities for all ages. The events change so you can go out a few times."

"The corn maze is different every year," Connor inserted. "And at night, it turns into a scary maze."

"Corn maze?" Max looked puzzled.

"Yeah, you know, after harvesting the corn, we mow down parts of it into a maze. You enter from one side and have to find your way through to the exit. We actually have a few different mazes. The children's easy, difficult, and scary. If it's done correctly, people can get really turned around, but there are maps and clues," Adam explained.

"Who designed it this year?" Connor asked.

"My grandfather. My brother and I did the hard work while he supervised," Adam answered.

"I'm thinking about going this weekend," Devan stated from behind the bar, casually clearing off the dirty glasses and refilling the drinks.

"I should ask my girlfriend," Max stated. Everyone turned to him in question.

"Who's your girlfriend?" Adam wondered. Like Connor and Devan, he had heard a few things about the new guy in town, nothing positive.

"Rachel MacKenzie," Max answered proudly.

"Really? You and Rachel?" Adam looked to Connor in confusion.

Connor gave a subtle shake of the head, telling him not to comment.

"Well, we aren't really serious yet. She's the main reason I'm relocating here. We met in the city and became fast friends. I wanted to help her out since she lost her mother. I didn't realize her family home was so big! She must have a lot of upkeep on her place," Max stated.

"She's got Chase to help her out with all that," the older man on Max's other side informed him before he sipped his beer.

"Maybe, but she knows I'm also here for her. I just need to get her bitch of a best friend away from her. She's always telling Rachel I'm not good enough," he continued. "Just my luck she also decided to move back."

"Are you talking about Clara?" Adam's eyes widened in confusion as he glanced toward Connor again.

Connor kept quiet, sipping his beer. Maybe coming down to Memories wasn't such a good idea.

"Yes! Don't you think she's a bit stuck up? She's always parading around like she's better than others. I just saw her earlier with her boyfriend and kids. She didn't even look over when I called out to her. She would never give me the time of day when we ran into each other at the gym in the city," he reported.

"That doesn't mean anything, she's always been reserved. It's because of her hearing loss. She does better in a smaller group once she knows you," Adam explained while Connor and the older man nodded in agreement.

"I don't think she's hearing impaired, she's just a stuck-up bitch," Max confirmed with confidence. "But Talia? You know her?"

"Difficult not to," Connor answered while the others chuckled.

"She is hot! I can't believe who she's married to! She should just dump him already. I can help her get a good attorney and she'd get the house. Run his sorry ass out of town," he declared as he finished off his drink.

"I don't think it works that way," Adam shared, surprised Connor remained silent as he finished off his drink.

"Hey, Devan, can I have another? And please, take care of my new friends." Max gestured with his empty glass.

"I'll pass," Connor stated when his dinner was placed in front of him. When he stood up, he nodded at the older man on Max's other side and slapped Adam on the shoulder. "Adam, great seeing you again. Give your grandmother my love."

"I better not, she's already told my grandfather she's just waiting for your proposal and she'll dump him on his sorry ass," Adam stated as the others chuckled. "Have a good night, sir."

"You know Connor well?" Max asked after Connor left.

Adam had waved off the new drink as he looked over his texts but looked up when he answered, "Sure. We're both from here."

"But you called him sir. Isn't that a bit formal for this town?"

"Never really thought about it. He's my boss so I usually call him doctor," Adam informed him as he, too, left money on the bar and donned his jacket. "But if I could give you some advice, you should really be cautious about what you say in the company of others. Everyone is hoping the new Y will be a success."

Adam nodded to the other men before stepping away.

"What did I say?" Max asked in confusion to the older man on his right.

"A lot, actually. The poor guy has had a rough couple of months. He sits down to a relaxing evening beer and you bad mouth his girl. Not very neighborly. Clara has always been intuitive and she certainly knows a bad apple when she sees one."

"Wait a minute, Clara is his girl? But I saw her earlier today with another man," Max argued.

"Yes, likely Rob. They have always been close friends," he dismissed, grabbed his newly refilled drink and started to turn in his stool. "And as for Talia, seriously? The man introduced himself with his full name. You didn't familiarize yourself with those who interviewed you for the job?"

"Talia's last name is Emerson? How was I supposed to know?" the younger man tried to defend himself.

"How many Talia's do you think we have? Like Adam says, caution when talking with people. You never know how they are connected," he stood up. "A freebie, the bartender is Connor's cousin."

Max sat in silence as the older man walked away to join another group sitting at a table.

Devan came over to clear off the vacant area. He paused when Max attempted to apologize, thoroughly perplexed. "I didn't mean to insult anyone. Are you really Connor's cousin?"

"Second cousins, our mothers are first cousins, close growing up," Devan nodded with his explanation.

"Second cousins? Who keeps track of these things? How could I know?"

"Maybe not but weren't you ever told to keep your thoughts to yourself, especially inappropriate ones?" Devan asked while he wiped the bar clean.

"Who was that, anyway, Clara's father?" he wondered out loud about the older guy that was sitting beside him.

"That's Mitch Foxwood," Devan answered, realizing he had yet to lay eyes on Carl Gibson.

"Shit! That's Chase's father?" Max's eyes turned toward the older man laughing with others at a table across the room.

"No, his uncle." He gestured with his head, amused at how Connor's nickname from years ago seemed to stick. "He's the father of the *boyfriend* with Clara."

"Fuck! Can you apologize to your cousin for me? I didn't know," Max explained.

"Seems doubtful. It's not likely to change his mind about you now. Both Connor and his brother are protective of their women. Just last spring, Connor threw his other cousin up against the wall for making inappropriate advances on Clara," Devan explained. "And honestly, there are many guys and gals around here that feel that way about their other halves. I suggest you tread lightly."

"Wait, I heard about that," Max said thoughtfully. "Didn't Connor cause Clara to break up with the guy?"

Devan paused before he turned away. *A lost cause*, he thought but remembered Max had been seen around town with some of Eric's friends. They would likely have provided misinformation. The small town secrets were difficult to keep under the hat and often exaggerated with the wrong details. "Actually, he was arrested for stalking her. They were never together as a couple."

"That can't be right. That's not how I heard it," Max argued with certainty.

"I was there when his body was slammed into the wall. I saw the sheriff arrest him," Devan answered cautiously. Now knowing Eric had been getting out despite being under house arrest, he wondered how close the two had become.

Still skeptical, Max paid his check and left. He decided to try his luck at The Lantern across the street. There were usually younger and more willing girls there.

Devan watched him leave as he pulled out his ringing cell. "Hello?"

"Devan? Don't hang up, please. I was hoping we could talk," he heard Shannon's voice.

"Now's not a good time. I'm working," he answered, wiping the bar with his other hand.

"Please, Devan. I want to talk with you, explain a few things. It's important to me," she pleaded.

"Can I call you after I get off?"

"Well, I was hoping I could meet you at your place."

"What?" Devan quickly looked around before quietly stepping away from the bar. "You're driving here? With your bodyguard?"

"No, he stayed in the city. The case was settled out of court and I'm free. It's just me. I did promise I'd text him when I arrived," she clarified. When Devan remained silent, she asked again, "Please Devan? Can we talk? I can be at your place in a half hour."

"Where are you expecting to stay?"

"I don't know," she admitted, hurt at the realization it wouldn't be an easy battle. "I guess Clara's until I get my own place."

"Her place may be getting a bit crowded," Devan commented as he looked around the restaurant. It wasn't that busy.

"Yeah, you're probably right. Connor wouldn't like it. I could probably stay at the farm," she speculated.

Devan hesitated, much had changed in the short amount of time Shannon was gone. Lila was permanently staying with Dallas. Connor was sleeping alone upstairs at his loft while Rob was not willing to step foot on the farm. He wasn't going to start on the rumors of the older Foxwood couple.

"You really haven't been in contact with any of your friends, have you? I guess I could meet you."

"Thanks, Devan. You won't regret this," Shannon assured him before hanging up.

That remains to be seen, he thought, returning his cell to his pocket before searching for the boss. It wasn't like this was his day job.

When Devan pulled into his driveway, he was surprised to see Clara sitting alone on the steps of her porch. He walked over as she greeted him.

"What are you doing alone out here? You and the boyfriend arguing?" Devan teased.

"Hardly," Clara answered with a laugh as she patted the spot next to her. "I can't believe Connor's nickname stuck for so long. You know Rob's never been my boyfriend, right? He's taking the kids on a bike ride. Well, Reese is on his bike and Hailey is on her tricycle. Rob's walking alongside of them. I can't keep up."

"How are you feeling?"

"Getting there, slowly," she answered. "Are you just getting in from the office? Learn anything new?"

"Waiting for lab results," Devan answered vaguely. "But I was working behind the bar at Memories. It helps to remind me there is good in the world. Met your nemesis today."

"You met Isabella Daynee?" Clara asked with surprise.

"Who?" Devan asked. Then he laughed, as he remembered meeting the woman over the summer. "No, I already met her. I mean Max. He claimed to be Rachel's boyfriend so I guess he's actually Chase's nemesis."

"I can't believe he's actually moving here. Max won't last long. The town is too simple for him." Clara looked at him. "Why do you think he's my nemesis? Oh, wait, don't tell me he's actually complaining about me to you. I don't know why, it's not like I've seen him since he arrived."

"Well, let's say he wasn't talking to me and I'm sure you already know he believes you're the one keeping him from his perceived other half," he reported.

"Oh, man. Who was he talking to?" Clara looked over as Devan smiled. "Damn! Connor? He didn't hit him, did he?"

Devan chuckled when she laughed. "No, Connor showed incredible restraint, he walked away. After Max more or less hinted he wanted to move in on Talia. It was Mitch Foxwood who explained to the simpleton who Connor is."

Clara was laughing as she clutched her side. "Oh, no! He was talking about Rachel as his girlfriend to Mitch? And is actually talking inappropriately about Talia to Connor?"

"He said he knew a good lawyer to help Talia with the divorce and help her get the house," Devan continued, "the guy really has no sense of polite conversation, does he?"

After a few minutes of laughing, Devan asked again how she was holding up.

"Taking it one day at a time. It was good to laugh but it still hurts," Clara admitted quietly, she understood what he was really asking.

"Are you ready to tell me what happened?" Devan regretted the sadness he brought back into her eyes. "We need to get your formal statement."

"Haven't you already talked to Rob?"

"Yes. He gave his statement at the hospital after he woke up. Clara, we need to hear from you what happened. You two weren't together the whole time. We need to know everything that happened," he patiently explained. He couldn't understand why she was so hesitant to talk.

"I don't really know what happened," she admitted just as Reese came into view on the sidewalk. Rob was close behind, carrying Hailey in one arm and her tricycle in the other. "I can't seem to make sense of the few memories I do have. I wouldn't know how to explain them."

"You know more than you realize. We know you were drugged and your perception of events are probably altered, but you could still give us important details. You pick the place and time, Clara. It could be just me or my boss."

"Does Connor have to be there?"

Devan looked at her a moment before he shook his head. "No, but he'll likely hear about it."

Clara looked down at her hands as she nodded her understanding. Devan reached out to touch her arm. "Clara, you didn't do anything wrong, you know that right? Nothing you did or didn't do is going to change how he feels about you."

"Perhaps," Clara allowed sadly as Hailey and Reese ran over to the porch. Rob walked past to bring the bikes into the garage as Devan stood up and reached out to assist her in standing. "Devan?"

"Yes?"

"Do you know where my dad is?" When Devan shook his head, she asked, "Could you find him, if you wanted to?"

Devan didn't say every law enforcement officer in the county was on the look out for him after his finger prints were found at the Howell cabin. It was widely believed he either left the area or he found a new place to hole up in. And they knew he'd been squatting at the Hawks House. No signs of him since the tunnels were discovered. Hopefully, Carl Gibson wasn't permanently hidden.

When Rob came back out a moment later, he held his annoyance at Clara holding Devan's hand as he assisted her up the porch steps.

Shannon paused for a moment to take a deep breath before knocking on Devan's door. She smiled when he answered. Without a word, he stepped back as she came inside. After he closed the door, he gestured towards the family room.

"It's great to see you again," she said as she stepped close to kiss him. He turned his face, causing the kiss to land on his cheek instead of his lips. *Damn*, she thought. This would be difficult. She went to sit on the sofa as he sat on the chair.

"You are really going to make this difficult, aren't you?"

"I haven't done anything wrong. You asked for the meeting," he shrugged. Devan had debated offering a drink but decided to wait. He was too curious to hear what she had to say.

"I want to apologize for my behavior last summer," she started quietly. "I hadn't considered I was lying and sneaking around until you called me on it. You were right; I was secretly seeing Joel but it was only that weekend. Not that it makes a difference if it was one day or a whole month, it was disrespectful and wrong. For that, I am truly sorry I hurt you."

Shannon's green eyes stayed on his hazel while she talked. She was starting to lose her nerve when he remained silent and still. She continued onto the other argument they had after the incident in the radiology department. "Please don't hate Rob. He's always been a good, reliable friend. He was there for me when no one else was."

Feeling restless, especially after the long drive, she stood up to walk towards the window. "I don't think you were in town the night the movie theater exploded."

"Wait, you were there?" Devan asked as he scooted to the end of his seat.

"No. I was supposed to be. The plan was Rob was going to drop Clara and Lila at the theater to get the tickets before picking me up at the hospital," she turned back towards the window. "My mother had been admitted earlier in the week because of an infection. She was doing well and expected to be discharged the next day. Instead, she passed while I was visiting her that afternoon. I wasn't prepared for it, which really was stupid of me. She had stage four ovarian cancer."

Shannon felt a tear slide down her cheek as she tightened her arms across her chest. She never talked about the evening her mother passed. "I was visiting with her, talking about the cute guy in my math class, while I painted her nails and she listened. I didn't even know she passed until the nurse came in. No idea how long I remained sitting there with her before I kissed her one last time. Then I ended up downstairs in the lobby, totally oblivious to the world. Suddenly, Rob was squatting down in front of me.

"I didn't even have to say a word, he knew," her voice cracked as spoke softly. "He sat beside me and held me as I cried. Again, no idea how long we sat there. I don't remember him walking me to his truck or getting me home. He stayed with me that night until my grandmother and my uncle arrived the next day. I didn't know about the theater until later. After the funeral, I asked him why he stayed with me when his sister and best friend were trapped in the rubble. He simply shrugged and said he was exactly where he needed to be."

Shannon chuckled as she wiped the tears from her face. "I consider him one of my close friends. Guys were never understanding about our relationship so I didn't talk about it. Our whole group was close, we would all turn to one or the other depending on what was going on and who was around. He's never crossed the line with me but I realize what I was comfortable with would not have been the same with Chase. There were times when we spent the nights together but we literally slept, nothing else."

She turned around to face him again. "Last summer when you kicked me out, I didn't even plan to go to him. I drove out to the farm and there he was. And since you already dumped me, it's none of your business what goes on between us. Rob is one of the most supportive people I know. He knows how to be there without being overly so. And he's never let me down. Ever."

Devan sat back in the chair as his mind replayed the many scenes with Rob. The way he defended Clara in the parking lot, when they were found in the shrub, damn! The guy was not popular with other guys around town, but his female friends loved him.

He stood up, slowly closing the gap between them. "I have been hearing a lot about him lately. Do you want a drink, something to eat while I catch you up on everything?"

35

one step at a time

The next morning, Rob was up before dawn. He usually slept the first couple of hours in his bed, until his pleasant dreams of riding in the woods turned dark with shadows moving out into the clearing. Each night, the dreams started out simple, usually he was riding on his favorite horse. Sometimes he was alone and other times he had company. But he always found himself suddenly alone, galloping into the darkness of the forest. The shadow always caught him by surprise, standing between him and Clara. And his greatest fear was realized when he could never get to her in time.

And like every night, he would awaken alone in the darkness of his room covered in sweat. He could still hear the echoes of the footsteps as if the shadow had just stepped out of his room. Rob would get paranoid that someone else was in the house. To diminish his fear, he'd retreat downstairs, after checking on everyone.

Convinced the house remained secured and locked, he'd spent the remainder of the night on the sofa. And like most nights, he would remain restless until Clara, likely also restless from her own night terrors, snuggled close beside him. Then, he would be able to rest without being haunted by shadows.

As he climbed the steps, he mentally thought of what to prepare for breakfast. He paused at the top of the stairs to listen. Did he hear a door close? As he turned towards Hailey's room, surprised to find the girl's bed was empty. He noted the closet door was partially open. Peeking inside, he was relieved to see the toddler was playing with her favorite stuffed animal. She looked up when the door opened and waved with a smile.

"Hailey, why aren't you in your bed?" Rob asked, squatting down in front of her. To his amusement, she answered, not that he understood a word. "You want to help me make breakfast?"

When the little girl nodded, he reached out for her hand. He listened to her gibberish talk as they first stopped in his room before heading down towards the kitchen.

Down the hall, Evil faded back into the shadows to avoid being seen.

Next door, Devan was up early getting breakfast started. He had been allowing Jack Ruddy to crash at his place and was relieved he had the common sense to have the bedrooms furnished with a bed and dresser. Surprising no one more than himself, Devan suggested that Shannon stay in the fourth bedroom.

When she walked into the kitchen, she stopped when she realized Devan wasn't alone.

"Shannon, good morning. This is Jack Ruddy, my boss. Jack, Shannon," Devan introduced the two as he gestured her toward the table. Once seated, he poured her a cup of coffee and passed the food in her direction. "Do you have any plans for today?"

"Not really," she answered cautiously. While Shannon had been given the all clear to return to town, she had been instructed to stay alert. There could be others out there, still loyal to her old boss. The last thing she needed was to drag her friends into harm's way, again. Shannon was never going to forgive herself for what happened to Clara and Lila. She was very hesitant to contact any of her close friends.

"Clara is home next door, I'm sure she'd love to see you," Devan commented, as if reading her mind. "She's been asking about you."

"Do you think it'll be safe? I can't be the cause of anything else happening to her," Shannon whispered.

"Shan, we'll make it safe. You're surrounded by the FBI. Clara's never alone," he assured her. "You know how protective Rob and Connor are with her."

"You really think it'll be alright?"

Devan was already nodding as he handed her his cell. "Text her. You can even enter through the back deck."

Shannon hesitated for a minute before sending the text. While she waited for a response, she finished her breakfast.

"Devan says you're an accountant. Are you interested in looking over some books for us?" Jack asked.

"FBI stuff? Is that legal?" Shannon looked between the two men. Devan had been silent while he ate his pancakes.

"We can have you sign on as a consultant," the older agent answered, studying the woman across from him.

"Sure, why not? Where would I need to go?"

"Upstairs into the office," Devan answered with a smile.

After breakfast, Clara assisted the children with getting ready for school. Since her return home, they only went a couple of times a week. But today, she decided she was no longer a victim. Her friend Chloe was coming over for a session. She wasn't sure what it entailed but agreed it couldn't make anything worse.

Rob agreed to drop them off before continuing with errands around town. After she closed the door behind him, she received a text message. Once she realized it was from Shannon on Devan's phone, she hit the call button.

"Shannon? Are you really next door?"

"Yes, I arrived last night!"

Clara was already stepping out the back door, looking over towards the neighboring deck. She cried out with happiness when she saw her newly discovered half-sister. "Shannon! You're really here!"

"Clara!" Shannon was quickly beside her, both hugging as if it had been a lifetime since they'd last seen each other but it hadn't even been two months. "I'm so sorry for everything. The accident and the shooting, all my fault. You and Joel both warned me to be cautious and I ignored it. My stupidity almost killed you!"

Shannon stepped back when Clara gave a soft groan. "Oh my God, Clara, I'm so sorry. I didn't mean to hurt you."

"Shan, I'm alright, really. Still just a little sore, but that's not your fault," Clara squeezed her hand, "you know, we never really talked about us being sisters."

"It's weird, isn't it? It seems to be the only good thing to come out of us all having our DNA tested. It didn't bring us any closer to finding out who my father is," Shannon commented. "I was so sure once I learned who my paternal half-brother was, I'd know who the father was, but it's all such a mystery."

"I can't believe you and Jason are half-siblings," Clara agreed. "Shan, I have to confess, I wasn't going to tell anyone about this, it's your news to share or not. But I talked with Connor and his brother. I wanted to know if he knew who your father was."

"Matt? Really? Is it him?" Shannon asked hopefully. Matt Emerson was an honorable person. But Clara was already shaking her head. "It wasn't him?"

"No, he knew of the pregnancy but not who the father was. He claimed my mother never told him. But he was the one to bring Mom to a clinic," she explained. "They were both surprised to hear you and Jason were both half-siblings. I think he may have an idea who Jason's mother was but he didn't say. Listen, I have an appointment in a few minutes, what are you doing? Where are you staying?"

"For now, at Devan's," Shannon explained but then she shook her head. "No, we aren't back together. I probably ruined that last summer. For now, I'm doing consulting work until I figure out my next step. I need to get back inside, we'll catch up soon. And for now, wait to talk to Lila and Rachel. I need to know what's what before I potentially expose them to danger again."

"At least call them! We've all been worried about you." Clara leaned in to hug with her good arm. "I'm so glad you're back."

When Clara stepped back inside, the doorbell rang, Chloe stood on her porch with a massage table and a large bag.

"Good morning! You are certainly looking better," Chloe greeted with a bright smile as she started to lift the table into the house.

"Let me help you with all that," Clara offered.

"Oh, no, I have this. This is what I do," she declined the assistance as she lifted the heavy massage table with ease. "I was told you have lifting restrictions."

"True," Clara admitted. "But I wanted to help you. When Dr. Taylor mentioned you, I had no idea what to expect. I don't know what kind of therapy you give."

"This is simply a relaxation exercise, Clara. You have been through so much these last few months. We are going to stretch, breathe, cleanse your mind, and massage those knots. This room will definitely do." Chloe gave her a bright smile after looking around the family room before she started setting everything up.

Clara watched in awe as the petite woman moved around with a graceful ease, setting up the massage table, placing candles around the room, and a noise maker set to the sounds of the ocean waves.

"Alright, so that handsome man you are currently living with is not here, correct? When do you expect his return?"

"A couple of hours, I guess. I don't know if I can be lying naked here. What if he comes back early," Clara expressed her concerns with the massage table in the center of her family room, within view of the front door.

"Clara, what are your goals? What do you wish to accomplish?"

"I have no idea," she answered honestly. "I don't know what is possible. I want to be able to sleep a full night without disturbing dreams; I want to be able to walk without pain; and I want to be able to move freely around town without fear. I am tired of playing the role of the victim."

Chloe's short blond wavy hair nodded as she studied her friend. They had gone to high school together, both leaving the town for college. When they ran into each other a few times, they always reconnected where they last left off. Chole loved that Clara was never judgmental about her decision for a more holistic approach to life. Sitting beside her on the sofa, she leaned over to squeeze her friend's hand.

"Those are excellent goals. We certainly have our work cut out for us. We won't be able to resolve everything during this session but I will give you tools to start down your path.

"Today's focus will be meditation, yoga, and massage. I know you're familiar with each of the areas, but today, we'll tap into each with a focus on clearing your mind, stretching your body, and easing the pain. Grayson has informed me of all your recent injuries. Every one, except your feet, is on the left side of your body, correct?" When Clara nodded, she continued, "You know breathing is essential, so I believe we will begin there, followed by the yoga and finish with the massage. And since you won't be able to relax while naked on the massage table in the middle of the family room, why not call that handsome hunk? Have him bring lunch at noon, when he returns back."

Early afternoon, Rob returned back to Clara's with the lunch order as instructed. He was not prepared for the family room to be altered into a spa when he came inside, after texting to assure an all clear. Somehow, he found himself almost naked on the massage table with Chloe's surprisingly strong hands massaging kinks he never knew he had. When she was finished, he was shocked how much better he felt.

Over lunch, each of her new clients were instructed to drink water first, and she provided homework they were to complete before their sessions the following week.

"I'm leaving everything but the table. You can each meditate and stretch separately or together. When you're up to it, I'm inviting you to my classes."

As Rob insisted on carrying out the massage table, Clara checked her text messages, happily surprised one was from Connor. He was asking if this evening would be a good night to attend the Fall Festival. With a smile, she quickly responded.

Chloe was right, if she no longer wished to be the victim, she needed to stop thinking like the victim. Instead of allowing herself to be held prisoner to her fears, she needed to start living her life. Taking a moment to think about what she wanted, Clara slowly stood up and went upstairs to assess.

When Clara entered her bedroom, she was surprised by the sudden burst of energy as she looked around. She had much to do: change the sheets, clean the bathrooms, vacuum the rugs. The list was endless!

"What are you doing?" Rob asked from the doorway. There was a pile of towels on the floor near the door and her comforter was pulled back.

"What does it look like I'm doing? I'm cleaning this damn house! I don't know when the sheets were changed last, the floor vacuumed nor the bathrooms scrubbed," she answered while pulling the sheets completely from her bed.

"Want help?"

By late afternoon, all the beds had clean sheets, the bathrooms were both cleaned, and the rugs were all vacuumed. While the two worked together, Clara was tempted to share the exciting news of Shannon's return, but it wasn't hers to share. Instead, she explained her plans for her therapy gym. She wanted to make changes in the room but had no idea of the expense for the budget.

Rob contacted Chase about meeting up later to discuss some ideas before heading down to the basement. After switching out the loads, he returned upstairs with the clean sheets when he realized how late it was getting.

"Should I go get Reese and Hailey?"

"Connor just texted. He's picking them up on his way here," Clara answered as they folded the sheets together. "Are you sure you don't want to join us tonight?"

"I'm sure Connor would rather see you and the kids," he answered. "I'm meeting Chase later to discuss plans for the therapy room. Are you excited about seeing Connor tonight?"

"Yes, I am." Clara smiled as she laid the folded sheet on the pile before reaching for another. "Thanks for helping me today. I really appreciate it."

"Why wouldn't I help? I've been staying here. I'm embarrassed I didn't think about all this myself." Rob paused as he carried the pile of sheets to the linen closet, and ensured the door was closed before returning back. "I won't say anything about us sleeping together on the sofa."

"What?" Clara looked up in surprise as images of her recurrent dreams flashed in her mind. Eric and Jason both in her bed with similar features. The dream always ends with her going downstairs to find Jason sleeping on the sofa. In the morning, she wakes up alone.

Or does she? Rob's always been an early riser. But they each go upstairs to bed at night.

But, he's likely to be having nightmares too, a voice said.

"I didn't say anything before but it helps me sleep better. I just figured it did the same for you," he explained as he looked around the room one last time before they headed down the stairs.

Clara could only stare at him, distracted as she pondered the significance of what her mind was telling her. Shit! She mentally viewed Rob, Eric and Jason's faces, physique and mannerisms. How did she not see this sooner? Didn't anyone else see it? Knowing what she now knew, she stopped on the last step as she watched Rob walk through the family room.

Rob's biological father is Zachariah Thompson. That makes Rob first cousins with Sean Black, Sammy Black's younger brother. Sean's mother is Sarah Thompson Black, sister of Zachariah. She must be the other young teen that gave up her son at birth, Jason.

She visibly shuddered as she continued with her thought process: Eric was half-siblings with Jason! There's too many similarities for it not to be true.

Clara gasped in shock at the realization, causing her to miscalculate the last step as she stumbled to the floor. She refused to acknowledge the next part, the most obvious conclusion.

"Clara? Are you alright?" Rob was quickly at her side. "You definitely did too much today. I think you're overdue for your pain medicine. When did you last take it?"

She looked up into his eyes as he touched her cheek. "Clara? What's wrong? You look like you've seen a ghost."

"I, ah, I'm fine. You're right, there was a lot of activity today. Too much standing and using my left arm." *And too many revelations today,* she thought. "I just need to get off my leg and probably ice my shoulder."

"Here, let me help." Rob placed his arm around her waist and lifted her from the floor, then carried her to the sofa. "You rest before the kids get home. I'll get the ice and pain pill."

In his rush, Rob didn't see the tears.

Clara watched his movements, so similar to Jason's. *Just like his softer side*, she thought. Rob's always so good with the children and me. She quickly wiped her tears as she closed her eyes and breathed.

The meditation certainly cleared up the cob webs. How did I not see this before? Why didn't anyone else? As she watched his mannerisms, Clara knew she was right. No one else knew all three of the guys, Jason, Rob and Eric, as well as she did. Only Shannon really knew Jason and Rob, but not really Eric.

What do I do with this? Who do I tell? More importantly, is it even something anyone would want to know?

Reese and Hailey were both excited to see Connor at daycare. He listened to the chatter as the young boy gave a detailed account of his day. When he learned he would be visiting the corn maze later that evening, Reese's excitement grew.

"Mommy? We are all home! We found Connor!" the young boy shouted from the door, rushing into the family room. "Guess what? We are all going to the Fall Harvest tonight! Connor said we are going! I can't wait."

After sitting down beside her for a hug, he continued to talk while his sister climbed up.

Connor remained in the entrance of the family room, watching Clara listen to the children talking about their day with a smile. *She's so beautiful*, he thought. When she slowly scooted from the seat to stand, he tried to assess her pain levels.

Clara stepped over to Connor, greeting him with a kiss before heading upstairs to assist the children with changing their clothes. It was expected to get cooler in the evening.

"Can I get you a beer while you wait?" Rob asked as he silently assessed Clara's movements towards the stairs. The fall earlier had him concerned but he knew she wouldn't allow assistance.

"Sure," Connor agreed. He waited until Clara and the kids were out of sight before following into the kitchen.

"I'm glad you two are patching things up," Rob commented, placing two beer bottles on the table. "She misses you."

Connor first took a sip from his beer before answering. "Clara needed space so I'm giving her space. She'll let me know when she's ready for something more."

"Yeah, I'm sure she will. It's just I don't think she's sleeping well at night. She's either on the sofa or wandering around at night." Rob shrugged as he sipped his beer, not mentioning he was also on the sofa.

"She walks around at night? Are you sure it's her? I would think she has too much pain to be pacing around all night." Connor eyed him. "Did you get up to check on her?"

"No, I'm giving her space and privacy," he answered, unable to meet his eyes but realized, he hasn't done anything wrong. But there was something in his tone. "If it's not her, who else would it be?"

Before either could say anything else, Hailey wandered into the kitchen. She pulled herself up into Connor's lap and immediately reached for his beer bottle as she announced, "Me lala, Na-na!"

"No, Hailey, you aren't drinking beer." Connor quickly grabbed the bottle from her hands as Rob chuckled. Keeping the young girl in his arms, he went to the cabinet to retrieve her cup. Once it was filled, he handed it to her to drink.

When Clara entered the kitchen a few minutes later, she stopped at the doorway. Rob was sitting at the table drinking a beer while Connor was leaning into the counter, holding her daughter. That was when she realized how crazy it was to have both Connor and Rob in her house. She sighed again as her mind replayed the scenes from her recent dreams.

"Are we all ready?" Connor's question interrupted her thoughts. She looked into his refreshing brown eyes and smiled with a nod.

"Uncle Rob, aren't you coming?" Reese asked.

"No, buddy. I'm meeting with Chase later," he answered. He couldn't bring himself to call him cousin just yet. "You have a good time and don't let the scarecrow scare you."

"No, he only scares the crows. I'm not a crow," the little boy answered with a giggle as he hugged Rob goodbye.

Connor remained standing with Clara at the doorway, watching the interaction with a smile before they all walked out together.

As the evening progressed, Connor was pleasantly surprised Clara was able to keep up with the festivities. Without expecting it, they ran into Matt with his family. He introduced his nephews: Alex, Colton, and Hunter to both Hailey and Reese. Colton offered to take them into the kiddie maze.

"That's a big responsibility, wouldn't you rather enjoy yourselves?" Clara asked.

Both Connor and Matt noted the concern in her eyes when she spoke.

"We are, it'll be fun. I'll keep Hailey's hand while Hunter holds onto Reese's. We only have to worry about Alex straying off with the girls," Colton reported. He was rewarded with a shove from his older brother.

"How about you guys go ahead of us, we'll follow behind," Connor suggested, his eyes on Clara's. He was also apprehensive about the children being without either adult in such an open public space at night.

When Colton looked like he wanted to argue, Matt signaled to his middle son with a slight shake of the head before handing him cash. "Sounds good to me. Colt, you make sure you don't let those kids out of your sight. We'll be behind you and meet at the ice cream booth after."

Clara watched her children walk with Matt's kids towards the maze entrance. They looked so excited to be hanging out with the older children. Hailey won't be a baby much longer, she sighed.

Rob was hesitant as he opened the door to Memories. It was his first time out at night since the kidnapping. But Clara was right. He needed to decide what he wanted to get accomplished before he could continue with his life. Why wouldn't he want to continue working with Chase? As he entered, his eyes quickly adjusted to the dark room. He waved back as he made his way over to the table.

"Rob! I'm glad you came out," Rachel greeted him with a hug.

"Thanks for inviting me," he answered. Rob studied the menu, as if he didn't already know everything on it. *Another reminder*, he thought as he looked around the restaurant, *nothing has changed. Same items on the menu, same people sitting around talking, probably having the same conversations as a month ago.* And sure enough, the same server as the last time he was here.

How can so much be the same when everything's changed?

The last event of the evening was the hayride. Connor wasn't too surprised Clara and Hailey both fell asleep from the slow rocking of the wagon. He was amazed the little guy was still going! He sat across the wagon with his new friend Hunter, 6 years old, as they discussed various action figures.

He was content to have Clara snuggled up beside him while Haily slept in his lap. When his eyes continued on from Reese to each of his nephews, his eyes met with his brother. Matt smiled as he raised his eyebrows in question.

When the wagon came to a stop at the parking area, the boys hopped off while Matt assisted his wife. Clara's eyes were open before she slowly stretched. Connor noted a slight wince as she came to her feet, but didn't say anything. After he stepped down to the ground, he reached up for her hand to assist. When she reached the second to last step, she stopped to kiss him.

"Are you able to walk to the car? I can bring it closer," he offered.

"I'm alright, as long as you don't mind going slow," she answered as she squeezed his hand. "I'm amazed Reese is still going. I thought for sure he would fall asleep during the hayride."

Connor chuckled as the boys all raced towards Matt's vehicle.

"Maybe you should go ahead and make sure Reese doesn't leave with Matt and Talia," Clara commented.

"I think they'll notice an extra kid in the back," Connor dismissed. He didn't want her walking alone in the parking lot. When they reached his car, Matt was carrying over a sleeping Reese.

"Yes, he climbed in to sit next to Hunter and immediately fell asleep," Matt answered as he waited until the door was unlocked before placing the child in his seat.

When he turned back, Clara was beside him. "Thanks Matt. We had a great time. I'm glad we finally met your children. They're wonderful. You're alright with everything for Monday morning?"

"Absolutely. I've already told you it's your department. You have the proposals ready for me to review and we can move along with anything that needs to be changed," he answered as he opened her door. He waited patiently as she climbed into her seat before he closed the door.

Matt went around the SUV to wish his brother good-night as his boys yelled good-night from the opened door the next space over. When he finally sat behind the wheel, Connor looked over at Clara sleeping in her seat. He gently squeezed her left knee before he pulled out of the spot.

After pulling into the driveway, Connor was sure everyone was asleep. He debated who to carry in first when Clara's hand reached over for his.

"Connor, thank you for taking us. We had a great time."

"Me too," he whispered, reaching over to touch her cheek before he kissed her. "I'll carry in Sleeping Beauty and come back for the Scarecrow before I head out."

Clara held onto his hand before he could step out. "No, Connor. I don't want you to go. Stay. Stay the night with me."

He looked at her, trying to read her thoughts in the dim porch light. "Why? Why do you want me to stay?"

"Because I miss you. I miss having you next to me when I sleep and seeing you when I wake up. I miss having you here each day. I don't like this separation. I want us back together." Clara looked down at her hands, nervously playing with his before she looked back into his eyes. "I know I have a lot to work on and I'm grateful for your patience. I don't know yet exactly what I want for tomorrow or next week but I do know I want you. I sleep better when you're in the house, regardless which one it is. I love planning the day and weekends with you. I love you."

Connor felt his heart skip a beat as he looked into her eyes. His lips turned up into a smile before he leaned in to kiss her. "Alright. Your wish is my command. I'll stay."

Suddenly a small voice was standing behind them. "I miss you too, Connor. But if you let me sleep next to you, I will let you know if I sleep better."

Connor and Clara both looked back, Reese with his scarecrow painted face was just mere inches away, standing with his head between their seats.

"Reese, are you having trouble sleeping?" Connor wondered.

"Not at all," the young boy dismissed.

Once the children were changed and in bed, Clara started to prepare for bed. As she stood at the sink brushing her teeth, Connor came in behind her.

"Is it alright if I take a shower?"

Clara's green eyes met his brown in the mirror as she nodded her head. "Go ahead. You don't need to ask."

Clara watched in the mirror as he undressed. She had debated joining him, but suddenly felt shy.

After the shower, Connor stepped out from the bathroom to find Clara on the floor stretching wearing a dark violet nightie with a low neckline. He was confident it was not something he'd seen previously.

Clara, sensing his presence, opened her eyes and looked up to see him standing beside her with only a towel wrapped around his waist. She smiled suggestively as he lowered a hand to assist her up onto her feet. Once she was standing, her good arm went up around his neck to pull him down toward her as her other hand touched his chest. When his lips met hers, her left hand slowly lowered, releasing the towel...

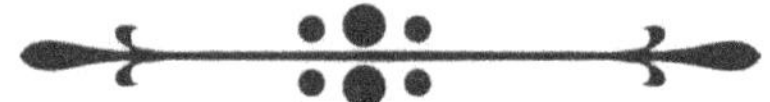

like old times

When dinner was over, Rob wasn't ready to return to Clara's just yet. He decided, what the hell, and crossed the street to The Lantern. He considered ordering a whiskey but reminded himself he was staying at Clara's. It wouldn't be appropriate. Instead he ordered a beer, taking it to an empty table in the back. He sat alone in the corner to watch those around him.

"Well, hello, handsome! It's certainly been a while since you've been out and about. What happened? Did your girlfriend kick you out," Isabella Daynee inquired as she plopped down in the chair beside him.

Like half the town, she had spent the evening at the Fall Festival. Her children had been begging her all week. She saw *perfect Clara* limping around with the gorgeous doctor. After dropping her kids off at her sister's, Isabella headed out for the rest of the evening. She never expected to see Rob out by himself, in The Lantern, of all places. Her night was about to get magical!

"Clara's not my girlfriend," Rob responded as he pushed the hand creeping dangerously high up his thigh.

Isabella wasn't discouraged, he never consented the first time. Rob always required multiple approaches before he finally succumbed to her charms. She chuckled as her other hand played with his collar, slowly making its way to his neck as she gently massaged. "You can buy me a drink before we head out for the night."

Rob looked over at the girl he dated twelve years ago and wondered what he saw in her. How did he remain with her for the summer? A whole summer! Her bleached blonde hair was thinning and brushed into her heavily made face. He had thought her green eyes were pretty back then but now they seemed tired. She appeared to still be wearing an outfit from her high school days, a short denim skirt with a hot pink tank under a cotton shirt, tied at her waist. While she looked good then, the extra forty pounds squeezed into three sizes too small made her look tacky and cheap.

"Come on, Rob! When was the last time your girlfriend gave you a blow job? I bet she's never done it, am I right? So prim and proper! I bet she's a prude in the bedroom. Let's head out to your truck, unless you'd rather just go straight back to your farm." She chuckled as her hand again rubbed his thigh, getting dangerously close.

Again, Rob stopped her hand with his as he pushed it away. He was relieved the details of his attempted demise weren't common knowledge around town. "Don't. This isn't the time or the place."

"Oh, come on now, Robbie. Why are you always ignoring me? If your girlfriend was pleasing you, you wouldn't be out alone tonight," Isabella pouted. "I don't understand what you guys see in her, anyway. She's always been so high and mighty, and prudish. You and Eric have always been whining that she doesn't treat you right. But honey, I'm right here. I can give you anything you want."

"When have we ever talked about Clara?" Rob demanded, scooting his chair back slightly, making it too awkward for her to lean into him.

Sighing, Isabella thought about it. "You're right, I guess. It's usually Eric and Danny. They finally stopped their whining then she moved back! Last summer was tiresome. Can you explain what the damn turn on is? What is so great about her that makes all you guys pant over her?"

When Rob only gave her a look, she continued talking. "Eric always talks about how pretty she is and what he likes to do with her in bed. Personally, I think she sounds like a prude. But Danny, he's never gotten his hands on her which is probably why he's so grumpy. So tell me, hotstuff, what's the attraction to your girlfriend?"

"She's honest and sweet, there's no hidden agenda with her. But Clara's not my girlfriend. We're just friends," Rob admitted, wondering for the first time why everyone always referred to him and Clara as boy/girlfriend back in high school. They never dated, even back then. "I don't know why either Danny or Eric were interested. You'd have to ask them at your next hookup."

"I doubt there'll be a hook up any time soon. Eric's been arrested again. Rumor has it he's not expecting to get out on bail. He's violated his previous bail terms."

"When was the last time you saw Eric? I thought he was on house arrest," Rob asked before sipping from his beer.

"He was on house arrest, not in jail. Not too difficult to visit at his place. His parents weren't around, but his grandfather is a bit creepy. Did you know the windows from Eric's rooms on the third floor give an awesome view into the house you're working on? With the binoculars, it's almost like I'm right there with you," she purred as she leaned her oversized chest towards him.

"Eric keeps binoculars at his window to spy on me? That's not creepy at all," Rob responded, relieved Clara's bedroom was on the other side of the house when she was growing up. "And he's not bothered by you spying on other guys during your visits?"

"Maybe I'm going over there so I can see that hot body of yours. It's not like you take me out anymore. But sometimes we meet at other places. Not like the stupid ankle monitor could actually keep him inside. Don't you miss me just a little? My sister has the kids until the morning." Isabella let the sentence hang as she scooted her chair closer. "It'll be like old times. You and me, all hot and heavy together."

"Isn't Danny out on bail? Why don't you give him a call?" Rob suggested, his eyes again searching the room. He was annoyed that the dim light did not allow him to make out everyone in the bar. He didn't want any surprises.

"Danny's still mad at me for getting pregnant again," she answered with a quick dismissal.

"You're pregnant?" Rob asked with alarm, his steel blue eyes looked disapprovingly at the drink in her hand. The last thing he needed was to get tangled with Danny's baby mama. He knew better. One of the many reasons he stopped seeing her years ago was because of her infidelity. He and Danny didn't need any more reasons to fight.

"Don't judge me. What makes you think my oldest isn't yours? He has your blonde hair and blue eyes," she announced as if it was new information. Rob had been relieved years ago to discover the child had been born ten months after they broke up.

Rob sighed, it was stupid to be sitting here beside her. And the recent information about his paternal makeup made him realize, there was an excellent chance any offspring of his could look similar to Danny's. Their children would be second cousins. Being related to the bastard was another reason he was constantly wishing for a shot of whiskey.

"Isabella, thanks for reminding me why we stopped seeing each other back then. Definitely not starting that up again."

Before he could push away from the table, she grabbed his hand. "Rob, why can't we tonight? For old time's sake? Head out back with me."

Seeing the panic in her eyes, alarms went off in his head. Did she agree to lure him out into the alley so one of the Thompsons could get a jump on him? "Which of the Thompsons are waiting for me? Is it Danny or one of his brothers?"

The look of shock in her eyes answered his question as he shook his head. "Just like old times, hmm? I will definitely pass. My lawyer has cautioned me against fighting with them. You get home safely."

Rob grabbed his beer before heading to an empty seat at the bar. "If I didn't know better, I would think you're following me."

Agent Jack Ruddy simply laughed as he sipped his ginger ale. He glanced over his shoulder at the woman pouting alone at the table he just vacated. "Trouble?"

Rob was busy texting Anthony, the deputy, to see if he'd run a patrol through the back alley. Maybe he could get the stupid Thompsons arrested. When he looked up, his eyes followed where the agent was looking.

"Not at all. She's just trying to lure me out into the alley so her boyfriend can jump me. Just your typical Friday night, same bullshit, different night. Nothing's changed in the last decade. You may want to talk with her, Isabella seems to have some intimate knowledge of Eric getting out of the house all summer."

As the two continued talking, neither were aware of a shadow sitting in another corner, watching everything.

A shadow tucked away in the corner remained still with a hand resting on the glass of scotch neat. The eyes watched with annoyance at the whore sitting alone at the table. She's certainly completed her cycle of usefulness, not really much point in keeping her around. The recent rumor she is once again pregnant was proven true. This had to be the fifth one, when will the stupid girl learn?

The glass was lifted as the front door opened again. Almost everyone turned to watch as the newly hired personal trainer walked to the bar. After he received his drink, he scanned the room. The blue eyes watched as the newcomer joined the whore in the back.

Speaking of usefulness, an idea formed as the glass was lowered to the table. The two seemed to hit it off as they stood and exited the bar together.

Connor was awakened by the sound of the front door opening, he was surprised by the late hour Foxwood was returning home. Had he been going out every night? He felt Clara shift slightly beside him. He opened his eyes as he touched her gently, whispering in her ear. "Clara, I'm here."

His words seemed to help ease her anxiety, he listened to her breathing as her body snuggled closer. A few minutes later, he opened his eyes again when the door was pushed open by a short shadow. Once it stepped closer into the range of the dim light, Hailey's bright blue eyes stared up at him as she climbed up into the bed beside Clara, touching her shoulder.

"Mama? Mama?"

"Hailey?"

To his amazement, Clara was instantly awake before he could say anything. She reached for her robe and her hearing aids as the toddler grabbed her hand to lead her out of the room.

Ten minutes later, Clara was sitting at the kitchen table with her daughter on her lap eating grapes and cheese. She smiled down as the young girl reached for another grape.

"Everything alright?"

Rob was standing in the doorway wearing only his jeans. The little girl waved. Clara smiled as he went to the fridge for a drink.

"Oh, yeah. She's absolutely famished! I think she had too many sweets at the festival. Her blood sugar probably dropped."

She watched as he sat down across from them. "You ok? We didn't mean to wake you up."

"I'm alright. I just got home, I wasn't asleep yet. Heard you both talking as you went down the stairs. I didn't know we were having a feast," he said in a silly voice he used when reading to the children.

His hand quickly reached for a grape rolling from the plate. Hailey put her hands on her hips, pretending to be mad as she made a pout face. Rob winked at her.

"I met with Chase and Rachel for dinner at Memories. We need to stop at your gym so he can take some measurements. Would you have some time tomorrow?"

"We could stop in around nine before Reese's party. That's at eleven, will that be enough time?"

"Should be," Rob agreed, as he grabbed another grape directly from the toddler's dish.

"No no lala! No no!" Hailey yelled, pulling the bowl toward her to keep her grapes safe from Rob. "Mine!"

"Hailey, share your grapes," Clara instructed. "There's plenty."

"Mine, mama, mine!"

"She has the word pronounced and used correctly," Rob observed with a chuckle. "Chase asked me to be his best man."

When Clara didn't say anything, he continued, "And you already knew he was going to ask."

"That's not really a surprise is it? Who else would he ask? You two have always been close. It'll be a great wedding," she predicted. "And I'm the maid of honor."

"Yeah, not really surprising, is it? I think those two waiting so long is more of a surprise. How are things going with you and the good doctor?" He grinned as he raised his eyebrows in question.

"Rob, you aren't going to be weird about him being here, are you?" Clara whispered.

"No, Clara, I promise. I'm happy you two are back together. He's a great guy," Rob answered as he looked down at the sleeping toddler. "It amazes me how quickly the kids fall asleep."

"Yeah," she agreed as she silently debated how she would carry her upstairs.

"Here, I'll carry her up," Rob suggested as he reached for the young girl. He waited while Clara placed the dishes in the sink and turned off the light. He paused when he saw a shadow move across the floor from the back door leading to the back deck. Rob waited a minute to see if it moved again before he went over to make sure the door was locked. He was surprised when Clara didn't say anything but slowly continued ahead of him towards the stairs.

After he lowered Hailey down onto her bed and pulled up her covers, Clara leaned over to give her a kiss. In the hallway, she reached up to kiss his cheek. "Thanks, Rob. Have a good night."

He nodded his head as he squeezed her hand. Rob watched as she limped down the hall into her room before he returned back downstairs. He needed to be sure all the windows and doors were indeed still locked from when he last checked before leaving the house earlier in the evening.

Clara slowly closed the door to her room. She knew Connor was a light sleeper. After she removed her robe and hearing aids, he lifted the covers. Once she was snuggled up beside him, she could feel his breath in her ear as he likely asked her a question. She shifted slightly to allow her legs to weave with his before quickly falling asleep.

When he arrived at the kitchen, Rob first checked the door leading to the garage before heading down into the basement. Returning back to the kitchen, he stopped at the fridge for a beer. Before he could twist off the cap, he froze to watch a shadow move across the floor. His heart started to pound into his chest. Slowly inching towards the window, he cautiously peeked out into the yard.

Clara had been advised to keep the back lights on to allow better monitoring of the doors and windows. It was difficult to see beyond the scope of the light. He immediately dismissed the idea of stepping out into the cool night. He did not want to find himself sinking to the bottom of the lake again. Instead, he assured all the doors and windows were locked in the kitchen and the security alarm set before he made his way into the family room. The lights were dimmed before he settled on the sofa with his beer.

He remained in the dark listening for any sound of footsteps or doors moving throughout the house. Rob was reminded of the first time he slept on the sofa many months before. He could have sworn someone had been in the room with him then.

After everything that's happened, it was no longer easy to dismiss.

. . . .

Evil watched from the shadows of the backyard. He was once again irritated by the intrusion on his time with his Babydoll. He wanted so badly to spend the night with her. He waited patiently as he watched the figure inside moving around in the kitchen. He willed as strongly as he could, that he would come outside so they could fight another round. It didn't matter if it was frick or frack. It would be good fun either way, not at all feeling over confident in his abilities to fight despite his still healing injuries.

He gave up all efforts when twenty minutes passed without a door ever cracking open. Evil faded further into the shadows, debating where to spend the remainder of the night. It had been foolish to leave the comfort and warmth of the attic while still recovering from his injuries. He wasn't aware until it was too late, the locks were all changed. His spare key no longer worked.

Hours later, Isabella stepped out into the cold October morning, wishing she had the luxury of sleeping in on a Saturday. Instead, she had to roll out of the personal trainer's bed and hurry to pick up her kids. The warmth of his bed was nice, but the guy himself, not so much. He was apparently developing a reputation for being prince of one-night stands, now she understood.

Max wasn't particularly creative in the bedroom nor did he have any concerns about pleasing her. She was surprised, honestly. While he had the physique of a gym god with charm to melt your heart, he didn't have any warmth or humor to carry on a conversation once they left the bar. *He could officially be checked off as one and done*, she thought with a hard chuckle.

Mornings were when she missed Danny the most. Until this last year, he would spend most nights beside her and even hang out for a bit to play with the children while she prepared breakfast and the children for school. For a while, she thought he would finally settle down and they could raise their family together.

Granted, Danny had doubts about the paternity of each child, especially Ryder, her oldest. He was convinced the boy was Foxwood offspring. Rob denied it, rightfully. Try as she did to get pregnant by him that summer, Rob was always cautious. And when he first saw the child, looking so like him with his blond hair and blue eyes, he immediately asked about his birthday. Unfortunately, Ryder was born exactly ten months after the last time they were together.

As she turned the corner, she became aware of a car slowly following. Isabella turned to see who the driver was before debating whether to hurry on or not. Her sister's place was just around the corner. She could not be late getting there or she would risk losing the only babysitter she could afford.

As the car pulled to the curb, the window rolled down. "Isabella? What are you doing out here in the cold? Jump in. I'll give you a ride."

Isabella Daynee made many mistakes in her life. This one would be her last.

When Monday morning rolled around, Connor was relieved his relationship with Clara was back on track. He enjoyed the weekend they all spent together. Everyone attended the birthday party on Saturday before heading to the lake house for the night. And on Sunday, they went to Matt and Talia's lake house for lunch. He wasn't sure how he felt about Clara forming a close relationship with his sister-in-law, but decided not to comment just yet.

When he arrived at the nursing home late morning, he was taken aback to see Clara sitting at her desk in her gym while the Foxwood cousins were meeting with his brother over blueprints.

"Clara? How long have you been back to work?" Connor hoped his tone wasn't too judgmental. He leaned on her desk as he studied her face. She still looked as refreshed as she did before the weekend started.

"Connor! Hi," she responded as he kissed her forehead. "Today's actually my first day. Don't worry, I'm not treating yet. Dr. Taylor approved my returning to work at my appointment this morning. I am only allowed to do the management stuff like paperwork and phone calls. I need to get my budget approved before the deadline and complete the interviews. Keep your fingers crossed Matt approves the minor construction in the gym," she whispered.

Across the room, Matt continued to listen to Chase's proposal as he watched the interaction between his brother and Clara.

Chase continued with his presentation fully aware Matt's attention was diverted. He wondered again what the deal was between the man next to him and Clara. Men, his cousin included, seemed to have a strong gravitational pull towards her.

"I wasn't aware you had an appointment this morning," he started but caught himself before he said too much. "I would have driven you. Do you need a ride home when you are finished?"

"He also cleared me to drive," she answered with excitement. "I'm only taking antibiotics and tylenol for pain. I am no longer a ridiculous burden to everyone. Unfortunately, I still can't do my job completely or lift with the left arm, but it's certainly a start in the right direction."

"You aren't ever a burden, Clara," Connor stated quietly. "It is good to see you back in your chair. I only have rounds today. Do you want me to pick up the kids and bring home dinner later?"

"I already have something in the crockpot," she announced with a smile.

He tilted his head as he again studied her face. "Who are you and what have you done with my girl?"

Clara laughed as he kissed her hand before heading out of the room.

A bit later, Connor was sitting at his desk down the hall when his brother entered the room to place the Foxwood proposal on his desk.

"What's this?"

"It's the proposal Chase prepared," Matt answered as he closed the door before sitting down. "I want to know what you think."

"You've never included me in the decisions before, why now?" he asked with irritation.

Matt studied his brother for a moment as he sat in the chair across from him. "I just wanted to be sure you'd be alright with the Foxwoods completing the job down the hall. As it is, the one is already staying with you and Clara. Wasn't sure you'd be alright having to see him at work as well."

Connor looked at his brother, debating if he should share his issues. Up until now, he kept his jealousies contained.

"Anything you care to get off your chest?"

"I don't know." Connor leaned back in his chair. "Clara's always been close to Foxwood and it's never really bothered me. But now, she's different. They are both different. He seems to be more open and she seems to be hiding something."

"Hiding something? As in something with him?" Matt speculated. "You think something is going on between them?"

"I don't know. From what I've learned, it could just be emotional. Hell, I can't begin to imagine what he's been going through with the news about his biological father," Connor stated. Seeing his brother's confusion, he explained.

"No kidding? Mitch Foxwood isn't his father?" Matt repeated. "That's harsh. And to learn he's actually a Thompson? That would shatter anyone's world."

"Yes, it would. Seems to be a lot of that going around these days, isn't it? First Dallas, then Shannon and now Rob? Hell of a group Clara has," Connor summed up. "I wonder if she's learned who Shannon's father is."

"You think she would keep it a secret? Why?"

"It wouldn't be her story to share," Connor answered quietly. But he kept to himself, it could also identify the shadow and her mother's killer. He wondered what she'd do with the information, who would Clara confide in? "Go ahead and let them do the construction."

Eric paced the small cell in frustration. What the hell was taking so long? Why didn't he have his lawyer yet? What was his mother doing? Did she really side with his father? Was it their plan all along?

"Eric? You have a visitor," Anthony, the deputy, was suddenly on the other side with keys in his hands.

"It's about damn time!" Eric mumbled. "Is it my lawyer?"

Anthony, without a word, gestured toward the small hall to the interrogation room.

Eric stopped at the door when he spotted his mother. "Mom! What the hell is going on?"

He stopped when she raised her eyebrows and looked over at the deputy. Without a word, the door was locked behind him.

"Eric, sweetheart, how have they been treating you? Are you getting enough food? They aren't keeping you in a cell with a hardened criminal are they?" Kathleen was quickly up on her feet hugging her son.

"Mom, where's my lawyer?"

"Sweetheart, I got you something better than a lawyer."

Eric quickly pulled back excitedly. "You got the charges dropped? How?"

"Never mind how," his mother dismissed with a wave of her hand. "It won't be much longer before they have no choice but to release you."

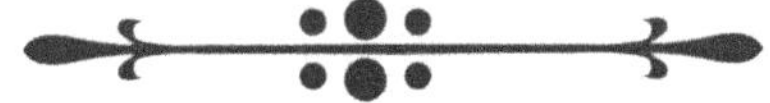

38 friends

As the week progressed, Clara and Shannon met up for coffee or lunch each day. By Friday, lunch included Lila and Rachel at Lila's cabin in the woods. The friends were happy to all be together again.

Shannon had decided to share her DNA results with her friends.

Lila was shocked. "Wow! I can't believe how much has changed since we took the DNA tests. You and Clara are half-sisters and Rob isn't even my full brother. Hell, Rob and Chase aren't even cousins! This is crazy!"

"I feel bad about dragging Rob down like this, that was never my intention," Shannon started to apologize.

"Nothing for you to feel bad about, Shan. None of us did anything wrong. You were looking for answers and, unfortunately, we all got more answers than we expected."

"Is it true your mother moved out? Where is she living? And how is your dad?" Shannon had so many questions.

"Yeah, she moved out and right into Zac Thompson's place." Lila looked around the group with disbelief. "If you told me a year ago my brother was a biological Thompson and my mother would be living with

Dallas's dad, the man that more or less raised him, while the rest of my family welcomed Dallas with open arms, I would have asked what you were smoking. The craziest part, my dad and Dallas are building a barn for the horses!"

They all turned to look out the large picture window overlooking the back of the land. The foundation for the barn had already been laid earlier in the week, with the studs already framing the building.

"It really is crazy," Clara agreed. "All this time, Dallas has been living with fear of a sudden violent death."

"Chase says nothing has changed, everyone is the same as before the DNA testing, but everything has changed. Rob was awkward around him and wouldn't even talk to him, then suddenly out of the blue, he calls Chase and now they are planning to work together again," Rachel shared. "They still have awkward moments."

"I bet," Lila agreed. "Clara, is Rob still staying at your place? With Connor?"

"Both are at the duplex with me and the kids now," Clara admitted. "It was a bit weird at first, but it's actually working. You all know we tend to move around every few nights. Rob doesn't always go with us to the loft or the lake house. I think Connor likes someone else at home so I'm never alone. I doubt it'll be much longer."

"I don't understand why Rob won't return back to the farm," Shannon commented. "Did your dad disown him?"

"Not at all, quite the opposite," Lila answered. "I think deep down, Dad always suspected, but he's never considered disowning Rob. Hell, Rob was meant to inherit the farm. I've not heard anything about that changing."

"Would it go to you, if not for Rob?" Clara wondered.

"Not me, Chase, probably," Lila speculated.

"Chase doesn't want it," Rachel shared. "Don't get me wrong, he loves the farm and the animals, but his heart is in the construction business he inherited from his dad. He loves the renovation work at your place, Clara, and can't wait to start on the Taylor House."

"What kind of changes are you going to make at the Taylor House, Rach?" Lila asked.

"Nothing drastic, we don't need the updates the Hawks House needs, the plumbing and electric is all up to code. It's mostly cosmetic, repaint the walls, redo the hardwood floors, and add an elevator for my grandmother. I think the biggest project will be going through all the trunks and closets on the third floor and even half of the rooms on the second floor." Rachel looked around the room. "I never realized that half the rooms have been closed up my whole life!"

"It is a lot of space and probably easier to manage," Lila agreed. "I can't imagine how long it would take to just vacuum the bedrooms! A hundred years ago, the house had live in help to assist with the cleaning."

"A hundred years ago, they didn't have all the cleaning tools: no vacuum cleaners, washing machines, or dryers! But now with less people staying in the house, less traffic to clean up after," Clara explained.

"Exactly," Rachel agreed.

"How is all the work going at the Hawks House?" Shannon turned towards her sister.

"I have no idea, I haven't been there since the summer," Clara answered.

"I don't understand why you and Chase are staying at the farm when you have the whole Taylor House to yourselves," Shannon turned to Rachel.

"Chase has been weird about that with everything that's been going on lately. He works longer hours than I do. He doesn't want me alone at that house. I can only be there if he's there," Rachel explained. She was about to explain about the secret passages and tunnels connecting the four grand homes on Park Ave, but her friends all nodded agreement.

"Of course, he wouldn't want you alone with the Howells next door," Lila commented. "Even with Eric in jail, the others in that family are just plain creepy!"

Sunday night, Connor returned home after everyone was already in bed. It seemed his head had just hit the pillow when he suddenly sat up to a loud piercing scream. Immediately, he was up on his feet and running from the room.

Clara had been sleeping, vaguely aware of Connor's presence beside her but was instantly awake when he leaped from the bed. When she followed him down the hall into Hailey's room, her daughter was sitting up in her bed screaming with her finger pointing to the wall.

On the wall, the nightlight gave the impression of a large shadow of a spider, half the size of the wall.

Connor grabbed the young girl. "It's only a spider, Hailey. It won't hurt you. You want me to get rid of it?"

She nodded her head as she continued to cry, reaching out for her mother.

"Is she alright?" Rob asked as he entered the room, to Connor's ongoing annoyance, wearing only boxers.

"It's only a spider," Connor answered as he handed the young girl to her mother. After he was sure she was only using her right arm, he disposed of the offensive spider.

"Hailey, what happened? Did the spider bite you?" Rob asked from behind Clara.

Hailey paused in her wailing, appearing to be telling a story with her hands dramatically moving around, neither adult was able to understand.

"Did she get bit?" Connor asked when he returned to the room. Quickly assessing her skin for any bites, but not seeing any, he asked if she wanted a drink. When she nodded, she reached her arms out to him. As they all started down the stairs, he looked directly at Clara and commented, "She certainly is your daughter."

"Hey, I was only five at the time. And it was a really big spider," Clara defended after reading his lips.

Connor chuckled as he turned on the kitchen light. He prepared a drink for everyone after he placed the child on her mother's lap.

"What happened when you were five?" Rob couldn't help asking, making sure Clara could read his lips.

Chuckling again when Clara appeared to make the same pouting face as her daughter, Connor explained, "Like she said, Clara was only five at the time. It was summer so the windows were open. I'm asleep in the dead of night and I'm suddenly awakened by this blood curdling screaming. I thought for sure Clara was being tortured. I ran to my window just as her bedroom light went on. Her parents were both there. The next day, she's telling me about this huge monster in her room that tried to carry her off while her mother explained it was only a spider, no harm."

Both men chuckled as they looked over at Clara. She decided to keep her comments to herself. She still remembered the incident. While the spider did bite her arm, she was confident someone was really in her room. She had tried to explain, but her father simply declared the spider was harmless. Her mother had been too sleepy to even attempt to talk to, but since they allowed her to spend the remainder of the night in their room, she was able to get more sleep that night.

. . . .

As everyone chatted quietly downstairs, Hailey's closet door shifted open. Evil emerged and paused for a moment to retrieve the candy wrappers on the floor before heading slowly and quietly down the hall. He slipped into the linen closet. The door secured behind him.

"Looks like the little princess is asleep. Are you ready to head back upstairs?" Connor asked before reaching over to retrieve the little girl. He waited at the doorway as Clara said goodnight.

"Tomorrow's a big day. Are you ready to return to work?" Clara asked as she placed her hand on Rob's shoulder. When he nodded, she squeezed his shoulder. "Sorry we woke you up. I'll see you in the morning."

Rob reached her hand on his shoulder. "I'm relieved it was only a spider. Clara, thank you for letting me stay here. I'll start looking for my own place and get out of your way soon."

"Don't be ridiculous. There's no rush. Stay as long as you like, I like having you close," she answered as she leaned down to kiss his cheek. "Sleep tight."

Great, Connor thought as he turned towards the staircase. How long will he need to continue putting up with Foxwood? He paused at the base to allow Clara to start up before him. He watched her slowly negotiate the steps, unaware of her silent dilemma.

Should Clara share who Shannon's biological father was? Who she believed was Jason's biological mother? Should she approach the woman? What good would it bring? She would get to meet her grandchildren, part of her argued. But would Sarah Thompson Black want to be reminded of a dark moment in her past? Was it even her place to share what she knew? She shook her head as the internal battle continued in her head.

Clara remained in the doorway as Connor gently lowered the young girl on her bed. She looked around the dimmed pink room. The closet door was slightly ajar. She went to open it, almost expecting someone or something to jump out at her. Instead, a flash of a memory jumped out, but was gone before she could fully grasp its meaning.

Connor turned when he heard a gasp. "Clara, what is it?"

Clara stepped back as she shook her head, quietly closing the door. "Nothing."

The wall blocking the harsh memories of her childhood was slowly weakening as her unconscious fought to keep it all contained.

39

the hawks trust

Monday morning, Clara sat across from Matt in his office. They had so much to go over. He decided to first address her recommendations for the many new positions in her rehab department.

"I've read over the applicants. All have cleared the preliminary background checks. You can go ahead and contact them for the hiring process. Judy in HR can help you coordinate the drug tests, paperwork and fingerprints," he started, placing the files in front of her. Matt leaned back, his eyes were on hers. "What does Connor say about your final decisions?"

"I didn't discuss it with him, do I need to?"

"No, not at all. He's never troubled himself with the hiring before. I'm surprised with your final choice for the full time OT position. This other one appears to be the better candidate," he explained with a tap on a file from the not hiring pile.

"Maybe on paper," Clara dismissed, remembering the interview. "I just didn't have any interest in working with someone I could smell long before I could see him."

When Matt's eyes widened in surprise, she laughed while explaining. "It wasn't offensive. It was just too much cologne for a healthcare worker in close proximity to older patients. Anyone with experience with the elderly population would know to limit anything that could be offensive. I could smell his cologne from my desk before he arrived at the doorway. You know my desk is across the room from the door! And, he was dressed more for night clubbing than a professional interview. I want my team to be made of individuals respecting the patients and giving them the attention they need. I don't want to be chasing after them all day to ensure they are actually doing patient care and not flirting with the nursing staff."

Matt laughed. His sources at the nursing home had informed him the candidate appeared to be interested in Clara, in a non-professional way. "Probably, just as well. I'm not sure you're aware, he's the brother of a woman Connor used to date."

"Oh, I'm aware. Amanda, right?" Clara asked with a nod of her head. Then it was her turn to laugh. "We've run into her before. Tell me, Matt, were they serious?"

"Not really on his end. Their relationship lasted longer than most. She was too confident he was planning a proposal and started doing things a wife would do, not a girlfriend," he answered, not meaning to provide too many details.

"Things a wife would do? What did she do, redecorate his place?" Clara wondered.

Matt chuckled. "She probably would have tried if she had a key. But close enough. She went to the city for a major shopping spree."

"That's not so bad."

"With his credit cards," he clarified. "Connor wasn't aware until his bank notified him of unusual spending, some expenses cleared."

"Wow. I'm surprised. He's always been so generous. Did he let it slide or was that the breaking point?"

"I think it was more the final straw." Matt felt the need to explain further. "Connor can be very generous, on his terms. If he wants to purchase a whole new wardrobe or even a vacation, no worries. I think there had been a lot of smaller purchases he learned about after the fact."

"I can certainly understand that. It's his money, he should do what he wants with it." Clara paused a moment as she silently debated sharing her concerns. "Sometimes I think he's too giving and doesn't stop to figure out if he's out of line."

"Connor's out of line?"

Suddenly restless, Clara leaned back in her seat, her right foot was tapping while her hands played together. Her green eyes looked up into his familiar blue eyes.

"We have the opposite problem. Initially, he was always paying for dinner or the drinks. I didn't think anything of it. He's old fashioned and has the money. His typical dating habits. But then, he bought carseats, which he justified by being able to pick up the kids at the last minute without having to play musical cars. I let it go. Next thing I know, the utilities are all paid up with auto payments from his accounts and my home is purchased outright."

Matt leaned back as he listened, noting the gradual increase in volume as Clara talked and suddenly all the pieces of the recent "break" made sense. Connor finally found a woman he wanted to shower with gifts, but she didn't want it. The irony made him want to laugh. Instead, he asked a question, "Since he appears to be back at your side, I take it you've both resolved your issues?"

"It's a work in progress," Clara admitted. "I just don't want to be *taken care of*, it's so degrading and suggests I'm weak and not capable. As a couple, don't you think he should discuss with me first before tackling projects in my own home?"

Matt was silent with his eyes squinted in thought, *what projects?* "Clara, what exactly did he do?"

"Well, where to begin? The security system, the gates to the backyard, and the resurfacing of the bathtub. He redid the bathroom and bedroom decor. Hell, he even refolds the towels in the bathroom!" She almost shouted. Clara realized she probably wasn't making any sense, *Matt probably thinks I'm a controlling bitch.*

With a sigh, she reluctantly explained. "After Jay's memorial service, I had trouble sleeping. So, I painted my bathroom a different color every few nights. In the process, paint splattered into the tub and a few other places. Connor never said anything about either the paint in the tub or the different color walls, except the one time it was a bit bright, smiley face yellow. Other than that, nothing. And I understand he's a major Type-A personality, a fantastic surgeon with a need to control the situation. But in my house, if I want the bathroom walls a different color every week or fold the towels a specific way, it's my choice. I don't appreciate it when he goes in after me and refolds the towels!"

"I didn't realize he was that OCD. Connor's always been neat and organized. He's never refolded the towels when he's at my place," Matt commented. "But the security system was more a group thing. Connor and I paid for it based on Devan's recommendation." He didn't say they were actually provided with three different options to choose from and Connor picked the strongest and most expensive: cameras covering all the doors and windows.

"Well, of course he doesn't refold the towels at your place. You two were raised in the same household. You probably fold the towels the same anyway," she dismissed. She sighed again when she realized she was overreacting. "You know, I think all the drugs have been messing with my thought process and emotions. The first time he refolded the towels, I just laughed. I didn't realize how much it bothered me until we had the big argument. But when I look back on it, it wasn't us both yelling at each other or even a simple discussion with open dialogue between two people. It was me suddenly losing control and listing every grievance I've ever had. He didn't even try to argue back. He never even raised his voice, not even when I told him to leave."

Matt decided he needed to get the purpose of the meeting back on track. He was also going to have a conversation with his brother. He found the resurfacing of the bathtub and refolding towels a bit odd and out of character, even for Connor, a true definition of A-type personality.

"Matt, I'm sorry. I shouldn't use you as a relationship counselor and I especially shouldn't complain about your own brother. That is totally unprofessional of me." Clara paused to close her eyes. Taking a deep calming breath, she willed herself to let it go before opening her eyes. When she did, she smiled before asking, "So what is your final decision on the candidates to hire?"

He was amused by her Zen moment and impressed with her ability to suddenly shift her emotions as well as her focus. With a lot left to discuss, Matt decided to play along. Now that he understood the issues between Clara and his brother, he knew what to keep an eye on.

"Ultimately, Clara, your department is yours to do as you see fit. I trust you and as long as everyone clears the full background checks, you have a go," he stated as he pulled another file over. "The other reason I set up this meeting, is that we have both Jason's and your mother's wills to go over."

Matt regretted bringing the sadness into her eyes. "Jason's first. I'm sure there are no surprises, he left everything to you and your children. Since it was proven he never officially quit, his life insurance policy from work is left to you. He had a separate policy, to be doubled if his death was unexpected. Suffice it to say, it was. That policy is to be divided equally between both Reese and Hailey into trust funds. They are allowed to access the funds only for schooling purposes until they reach thirty years of age. At that time, they will be provided with a monthly allowance."

He had initially been surprised by the setup, until he read her mother's will. Then Matt understood Jason had somehow accessed Susannah's will. He quickly reviewed the stocks and the savings. Not surprising, as the man was good with money, he left his young family quite comfortable.

After a few minutes to absorb the information, he shifted to her mother's will. Matt wasn't willing to admit he was the one that needed the moment.

"Now your mother's will," he softly announced. "She left everything to you."

"The house with all the furniture and jewelry, right? I still need to decide what to do with all that. Chase has temporarily stopped the renovations," she commented with an equally soft tone.

"The house, while an impressive estate with its own trust to cover any and all expenses, is only a small percentage of the Hawks Estate. You also have all the real estate and trusts built up, and added to, by each of your great-grandfathers before your grandfather. When you turn thirty in two months, you will be in full control."

Clara simply stared in silence at him a few minutes before she leaned forward. "What?"

"Oh, I'm sure you heard it correctly. Upon your thirtieth birthday, December twenty-fifth, you will be in full control of all the Hawks real estate and trusts." Matt repeated as he leaned back in his chair, watching with amusement at her reaction.

"There's real estate? And trusts? Plural? What are you talking about? My mother never talked about any of this. Hell, she never even mentioned the jewelry. Why didn't she?" Clara demanded as she remembered the comments previously made. Felicia Thompson was upset when her father broke it off *'just as the money is coming to us.'* And her father's comment, *'Connor is only interested in her because of the money.'*

Clara never knew about the money. And as her mother's spouse, her father would have been aware of the money, wouldn't he? Why didn't he tell her?

Matt gave her a moment to process the information. Susannah died, literally, days before her thirtieth birthday. She never had control of the trusts. While she lived in the house, all expenses paid, she did receive a somewhat generous monthly allowance. But the allowance was meager compared to the whole of the estate. Graham Hawks had plenty to leave to both of his children, if only either had survived to receive it. With her disappearance, the funds remained untouched while interest continued for a whole generation.

Matt was literally looking at the richest person in the county. Once December twenty-fifth arrived, Clara Noelle, the only heir to the Hawks estate, would be thirty years old. Two months away.

Everything was finally making sense.

A few blocks away, Angelica Daynee had just dropped off her nieces and nephews at school before heading to the sheriff's department. She wanted her sister arrested for child neglect and abandonment. It was one thing to ask to babysit for a few hours on a pre-planned evening, but it was another to totally forget to pick them up!

This was the last straw!

Angelica was filing charges! Then, she would see a lawyer to secure custody papers. As their legal guardian, she would be able to better plan her life around the children's schedules. She shouldn't have any trouble since this was not the first time her sister disappeared for a week at a time without any concerns for her children.

The sheriff was late getting into the work that morning. Before going into his office, he made a stop in the breakroom for a fresh cup of coffee. Having the FBI, more or less, take over his department was bothersome, but they sure knew how to make great coffee, he thought with a smile. He paused to sip again when he heard yelling from up front.

"Damn it, Maggie, I need to talk to someone now!" a female voice yelled.

"Ms. Daynee, what's all the fuss?" the sheriff asked.

"Sheriff, I want to file charges against my sister. She's again abandoned her children. I want her found and arrested with a court order to keep her away from those kids," Angelica demanded from across the room.

Tony Mancuso nodded as he motioned for Angelica to be allowed through. Without a word, he led her back into his office and asked her to start from the beginning.

After explaining how she was asked to babysit for the evening, which was actually code for the night since her *evenings* always continued through to the early morning hours.

"Sheriff, I want it on record that I am often the one getting those children up and ready for school in the morning before I head into work. I take them to practices and games. I can't sign any permission slips or even take them to their appointments without her consent. She's always been unreliable and those kids deserve better. I am done playing games. I am going after custody. I have an appointment with a lawyer tomorrow."

"You haven't seen her since Friday night?"

"A week ago Friday night. It has been ten days since I last saw her," Ang clarified.

"Ten days is a long time, don't you think? Why didn't you report this sooner?"

"Because last week when I tried, Maggie said she would turn up and to stop wasting your limited resources on a woman with a history of going off with men for days at a time. I've already searched everywhere I can think of. She hasn't been to work, unlike her to not at least call in. Danny hasn't seen her. Eric is still in jail. And honestly, I don't keep up with her current men," she stated as she paced the office. "She hasn't been back to her place either."

Warning bells were going off in Tony's head at the mention of Eric Howell. Too many women have disappeared or turned up dead in connection with him. He kept his thoughts to himself when she finally sat down.

"Angelica, let's fill out a missing persons report instead of filing charges." He held up his hand to explain when he saw the look of concern. "A missing persons will activate a more immediate investigation to search for your sister. Then you can file the charges."

He reached for his cell to send a text. Minutes later, his son was standing at the door.

"You need me, Dad?" Anthony asked as his eyes darted between his father and Angelica.

"Anthony, I want you to assist Ms. Daynee with filing a missing persons report. You will take lead on this," Sheriff Mancuso instructed, using code for the urgency of the matter. He hoped he was wrong about this.

Tony stood up to go address the stonewalling issue with his receptionist. No one, regardless of her reputation, should be allowed to go missing for ten days before reporting it. Not with everything else going on right now.

The next issue to address was Eric Howell. He's been locked up since his arrest the week Clara and Rob went missing. He denied killing Billy Kingsley last spring, Lauren McDonald, or even Shiloh Prentiss. But this current missing persons case was undeniably related to Eric.

The town had an ongoing debate over who fathered the many children of Isabella. The general consensus was Danny Thompson and Eric for the younger three, and Rob Foxwood for the oldest, perhaps causing the ongoing issues between the men. With eyes currently on the latter two, it was time to look deeper into Danny Thompson's whereabouts.

Danny Thompson, thirty years old, was born and raised in the area. His family owned farm land and the diner on Main Street. He was a lifelong friend of Eric Howell. Over the summer, Danny was arrested after initiating a bar fight with Rob Foxwood. After he was thrown out, Danny proceeded to slice open all four of Foxwood's tires on his truck. Just before the sheriff's department arrived, Danny pulled a knife out on Foxwood while Clara O'Reilly was standing beside him.

His grandfather, Ernie Thompson, had been fed up with the youngster's behavior. Determined to teach him a lesson, he refused to bail him out, and forbade his family from doing so as well. He did pay for the damage. But on the last day of September, Danny's oldest brother ignored his grandfather's warnings.

Danny Thompson was out on bail for almost a month.

Where was the lad now?

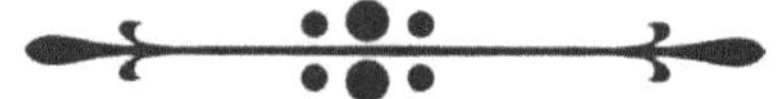

shocking news

Clara remained silent as she listened to the extent of the estate left to her. She literally owned half the buildings on Main Street! The broken down and not repaired side, she acknowledged. All that was going to change. She sat in amazement pondering the size of the estate. Unable to process everything, she only stared at Matt while he talked. He had shifted from the trust funds to the real estate and now to the stocks.

She was starting to process what else was not stated. Her mother was killed before her birthday when she could take control of the estate. She, herself, was also almost killed before she could take control. Was this connected or a sick coincidence?

The bugging of her home, did the Howells have prior knowledge of her family's sizable estate? Did her father? Was this the real reason for her mother's death? Her mind searched again for any memory of her childhood that would prepare her for this moment. Instead, shadows of the past surfaced to haunt her.

When Matt concluded the list of her estate, he realized Clara had remained silent and impassive. He worried she also connected the circumstances of her mother's death and the various events from the past summer. He needed to figure out who else knew of the value of her estate and how to protect the descendants of Graham Hawks.

But first, the final piece of the will. It was a shocker.

"Clara, all this has one stipulation." Matt paused as her green eyes met his. "You have to continue to pay for the care of your great-grandmother."

Lila slowly negotiated the steps down from the porch. She clicked her tongue and motioned for her new puppy to follow. Instead the small yellow lab stumbled down, somehow landing on his chest. Immediately, he popped to his feet and wagged his tail while looking up proudly.

"You are getting better! Before we know it, you'll be leaping down without any trouble. Come on, lets go check out the new barn. I can't believe Dad and Dallas finished it so quickly." Lila continued towards the barn with the puppy running along side her feet.

Inside the barn, Dallas was shoveling up the old hay while the horses were already out in the fenced in area.

"Need any help?" Lila asked.

"Naw, it feels good to be working in the barn first thing in the morning before work," he answered. "I never realized how much I missed this until now."

"Don't think you have to do all the work around here, I can help," Lila said.

"I think you have your hands fill with the little guy. Have you decided what you want to name him?" Finished with the task of cleaning up, Dallas started to spread out the new hay.

They both looked down at the puppy chasing and wrestling with his feet as he worked. Whenever Dallas remained still for a minute, the puppy started to play with his laces.

"Not sure, so far I'm thinking maybe Stormy or Rascal because Dallas, I don't think this little guy is going to make our life easier. He's already been into the bathroom trash, locked up in the pantry, and crawled into the refrigerator."

Dallas chuckled. "We should put the trash bin under the sink. Keep the temptation away. I like Stormy. Stormy Weather Thompson."

Shaking his boot loose of the puppy, Dallas walked to the other side of the barn and called with hand signals, "Stormy, here!"

Stormy immediately ran towards him and sat at his feet. Dallas squatted down to first give him praise with a pat on the head before giving a treat.

"You carry dog treats in your pocket?" Lila laughed.

"Sure thing, dog treats in the left pocket and horse treats in the right." Dallas looked up with a grin.

In town, Shannon was sitting down with a fresh mug of coffee. She was looking forward to reviewing the next section of records. With a happy sigh, she rolled her shoulders and stretched her hands before her fingers touched the keyboard.

As she reviewed the numbers, checking and double checking the math, Shannon started to see a pattern and her mind immediately closed out her surroundings.

Across the room, Devan watched with amusement at her actual excitement.

Jack entered the room. "How's Shannon doing? Has she gotten bored with the job yet?"

"Doubtful," Devan answered. "She seems to be enjoying this too much. It'll take some sorting through, I think there's years of accounts that need to be reviewed."

"Do you think there will be anything we can use or are we wasting her time at the taxpayers expense?"

"No idea," the younger agent shrugged. "But if there's anything conflicting, Shan will find it. She's apparently in her element. I never realized what a nerd she is."

Clara remained shocked as her brain tried to process what Matt said. After a few moments she whispered, "I have a living great-grandmother? Where? Why has this been kept a secret?"

"Shelby Hawks is the mother of your grandfather. She married your great-grandfather, Clarence Hawks, who I believe you were named after since you both share the same Christmas birthday. She's been under the care of a doctor, as far as I can tell, for the last forty years. She is ninety-eight. I'm not sure why she's been living secretly in the city," he answered honestly.

"I remember her. Like the others, she raised her family in the house. When the house was turned over to your grandfather, she moved permanently to the city address but often returned to the house in town for extended visits. I'm not sure when or why she moved to the facility where she currently resides."

"What kind of facility?" Clara demanded, ignoring the comment about the city address.

"The Palace," Matt answered as he kept his eyes on hers. "It's a highly secured community for the wealthy with extensive medical issues."

"Medical issues? Like assisted living or psychiatric medical issues?" she asked, attempting to understand what he wasn't saying. When he nodded, she asked, "Which is it? Why the high security?"

"I'm not really sure which or a combination of psychiatric and elderly care. From what I've learned, it's a way to protect the vulnerable from being targets of scams as well as protect their privacy," he answered. It made more sense when one realized the extent to what she was worth.

"But why would my mother consent to having her grandmother living there when she had plenty of money and resources to keep her here?" When she saw a flicker in his blue eyes, the answer came. "She didn't know about her, did she?"

"I don't think so. I doubt the will was discussed extensively. She knew her thirtieth birthday would give her access to the money. She likely didn't know the details yet," he speculated, knowing what her next questions would be.

"What are her extensive medical issues?"

"I was unable to get the information since I'm not a family member. However, as her next of kin, you can," he answered.

"How soon can I go visit her?"

"I can take you today. I'll call ahead so they will be expecting us," he answered.

"Give me time to call the applicants and set up arrangements for my children," Clara stated with a glance at the clock. "Will nine be soon enough?"

Matt also looked at the clock, he'd already prepared for this trip. His schedule had already been adjusted. "Absolutely. Where would you like me to pick you up?"

After they finalized their plans, Matt walked with her to the back door. As he watched the heir to the Hawks Estate slowly descend the stairs to the parking lot, he realized she had more traits of her grandfather than Susi would have liked. He also needed to complete his research. Who else knew the details of the will, as well as the size of the Hawks Estate?

C onnor was pleasantly surprised to find Clara in his office at the nursing home. He leaned into the doorway and admired the sight before him: Clara's brown curly hair down around her shoulders; she wore a dark green blouse with black dress pants. *Very beautiful and professional*, he thought with a grin.

Clara was sitting behind his desk on the phone. When she saw him standing at the doorway, to his amusement, she waved him in.

Nothing like being permitted into your own office, he thought as he stepped around to join her, leaning onto the desk. As she appeared to be finishing her call, he glanced over the files.

"I look forward to seeing you, have a good day," she stated before hanging up. "Connor, I'm glad you're here. I was just about to text you."

"Don't you have your own desk? Did Matt give you my office? Have I been demoted?" he teased.

"No, I needed a quiet place to make some calls. Rob and Chase started on the construction in the therapy room and the dining room is currently the gym," Clara explained, finally looking up at his face. "I hope I didn't overstep by coming in here."

"Not at all. Mi casa es tu casa. Or mi oficina es tu oficina," he chuckled at his own joke as he lifted her hand up to kiss. Within a minute, Clara was standing between his feet with her arms around him, kissing him. Her plans were forgotten, until a subtle cough brought her back to the moment.

"You two still can't keep your hands off each other? I really need to get the policy updated!"

When Matt's words registered, Clara stepped back and blushed, Connor chuckled.

"Clara, I'm ready to leave whenever you are," Matt announced from the doorway.

"I just need about five more minutes, then I'll be ready," she responded as she stepped away.

"Where are you two going?" Connor asked, noting the look they shared.

"You didn't tell him?"

"He just came in. Can you explain? I need to do one last task," Clara responded as she gave Connor a quick kiss before she left the office.

Both men watched her limp out of the office before Matt closed the door. "We have a lot to discuss, but now is not the time. I went over Susannah's will with Clara this morning. She just learned her great-grandmother is still alive and living in the city. She wants to go see her."

Clara entered the gym, slowly navigating the organized construction chaos. She stopped when both Chase and Rob turned in her direction.

"Hi, Clara," Chase greeted.

"Hi, guys. Rob, just letting you know I need to run into the city with Matt for a few hours. It'll be late when I get back. Michelle will be at home with Reese and Hailey after daycare closes," she explained.

"Why? I can pick them up myself and take them home," Rob answered.

"You've been doing so much lately, I don't want to intrude," she started to explain.

"Now you are insulting me. Toss me your car keys and I'll just use your car," he instructed.

"Are you sure?" When he nodded with a motion for the keys, she stepped in to hand them over but tripped over an extension cord.

Connor arrived in the doorway in time to see her fall prevented by Rob's quick movements. He was suddenly holding her in his arms. Connor again tried to contain his annoyance, watching Clara assisted to an upright position. First, she planned a trip into the city with his brother and then she literally fell into Foxwood's arms.

But the day was taking a turn for the better, he hoped. Though, the few comments from his brother had him worried.

"Clara?" Connor waited until she turned her face towards him before he continued. "Is it alright if I tag along on the trip?"

As he watched Clara's face light up, Connor's heart skipped a beat. He realized his ridiculous jealous streak was showing again. *I need to get a hold of this before she sees it*, Connor thought, reaching out for her hand to avoid another incident.

"Connor, that will be great!" She turned to Rob when she reached the door. "Rob, thanks again! I'll owe you."

Minutes later, Clara sat in the back seat beside Talia as the two chatted about everything and nothing. Connor sat up front as Matt drove.

When they arrived in the city, Connor and Talia went to a nearby coffee shop while Matt escorted Clara into the lobby of the facility.

Matt went to the desk to announce their arrival, while Clara studied the pictures throughout the room. Pausing to look at the familiar paintings, she realized she recognized the artist. She had a similar painting, the same garden from a different angle, hanging in her current home. *Damn, my great-grandmother is an artist*, she thought as Matt joined her.

"Her doctor will be down in a minute to discuss her care. I have the paperwork to assist with the transition to change her power of attorney," he reported, studying her face. Matt wasn't sure what to expect during the visit, but he wished there was a way to prepare her. When Clara turned towards him and smiled, he realized she was alright, it was his own anxiety for her.

"Mr. Emerson, Dr. Colbert will see you. Please follow me," a middle-aged woman announced from an open door. She led them past the receptionist's desk, down a bright homey hallway and into a large office. "Can I get you anything to drink? Water, coffee, or tea?"

Matt first looked over at Clara before shaking his head. "No, thank you. That won't be necessary."

The woman nodded before leaving the office. A moment later, another door opened from behind the desk, and a younger man entered. He was of medium height with broad shoulders. He had short brown hair and was dressed in business casual. His sharp blue eyes first looked at Matt before shifting towards Clara. Immediately, a smile spread across his face as he introduced himself.

"Mr. Emerson, Ms. Hawks, it's a pleasure to finally meet you. I am Dr. Evan Colbert," he announced as he first reached to shake Matt's hand before Clara's.

"Actually, it's Mrs. O'Reilly," Matt clarified as he watched the man before them assess Clara a bit too long. He handed over a file. "Here is the paperwork to shift Mrs. Hawks power of attorney and health care surrogate to Mrs. O'Reilly."

"But please, call me Clara," she instructed as he paused to smile before gesturing towards the sitting area.

Clara chose the small sofa, Matt sat beside her, and the doctor sat across the coffee table. He read over the paperwork before he commented. "Clara? Thank you. I understand you are Shelby's next of kin. I was sorry to hear about your mother's passing. It certainly explains why she's not had any visitors for some time."

"What kind of a facility is this?" Clara asked. "What level of care?"

"It's an assisted living facility. We specialize in those with mental issues," he appeared to be dancing around the issue. "Your grandmother requires a very special controlled environment that many are not equipped to provide."

"Such as?" Clara asked after looking first at Matt. He had leaned back, watching the interaction between the two.

"She lives in a constant state of denial and does not adapt to change in the world. My predecessor believed she led too much of a sheltered life and had trouble adjusting to certain unexpected life happenings, especially if it were negative," Dr. Colbert calmly explained. "Please, let me introduce you to her and then answer any questions you have afterwards."

Standing, he gestured toward the door he previously entered. Clara was surprised by the decor when she stepped into the hall. While the front was well furnished, it had the atmosphere of an expensive healthcare facility. But behind the closed door, she felt as if she were in someone's home.

"How many residents do you have here?"

Dr. Colbert smiled before answering. "You understand the difference between patients and residents. Are you in the healthcare field, Clara?"

"Yes, I am," she answered vaguely.

"The number of residents varies but currently we have forty," he answered as his blue eyes seemed to smile. "You have your grandmother's eyes. I must admit, you are younger than I expected."

"I'm her great-granddaughter. Her granddaughter, my mother, passed twenty years ago," Clara explained as they stepped onto the elevator.

Evan's eyes narrowed at the explanation as he looked between the two visitors. "And you two have never met? Your grandparents never brought you to visit?"

"If they did, I don't remember. They both passed when I was very young," she commented as she looked puzzled towards Matt. Did she ever visit, she wondered, but he only shrugged his shoulders, he didn't know.

When they reached the top floor, Clara and Matt were led down a long hall to the last door at the end. Dr. Colbert knocked on the door before entering. "Mrs. Hawks, you have visitors."

"Evan, thank you," a female voice stated. "Please come in."

When Clara stepped inside, she stopped as she looked around her. She felt as if she had stepped back in time. The room was filled with antiques. The soft blue wallpaper, Clara was sure, was from fifty years ago. But something about the room seemed very familiar. She paused to look at a painting very similar to the one hanging in the parlor when she was growing up. Admitting only to herself, she never really studied the various paintings and furniture in her home. Hell, she was rarely in the house after her mother disappeared. How would a young child ever learn to appreciate such things?

"Susannah! How wonderful! It's been ages," an elderly woman stood up when Clara came into her view. She wore a dark green polka dot dress that brought out her green eyes. The dress had a fitted top and flared at the waist. Her feet wore matching pumps with low heels. And around her neck, she wore a single strand of pearls with matching pearl earrings. Her hair was the same shade of brown as Clara's pulled back into a French twist with many curls escaping to frame her face.

Clara simply froze in place and stared, too speechless to respond. She felt as if she were looking into a mirror of what her future self would look like. She would never guess the woman before her was ninety-eight years old.

Shelby stepped closer with her hands out as she grasped the younger woman's hands. "You have certainly grown into a beautiful woman. And you brought Matthew with you!"

She turned towards the doctor. "Thank you, Evan, that will be all. I will ring when they are ready to leave. Charles?"

A man in his young twenties entered the doorway. "Yes, Miss Shelby?"

"Please bring the afternoon tea, my guests have arrived," she stated with the confidence of a woman used to running a household.

Chase was amazed with the amount of work accomplished on the first day. They were wrapping it up when Rob realized the late hour. "Shit, I need to get the kids before the daycare closes. I'll meet you tomorrow."

Within the hour, he and the children were safely home with dinner cooking. They were all playing in the family room when the doorbell rang. Rob quietly peeked out onto the porch, not expecting any visitors.

"Shit," he muttered under his breath.

"Shit!" Rob heard behind him. When he turned, Hailey looked up proudly with a smile.

"Figures that would be the one word you pronounce correctly," he stated with a sigh. *Clara will never let me babysit again.*

Rob took a deep breath before opening the door. Standing on the porch was his father. They still hadn't spoken since his world fell apart. While his father had tried to reach him many times, Rob continued to avoid both his parents, well, his mother and her husband.

"Rob, I am just here to drop something off for Clara," Mitch Foxwood explained as he opened the screen door to place a box on the floor, before reaching out for a second box. When he had everything inside, he closed the door behind him. "Is Clara home?"

"No," Rob answered. "What's this?"

Before he could answer, Reese scolded, "We don't let strangers in the house, Uncle Rob."

Rob sighed as his father chuckled. "Reese, this is my father, Mr. Foxwood. Dad, Clara's kids, Reese and Hailey."

"Uncle Rob, what do we call him? Uncle Mr. Foxwood?" the young boy wondered.

"No, you call him Mr. Foxwood, just like your mother did," Rob answered patiently.

"Just Mitch will also work," Mitch answered.

Rob closed his eyes, resigning to what came next.

"Just Mitch, what is in the box?" Reese wondered, trying to get a peek.

"That is an excellent question, Reese. I have something here to give to your mother. Maybe I can leave it with you and your sister?" the older man asked while he squatted down to open the loosely folded top.

When he reached inside, he pulled out a small yellow lab puppy. Mitch wished he had a camera to capture the excited faces when the children realized it was a puppy. He gently placed her on the floor before he instructed.

"Sit!"

The puppy's wiggling body sat on command. Hailey's little bottom immediately hit the floor as she tapped her chest. "Mine? Mine?"

The little puppy took the tapping as a release signal and was suddenly in her lap licking her face while her brother reached over to pat her head. "Just Mitch, who's puppy?"

"Your mother always wanted a puppy, but if you promise to help take care of it, I'm sure she'll share the puppy with you." Mitch reached into the second box and pulled out a toy to hand to Reese.

While the children were running around the dining room with the puppy, Rob felt a slight panic at having to explain why he let the one person he wasn't talking to into Clara's house. He wasn't prepared for his father's next comment. "Please tell Clara I'm sorry I missed her. I have to finish delivering the puppies. There's a total of eight in the litter, six are spoken for. Let me know if you want one. Everything the puppy needs is in this other box. Reese? Hailey? It was great meeting you, both. Take good care of the puppy."

"Thank you, Just Mitch!" Reese ran back towards the door. Hailey was beside him and hugged his leg, talking in her usual gibberish. "My sister also thanks you."

Mitch looked up at Rob who explained. "He's the only one that really knows what she's saying."

After he left, Rob sighed as he watched the children running around with the puppy chasing after them. He reached into the box for the bowls and puppy food before heading back to check on dinner. As he expected, everyone followed. Checking the oven to make sure he still had time, he sat on the floor while they debated puppy names.

"Your daddy must really love you," Reese announced with giggles when the puppy licked his face.

"Why do you say that?"

"He gave you a puppy!" the boy exclaimed with his arms out wide. Reese was practically dancing in place with excitement.

"No, he gave you and your sister a puppy. We still have to see if your mother allows it to stay. Besides, I'm still upset with my father," he explained. "We aren't really talking these days."

"Why? What did he do?" Reese asked with concern, all the happiness disappeared. "Did he take away your bicycle?"

"No," Rob answered as he filled the water bowl.

"Did he take away your crayons because you colored on the walls?"

"I never colored on the walls. Did you?" Rob was attempted to shift the young boy's focus.

"Of course not. Mommy bought me a coloring book. But Sawyer's daddy took his crayons away for a whole night!"

"Just a night?"

"Yeah, then he went to his grandmother's house. She let him have his crayons," Reese explained. "Did your daddy take your baseball bat because you broke the window?"

"No, Reese, he didn't take anything from me because I misused it," Rob answered absently.

"Then why are you mad at your daddy? What did he do?" The young boy was obviously puzzled.

Rob stopped short, what did his father do?

He gave me a roof over my head, fed me, taught me how to ride a horse, to care for the farm and he loved me! All along, he knew full well I wasn't his biological child. He could have dumped me on Zachariah Thompson's porch. The man that actually did kick a kid he'd raised since birth out of the house at the age of twelve, Dallas.

Shit! If anyone did anything wrong, it was his mother. But if Dad could forgive her, shouldn't he? Otherwise, he'd be at the mercy of the Thompsons! Rob visibly cringed at the idea of being best buddies with Danny Thompson, his true biological cousin and not Chase. The first time he allowed himself to acknowledge the horrible fact.

"Reese, you are one smart kid," Rob announced.

"I know," the little boy agreed. "We should have ice cream while we wait for dinner."

Unable to process, Clara allowed the older woman to lead her towards the sitting area.

Clara sat on the elegant Victorian chair with Matt sitting next to her in a matching chair. Across from an elaborate coffee table, her great-grandmother was busy adjusting her skirt. When she looked up, her green eyes sparkled.

Charles, dressed in a formal butler's uniform from a long gone era, stepped forward once everyone was seated. He placed a freshly poured tea cup in front of everyone and then placed a plate of tea sandwiches and a tri-platter of scones and biscuits. When his task was completed, Clara blinked in shock when he *actually bowed* before leaving the room.

"Tell me everything that's going on and don't leave out anything," the older woman instructed. "You are too young to be paired with Matthew and yet you look too like Susannah to not be related."

"You know I'm not Susannah?" Clara's eyebrows furrowed in confusion. "Why did you call me Susannah?"

Shelby gave a dismissive wave of her hand before reaching for her tea cup. "Evan and all the medical staff expect to see a spoiled rich senile woman. I'm just giving them what they expect."

Clara watched her move with ease of a young woman. "You are really the mother of Graham Hawks?"

"I am," Shelby confirmed. She looked each of her visitors in the eyes when she spoke. "I apologize, I know you are Matthew Emerson but I still don't know who you are."

"I'm Clara Noelle," Clara whispered without intending. Her eyes widen in surprise when her great-grandmother clapped her hands and laughed out loud before she could explain their relation.

"Clara Noelle? How delightful! Syliva must be turning over in her grave! She despised my husband"

"Why would my grandmother not like her father-in-law?"

"Oh, I imagine she had many legitimate reasons, Clarence was not the easiest man to get along with, I should know! I was married to the cantankerous, old grump for over forty years. He did the best he could with what little he had to work with." Shelby shrugged.

Unsure how to respond, Clara could only stare. She glanced at Matt for support but he was too busy helping himself to the food.

"I'm named after a grumpy old man?"

"Clarence wasn't a horrible man. He had a set way of how things were to be done. His expectations were ridiculous!" Shelby waved her hands in the air with dramatic flare as she talked. "Dinner had to be on the table at precisely 7:00 pm, children were to be seen and not heard and he counted *every* penny carefully. But what can you expect from someone born from generations of hardheadedness?"

"If he was such a bad guy, why did you marry him?" Clara wondered.

"Oh, he wasn't a bad guy, dear. Not at all! He was always a perfect gentleman, excellent dancer, and knew how to have fun. Of course, he only shared that side with a selected few. As much as he kept the purse strings tight, he was one of the most generous benefactors in town. He just always kept it anonymous. Clarence hated anyone knowing he was being helpful. 'If they knew where the money was coming from, they'd be constantly knocking on our door interrupting the dinner hour,' he always said."

Connor was sitting in the last corner booth with his coffee as he read from his tablet. When he glanced up, Clara and Matt were walking towards him. He stood up to give her a hug.

"Hey, how did it go?"

"Surreal," she answered before sitting. "She called me Susannah at first. I wasn't sure if I should correct her or not. She remembers Matt. Connor, she's still an active woman, still cognitively intact. I don't really understand why she's there."

He looked over towards his brother, Matt simply shrugged as he looked around. "Where's Talia? Did you two get into it again?"

"Not at all, she went shopping. I don't think she had any intention of sitting here with me while you both went visiting. Give her a text and she'll return," he answered. Connor didn't want to explain to Clara about their previous disagreements.

During the drive home, everyone assumed Clara was sound asleep. Instead, she was mentally reviewing her day. So much had changed since she woke up that morning! Or rather, nothing changed, but her world was so different! She had a living, breathing, spry, great-grandmother. And she had real estate. In both the city and at home. Matt assured her she had more money than Connor, but she didn't have any concept of how much either of them had. What was she going to do?

And more importantly, how did this affect her current life?

a crazy wednesday

Wednesday morning, two days later, Dallas watched as his wife secured the puppy in the mud room before they went out to the horses. He shook his head at the craziness of his life. Six months ago, he was living alone while secretly married to Lila, without anyone even aware of them being together.

Now, not only was their marriage out in the open, Lila was living with him! They had a puppy and two horses. When he stepped into the newly made barn, he breathed in the smells of horses and hay. *He loved his life*, he thought with a grin as he prepared the horses for their ride. Never, since he first started spending time with Lila that night in the caved in theater, would he have predicted their lives would turn out like this. The pessimistic side of him wondered if the other shoe was about to drop.

With a smile, Dallas watched her slowly walk towards him into the cool crisp morning. "Lila, are you sure you're ready to be riding?"

"Dal, it would be different if we were hiking, but riding? Oh, yeah! I am so ready!" Lila exclaimed with excitement. She spoke to her mare before allowing assistance up into the saddle. "I never thought I'd see the day my dad, Mitchell Foxwood, would not only assist you in building a barn, he would welcome you with open arms. Life is good."

After mounting his own horse, Dallas nodded in agreement. "I was just thinking the same thing. We'll keep it light, the shorter trail to the low ridge. We can stop for a rest before heading back."

He led the way into the woods, keeping the pace slow as they enjoyed each other's company, talking about the simple things in life: work schedules, dinner plans, and whether to repaint the half bathroom.

"Dal, I'm going out of my mind with boredom! The doctor is not likely to clear me to return to work for at least another four weeks! I promise it won't be too feminine," she pleaded her case.

"Li, I don't care if you want the whole house decorated in pinks and purples with flowers! That's not what I'm concerned about. It's you lifting too much and climbing up on a ladder. It's too much, too soon," he argued over his shoulder. When he turned back, his eye caught something partially hidden in the ground.

Lila was about to argue, but stopped when Dallas' hand came up in a motion to halt. Without a word, he slid off his horse. He squatted down and reached over to uncover a small piece of what appeared to be an earring. Without touching it, his eyes scanned the immediate area and stopped on a recently made trail. He motioned for his wife to remain on her horse as he cautiously followed the trail.

A few minutes later, Dallas reappeared back on the trail with his phone to his ear. "Devan, I'm sending you coordinates to my current location. I found a body. You'll need to use the ATV to get here. Tell Anthony the blue trail entrance will be easiest."

"Shit, another body? Do you know who it is or how long it's been there?" Devan asked.

"I would say days," Dallas answered as his eyes turned to his wife. Lila, hearing the news, slid from her horse. He used his body to block her path as she tried to step around. "It's Isabella Daynee."

"Damn it. All right, I'll keep you posted on our ETA," he heard the agent answer.

"Dallas, we need to help her!" Lila was trying to step around him.

"Lila, we can't go back there. She's beyond our help. It's a crime scene," his voice was soft. He watched the panic grow in her eyes.

"How do you know? She may need our help. She could have fallen while she was hiking," Lila's voice shook with fear. "How do you know we can't help her? What happened? Let me look."

"Baby, trust me. She was not out here hiking. She wasn't properly dressed for the low temperatures or the hike this far into the woods," he assured, leading her over to a large boulder. Once she sat, he tied the horses back off the trail before sitting beside her.

A couple of hours later, Dallas and Lila answered a few questions as both Anthony and Devan assessed the scene.

"Your leg must be healing up nicely to be riding this far so soon after your surgery," Devan stated. "You two head back to your place while we take care of things here, alright?"

Lila simply nodded, but didn't attempt to stand until Dallas assisted her onto her feet. She winced with her first few steps towards the horses. "You alright to ride? Want me to borrow one of the ATVs?"

"I'm alright," she assured him as she motioned for him to assist her onto her horse. "I don't want to take from the help she needs right now."

Gone was the joy of riding together as the late morning chill settled deep into her bones. Lila knew without saying it what they were both thinking. Someone was killed, practically in their backyard!

Why? Who would do such a thing?

The return trip seemed to drag on, taking longer than the ride in. When they arrived home, Dallas assisted Lila off her horse.

"Head inside and get warmed up. I'll take care of the horses."

Lila nodded with a sad smile before turning towards the house.

Dallas had just secured the horses in their stalls when he heard Lila scream his name. His heart stopped as he dropped, literally everything in his hands, before running to the back porch.

"Lila! Are you all right?" he yelled as he neared the porch steps. She was sitting on the floor, but he came to a halt at the sight of blood on the steps. "What the hell?"

Dallas cautiously climbed up, avoiding the blood trail. Once he reached the top, he froze as his eyes met Lila's in question.

Lying prone before him was a male body covered in mud and leaves. A pool of blood formed beneath him while Lila appeared to be applying pressure.

"Dallas, call 911. He's still alive."

Connor had just arrived for his shift in the ER with his nephew, Josh, beside him. He listened to the younger man list pros and cons of moving out as he reviewed the current list of patients awaiting care.

"Dad initially agreed to let me move out, but now he's saying it isn't safe. I don't think it's fair to go back on his promise. Personally, I think Talia talked him out of it. What do you think?" Josh wondered.

"I certainly understand your reasons for wanting to move out. Why not compromise? Fix up the apartment over the garage. It gives you distance from the main house with privacy and quiet to study. You'll be close enough to eat Chef's meals when you're hungry. Your dad will be able to get Talia to agree if you let her approve the decorating," Connor suggested absently.

Josh thought it over a minute. "That's not a bad idea. Talia would love the project and the security system is already installed. It'll only need a few repairs and paint. Shouldn't be too costly."

"Dr. Emerson, there's an ambulance en route: a man in his fifties with severe traumatic injuries," a nurse called over.

"Thanks," Connor answered as he checked the clock before leading the younger man over to don the appropriate PPE. They arrived at the doors as the ambulance pulled up.

Connor was surprised to see Dallas exit the passenger seat of the ambulance.

Without a word, Dallas opened the back doors and assisted Lila down before the paramedic hopped down. Both pulled out the stretcher. The man was strapped to a backboard with his head secured to prevent any cervical movement.

As everyone walked the stretcher, the paramedic listed off the vitals and medications administered, as well as the suspected injuries. When Connor glanced in Lila's direction, he noted her excessive limping and blood all over her clothes.

"Lila, are you hurt?"

"Not my blood," she dismissed as they arrived at the trauma room. Without thinking, Lila donned a gown and gloves before she continued to assist.

Once the man was transferred to the bed, Connor started listening with a stethoscope while his eyes finally looked at the face. His eyes immediately went to Dallas' then Lila's as he asked, "Does Clara know?"

"Chase is bringing her here, but they don't know why," Lila responded with a shake of her head.

"What happened?"

"No idea. We went riding this morning. I'll tell you about that later. When we returned, I found him on the back porch face down." Her eyes followed Connor's towards Dallas. He had remained suspiciously silent throughout it all. For once, she couldn't read Dallas' mind as he remained out of the way to watch. "He was conscious enough to crawl up the porch steps within the last four hours."

"Dr. Emerson? Clara is here," the triage nurse announced.

Connor's eyes met hers as he gave a slight nod. He turned to give Josh instructions to notify the OR before he stepped away to remove his gloves and gown.

Clara was irritated with being pulled from work by Chase. He announced his intent to bring her to the ER after stating the children were both alright. They were joined by Rob in the parking lot when he returned from an errand. Neither appeared to know anything.

"Clara, come on back," the nurse announced. "Just her."

Clara exchanged looks with Rob before she followed the nurse back. She listed off the people she knew it wasn't, obviously not Rob and Chase. Nor would it be Lila or Rachel. When she saw Dallas, she sighed in relief. But when their eyes met, she froze. She couldn't take another step as Connor appeared out of a treatment room.

Connor signaled Dallas to follow as he grabbed her hand to lead her into a quiet corner. He didn't have much time.

"Clara, your father was found with extensive injuries including a fractured leg and internal bleeding. He's lost a lot of blood. I'm not sure if he'll survive the surgery. I'm going to give you both a moment before we take him up, just in case."

When neither spoke, Connor grabbed her hand again to lead them to Carl's side. His team was silent as they stepped back, they'd done all they could for the moment. Lila remained at Dallas' side, while Connor's hand rested on Clara's shoulder.

Clara's mind was suddenly flowing with images from her childhood. Her father across the table as they ate, calling up to her before she came down the stairs, standing at her doorway watching as her mother read to her. Clara reached for his hand as she whispered, "I love you, Dad."

Connor had kept an eye on the monitor. When the two minutes were up, he announced they needed to take Carl upstairs.

Rachel arrived just after everyone sat down in the waiting room outside the OR. She first hugged Clara, sensing her need to be close. She sat down beside her, holding her hand.

"Lila, can you and your brother head back home to see to the horses and the puppy? I'm not even sure if they have enough water after the ride this morning," Dallas' voice was without emotion.

"Clara, want me to pick up Reese and Hailey?" Rob asked as he stood up with Chase. She simply nodded her head.

During the drive back to her house, it was somehow decided Lila would pack an overnight bag, just in case Dallas wanted to stay in town. They dropped the puppy off at Clara's while Rob picked up the children. He debated being at the hospital with Clara, but realized he was the most familiar with the evening routine.

When Lila and Chase returned to the waiting room a couple of hours later, there was still nothing to report from the OR.

Rachel was returning from the cafeteria with a tray of coffee and hot chocolate when her cell rang. She quickly handed Chase the tray to answer. "Hello?"

"Baby? I need help. I need a lawyer," she heard over the phone.

Chase watched Rachel's eyes widen in surprise as she turned to him in question. "Max, what's going on?"

"I think I'm being arrested for the murder of Isabella. Shit, I don't even know her last name," he cussed over the phone. "Rach, you have to believe me! I didn't kill her."

"Why would they think you did?" Rachel found herself asking. "Isabella? Isabella Daynee?"

"Yeah! They seem to think I'm the last one to see her alive," he admitted. "But I swear, Rach, I didn't kill her. Please help me."

"I don't think there's anything I can do," she answered slowly. What was going on?

"Rachel, please don't hang up. I need help. Can't you call that rich lawyer friend of yours? Please? I called you for my one call," Max pleaded. The call suddenly went silent.

"Oh my gosh!" Rachel exclaimed.

"What? Who was that?" Chase demanded.

"Max says he's been arrested for Isabella's murder," Rachel announced with confusion.

Clara's eyes widened in surprise. "Isabella Daynee? She's dead?"

"Why the hell is he calling you?" Chase wanted to know as he watched Lila and Dallas exchange looks. "Dallas, what's going on?"

"I totally forgot with everything else happening this morning," Dallas started to say.

"During our ride this morning, Dallas found her on one of the popular trails," Lila finished.

"You found her? What was she doing out there?" Rachel asked.

"She wasn't dressed for hiking or for the cooler weather," Dallas summed up.

Chase's eyes widened, fully understanding the meaning, but Rachel was confused. "Well, that would make sense, she never really dressed appropriately for any occasion, even back in high school."

"If she were planning to go into the woods, she wouldn't be wearing a mini skirt and heels," Dallas's tone was quiet. "She was likely brought there and left."

Everyone looked at him, expecting him to finish, but Dallas didn't say anything else.

"You mean she was killed there?" Rachel asked for clarification.

Dallas sighed, "Based on how she was dressed and the mud on her, I think someone left her to the mercy of the elements."

"Dallas, why didn't you say that before?" Lila asked.

"Not my investigation," he shrugged, "and honestly, I could be wrong. The immediate area where she was found suggested she was alone and panicked."

"Is this what happened to the others?" Clara wondered as she had flashes from her own time drugged in the woods. She saw herself wandering down a narrow path and losing her footing before falling, waking up after who knows how long. She wasn't properly dressed for the cold mountain temperatures either. Was this what was happening to all the others that went missing and were found dead?

"No, not everyone. Billy was killed differently," Dallas stated.

"By a guitar string," Clara stated softly.

"Clara, how do you know that?" Rachel asked as everyone turned to her.

"I don't really know how I know." She shrugged. In the past, she always seemed to know more details than others. It was something her friends seemed to accept without question, which was ironic considering she was hearing impaired. Clara often missed details in discussions.

Dallas had not seen this beforehand. But then, he wondered, how did he know to stop and assess the area and find the bodies?

Before anyone else could comment, Clara sensed Connor's presence. She turned to see him coming out of the double doors. She slowly stood up, trying to read his face. His brown eyes were on her green as he walked into the waiting room, he nodded slowly.

"We've stopped the bleeding, but had to remove his spleen. He's lost a lot of blood, and he's already had four units transfused. Later, we'll get an MRI to determine the extent of his head injury. He's stable for now. An agent is present to take pictures and collect his nail clippings, for forensics to assist with catching who did this to him. Once he's cleaned up and settled in his room, you two can go see him," he announced.

Connor didn't say anything about the drugs in his system. Carl Gibson was apparently on the same homemade hallucinogens as Clara.

Chase agreed to go to the Sheriff's department, mainly because Rachel was going regardless. He didn't want her alone with Max, but not because he believed the guy was the killer. First, the killings started before MadMax came to town. And despite being dedicated to his workouts, Chase believed Max was too lazy to go into the woods. City boy would never consider hiking as a form of exercise.

As they stepped inside, Anthony Mancuso was talking with the receptionist.

"Anthony? Can we have a minute?" Rachel called out.

"Sure, what's up?" he asked. Anthony was quiet while he listened to his friends explain the reason for the visit. "So Max is a friend of yours?"

"We met in the city. He was my personal trainer," Rachel answered vaguely.

"That's right, I remember now. Isn't he the guy that was arrested at the Emerson House when we were searching for Lila?" he continued when she nodded. "Can't really say I've had the honor of meeting the guy before today. He's a bit odd, isn't he?"

"I'd use different adjectives," Chase commented.

"What do you mean?" Rachel asked, ignoring him.

"Well, he's publicly referred to you as his girlfriend, but apparently he's developed a reputation as a player," Anthony explained. "What exactly is he to you?"

"He's a friend, nothing more. We've never really dated," she answered. When the men both raised their eyebrows in question, Rachel clarified. "We would see movies together and have lunch only as friends. Nothing ever happened between us."

"I heard you were kissing him in front of The Lantern not too long ago," Anthony reported. He knew he was riling Chase, but it was out of character for Rachel.

"Of course, you did. I hate the town's stupid gossip mill! Anthony, he's only kissed me like that three times the whole time I've known him. Two of those times, were in front of Chase, trying to make him jealous," Rachel explained, unable to contain her frustration.

"Rachel, I am only doing as I'm told. He's not been arrested per se. He was brought in for questioning and his rights were read as a formality," Anthony explained. "I'm surprised he called you instead of a lawyer."

"Me too," Chase answered.

"I'm not able to let you talk with him right now but you're welcome to wait."

Devan and Jack were heading toward the medical examiner's office. Both turned to see who entered behind them. It was Eugene Slater, the district attorney. He paused in shock when he realized who the men were.

"What are you doing here?" Slater inquired. "This area is off limits."

"Not for us," Devan answered as he pulled out his ID. "Federal agents. We're here to see Dr. McDuffy."

"Isabella's case is local," Slater stated after checking the ID's. "What the hell are you doing working behind the bar? Have you been working undercover all this time, without notifying the locals?"

"Isabella's sister filed a missing persons report. During the course of the investigation, it was discovered she was abducted. Once her body was found on federal property, it made it our jurisdiction." Devan shrugged. He wasn't going to expand on the fact that he was indeed invited in by the Sheriff, nor that multiple bodies implied a serial killer in the area. He was keeping his eye on this Slater guy, his appearance seemed too coincidental for his liking.

"I have a right to be involved in this investigation," Slater demanded.

"Not really. Tell me, were you acquainted with Ms. Daynee?" Jack asked, sensing something more than a tug over jurisdictions.

"Not really. We are both from here and went to the same high school," Slater cautiously answered.

"So you knew her. When did you see her last?"

"Is there a reason you are interrogating me?" the DA asked.

"Oh, this isn't an interrogation. You're a local, I'm simply asking you a few questions," Jack shrugged, "but if you're uncomfortable, we will be on our way. The medical examiner is waiting for us."

Devan smiled and nodded to Slater before he followed his boss into the back room. "What do you think that's about?"

"Something's going on for sure. This town has many different players, almost as many as the city. He could be the connection. He worked closely with the mayor," he answered as an idea formed. "Plus, he was at The Lantern the night in question. The sheriff was right to be suspicious of the district attorney's office."

"Really?" Devan turned towards his boss.

"Yes, I was keeping an eye on Rob while he was out that evening. After he met up with his cousin and Rachel for dinner, he went across the street. He was sitting in the back, brooding, when Isabella sat with him. From the looks of it, she was trying to hook up, but he wasn't interested. He left her at the table and sat beside me. DA Slater was sitting at a table near the dance floor. I didn't think too much about it, but he did leave shortly after Max came in and left with her."

"Interesting. Is he the one that reported Max and Isabella were together? I wonder if he remembers Rob being there?" Devan speculated. Further discussion ended when Dr. McDuffy entered the room.

Slater pulled out his cell once he stepped outside the hospital. "It's me. I didn't get here in time. The feds are here and I couldn't get inside to make the exchange. You're on your own now."

He paused a moment before he continued, "You should have thought that through before you started all this. Sorry, my hands are tied. Any further action will be suspicious."

As he ended the call, he looked over to see Lila sitting on the bench. "Lila? What are you doing here?"

"Slater? My father-in-law is having surgery. You?"

"District attorney, remember? Part of the job is checking in with the medical examiner's office," he explained as an idea began to form. He still could not believe Lila and Dallas had been secretly married all this time. He wished he knew that detail before her kidnapping. "I'm sorry to hear about Isabella. I know she was in your class and your brother's girlfriend."

"He dated her for a summer twelve years ago. It doesn't make her my best friend. I hardly knew her." Lila shrugged.

"Really?" Slater sighed a moment, suddenly acting as if she were the same naïve girl from high school. "I guess he didn't tell you. Can't really blame him. He was one of the last people to be seen with her. He was still seeing her on and off. I guess it's hard to let go of someone when you have a child together."

"What the hell are you talking about?" Lila demanded as she stood up, trying not to wince in pain.

Slater's eyes squinted as he looked down into her beautiful blue eyes, a part of him regretted agitating her but he had a job to do. "He never told you? Rob's the father of Isabella's oldest child."

"No, he's not. The child was born ten months after they broke up. She never pushed for a paternity test because she knew the one person that would actually support the child, was not the biological father," Lila stated as she folded her arms.

"Still doesn't change the fact he's one of the last people to see her alive," he shrugged, "believe me, I will see her killer is brought to justice."

"How? She was found on federal land. Doesn't that make it the FBI's case?" Lila speculated, watching his eyes widen in surprise. *What game is he playing?*

"How do you know that?" Slater demanded.

"You're obviously not fully aware of the details surrounding her death, are you? I can't tell you confidential information. Please excuse me, I need to get back inside," Lila dismissed before she limped away.

That wasn't weird at all, she thought as she headed back upstairs.

When she reached the elevator, Lila was surprised to see Devan and his supervisor also step in behind her.

"Lila, you're getting around pretty good these days. Horseback riding this morning and now walking all over the hospital. How's the leg?" Devan asked.

"Hi, Devan," she answered with a nod to Jack. "It's a bit sore but once I get upstairs, I'll be off it. How's the investigation going?"

"Which one?" Jack asked.

"Do you believe Isabella and Carl's are connected?" she asked as she looked between the two agents. "I should probably tell you about an awkward conversation I had with someone a few minutes ago."

"Would that be with DA Eugene Slater?" Devan speculated. When her eyes grew wide with surprise, he chuckled. "We saw him downstairs when we first arrived. How well do you know him?"

"Dallas knew him better than I did back in high school. I don't think they've run into each other much since we moved back but," Lila hesitated as they stepped off the elevator, "Slater seems to want to pin Isabella's death on my brother."

"Why?" Devan asked.

Lila looked around her before pulling them into an empty room to talk privately. She quickly talked about what she overheard while he was on the phone, before he saw her, and how their conversation turned towards her brother. "I have no idea why he would want to pin it on Rob."

Devan and Jack shared a look before he spoke. "Lila, we know Rob didn't have anything to do with Isabella's death. He's been under surveillance since he's been discharged from the hospital, not because he's guilty. Because he survived. It's for his protection. Jack saw them sitting together at The Lantern before Rob left her at the table to sit with him at the bar. Someone else joined her and was seen leaving with her."

"Max Kauffman, right?" Lila chuckled when they looked surprised. "He called Rachel in a panic while we were waiting for Carl to get out of surgery."

"Why would he call her?" Jack wanted to know.

"Not really sure. I think he's nervous. Chase is annoyed the guy keeps pestering her, but he's a player," she answered. "Max had two years to win Rachel over in the city and she never budged. Clara and I believe he considered her a failed conquest."

"What?" Jack stopped. He laughed after Lila explained her theory. "He's going through an awful lot of trouble for a one night stand, don't you think?"

"I did at first. Now, I believe he's set his sights on the Taylor House."

"Certainly an interesting theory. And he'd make an excellent scapegoat. Last person seen in public with the victim. No real support in the area. How is Carl doing?" Devan asked to change the subject.

"He survived the surgery, but hasn't woken up yet. It's pretty much wait and see now," she answered. After she sat in a chair, the agents questioned her about the morning events.

When they were finished, Lila walked with them to the ICU.

That evening, Devan returned home to find Shannon still working at the computer. When he entered the room, she shouted out excitedly, "I got you, you stupid bastard!"

"What's going on?"

Shannon quickly twirled around in her chair with her hand on her heart. "Oh! You scared me. I didn't hear you come in. How was your day?"

Devan suddenly felt bad about not keeping her up to date on the day's events. "You've been in here all day? Let's take a break. I have food downstairs."

"Wow, I didn't even realize what time it was. This is actually kind of fun," she commented after glancing at the clock on her computer screen before following him down to the kitchen.

"You like this kind of thing?" Devan inquired as pulled out various Chinese dishes. "It seems a bit too geeky for you."

"Devan, I am a geek," Shannon admitted. "So much food! Who are you expecting, the whole neighborhood?"

"A few agents. We'll be having a meeting to compare notes. Too many coincidences and a lot of things happening," he explained as he pulled plates from the cabinet. "Shan, it's important you keep quiet about everything you hear."

"You're going to let me stay?"

"Why not? You're working the case," he answered with a shrug. As Devan sat down, the front door opened, it was Jack and two other agents. After introductions were made, they all sat down to eat, each presenting what they knew from their part of the investigation.

"Whoever's laptop you gave me, he's skimming money off a trust fund. And he's being pretty stupid about it. I think someone discovered it," Shannon announced before she explained in further detail what she discovered. Before she concluded, "And let me tell you, whoever's money it is, he's pretty loaded."

"Emerson loaded?" Devan wondered.

"No idea what that really means. I don't know their worth, which is pretty interesting when you think about it," she commented.

"How so?" Jack wondered, preparing himself for another crash course in the town's history.

"The owners of the four mansions on Park Avenue are, more or less, the founding fathers of the town. They go back many generations. In the beginning, they were all significantly wealthy each in their own right, but they also were co-owners of successful business ventures which established the trust for each of the four mansions," she started to explain. "The wealth was well invested, so the principle is never touched and the wealth continues to grow.

"What I'm looking at doesn't let me know which family is which. You have family A, B, C, and D. Family A seems to be living conservatively throughout the years. Maybe an occasional splurge here and there but nothing compared to the others. Family C seems to be the most extravagant because they're siphoning from families B and D. Mostly B."

"But all four families have been withdrawing from the account over the years?" Devan asked.

"Yes."

"How?"

"What do you mean, how?"

Devan's eyes stayed on Shannon's for a moment as he thought about how to tactfully bring the information from abstract numbers to concrete people. They were the only two that really knew these families, she especially more than he.

"Shan, let's back up a minute. So the house trust is shared by all four families?"

"Correct."

"And how is that trust supplied?"

"By each of the individual family trusts. Each one contributes so much a year but about thirty years ago, there was a slight alteration in the amounts provided and given." Shannon walked over to a dry erase board on the wall.

She first wrote the four letters across the top and two circles below each one with a large square at the bottom. "The green circle is the account from each family placing money into the shared house account. The blue is the money going from the big account back to the individual homes. The wealth among these families is so significant, one probably wouldn't even notice the funds going into the accounts. It all appears to be set up automatically."

Shannon looked around the room before picking up the black marker. "Around twenty-five years ago, give or take, the money going from families B and D increased while C decreased. But, the money leaving the big account significantly increased to C while it significantly decreased to B. The B family is literally supplying family C's lifestyle."

Devan knew the moment Shannon was able to connect the letters on the board to real people. She stopped to study the board before she closed her eyes as a tear fell. Taking a deep breath before she concluded in a whisper. "And Jason uncovered this? He learned the Howells were living off the Hawks? That's why he was killed?"

Horrified, Shannon turned to Devan. "Lee Howell killed Jason and Susannah?"

Jack and Devan were the only two agents familiar with the names, leaving the other agents slightly confused.

"Wait a minute, who are Jason and Susannah?" the youngest agent asked.

"Jason O'Reilly was killed last January, in the city. He was an accountant hired to look over the trust records. Someone, I'd guess Matt Emerson, grew suspicious, for any number of reasons. Susannah Gibson was the present head of the Hawks House twenty-five years ago. She was killed twenty years ago. Somehow, Lee was able to alter the money from the accounts before he killed her." Shannon looked around the table of agents. "That is the motive for killing Clara's mother and husband."

Damn, she's good at this, Jack thought before he asked, "This isn't a theory, right? Do you have proof?"

"This only proves someone from the Howell household altered the trust disbursements to receive a substantial amount more," she answered as she sat down with a heavy sigh. "But it doesn't prove it was Lee. I would have to look further into where the money went. But I know it was him."

"But how do you know it was Lee Howell, not the father or the son?" the younger agent challenged.

Devan's eyes stayed on Shannon's as he answered, "Because the father is too old for the computer scene and the son was too young to have killed Susannah Gibson twenty years ago."

"Plus Eric's too lazy and transparent to scheme such an elaborate plan," Shannon answered. She was quiet for a moment as her brain processed everything she knew: the timeline, the deaths, and the drugs.

"Oh my God!"

Everyone stopped talking and turned toward Shannon as she suddenly left the room.

"What?" Jack asked.

"Not sure," Devan commented before following her up the stairs to her room. "Shannon?"

She was standing at the window looking out over the backyard, sobbing when he closed the door behind him.

"Shan?"

"I never should have started this! How can I ever forget it? It's so much worse than I could ever have imagined, Devan!"

"What are you talking about?"

Shannon turned around to face him. "What do you know about why Clara and I drove into the city that day?"

"Nothing," Devan answered cautiously.

"I am a child of a monster!"

That was the only sentence he understood as she sobbed hysterically, falling to her knees.

Devan reached out to grab her and carried her to the bed. Together, they sat with his arm gently around her as she sobbed incoherently into his chest.

After what seemed like hours, she leaned back. As she wiped her face with the back of her hands she tried to shift away from him but he wouldn't have it. "Hey, why are you pulling back?"

"I am horrified, Dev! This is so embarrassing. How can you possibly look at me? Touch me right now?" she whispered.

"Shan, I have no idea what the hell you're talking about," Devan answered honestly.

She leaned back to study his face. *Shit, he probably doesn't know,* she realized as she thought back to the previous summer. They were just casually dating when she convinced her friends to complete the DNA tests. They were already broken up when she received the results. She quickly explained about the tests.

"So that's why you and Clara were driving back from the city that day? You two are maternal half-sisters?" Devan continued when she nodded. "And you learned Jason, Clara's husband, is your paternal half-brother? How the hell did you conclude Lee is your father?"

"Clara's mother wrote in her journal about being pregnant, and she had no idea who the father was," she quietly explained. "And the talk of the drugs. Hell, it's not a big leap to conclude she was roofied and raped. Same as Jason's mother."

"Alright, I get how you landed on that, but I still don't get how you arrived at Lee Howell being your father," he repeated.

"He had a motive and all this started over thirty years ago," Shannon explained.

Devan heard the irritation in her tone, but he still couldn't follow her thought process.

"It doesn't matter how I know, I just do. How will I ever be able to look Clara in the eye again? My father killed her mother!"

"He killed your mother too, right? You aren't responsible for his actions. Just like Jason isn't responsible for the bastard's actions either." Devan was silent for a moment as he realized she didn't know the whole of it. He found himself quickly explaining Rob's version of his time in the woods with Clara.

"Clara killed him?" she tried to confirm when he was finished.

"I'm not sure. I've only heard his version. She's yet to talk about it. But there wasn't a body," Devan explained.

"Why hasn't she talked about it?"

"I don't know. She likely doesn't trust her recall of the events. She was heavily drugged when we found them," he kept his answer vague. "We need to talk to her, but I'm not sure if now will be the best time."

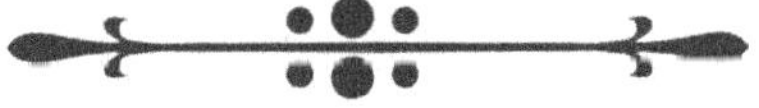

The next morning, Clara woke up alone in her bed. A quick glance at the clock confirmed it was still early, by most people's standards anyway. After a few minutes, she slowly started down the stairs.

"Mama!" Hailey yelled, greeting her mother with a hug at the bottom of the stairs. She pulled her by the hand towards the dining room.

After the late hour the night before, Clara invited Lila and Dallas to stay at her place in case the hospital called. Rob had offered his bed while he slept on the sofa. He didn't mention he usually spent the nights there anyway.

"Good morning, beautiful," Connor greeted her with a kiss before holding out her chair in the dining room. Once she was sitting, he placed the toddler on her lap before handing her an opened banana.

"Sorry I slept so long. Have you heard from the hospital?" Clara asked, looking over at Lila and Dallas sitting beside her at the table.

"Nothing yet," Connor answered quietly before returning to the kitchen.

Lila was watching from her seat as Rob pulled something from the oven and placed the items onto a serving platter. He handed Reese a platter with instructions to bring it to the table, as he handed another to Connor, before he also carried another dish from the oven. "How did you get them to get along so well?"

Clara's eyes met her friend's before turning to the kitchen. "I've no idea."

Rob and Connor passed the food to Dallas and Lila before sitting down. Connor assisted Reese in his seat next to his mother. Everyone was quiet as they dished up various foods when Hailey's banana fell in half.

"Shit!" the toddler exclaimed.

"Rob!" Clara looked over in shock.

"Why do you blame me?" He was immediately defensive.

"Because you talk shit all the time," Reese patiently explained.

Without meaning to, both Connor and Dallas started laughing.

Rob's eyes were on the young boy when he sighed. "Reese, I thought you were on my side. And now you throw me to the wolves. Besides, I say shit, I don't talk shit."

"That's what I said," Reese dismissed. "You always talk shit."

"Say, not talk," Rob tried to patiently explain.

"Don't they mean the same?" Reese clarified.

"Not in this context, no." A look from Clara had Rob sighing in defeat. "Your mother won't let us hang together anymore."

"Reese, you should not repeat the bad words the adults say. It will get you into trouble at school," Clara said with her eyes on Rob.

"It's just a word, I don't see what the big deal is," Rob muttered under his breath.

"Sawyer's mommy says fuck," Reese reported.

"That's even worse," Rob commented.

"I know," the young boy said expertly as he bit into his muffin.

"I don't want my daughter's first clear sentences to be full of cuss words," Clara explained.

"She's already said her first sentence," Reese announced proudly. When he looked around the room, he explained. "She says 'Reese is the best.'"

He pointed and nodded encouragingly at his little sister.

"Yaya la baba!" Hailey yelled out excitedly.

Reese beamed with pride at his sister, but everyone else around the table leaned in to listen with confused looks on their faces.

"I don't think that's what she said," Dallas suggested. Both Rob and Lila shook their heads in agreement.

"Sure it is. She said 'Reese is the best.' Hailey, say it again," the older brother pointed to his sister again.

"Yaya la baba!"

"I still don't hear it," Rob said. "It sounds to me like she's saying 'Rob is the best.'"

"Or even Dallas," Dallas put in, surprised when his brother-in-law nodded in agreement.

"Nope, it's Reese, isn't it Hailey?" Reese asked his sister. Everyone laughed when she nodded in agreement, clapping her hands.

"Uncle Rob, when is Just Mitch bringing your new puppy over?" Reese wondered as he looked down at the puppies at his feet.

"Just Mitch?" Lila repeated.

"Don't ask," Rob advised.

"Just Mitch came over again last night. He brought us ice cream and said he'd be back with a puppy for Uncle Rob. Uncle Rob has been a good boy because Just Mitch is letting him have a puppy too," Reese explained with a nod.

"Dad comes over here?"

"All the time," the little boy confirmed as he continued eating his eggs.

Lila smiled at her brother. "You two are talking again?"

"More or less," Rob admitted with a shrug. "Don't get me started on the other one."

Lila nodded her head in understanding. She still hadn't been able to bring herself to talk about her mother no longer living on the farm. She looked down as Dallas grabbed her hand to squeeze. She couldn't believe her mother was currently living with Zacariah Thompson! Never in a million years would she have guessed such a thing would happen.

Everyone turned to Connor when his cell chimed, he quickly read a text before returning a message. When he looked up, Clara's eyes were on him.

"I hate to eat and run, but I need to get to the hospital. It's not concerning your father. I'll see you there. Do you want me to drop off the kids?"

"We can do that when we go to visit Dad," Clara answered as Connor brought his plate into the kitchen. When he returned, he kissed Clara before leaving.

"Reese, I think the puppies need to go out. Can you help me?" Dallas asked as he also stood up to bring some dishes into the kitchen.

Both children immediately ran to grab their jackets before chasing after their uncle.

44 regrets

Felicia Thompson groaned as she stood up. She grabbed the table with both hands until she was sure her legs would provide the support. After a moment, she started to limp towards the open bottle of vodka she stupidly left on the counter. Once her glass was refilled, she stumbled into her living room.

She collapsed in Carl's recliner chair near the window. Closing her eyes, Felicia was sure she could smell his cologne. She sighed as she sipped her drink. *Where did it all go so wrong? It was never supposed to be this way, me all alone and forgotten. And worse, poor! The stupid bastard never kept his word.* She never should have allowed him to manipulate her the way he did over the years.

Felicia was surprised by the tears. She was never the weeping type, not while alone anyway. Tears did serve a purpose. But who was there to persuade now anyway? Damn him for dying. Damn him for thinking he could tell her it was over and move on so easily, she thought as she looked down at his picture in her yearbook.

Aaron was so good to me in those early months, always the gentleman treating me like a lady. No one ever treated me so well before or since, she thought, wiping away her tears. And if she were truly honest with herself, did she really love him? Or was it the promise of the lavish lifestyle in the glorious house with the most handsome man in town? All these years later, after all the broken promises, Felicia was finally able to admit, the young girl really loved him, but only as much as a naïve child was capable.

She lifted her glass for one final swallow before letting the heaviness pull her under. She mentally chuckled when she heard a vehicle pull into her driveway. Figures, he'd show up now. He's too late.

Always a day late and a dollar short.

Dallas pulled into his mother's driveway. He stared at the front door a moment before turning off the ignition.

"Are you alright?" Lila asked from beside him.

"I don't know, something feels off," he answered as he opened his door. He walked around to assist her down. Extending out his arm, he waited until she looped hers around before they both headed towards the front door.

After ringing the doorbell, Dallas waited a moment before using his key. He held the door open as his wife stepped through before following her in, closing the door behind them.

"Mom?"

"Dallas, call 911," Lila ordered, walking towards her mother-in-law. She noted the empty vodka bottle and the pill bottle beside the unconscious woman. Rushing to her side she called out, "Felicia? Felicia, wake up!"

Dallas was momentarily frozen as he watched Lila roughly rub his mother's sternum.

"Felicia! Wake up, damn it! Dallas, her breathing's shallow! We need to get her to the hospital now!"

He was suddenly shaken out of his trance as he looked around at the room. "Would it be better to drive her ourselves? The ambulance would take too long."

Lila stepped back as he leaned down to pick his mother up off the floor. She grabbed the empty prescription bottle and a blanket from the sofa before heading outside.

"Put her in the back, I'll sit with her as you drive."

Dallas cautiously placed his mother down on the blanket. He assisted Lila in before closing the door, then ran back to the driver's seat. As he drove, Lila called the hospital.

"Go away," he heard a voice mumble.

"Felicia, you need to stay awake," Lila's voice was firm.

"I never wanted him to die. He was never supposed to die," she whispered. "The bastard never kept his promises and just made everything worse! He killed him!"

"Who? Who did he kill?" Lila asked as she watched a tear fall from the older woman's face. Her panicked eyes met Dallas' in the rearview mirror as she silently pleaded for him to hurry.

"Aaron. Evil killed Aaron and so many others," she whispered before she faded out again.

Connor felt a slight case of déjà vu when he and his nephew stopped just outside the doors of the ambulance bay. The SUV was already there, they watched Dallas open the back. First, he assisted Lila down then he reached in to lift his mother out, placing her on the stretcher.

"What happened?"

"We found her passed out in her home beside empty bottles of vodka and this." Lila held up the empty prescription bottle. "She's barely responsive to a sternal rub, but she's been breathing on her own. When she comes to, she talks about Aaron being killed by Evil."

Connor glanced at the label long enough to see the date the bottle was filled, *shit*, he thought. He started to give out orders as he brought the stethoscope towards his ears. "Aaron? Aaron Hawks? His death was an accident."

"Not according to her," Lila answered as she started to initiate the IV line. "She says Evil killed him."

"Who's Evil?"

"Not sure, but I have theories," Lila admitted.

Connor's eyes met hers before he used a penlight to assess Felicia's eyes. "Felicia!"

"Who is Aaron?" Josh asked, totally confused.

"Clara's uncle. He was killed in an automobile accident shortly after he graduated high school. Felicia dated him," Connor answered as he placed the stethoscope into his ears. He listened to her heart and lungs before he listed off more orders. "Lila, we've got this. Take Dallas out to the waiting room."

Felicia finally opened her eyes in the late morning. She was surprised to see Dallas standing at the window.

"Dallas? What's going on?"

He turned, somewhat surprised at the sound of her voice. "Mom, you're finally awake. How are you feeling?"

"Confused. What the hell happened?"

"You overdosed on your pain pills and vodka," he answered quietly. He still wasn't sure if she actually meant to kill herself. It seemed too out of character for her. All his life, she always seemed to have a backup plan and an ace hidden up her sleeve.

"What? That's ridiculous. I've barely been taking the pills," she answered but stopped as she remembered her early morning visitor. "That bitch! She's finally getting caught at her own stupid game."

The next morning, Dallas was sitting in the dark, across the room from his mother, debating what to do. He watched her stir in her sleep, wondering if he was making the right call when he hit the send button on the text.

As the morning progressed, he started to pace the small room. Dallas turned towards the door when he heard it open.

Devan was surprised at the sudden turn of events. Felicia Thompson had agreed to talk. He wasn't really sure what information would be provided, but Dallas promised it would be well worth the FBI's time. He looked over at Jack before knocking on the door.

"This should be interesting. Felicia Thompson has always been dramatic."

"Ms. Thompson?" Devan inquired, making the introductions before he continued. "I understand you have something to share about the death of Aaron Hawks?"

"If I talk with you, will I be protected from the bastard? They weren't joking when they said the E in his middle name stands for Evil," she stated quietly.

The FBI made an immunity deal with Felicia. She would not do time for her knowledge of any crime, unless it was proven she had an active role.

As she talked in a raspy voice, Devan felt the hair on the back of his neck stand up. He couldn't believe the pieces were finally fitting together. Gone was the drama he'd always associated with this woman. Instead, she sounded defeated, as if she had to pick a side and lost.

"Aaron was everything everyone said he was. He was honest and hardworking, great looking, and had a wonderful personality. He treated me like a princess, but I was too caught up with promises of grandeur and the naïve belief it could never be taken from me. Our parents had agreed on our courtship with the likelihood it would lead to a formal engagement after he started at the university. He was always the perfect gentleman, always. So, when I was told he was stepping out on me, I was horrified," she paused for a moment, wishing she had a cigarette or at least a shot of vodka.

"We were at the prom. I had been looking around for him when someone else asked me to dance. While we were dancing, he told me about the indiscretion. Instead of confronting Aaron, I allowed the guy to lead me into another room. Things were getting pretty hot and heavy, when Aaron walked in on us. He was livid. We stood there arguing while the stupid bastard just laughed and left us. It was all a lie. The guy lied to me! Instead of working things out, Aaron dumped me.

"We had another month before graduation. I was so upset. I threw myself into Carl Gibson's arms. And he did his best to cheer me up. I told him everything." Felicia looked between the agents before emphasizing. "Everything, the money, the prestige, and the jewelry. Except the part about me cheating on him. He told his cousin, Lee. 'Lee Evil' he called him. He wasn't wrong. Aaron often said the E in his middle name stood for Evil."

"How are they cousins?" Devan wanted to know. He was not able to find any blood relation.

"Oh, I don't know," she thought for a moment. "Something obscure like Carl's mother was dating Lee's uncle. I don't know if they ever married before the mother was killed, but the uncle raised him.

"Carl was always charming, but Lee was even more so, until he got what he wanted or things didn't go his way. I learned that early on, but too late. I thought with the break up, he'd start courting me. Instead, he told me it was too soon after his wife's death, his first wife. I now realize he was likely already seeing Kathleen.

"Just as well, his taste was a bit too, I don't know, sadistic for me. Carl and I often hung out together, including visits to the Howell House. Lee and I occasionally snuck off together," she paused as she replayed many moments from her past.

"He told me he had a plan for Aaron and all would work out as it was intended to be. I thought he meant he would help me win him back. But Carl was right, Aaron would never have taken me back after catching me with Lee. And Lee's fascination was not with me or even Kathleen. He just wanted her money. The other woman, to his frustration, was too young and her father would not allow the match."

Felicia paused again to sip her water. "You know, I could never understand what everyone saw in that woman. All she ever had to do was smile and shake her lashes and the men all fell at her feet: her father, Aaron, Matt, and hell, even Carl. He actually canceled a date with me to go ice skating with her. She was in the family way before she graduated and Carl still stood by her. Claimed the baby wasn't his, all right, whatever. But when Lee asked me over the years to help keep Carl distracted, I didn't think anything of it. Carl was such a great distraction from my own marriage."

Devan first looked over at his boss before he tilted his head. "Let's go back to how Lee Howell killed Aaron Hawks."

"He cut the brake line in the car at the party before the boys all drove off. That caused the car to miss the turn," she answered sadly. "I didn't know about it until much later. By that time, I was already neck deep in distracting Carl from his wife. And when she left, my first thought was, finally!"

Felicia looked up with a sad smile. "I was finally going to be the lady of the Hawks House, stepmother to Aaron's niece. But Carl was too much of a wimp, he had no backbone to stand up to the trust. He wouldn't fight to have me stay at the house or even look into a divorce so we could get married. The stupid idiot was willing to take her back. As if that were ever going to happen."

"Did you know or assume Lee cut the brake line?" Jack asked.

Felicia paused for a moment. "It's been so many years, I'm not really sure. I didn't even think about it at the time. It was a casual statement he made, 'strangling was so much more personal than cutting a brake line.' That's when I started putting everything together."

"But you did not know about it, nor did he specifically state he cut Aaron's brake line?" Devan attempted to clarify. When she shook her head, he shifted gears to more recent times. "The afternoon you attempted to strangle Clara O'Reilly, what money were you talking about?"

"Who is Clara O'Reilly?"

Devan stared at the older woman a moment before answering, unable to keep the sarcasm out. "Clara Noelle Gibson O'Reilly, Carl's daughter, the heir to Hawks Estate?"

"Her last name is O'Reilly?" She simply shrugged. "Well, whatever."

"Ms. Thompson, I was there that afternoon. Hell, I even have it on video. You specifically stated, *He thinks he can break it off just when the money is coming to us?* I ask again, what money?" Devan's hazel eyes remained on hers as he watched her contemplating her answer.

"Aaron told me back in high school, the Hawks children would each inherit access to their trusts on their thirtieth birthday," Felicia whispered. "A substantial amount. As the oldest, he would also receive the house and most of the real estate."

"And how do you benefit from this?"

"Carl is Clara's father. I've been with him, on and off, over thirty years! Why shouldn't I have some of it? It was supposed to be mine anyway until Lee intervened, trying to win over the stupid Hawks girl," she gave a harsh chuckle. "And fifteen years later when she came to her senses, as we all do, the guy is psycho, she was killed."

"Susannah Hawks? You are talking about Carl's wife, Aaron's younger sister? A grown man of what, late twenties stalked a teenage girl for fifteen years? And you don't think to say anything about it, to anyone?" Devan asked, feeling nauseous as everything started to make sense, in a blood curdling way.

"Oh, please, she was just as charmed as I was or any of the other women he pulled under his spell. She even had his child. He loved lying there with her at night, rubbing her belly while the baby grew. It saddened him when she had to give up the baby for adoption. Her father would have disinherited her and he would have lost the money." She paused again in thought. "And when she returned back after giving birth in the city, her father agreed to the engagement with Carl. I was already engaged to Zacariah. Everything seemed to settle for a bit. Evil Lee married Kathleen Emerson."

"You didn't try to fight for Carl? Marry him?" Jack wondered.

"Oh, please, aside from being the best and by far the most creative in the bed, what else could he possibly bring to the marriage? He had no name, land, or money. Once married, he just had to wait it out until she turned thirty! The stupid bitch was threatening to divorce him. She had the gall to set it up so the papers would be served just before she turned thirty. Then she just disappears, leaving us with no choice but to wait for the little bitch to turn thirty. And now, even that's ruined," Felicia sobbed, surprising no one more than herself as real tears were released.

Devan quietly handed over the box of tissues, and waited patiently for her to continue.

"I'm so sorry. It's just difficult to believe, after all the ups and downs of our relationship, I really believed we would be together, grow old together. And now he's gone. She thought she could take him from me because the little bitch took him from her," Felicia sobbed loudly into the tissue.

Devan looked over at Jack with raised eyebrows, confirming he was just as confused. He understood the little bitch was Clara, but who was the other woman and who was taken from her? Before he could think of a proper way to ask the question, Felicia continued.

"Carl often went off on his own. I never asked where or with who. He always reminded me we weren't married. It finally dawned on me last summer he always kept a separate legal residence so we could never be considered common law partners! Thus I would never have *legal rights* to his money. An on and off lover of over thirty years stands no chance to inherit money," she stated in a mocking tone followed by another harsh chuckle, "and now suddenly, Carl has developed some smarts and figured out his cousin killed his *precious little wife*. Except, he can't find Evil Lee anywhere. Kathleen denied she knew where he was but Carl didn't believe her. The bitch has always been a liar. He followed her.

Stupid naïve man actually thought he could play the role of a hero and try to save the young girl."

She paused in an attempt to compose herself before she spoke it out loud for the first time. "Instead of saving the girl, he was killed. I loved the stupid bastard!"

Devan and Jack looked at each other a moment as they attempted to decipher the last piece of information.

"Felicia?" Devan spoke softly, waiting until her eyes met his before he continued, "Was the young girl Isabella Daynee?"

Her eyes grew wide in surprise as she nodded her head.

"Carl was trying to save her?" When she nodded again, he asked, "Who killed her?"

"Kathleen Howell," she whispered. "She wanted her husband back. Didn't care who he'd been with or what he'd done to them. She just wants him back in her bed at his house. The girl was a nuisance she needed to get out of the way."

"How?"

"She offered her a ride late one night, or maybe it was early in the morning when she left some guy's bed. Instead of taking her home, she drugged her and left her in the cabin in the mountains alone. Carl showed up, tried to save the girl but Kathleen killed him. She didn't go into details."

"You talked to her? She came to your place?" Devan asked, noting Jack sending a text. No doubt to get an order for a warrant to search her house. "Can we search your place?"

"Oh, absolutely," Felicia stated. "That woman should get what she deserves. Killing her own grandchild, she's worse than Evil Lee."

"Holy Hannah! I can't believe all the information she gave us! She opened so many cans of worms," Jack Ruddy stated when they left the room guarded by another agent with strict orders to limit visitors to a short list. "The woman didn't technically do anything wrong except continue a relationship with a married man, who she was already seeing before either were married."

"You believe her?" Devan was skeptical.

"I believe she believes it," Jack answered. "It gives us enough to ask questions. And more importantly, we have a better understanding of who the major players are. That is one screwed up family."

"You don't think she's guilty of letting statutory rape happen?" Devan wondered.

"I don't think she understands the concept. She was smitten by the attention of an older man, why wouldn't another girl be? As difficult as it is for us to believe, Felicia was also a victim before she graduated high school," the older agent answered. "If we do this right, we may get all the answers. We just can't let her know Gibson is still alive."

"We need to find Evil Lee's body," the younger agent stated. He sighed when he thought of all the details before he finally said what concerned him. "What if it wasn't just statutory rape but date rape? He's had access to drugs his whole life. He loved being in control. Young pretty girls, virgins."

Jack paused to look over the hood of the vehicle. "A psychopath district attorney then town mayor. He loves the power and ability to control without anyone the wiser. Scary to contemplate how many girls he's actually snarled into his trap."

"Worse, some may not even be aware." As they both got into the SUV, Devan continued, "I think it's best to not mention too much to Connor or even Matt."

"Why?"

"What if no body is found," Devan started. He wasn't sure if he should say out loud what he believed.

"You don't think Evil Lee is dead?"

Shaking his head firmly. "It would be too easy. Foxwood said Clara clobbered Evil Lee pretty good. Figured they were leaving him for dead, but he admits to not even checking to see if he was still breathing.

Foxwood, rightfully so, wanted to get distance between Clara and the bastard. He didn't think he could win another round with the guy. Smart. But who would be left to bring him out of the woods? Eric was home and the wife would never be able to carry him. Plus, she was also home at the time we arrested her son. And God help the bastard if either Emerson brother finds him before we do."

Devan stood with his uncle and cousins, Anthony and Joe, in the room behind the mirrors of the two interrogation rooms. In one room sat Eric with his expensive lawyer from the city.

Max Kaufmann sat in the other room alone. He continued to look panicked. All law enforcement officers were in agreement he was not only innocent of Isabella's death, but set up to take the fall. They just didn't understand why.

They were waiting for the forensics to get back about what was found in Felicia Thompson's home. Before they could confront Kathleen Howell, they needed all the facts confirmed.

"Just to see if I'm understanding all this, we think Kathleen killed Isabella? Why?" Anthony asked.

"She was pregnant with her grandchild," Devan speculated with a shrug.

"So? Illegitimate grandchild isn't the end of the world," Joe answered. "If she was indeed pregnant."

"And Carl Gibson got in her way when he tried to rescue her? That's why he was beaten and left for dead?" Anthony asked.

"Connor says Gibson's injuries are more consistent with a pedestrian hit by a vehicle. Once we confirm a few details, we'll be getting a subpoena for her arrest for the murder of Isabella and attempted murders of Felicia and Carl," Devan answered quietly.

"We don't believe Eric killed Shiloh," Joe continued. "Because he was kidnapping Clara and Rob at roughly the same time. So we get him for attempted murder and kidnapping. But we don't have any evidence he sunk Rob in his truck."

"No, sadly we don't. If we can get him to confess to his whereabouts while we continue to accuse him of the girl's murder, he might slip up," Devan explained. "And the big shot expensive lawyer from the city may have to choose which client he wants to represent. Since we are presenting as if we're solely focused on Eric for all the murders, he will learn who really loves him. His father set him up to take the blame for Shiloh's death and the mother set him up for Isabella's."

"Wait a minute, there's no way we would possibly think Eric killed Isabella. He's been in the county jail since after we found Rob and Clara. He was arrested for violating the terms of his bail. We'd never believe he was Isabella's killer," Anthony argued.

"But why would anyone want to kill Isabella? Or for that matter, Billy, Tonya, or Lauren?" Joe speculated. "Do we believe everyone was killed by the same person? Because if we do, then the killer isn't Eric. Not with Isabella killed while he's in custody…"

His brother cuts him off, "His mother may have killed Isabella to dismiss Eric as the killer. She believes *we* think he killed everyone. But why kill the others?"

"This goes back years," Devan speculated. "And we may never know the extent of the killings nor the actual reasons why. Billy Kingsley was caught inside Clara's house and also injured her. His death may have been a punishment. Lauren's arrest for stealing brought an investigation into the nursing home. She was likely also killed as a punishment. These deaths all involve strangling and something Felicia Thompson said helps to explain it, Evil Lee was into strangulation. Some of the female deaths could have been accidents, letting things go too far, but that's not the creepy part. Or I guess, creepiest."

Devan paused, looking around the room before he spoke. "Evil Lee seemed to form an unusual attachment to Susannah Gibson at an early age. And when he killed her, likely an accident since she wasn't yet thirty, he projected those attachments onto Clara."

Before anyone could comment, Joe read a text from his father:

'Kathleen is requesting a meeting in my office.'

"She can't be that stupid?" Anthony spoke first.

"Only one way to find out." Devan closed the door and pulled out his cell.

Kathleen Howell ignored the towing zone sign when she parked in front of the sheriff's department. When she pulled open the door, she informed Maggie at the receptionist desk she wanted to talk with the sheriff.

Within five minutes, she was seated across from the sheriff in his office.

Since he didn't request the meeting, Tony Mancuso remained silent.

"Sheriff, I've been patiently waiting for you to drop the charges against my son and release him!" Kathleen's tone was condescending.

"On what grounds would I be releasing him?" Tony wondered.

"There was another murder while my poor Eric has been rotting away in a cell!" She leaned forward and slapped a hand on the desk. "You have no right to keep him here!"

"Kathleen, let's go talk with Eric, shall we?" He stood up and gestured towards the interrogation room.

Eric was getting used to sitting in the small room with the mirror. His excitement at finally having the charges dropped was almost too much to contain. The presence of his lawyer proved it was all about to happen.

When the door opened, he was tapping his hands to the song he was singing. At the sight of his mother, he jumped up.

"Mom! Finally, when the hell are you getting me out of here?"

"Right now. There's been another murder! You being held here has actually been your alibi," Kathleen announced, obviously pleased with herself. She reached up to brush her son's hair with her hand.

"Kathleen, be careful of what you say in here," the lawyer cautioned.

"Nonsense, Hank. Lawyer and client privilege. They can't touch him with you in here," Kathleen dismissed.

"It can't be this easy," Devan muttered from behind the two way mirror as the sheriff joined them.

"The real question is, did she take the instructions from Eric or act on her own?" Jack wondered.

"Who was killed?" Eric asked. He was genuinely interested.

"Isabella Daynee, the stupid tramp!" Kathleen announced, as if she were bragging.

Hank's eyes flew to the camera in the corner and tried to shake his head in warning to his former classmate.

Eric dropped into his chair, his face paled. "No! Not Isabella? Why? Why? What happened?"

"She was picked up by that new friend of yours. The one hired for the YMCA. He brought her up to the cabin and left her alone without any way back to town. She was stupid enough to try to walk back."

Unable to correctly read her son's reaction, she continued, picking lint from her skirt as she talked. "They found her on the lower trail yesterday morning."

"That can't be right," Eric whispered. "That's not what happened."

"Sweetheart, you can't honestly be upset about this. How could you have known your friend would recklessly leave her there?"

Eric's eyes became razor focused on his mother. His head tilted slightly to the side before he asked, "How did Max learn about the cabin?"

"No idea! It must have been your father," she dismissed.

"Doubtful," Eric stated in casual conversational tone. "Dad never told anyone about the cabin. All the shit he does up there, he wouldn't risk others finding it."

Hank sensed something huge was about to go down, he leaned back in his seat. His subtle attempts to keep his client quiet failed, until he realized who his real client was.

"Shit! Eric figured it out!" Devan ran out of the room. He could see the signs that all hell was about to break loose. Anthony and Joe were on his heels.

Jack and the sheriff remained behind the mirror.

"You killed Isabella? Why?" Eric's head tilted the other way. The violent storm brewing in his eyes.

"What do you mean, why? To clear you of murder and get the charges dropped!" Kathleen patiently explained, still oblivious to the change in her son.

Without any warning, Eric was on his feet and the table was shoved to the side as the door flew open. Devan and the deputies flooded the room while he leaped towards his mother. His hands were wrapped around her neck.

"You fucking bitch! I'm in jail because I left the house to go see my girl! I didn't kill anyone! Your husband did all that! That stupid fuck killed them! Not me! I didn't kill anyone! The one time I tried, he escaped and swam to shore. I didn't kill anyone!" Eric continued to shout.

Hank stepped into the corner out of the way.

Devan and Joe were on either side of Eric, profanity flowing from his mouth.

The second Eric's hands were peeled away from his mother's neck, Anthony tried to escort Kathleen out of the room. Instead, he had to shove her out the door while she screamed back at her son over his shoulder.

"She was trying to ruin you with all the stupid brats! You knocked her up again! She was going to go after your money!" she yelled.

As if a switch was flipped, the fight instantly left Eric. He stood calmly in the center of the room next to the table lying on its side. His voice was so gentle when he spoke, "You are as heartless as your husband, aren't you? You would kill your own grandchild? My child? But the joke is on you. It wasn't mine!"

Tony and Jack stood in the hall when Anthony was finally able to pull Kathleen out of the room.

Kathleen was busy adjusting her clothes. "Well, that was certainly unexpected."

After he received a nod from his father, Anthony pulled out his handcuffs. "Kathleen Howell, you have the right to remain silent."

Her head shot up. "What? What are you talking about? What charges?"

The deputy continued citing her miranda rights during her rant as he turned her around and handcuffed her. Her pleading blue eyes met the sheriff's brown.

"Kathleen, you are under arrest for the attempted murder of Felicia Thompson and the murder of Isabella Daynee," Tony explained. "I suggest you think before you say another word."

Inside the room, Eric was shaking his head at the closed door. "I don't understand how my mother thought killing Isabella would set me free."

"She thought you were here for Shiloh's murder," Devan commented, wary of his calm demeanor.

"I didn't kill her," Eric muttered.

"We know you didn't."

"I was with Clara," Eric sighed before facing Devan and Joe. "We had a magical night until my father ruined it."

Without another word, he sat in his chair and listened while Devan informed him he was arrested for the kidnapping of Clara O'Reilly and the attempted murder of Robert Foxwood. When Devan stated the drugging charges, Eric shook his head.

"No, I didn't drug Clara. That was all my father's doing. I'll sign anything you want regarding the golden boy and my magical night with Clara but I will not take the blame for my father's misdeeds."

road to recovery

Clara had no idea of the activities going on behind the scenes. She wasn't aware of Felicia's potentially fatal overdose, nor the events leading up to her father being in the forest. She wasn't aware of Shannon's awkward quietness as she also struggled to accept a few secrets of her own.

The only thing Clara knew, she was emotionally and physically drained. The last few days were exhausting for her. Unable to eat or stretch, she was feeling weak and in pain. Even sleep was unattainable. All the recent events since the kidnapping seemed to weigh her down more than the shooting, the accident and the kidnapping.

The news of having a living great-grandmother brought her great joy. Potentially being the wealthiest woman in the county brought her fear. And finally understanding her husband's past was overwhelming. Clara still felt like there was something else, a constant shadow hanging in the peripheral of her memories. A shadow from her past, the one she'd been blocking over the years, continued to fight its way to the surface.

It was time to open the vault and release the shadow into the light.

"Hey, beautiful, what are you doing sitting out here?" Connor interrupted her thoughts as he sat down beside her in the isolated waiting room.

"Connor, any changes?"

"No, nothing yet. It's still a wait and see. It's all up to your father at this point," he explained. Placing his arm around her as he spoke. "You look tired. Why don't you go home, get some rest. I'll pick up the kids and get dinner."

"Are you sure?"

"Definitely, it's nap time now and your dad is stable. I'll notify you if anything changes," he answered as he pulled her in for a hug. "Josh can give you a ride."

"Even if he wakes up?"

"Especially if your dad wakes up," he assured her. "I have a few minutes. I'll walk you out."

When she arrived home, Clara thanked Josh for the ride. She went inside and crashed on her sofa. It was a few minutes before she remembered why she came home before everyone else. She went upstairs to change her clothes. Clara paused to light up the candles before settling on the floor with her meditation pillow.

She focused on her breathing, visualizing the purple as she inhaled and black as she exhaled until she saw only purple.

• • • •

Evil slowly walked throughout the main floor and surveyed the rooms. Eventually, he worked his way up the steps, whistling as he went. It was so much easier getting around when everyone was out for the day. With both the doctor and the farmer staying on, he didn't like chancing his movements during the night. Though the little girl was definitely a joy to be around. Her dimpled smile and innocent sky blue eyes reminded him of another girl a while back. Was it Jenny or Jessica? Oh, who could keep track anymore?

Once he reached the second floor, he noted the door was partially closed. Was his Babydoll home? He smiled at the thought. He pushed open the door and grinned. Looking at her beautiful face, he sighed with contentment.

Rob was exiting the ICU when he bumped into Connor. "Have you seen Clara?"

"Yeah, she was getting tired. I had Josh drive her home to let her recoup for a bit while I get Reese and Hailey, and grab dinner. You want a ride back?"

"Sure," Rob agreed as he sent his sister a text.

As they headed together to the daycare, the talk between them was easy as they discussed dinner options.

"I've been meaning to ask you about the master bath tub. How did you get Clara to agree to clean off the splattered paint?" Connor asked. "And change the color?"

"What are you talking about?"

"Over the summer, she would paint her bathroom the craziest of colors. Sometimes a different color on each wall. I figured it was her way of dealing with her grief after Jason's death. The bathtub was stained. I didn't have the heart to ask her if I could have it cleaned. But when we returned back after her accident, the splatter's been all cleaned off and the walls are different. Not a color I would expect her to pick, but it's alright," he stated as they stepped into the daycare.

"She gets picky about some of the strangest things, Connor. I would never have suggested a change nor have I been into her bathroom," Rob assured him.

"No? I guess I figured when Lila and Rachel picked up some things for her and the kids, they saw it and had you and Chase clean it up," he explained as he went into the toddler room and Rob into the preschooler room.

A few minutes later, everyone was strapped in and the discussion led to dinner. Rob called in to order the food as Connor drove.

Once everything was picked up, the men were quiet, listening to the conversation between brother and sister in the back, until a cold chill caught their attention.

"No, I don't see him. Is he there every night?" Reese was asking. He paused while Hailey spoke in her gibberish language. "He's the one that brings you all the gifts? How come I don't get any gifts? Connor, it's not fair."

"What's not fair Reese?" Connor asked as he pulled into the driveway.

While Clara focused on her breathing, her mind shifted without any concerns to where. She found herself watching a reel of her memories from when she was a child. She was in the kitchen with her mother, running down the stairs to greet her father when he came home. She was climbing out of her bed in the cold room, following the shadow as it led her toward the kitchen. She squatted down behind the banister as she watched her mother get hit and knocked to the floor. She froze in place as her mother was lifted onto the cornflower blue tablecloth. She continued to watch as the shadow moved out of the room and came back again. And when he returned, his violet blue eyes looked adoringly down at the beautiful young woman before him. He gently caressed her cheek before he kissed her lips. He wrapped her up before he dragged her feet first out the back door. As he was turning towards the door, her green eyes opened.

Clara gasped, feeling a slight breeze with the faint familiar scent of cologne mixed with bleach and alcohol. Then she felt a slight touch on her cheek. She froze as she heard his voice for the first time…

"Babydoll, you are looking good these days. Just as good when you were dancing for me in the bathroom so long ago. I knew then, you and I were meant to be. I have to be away, but I will be back for you."

"Why the shadow man brings Hailey gifts and not me," Reese complained with a pout as he crossed his arms over his chest.

Connor and Rob paused before getting out, looking at each other then back over their shoulders at the young boy.

"Reese, what are you talking about? What shadow man?"

"You know, the one that walks around the house every night and brings Hailey gifts. Why don't I ever get one?"

And then they heard a scream coming from inside the house!

coming soon

Small Town Secrets Book 3
SHADOWS OF THE TRUTH

acknowledgments

So many people in my life, personal and professional, have supported me on this long journey of completing the Small Town Secrets series. First, I want to thank all those that have read my first book, *Shadows of the Night!* Your support and comments have helped me to continue with the series. I hope you continue to enjoy the second book!

I want to thank my children: **Hannah and Cody.** You both continue to support me with endless discussions as I plan out a scene and decide a character's fate. You are the best IT support anyone can ask for! Thank you for all you've done to assist with the marketing! I love you both and am proud to call you each mine!

To my nieces: **Cassie, Alysa, Camilla, and Andrea.** The love and support you've all provided over the years has been priceless! Thank you!

Marcey, my friend, boss, and consultant! Your continued encouragement and promotion of my work have been inspirational. Without you, I may never have gotten the courage to seek out publishing these books! I appreciate all the time you've spent reading the various drafts! Thank you for showing up to all the endless meets!

I want to thank everyone at **Two Penny Publishing** who has assisted in making this book: Jessica, Kaylee, Jodi, Sarah, and Holly, just to name the few I'm in contact with throughout the journey of publication. Who knew all the different steps? Thank you for your always positive encouragement and comments. But mostly, thank you for your patience!

Another thank you to **Dr. Nada Hana**, for helping me reenter the hearing world and for pushing the limits of the sounds so I could finally hear what I'd been missing since before my cochlear implants. We still need to meet up for coffee!

Since parts of the second book were initially written years ago: thank you to my many friends and co-workers who helped me debate the many options a scene can go: **Lisa, Deanna, Traci, Heidi, Harpreet, Amber, Kim, Valentine, and Pierre**.

And also to the people of the small town that helped to inspire this story. I learned over again, no such thing as secrets in a small-town. They always have a way of getting out!

about the author

JULIE ANN KEADY has been hearing impaired since an illness when she was an infant. She started wearing hearing aids when she was five years old. Later in adulthood, she got cochlear implants in both ears and re-entered the hearing world with a different view on life, including a new appreciation for music and background sounds. Today, Julie loves to read, write, and travel.